CAUGHT UP IN THE RAPTURE

LISA G. RILEY

Genesis Press, Inc.

Indigo Love Spectrum

An imprint of Genesis Press, Inc.
Publishing Company

Genesis Press, Inc.
P.O. Box 101
Columbus, MS 39703

ISBN-13: 978-1-58571-344-8
ISBN-10: 1-58571-344-9
Manufactured in the United States of America

First Edition 2004
Second Edition 2009

Visit us at www.genesis-press.com or call at 1-888-Indigo-1

DEDICATION & ACKNOWLEDGMENTS

For Ms. Gloria B. Riley (1938-2000). Thank you, Mom, for being "the best mom ever." I love and miss you.

Thank you, Sydney Rickman, for being such a thorough editor. Thank you, Niani Colom, for being a publisher who believes in the work.

To my grandmother, Ms. Helen Mitchell, I love you. I love you too, Auntie Dean, Uncle Herbert, Auntie Marva and Uncle Rudy.

To my nieces and nephews, a small, but vocal group of brats who complained when they weren't included on the dedication page of *At Last*. More than half of you aren't even old enough to read this book, but here you go: Jennifer, Barry, Johnny, Christopher, Tyrell, Kelsey, Tyrone, David, LaJé, Lanesha, Briahna, Geneva, Mikala and Baby Gloria (GiGi). I love you guys and I thank you for loving me.

And the queen bee and oldest of all the nieces and nephews: Nerak. I love you too, Rakky, but I knew you'd kill me if I listed you with all of your underage cousins.

Merci, Rahsan Lindsey et Lisa Bueno pour le francais.

Obrigado! Carlos Bueno por le portoghese.

To my siblings: Karen, Tricia, Val, Pam, Kesha, Gloria and Jason, just because.

To my friends: Mrs. Anderson, Anjuelle, Brenda, Carey, Gwennie, Jenn, Lavida, Letena, Marsha, Olivia, Stacy, Tasha, Terry and the BDBs, also just because. I'm always thinking about you guys!

PROLOGUE

Thirteen years earlier

Jack Winthrop stared hard at Julie Emery. There she stood in the middle of her parents' richly appointed parlor looking like the ultimate high-society debutante. But she was using again; he could tell. His trained eye spotted the signs. Her eyes darted about the room, never landing in one place; her skin had the cast of an addict and her too-thin body practically vibrated as she paced jerkily from one end of the room to the other.

Jack gently grasped her shoulders to hold her still. "Julie, you're doing cocaine again, aren't you? Why, honey, after all the work we did to get you clean and back to your parents?"

Julie swallowed and looked down. Refusing to look at him, because she never could and lie, she broke away from his grasp and stumbled back. "It's r-r-really none of your business what I do, Jack Winthrop. I-I-I don't need your help. I'm doing fine on my own. So why don't you go back to Chicago and do what you do best—be a cop. You're not my social worker!"

Jack looked cautiously into her green eyes. He'd first run across her two years ago when she'd been a 19-year-old University of Chicago dropout selling her body to get the drugs she so desperately craved. He'd been a rookie cop who'd thought he could save the world. Because she'd really seemed to want to get help, he'd taken an interest in her. He'd gotten her into a shelter and into a drug treatment program. He'd even helped her find a job so that she could make the money to go back home to Boston.

She'd been afraid to ask her wealthy parents for help, saying that they wouldn't take her back until she showed them that she'd made the effort to turn her life around.

With a lot of hard work, she'd done it and six months ago, he'd put her on a plane to Boston, promising her that he'd keep in touch and come visit whenever he had a chance.

Well, here he was and there she was, looking as if a good, stiff wind would blow her over. "Julie, what happened?"

Julie swiped at the mucous that was perpetually dripping from her raw nostrils. She wished Jack would just leave her alone. Why couldn't he and her parents understand that she was fine? "Nothing happened, okay?" She avoided his eyes. "Just go away, Jack, and don't ever come back! I don't need you or your self-righteous help. Go find some other cause to get behind, because I'm getting married and I don't need your help anymore. Everything is fine." She swiped at the mucous again in agitation.

Jack pulled his handkerchief out of his pocket and gently wiped the blood from her nose. Blood that he was sure she didn't even know was oozing from her nostrils. "You're bleeding, Julie. Here, hold your head back."

Julie snatched the handkerchief and moved away from him. "I don't need your help, Jack!" she repeated in a muffled voice as she held the handkerchief in place over her nose. "This doesn't mean anything. Everyone has nosebleeds. It's perfectly normal." God, she wanted a fix so bad, she could almost taste it.

"Do your parents know that you're using? Your fiancé–does he know?"

"Leave my parents out of this. As for my fiancé, I've known him since we were children and he understands me. He's a very generous man because he loves me. He gets whatever I need from his cousin."

Suddenly, she desperately wanted him to understand and she tossed the handkerchief aside to grab his hands. "You don't have to worry, Jack. It's not like it was in Chicago. I'm safe. Kevin's cousin Alex has the finest powder on the eastern seaboard. He supplies all of my friends. We don't have to go out looking for it, it comes to us."

Jack sighed. "What have you gotten yourself into, Julie? Is that why you're marrying this guy? For the drugs he can get you? Come with me. I can get you into another treatment program."

Julie's face twisted in anger and she threw his hands away from her. "Screw you, Jack! I love Kevin Brickman and he loves me. My parents like him as well. He's from one of the finest families in the state and I'm not going to let you screw this up for me! Get out before I have you thrown out!"

Jack turned away to leave, but said over his shoulder. "You know how to reach me if you need me. Call me at any time, day or night." He left.

Four months later, Jack came across an article in a news magazine. The title read, *From Debutante to Strung-Out Prostitute: How a Child of One of Massachusetts' Most Prominent Families Ended Up Dead in Back Alley Boston*. Underneath the title was a picture of a smiling, healthy Julie, blonde hair shining, green eyes sparkling. Jack hurled the magazine across the room. The bastards had killed her. He knew that Julie's fiancé and his cousin were responsible for her death as sure as he knew his own name.

CHAPTER ONE

Jack opened the door to his Parisian flat and dropped his carryall on the floor. He was disgusted, exhausted and supremely pissed off. He sighed and walked over to slouch on his sofa. That Brickman bastard was just too slippery. He'd been chasing Alexander Brickman for eight months now. This time around, anyway. In the grand scheme of things, he'd actually been after Brickman for thirteen years. This last round, he'd started in Chicago, then on to the Bahamas, where a rookie mistake had made him lose him. Then it was on to the Cayman Islands and now, here he was in Paris.

Brickman's trail was getting harder and harder to follow. The man was a criminal genius and the time Jack had to catch him was fast running out. As it was, the money for this trip to Paris had come out of his own pocket. After he'd lost Brickman in the Cayman Islands, his "boss" at the agency had said he was on his own. She'd given him two weeks to "find the slug and get your pretty-boy ass back to Chicago, or else you'll be out of a job! I don't care if you are only freelance!"

She'd hung up before he could point out that as an independent, his time was his own and he could take two months or two years if he wanted. He'd turned in his resignation with the department all those months ago specifically so he could go freelance and not worry about the bureaucratic red tape that came hand in hand with a "government job."

Jack rose and went to look out the window of his flat. The view was magnificent, but he barely took notice of the Seine or Notre Dame. Catching Brickman and putting him behind bars were the only things on his mind. No one understood his obsession because he'd never told them about Julie and what Brickman had done to her. No one needed to know; it was enough that he did. The fiancé was already taken care of. He'd died of an overdose several years before. Jack went up the stairs to his bedroom. Brickman was long gone for the day. He'd track him again tomorrow, but for now, he'd just go down to the café, let his uncle know he was back in town and enjoy an early dinner.

He was sitting in a far corner with his back to the wall when she walked in. It was Jack's usual spot in his uncle's bistro whenever he was in town. He looked up to briefly take notice of her, just as he did with everyone who walked in. In the span of a few seconds, Jack noticed that she was an African-American of average height, wand-slim and seemingly attractive.

Seemingly attractive because her large sunglasses obscured her face, and *American* because he could spot an American on foreign soil a mile away. It was all in the way they carried themselves. He watched Henri seat her a few tables away and then he went back to reading *Le Figaro*.

But when she thanked Henri in a voice of husky resonance that instantly brought to mind a dimly lit room empty of everything but a huge bed with satin sheets, he lifted his head again. He wasn't the only male in the room affected by her voice. He watched as several heads swiveled in her direction. If she noticed the attention, she ignored it. Jack knew he was staring, but he couldn't help it. He was eager to see the face that went with that voice.

She settled her purse and guidebooks, ran slender fingers over black hair that was styled in a complex but beautiful twisty fashion that only black people seemed to be able to pull off, and then finally he and every other male in the room were rewarded. She took off her sunglasses. He felt as if he'd been sucker-punched and as he heard a quick whoosh of breath being released from male lips, he hoped it hadn't come from him.

Her eyes grabbed a man by the gut and despite the pain, made him thank God and beg Him not to be released. They were so dark that they looked as if light would simply be absorbed *into* them to disappear altogether. Rimmed with thick, dark lashes and set in a light brown face with a patrician nose, high cheekbones and a beautifully full mouth, their effect was startling.

Jack forced himself to stop staring and went back to his paper. However, he listened intently as she started speaking to Henri.

"Parlez vous espagnol?" she asked hopefully.

"Je regret, mais non." Out of the corner of his eye, Jack watched the woman's face fall in disappointment as Henri shook his head in the negative and apologized for his lack of knowledge of Spanish.

"Italien?" she asked.

"Je regret, mais non."

"Allemand?" she asked with hope and hesitance. *"Swahili?"*

Jack looked up, impressed that she knew how to speak German and Swahili.

"Je regret, mais non," Henri said for the third time.

She started to speak again, but thought better of it and snatched up one of the books she'd put down earlier. She hurriedly flipped through the pages until she found what she was looking for. Putting the book down again, she looked at Henri and said with a triumphant smile, *"Je parle un peu le portugais. Et vous?"*

Jack's brow winged up in surprise. She spoke a little Portuguese, too, huh? Interesting.

"Je suis désolé, madame," Henri said with a sad smile. He put his hand over his heart for emphasis before saying, *"Vraiment."*

"Oh no, so now you're desolate. We can't have that." Her American English rushed out in a voice filled with laughter before she put her face in her hands and shook her head. "My God." She picked up her book again and said softly, "*Vraiment, vraiment, vraiment.* Ah yes, there it is. You are *truly* desolate. Or is it truly sorry? It doesn't matter, because so am I," she said wryly and chuckled. "You'll never guess how much." Still chuckling to herself, she started gathering her things.

Resigned, she said, "*Merci, monsieur. Au revoir.*"

Henri stood at her table indecisively, feeling sorry for her. Jack knew the instant Henri remembered that he was there and could speak several languages, because Henri straightened in military style and turned to him with a smile. Jack forestalled him with a small shake of his head and stood. He decided that he wouldn't let her know that he was French-American with dual citizenship in America and France, because she would probably latch onto him when she found out and he had Brickman to worry about. He cloaked himself in his French heritage and walked over to her table.

"*Scusi, signorina,*" he said in flawless Italian. "You seem to be in need of assistance." She lifted her head and gave him a brilliant smile and Jack's breath caught in his throat.

"You are Italian," she said in the same language.

"No, I am French. I speak many languages, but we will converse entirely in Italian, if you'd like. I am Jacques."

"Yes, let's do that," she said in Italian. "I'm Tracy. Please, sit." She indicated the chair across from her. After that, she said nothing, but just looked at him.

Jack was used to people staring at him. He knew, without conceit, that he had an unusually handsome face. Teased mercilessly by friends, stared at by strangers and lusted after by women, he had even been called beautiful. His hair was pitch black and long enough to brush his collar; his forehead was high and wide and his nose and chin looked as if some Greek sculptor had created them. His cheekbones were angled and his eyes, with their double lashes and indigo blue color, had caused many people to ask him if he wore color contacts. He knew what Tracy was seeing, but he didn't know what she was thinking.

He sat quietly and waited her out. It was no hardship, because he found her fascinating and realized in surprise that he wanted to spend time with her. Unfortunately, with Brickman in Paris, he didn't have the time to indulge in the rituals of courtship.

"Pardon my asking, *mademoiselle*," he again spoke in Italian, "but how is it that you know so many languages, but you have not mastered such a beautiful language as *francais*?"

She laughed in self-deprecation. "It's my fault entirely. I wanted to learn it before I took my trip, but I didn't make the time. So as punishment to myself, while in Paris, I am allowing myself to speak only in languages not native to me. I am American, you see. I told myself that if I needed help while here, I would ask for it in the languages I learned after English, and if no one could speak any of them, then I would just have to suffer and not get what I wanted."

"Ah, but that seems rather a harsh punishment for a simple oversight."

"No, I don't think so. I deserve it for my unintentional lack of respect for this beautiful country and its language. You see, I planned my trip months in advance and I signed up for French language classes, but never made it to a single one. I let myself get sidetracked by work and other things. I think it's extremely rude of me to visit your country and not know your language. It's like entering someone's home and not saying hello to the owner. It's simply illmannered and unnecessary."

Jack sat back in surprise at her attitude. Too many Americans didn't feel the same way, and in fact, felt that they were the injured party when people in the different countries that they were visiting didn't know English. She was refreshing. "Come, *ma petite*," he said softly. "Do not punish yourself so. You must forgive yourself. Surely you have learned your lesson, no?"

She suddenly threw her head back and let out a delightful peal of laughter that had every head in the restaurant turning towards them. Jack watched her with a solemn look on his face as whatever had amused her caused the laughter to just bubble out and fill the corners of the restaurant. He felt the pit of his stomach tighten up in defense against the urge to just grab her, put his mouth on hers and swallow up all that delicious, sexy laughter. *Sacré*, she was criminal.

When she finally calmed down, and was wiping the tears from her eyes, she looked at him through her fingers. He, apparently, was hilarious, because she started laughing again, so hard that she bent over and held her stomach with crossed arms.

"Oh, I apologize profusely," she said in Italian as she wound down. "That was unforgivable. It's just that you inadvertently made a joke at my expense."

Jack smiled. "How is that, *ma petite*?"

Tracy chuckled again. "You called me *petite*…small. You just don't know how appropriate that is. You see, this is the third restaurant I've been to in trying to get something to eat. Because I've imposed this punishment on myself and no one has spoken any of the languages I speak, I haven't been able to find a place to eat yet. So your calling me *petite* is fitting, because that's exactly what I will be if I don't get something to eat really soon!" She finished and laughed again.

"Have you not eaten at all today?" Jack asked in concern. Maybe the hunger was making her delusional, because the joke wasn't *that* funny.

"I had a delicious pastry for breakfast, but that was hours ago and I'm starving!" she said.

Jack moved his chair around the table to sit next to hers. He picked up the menu. "You must allow me to translate the French into Italian for you."

"Oh, would you?" she asked. "I was hoping you would." She bent her head toward the menu.

He translated and helped her to order a chicken dish with bread and wine. When the food arrived, he looked at her expectantly and said, "*Mange, mange!*"

She picked up her fork. "Okay, I'm eating," she answered in Italian.

Tracy Adamson slid out of bed, trying not to wake the man beside her. She couldn't believe that she'd just spent the night with a man she'd known for only three days. She didn't know what had gotten into her—okay, maybe she did. He was just gorgeous! He was probably the most beautiful man she'd ever seen in her life. Plus, she was in the City of Light. Wasn't Paris meant for lovers? Still, that wasn't all. She genuinely liked him. Sure, she hadn't known him that long, but in that short period of time she'd talked with him, laughed with him, and gotten to know him somewhat.

She crept silently around the room and gathered her things. Walking on tiptoe, she stealthily left the bedroom and went into the guest bathroom, where she washed and dressed, grimacing in distaste as she put on her clothes from the night before. She looked at herself in the mirror. Her light brown skin was whisker-burned around her mouth and there was a red mark on her neck. She sighed in disgust and chastised herself quietly. "You always did take things too far, Tracy! The one time in your life you decide to test yourself outside your boundaries, and you go and sleep with an almost-perfect stranger." She couldn't feel too bad, though. The whole purpose of her trip to Europe had been to leave the old behind and embark on the new. Well, she'd certainly done that!

She couldn't even claim love at first sight; it was just lust, pure and simple. From the moment she'd laid eyes on Jacques, she'd wanted to jump his bones. "Thank God we used protection," she whispered to herself and rolled her eyes heavenward. She couldn't resist one last look and she crept back to the bedroom to peek through the slightly opened door.

She looked at his over-six-foot length stretched out on the bed and closed her eyes in delight at the memory of their lovemaking. They'd gone at each other like minks the entire night and now she winced as she felt a soreness that she hadn't been familiar with for more than a year. Boy, did it feel good, she thought with a private smile. She sighed in regret, lifted her hand to her lips, blew a kiss and shut the door before he awakened. She was a bit embarrassed, but a lot delighted.

She was leaving for Chicago in two days, so she wouldn't have to face him again. That was a relief. To be sure, a man who could steal her control the way he had was not a man she intended to be around. "I never thought I'd be attracted to anyone outside of my own race, but Jacques, you certainly proved me wrong," she whispered. She laid her hand gently against the door and was gone. And if her hand lingered on the door for a moment, so what.

Jack rolled over and reached for Tracy. He opened his eyes when he felt nothing but sheets. He knew instinctively that she had left the apartment. He wasn't really surprised because he'd known that she didn't normally indulge in sex with strangers and was probably embarrassed. But there was still a small part of him that was confused, because they'd had an unusual connection and he thought women usually went for that kind of thing. Hell, *he'd* fallen prey to it, even giving up his obsessive search for Brickman to be with her.

She'd been extraordinarily responsive to his touch, his moods and his needs. Just as he had been to hers. No woman had ever pulled things from him the way Tracy had and he instinctively knew that no other man could make her respond the way he had.

That's why he couldn't quite believe she'd just left without a word.

He chastised himself. "You should be thrilled, you idiot. You had great sex and she expected nothing in return. It was perfect." So why did he feel disappointed that she'd left?

CHAPTER TWO

Tracy sat back and relaxed on her flight back to the States. As she'd done repeatedly over the past two days, she thought about Jacques. From the very first, there had been not just a spark, but a full-fledged flame between the two of them. She'd barely been able to control her attraction to him from the moment they'd met in what she'd later learned was his uncle's bistro. She'd felt a weird connection from the second he'd introduced himself in Italian until the second she'd sneaked out of his apartment like someone who had committed a crime.

Her senses had gone on full alert at how gorgeous he was—not just his face, but his tall, muscled body as well. She'd never before felt such a strong, instant attraction. She'd immediately wanted to touch, see, smell and taste all at once. All of her wishes had come true *over and over again* during her one extraordinary night with him. Even as her cheeks heated, Tracy bit her bottom lip and closed her eyes in secret bliss as her mind called forth images of that wonderful night.

She didn't believe in love at first sight. Not for a practical, no-nonsense person like herself, anyway. That sort of thing was for people like her friend

Caroline, who had found her true love more than a year before. Tracy didn't even want it to be love. She preferred to call it what it was—a wild, mad lust that had almost seemed unquenchable.

True, she did have a good time with Jacques during the time they spent out of bed. He was warm, intelligent, good-humored and easy to talk to. But that had only served to help her feel less guilty about sleeping with him. It didn't make her think of songbirds or wedding bells. In fact, as she now relived their time together, she was again relieved that she was American, he French, and that thousands of miles of ocean and land separated them. Despite her feelings, she still smiled foolishly as she remembered how everything had gotten started that second day when they'd met to go to the Musée d'Orsay.

Waiting patiently in front of the bistro where she'd first met Jacques, Tracy was surprised that she felt a bit nervous. She hadn't felt nervous about a male since she'd had her first real crush at sixteen. It was a weird sensation. She looked down at her clothing and gave a smile of satisfaction. Her loose, white linen pants and jacket were perfect for a museum tour. She'd paired the outfit with a lemon-yellow shirt with shoes and purse to match. She had her sunglasses, her camera and her guidebook to the museum. All she needed now was her human guide.

She felt her stomach drop to somewhere in the vicinity of her knees as she looked up and saw him. Her body exploded in heat and her tongue felt like lead as it peeked out to lick suddenly dry lips. *Good Lord!* she heard her brain shout inside her head. The man sure knew how to showcase his God-given gifts. Like her, he wore linen. That long, limber frame of his was encased in black trousers and a loose-fitting, short-sleeved, indigo-colored shirt. When she spotted the diamond he wore in one ear, she almost groaned out loud. He was just obscenely sexy.

"*Bonjour, ma petite,*" he said in his deep, rich voice that made her stomach turn somersaults. He took her shoulders in a firm grip and kissed her European style—a kiss on each cheek. She froze in his grip and then tamped down the urge to giggle like a schoolgirl. Wickedly, Tracy wondered what it would be like to kiss him French style.

Shocked, she shoved the surprisingly vivid image out of her head and swallowed several times before saying, "Ah, *bonjour.*" That was all she attempted in her limited French, before rattling on in Italian. "I do hope this is not an imposition for you, Jacques. I don't want to take up your time."

Jacques smiled and spoke in Italian as well. "Do not trouble yourself, *ma petite*. It would give me nothing but pleasure to spend the afternoon showing you the wonders of Paris."

"I'm so glad," she said with obvious relief. "I'd have managed, I'm sure, but it would have been difficult for me to get around without your help today. Yesterday, I was beginning to think that speaking other languages wasn't a priority for Europeans, though I'd always thought it was. I thought I'd have to spend my time in Paris hungry, lost and uncultured."

"Of course not, *ma petite*. I am more than willing to help you." Jacques had a mischievous glint in his eye as he took her hand. *"Preferisci italiano o Ridhaa wewe penda zaidi kiswahili?"*

Tracy was speechless for a moment and then she laughed in delight. Switching effortlessly from one language to the other, he'd asked her if she would prefer he speak in Italian or Swahili. "Why, Jacques, you're just full of surprises," she said in Italian before quickly switching to Portuguese, *"Parlare portoghese anche?"* she asked hopefully.

He raised his brow in question. *"Scusi?"*

"I was asking you in Portuguese if you spoke Portuguese. I have my answer," she said in Italian. "Too bad, I was hoping you could help me improve my command of the language. *C'est la vie,"* she finished with a shrug of her shoulders. She continued in Italian, "We'll just stick with Italian, no?"

"Si, bella."

She blushed because he'd called her beautiful and they were off to the Musée d'Orsay. Not as well known as the Louvre, the Musée d'Orsay was, to Tracy, of more interest. It was housed in a renovated, ornate train station dating back to the late 1800s. The collection was comprised of nineteenth century art and included everything from the works of Manet to Monet to Degas to van Gogh.

Of the three floors of exhibits, Tracy enjoyed herself most on the upper level. As she went from one masterpiece to the next, she marveled at the immense talent of each artist. The roomful of van Goghs took her breath away and she was in sensory overload by the time they got around to looking at works by Cézanne and Gauguin.

"I can't believe one museum has so many of the great artists in one place," Tracy said to Jacques as they stood looking at Monet's *Cathedrals*. "I mean, there's work by Degas, Manet, Seurat, and even Whistler. It's almost criminal to have so much beauty located in one place."

Jacques stared at her as they made their way to the restaurant. Just when Tracy was about to squirm under the intensity of his gaze, he said quietly, "Yes, so much beauty can overwhelm one and make one do and say things he normally would not do or say."

Tracy just *knew* that he wasn't referring to the artwork and shot him a look filled with nerves and desire from beneath her lashes before saying, "Yes, well, uh, not just a man, but a woman as well. There's so much here that I don't know if I'll be able to take it all in. I may have to come back here and skip the Louvre all together."

Jack had caught her look, but was distracted by what she said. "You have not yet visited the Louvre? Ah, *ma petite*, but you must before you leave. It is one of the best museums in the world! The extent of its collection is staggering."

"Yes, so I've heard. I have a friend who's an artist and she'd live at the Louvre if she could. As it is, since her twenty-fifth birthday, she's tried to make a trip to Paris to visit the museum at least once a year. She's in love with the place."

"Your friend sounds like a discerning lady. No other museum in the word compares to the Louvre."

"Well, it depends on what you're looking for, I guess. For instance, I would love to see the *Venus de Milo* one day. And of course, who can visit Paris without seeing the *Mona Lisa*? I'll make my way over there before I leave, but for now, I don't feel like the crowds."

"Ah, but what is a crowd compared to getting to see some of the most beautiful artwork in the world? You must decide if it is worth it."

"I have. I've just said that I'll get to the Louvre before I leave Paris." Tracy was suddenly irritated and she knew exactly why. Being around him so much was making her crazy and she was starting to resent him and his damned sexiness that made her want him so much.

"What is the matter, *ma petite*? I am sorry if I have offended you in some way."

He sounded so contrite that she felt guilty and rushed to apologize. "No, no, it's not your fault, Jacques. I'm sorry for snapping at you. I'm just a bit tired. I'm sure I'll get my energy back and feel better after we've eaten."

"Wonderful, because I would like to show you something that one should not leave Paris without seeing."

"Not the Louvre, please. I don't think my system could take in much more beauty and really appreciate it."

"No, it is not the Louvre. But I promise, it is something you will appreciate," he said with a mysterious smile.

He took her to a cemetery. She stood stock-still at the entrance and refused to move when he tugged on her hand. "You're not serious, Jacques. Tell me that this isn't what I think it is."

Jacques laughed and pulled her hand harder. "What do you think it is?"

"Obviously it's a cemetery and obviously I'm not going in there."

"It is not just any cemetery. It is the Cimetière du Père-Lachaise. It is one of the most beautiful cemeteries in the world—"

Tracy interrupted him. "I wouldn't know, since I don't make it a habit to visit cemeteries as a form of entertainment." She resisted the tugs.

Jacques continued as if she hadn't spoken. "...And some of the most celebrated people from the arts world are buried here, including Jim Morrison, Gertrude Stein, Proust, Edith Piaf and many others.

You will enjoy a tour, I promise. Trust me, you'll love it."

"I don't know, Jacques. It seems a bit macabre." But she'd stopped pulling away from his hand.

"Trust me," he said again. And so she did and was pleasantly surprised at the beautiful sculptures that adorned the place, along with shaded paths and beautiful landscaping. In addition to the ones he mentioned, they also visited the graves of Isadora Duncan, Bizet and Oscar Wilde.

Afterward, they walked up Paris' most famous avenue, the Champs-Elysées, to the Arc de Triomphe. He tried to talk her into slipping into the Louvre, which was "just a little ways away," but she adamantly refused. They went to the top of the arch so that she could see the view. She sucked in a breath when Jacques pointed out that looking in a straight line would give her the opportunity to see the Louvre, the obelisk in place de la Concorde and the Champs-Elysées all at once. The view was simply dazzling.

She caught her breath again, but not because of the view. Jacques had moved behind her, and in effect, was embracing her. He stood behind her with his arms stretched out on the balustrade on either side of her. She shivered and then became still when he pressed closer. He bent his head and said directly into her ear, making her shiver even more, "Cold, *ma petite?*"

She wished, but she was anything but cold. She was, in fact, the exact opposite. Her body temperature was several degrees higher than what would be considered chilled by *any* stretch of the imagination. The sexual tension she felt was screaming for release. So before she gave in to temptation and pressed back into the shelter of his sexy, wide chest, she shook her head no and ducked under his arm. "I believe I'm ready to go back down now."

He smiled knowingly. "As you wish, *ma petite*. Perhaps you would like to stop in the Jardin des Tuileries for a rest before I take you back to the café," he said.

"Jardin des Tuileries?"

"It's one of our beautiful gardens. The name comes from the clay earth beneath it. The earth was once used to make roof tiles. There are beautiful statues to enjoy and you may rest for a bit in the shade if you are tired from our day. Will you join me?"

"It sounds lovely. Yes, I think I would like to join you."

They walked over and it was while they were walking that Tracy decided that she would enjoy herself. So, she let Jacques hold her hand while they walked, let him quickly kiss her laughingly after she made some silly comment and casually twirl one of the twisted locks of her hair around his finger as they strolled through the garden.

The most daring thing she did came later as they were walking through the garden on their way out. As they walked behind a statue, Jacques suddenly stopped.

"What?" Tracy asked in surprise.

"I am glad you like my city, *ma petite*. Will you come back soon for a visit?"

Startled, Tracy chuckled. "Well, I don't know. I hadn't actually planned on it, not anytime soon, anyway. This is my first real vacation in more years than I can count. I've been away from home and work for almost six weeks."

"And what is this work you do?"

"Please, let's not bring that up," Tracy said in a strained voice. "I'm an accountant, but I don't want to talk about it. It's been too nice a day."

"Ah, you are tensing up, *ma petite*," he said when her hand clenched in his. "Do you hate your work so much, then?" He took her left hand in both of his.

"I took this vacation to reassess my life, to figure out what I want to do besides accounting," Tracy said.

"And have you figured it out?" He started massaging the base of each of her fingers with the pad of his thumb. After massaging each finger from the base to the tip, he began to work on her palm, moving his thumb in deep oscillations across the surface.

Tracy found it hard to concentrate. "Uh… uh…" She tried to remember what he'd asked. When she felt the soft, inner skin of his fingers gently sliding against hers as he entwined them and slowly slid them through one another over and over, she just gave up trying to remember the question at all. "Uh…I'm sorry, but what was your question?"

Jacques released her left hand and picked up the right one to begin the massage. "I asked if you had figured out what you want to do."

Tracy snatched her hand away and put it in her pocket. "If you keep doing that, I won't be able to concentrate enough to have a decent conversation."

Jacques smiled. "The massage feels good, no?"

"You know perfectly well that it does. In fact, it feels *too* good."

Jacques laughed outright. "I was hoping it would."

Tracy looked at him with serious eyes. "You're a troublemaker, Jacques, and I make it my business to stay away from troublemakers. We should be going. It's late."

Jacques stilled her with his hand on her shoulder. "But sometimes a little trouble can be good for you," he said, his eyes just as serious as hers had been. "Do you not want to know what it would feel like, *ma petite*? Not even just a little bit?"

Tracy took a deep breath and said, "What exactly are you talking about?"

"Do not pretend ignorance. I am referring to kissing. Are you not curious to know what your lips will feel like pressed to mine?"

Tracy tried not to close her eyes at the sexy way his words caressed her. "I was not pretending. I didn't know what you were referring to. Now I will answer you. Yes, I would like to know what it feels like, but that doesn't mean I'm going to find out."

"Ah, *ma petite*, why not?" he asked persuasively. "We both want to."

"Because I'm not the kind of woman who goes around kissing men that I've only known for a day and a half!" Tracy said vehemently to snap the spell he was casting.

"Nor am I usually that kind of man, but there is always room for change. For growth," he said charmingly.

And unwillingly charmed, Tracy chuckled. "Well, you're clever, I'll say that much for you. And as for what kind of man you usually are, I really can't say."

"You're not calling me a liar, are you? I have not done or said anything to make you think that."

"That's just my point, Jacques. I haven't known you long enough to be able to judge. And besides, I'm not looking for a relationship."

"It's simply a kiss, *ma petite*, not a proposal of marriage."

Tracy was quiet for a moment while she studied him and thought about what he'd said. She really, *really* wanted a taste of him and whom would it be hurting? They were both unattached adults, after all.

"I am not a married man, as you know. Why do you hesitate?"

"You're right," Tracy said slowly as she made up her mind. "It's not a proposal of marriage. It will simply be a kiss and besides, you live here and I live in the States, so this can mean nothing to either one of us." She stepped closer to him.

When she was close enough so that they were touching, he removed her purse and her sunglasses and laid them at the foot of the statue. When he straightened, she slid her hands up his chest, looked up at his mouth and smiled seductively. "Is it true, Jacques, that a Frenchman's kiss can be as satisfying as…making love?" She licked his lips.

Jacques groaned. "Trust me, *bella*," he said as pulled her closer, "a kiss will not be enough for you and I." He covered her mouth hungrily with his own.

Tracy eagerly opened her mouth for him and accepted his tongue, standing on tiptoe to take better advantage. *Instant, burning heat.* She let her eyes fall shut and just experienced. His taste went straight to her head and she clutched at his shoulders, softly moaning as his tongue again and again stroked the sensitive roof of her mouth. Taking charge of the kiss, Tracy used her teeth and her tongue to seduce and become seduced. They inched closer to one another until Tracy thought she would just sink into him. She couldn't seem to get enough of him and simply gave up thinking that she ever would.

Jacques ended the kiss, only to bury his lips behind her ear to trace a path down her neck. When that became too much for her, Tracy mustered up the breath to say, "We'd better go. I need to get back to my hotel." She was too flustered to say anything else. They planned for the next night's dinner at a restaurant he named and then they parted. Tracy took a taxi alone to her hotel room, where she ordered room service and sat up for most of the night reliving the kiss and wondering what had come over her.

The next night, Tracy nervously made her way to the bar of the restaurant where she was meeting Jacques. She was early only because she'd left her hotel before she could talk herself out of meeting him. Her attraction to him scared her and emboldened her at the same time. He'd told her that the restaurant was classy and she'd dressed accordingly in a silky, sleeveless, fitted black dress that stopped just short of her knees. She'd taken her hair and pinned it up, highlighting the darkness of her eyes even more than usual.

To her surprise, Jacques was already there, leaning against the far end of the bar. Their eyes connected as soon as she walked in. She stopped and just stared, caught in the snare of his gaze. She felt her fingers go numb as she gripped her clutch purse in her hands. She was at a loss and stood there. He started to walk towards her and his movement jarred her out of her momentary paralysis. Completely unnerved now, she hastily moved to the end of the bar closest to her, which was away from him. She closed her eyes and gripped the bar with her free hand when she felt him step up behind her.

"Good evening, *ma petite*," he whispered in Italian in her ear, making her shiver.

She turned her head, unsure if she was grateful for her three-inch heels or not. She didn't have to crane her neck anymore, but when she turned her head, her eyes were level with his lips and looking at them made the desire, which had been burning low since she'd left him, explode in her stomach. She turned away again to stare vacantly ahead. He grasped her shoulders and turned her fully around so he could see her face.

"You feel it too, no, *ma petite*? This craving. This longing. This voracious hunger." He took her hand in his and held it to his lips.

Unable to be anything but honest, Tracy nodded her head helplessly. "God, yes. I want you so much, I can almost feel you moving inside me."

Jacques groaned and gently bit the palm of her hand. "Tracy, you must not say such things if you do not plan to spend the night with me."

"I wouldn't," she whispered softly, her decision already made. "I couldn't."

As though he couldn't help himself, Jacques bent his head and captured her lips. His tongue quickly explored the caverns of her mouth, leaving her clutching at his arm for balance. She met his tongue with hers, stroking back and forth in rapacious need and then greedily sucking his tongue into her own mouth.

"Take me home, Jacques," she whispered against his lips. "Now."

Needing to touch, to feel, they leaned into one another from breast to knee in the taxi on the way to his flat. Their fingers entwined and Tracy rested her head on his chest. "My God, this has never happened to me before. I've never been so attracted to anyone in my life. I don't know what it is about you." Trying to keep from touching him all over, she reached across him, took his other hand and held it on his thigh.

"Yes, it is wonderful, is it not?" He pressed a kiss to her brow. "Have I mentioned how beautiful you look tonight? Your eyes take my breath away."

"Thank you." She lifted her mouth to kiss him, curling into him and pressing her breast into his arm. The hot and fervid kiss had them both panting with need.

"God, I love your mouth. I could make a meal of it," Jacques said and licked her lips…the corners of her mouth…her chin. The taxi lurched to a stop and Jacques pulled some bills from his wallet and practically threw them at the driver in his hurry to get her inside his building. He rushed her in past his startled doorman, hustled her into the empty elevator and pressed the button for his floor.

Pressing her against the wall, he placed a hand on either side of her face and latched onto her mouth as if he were a dying man. Tracy wrapped her arms around his waist and tried to melt into him. "Closer, Jacques," she mumbled huskily, the feel of his slacks against her bare legs intensifying her need. "I need more."

Devouring her mouth, Jacques pressed into her, at the same time lifting her onto her toes. Tracy's eyes closed lethargically as she felt him settle in right where she needed him. Her breath caught in her throat and she spread her legs wider to better accommodate him.

Still needing more, she lifted one leg to wrap around his hips and moaned when he established himself even more firmly.

Jacques was far from satisfied and he grasped her underneath her thighs and lifted her so that both of her legs were wrapped around his waist. "I could be inside you now, taking you slowly…" He moved painfully slow against her, "or quickly…" He pushed hard and fast against her. "Or at some speed in between the two." He moved moderately against her, making her cover her mouth to keep frantic noises from escaping.

When the doors opened, Jacques spun around with her in his arms and walked off the elevator. Panting heavily because every time he moved, he *moved* against her, Tracy barely noticed where they were. She grasped his neck with both hands, crossed her ankles more tightly behind his back and began to rock against him, moving up and down in conjunction with his stride and driving them each more mad with lust.

She felt orgasm rushing towards her and surprised, she tried to slow things down. She stopped moving completely. It was too late. "Oh God, Jacques—" Her words cut off as her body became stiff and straight and she pressed her opened mouth against his shoulder to muffle her satisfaction. Boneless now, she let him take all of her weight and buried her face in his neck. "I'm so sorry," she said sheepishly. "I didn't mean for it to happen without you, but…"

Jacques stopped walking and turned so that her back was against a wall. "Do not worry yourself, *ma petite,*" he said and slid a finger underneath the leg of her panties. "I will get you started again." He slipped his finger inside her and began moving it in and out. "You will *ride* again, no?"

Incredibly, Tracy felt desire take hold of her again and she grabbed hold of his shoulders, pushing back against the wall. "Y-y-yes," she got out as he took her higher and higher. "Stop. Your neigh…neighbors will hear."

"No fear," he said with a sly grin. "I have no neighbors. The top two floors of the building belong to me. So you see, we can do whatever we like, *wherever* we like." He slipped another finger inside her to join the first one.

"I see," Tracy said between breaths as his fingers moved progressively faster inside her. She reached down and grabbed his hand to still its motion, so she could concentrate better. "But I don't want to make love in a hallway, Jacques." She bent her head and gave him a kiss that was completely sexual. "Please, let's go inside." She became pliant against him when he removed his fingers and began walking again.

"Hurry, Jacques, hurry," she breathed as he unlocked the door and walked inside. She lifted her head briefly to take in her surroundings, but then tucked it to place openmouthed kisses on his neck as he started walking up the spiral staircase. Each step he took pushed him more intimately against her and, with her mouth open against his neck, Tracy struggled to breathe.

She felt the up and down movement stop and then found herself lying flat on her back on a huge bed with him on top of her. He rocked against her and she bit her lip before muttering, "If you keep doing that, I'll have my turn before you're inside of me and I don't want to do that again."

Jacques smiled and said in English, "Do you realize that everything you've said since leaving the restaurant has been in English?"

She smiled back. "Well, I can hardly be expected to speak in anything but my native language when I'm so...preoccupied and overwhelmed, can I?" She lost her smile and closed her eyes when he moved against her again. "It's hard to concentrate. Ah...ah, Jacques. Please tell me you have condoms."

"Yes, of course." He helped her to remove her dress, strapless bra and panties. She was left in nothing but high heels and jewelry. "You are magnificent," he breathed as he bent his head and took her breast into his mouth.

She wrapped naked limbs around him and heard herself say plaintively, "Jacques. Please. *Get the condom.*"

He released her, straightened and began undressing. Lassitude overtook her and she lay there naked with her legs hanging over the bed, knowing and not caring that she looked decadent. She *couldn't* care as she watched him take his clothes off, revealing his gorgeous body to her, one splendid part at a time. His wide, muscular chest was sprinkled sparsely with hair that became one thin line of black as it grew further down. He removed the shirt completely to reveal a hard, flat stomach. He didn't even bother to remove his pants; he only unbuckled the belt and unzipped them. Tracy closed her eyes in anticipation as she saw what waited for her.

She heard a drawer open and then he was back, prepared to take her. She opened her arms and body in welcome. As he sheathed himself within her, filling her so completely, her climax, this one bigger and stronger than the last one, took her immediately and she screamed. She heard his shout as she faded out.

Tracy awoke (or came to, she didn't know which) to find Jacques still lying between her legs and smiling down at her. She smiled back hesitantly. "That was strange—I've never passed out from having sex before. I mean, I've fallen asleep before, but never so quickly after."

"In French, we call this *la petite mort,* the little death. The pleasure is so intense, one feels like he is dying."

Tracy tried it on her tongue. "*La petite mort.* I like it. Did you experience it too?"

Jacques scoffed and reared back in pretended arrogance. "I? A strong, virile Frenchman experience *la petite mort*? Madam, I am offended by this suggestion! I am completely taken aback! I am...I am..." He came back into her arms, looked into her laughing eyes and said sexily, "I am ready to experience it again and again and hoping you feel the same."

Tracy couldn't help it; she smiled helplessly up into his eyes, wrapped her arms around his neck and felt like promising him anything he wanted. "I feel the same and I'm ready when you are."

Jacques stood with her in his arms and laid her at the head of the bed. "Madam," he said as he sat near her hip and began slipping her sandals off her feet. "You have only to say the word." He removed the rest of his clothing, pulled a fistful of condoms out of the drawer and tossed them on her stomach.

"Well, well," Tracy said around deep, sexy chuckles, "it appears that you could go all night if we wanted."

Jacques pushed the condoms so that they fell to her side and then lay between her legs. "Yes, we want. Do you not feel how much *we* want?" He moved against her.

She looped her arms around his neck again. "You are including me in that we, aren't you?"

"God yes, it can't be done without you." He bent his head and slowly laved her nipple with his tongue. "Only this time, we will add a little more finesse and take our time." He looked up from her breast. "I would love to hear you speak Portuguese. It sounds so beautiful coming from your mouth and when the language fell from your lips yesterday, I wanted to take you away from the noise of the city and run off with you to my family's country home. There, I would strip you of your clothing and make sweet, thorough, hedonistic love to you while you spoke to me in the language of the Portuguese."

Thoroughly charmed and turned on by his words, Tracy wrapped her legs around his waist and pushed against his chest until he flipped over so that he was on his back and she was on top of him. She slid down his body until she was sitting on his thighs. Picking up a condom, she used her teeth to open the package. "*Querido,*" she said huskily in Portuguese as she began rolling the condom over his erection.

"*Eu quero faze amor para você.*" She made a trail of kisses up his stomach, stopping to lathe his navel with her tongue. "*Eu quero faze amor para você,*" she whispered again against his skin as she crawled up his body like a hungry cat. She reached his nipples and took one between her teeth to bite gently and then tease with her tongue. She gave the other nipple the same treatment before adjusting herself over him and taking him inside her, inch by inch. As she slowly rode him and began to succumb, she said softly, "*Repetidas vezes. Repetidas vezes. Repetidas vezes...*"

Jacques held her hips still while he pumped his hips upward into her again and again until spent and satisfied, she covered him like a blanket. He pumped his hips one last time before succumbing himself. When he was able to breathe normally again, he asked, "You will spend the night with me, yes?"

"Mm hmm." The barely audible reply came from the vicinity of his neck.

Jacques smiled and trying not to disturb her, he reached around until he felt the top sheet. He spread it over their bodies and soon followed her into sleep.

Sleeping and waking to make love became the pattern during the night, until they both had had enough and fell into an exhausted, satisfied stupor.

CHAPTER THREE

Jack sat in the Paris offices of GLEA, the Global Law Enforcement Agency, and waited to speak to one of the commanders. He knew he should have gone to the offices when he'd first gotten to town, but he'd wanted to wait and get a good fix on Brickman. Unfortunately, he wouldn't be able to get Brickman back to the States without the agency's help and the help of the Parisian police. He wished things were different, but he couldn't just march into another country, arrest a criminal and take him back to Chicago. There were the matters of extradition and international laws.

He sighed impatiently at Commander Tragier when she finally returned. "It's about damned time you came back, Veronique," he growled. "What took you so long?"

Veronique stared at the man whom she'd played with every summer when they were children. Even when he irritated her, she was still forced to admit to herself how handsome he was. "So, you still have the rash habit of wanting to run outside when you are not fully dressed, eh Jacques? Your impatience will get you killed one day. Did they not teach you this during your American training?" she asked with a smirk.

"As much as I usually like to debate the merits of American law enforcement training with you, Veronique, that's not what I'm here for today. Does your organization have anything on Alexander Brickman?"

"Yes, of course," Veronique said as she slid in to the chair behind her desk and handed him the folder she'd been carrying. "But you must understand, he does not rate much of a file here. Most of his crimes have been committed inside your other country's borders and on your side of the world. So while we have an interest in him, it has not yet reached deep concern. You say that this Brickman is here in Paris? The file says he presumably blew up on a yacht in Boston Harbor five years ago."

Jack looked up in distraction from Brickman's file. So Brickman dealt in drugs, weapons and killing. There was nothing there he didn't already know. "Yes, I tracked him here almost two weeks ago. But I haven't had a lot of luck in finding him. My gut tells me that he is still here. If not in Paris, then the countryside."

Veronique's brown eyes sparkled with anger. "Your respect for our authority is underwhelming. This is not your American wild west of yesteryear! You must notify us and the Paris police when a known criminal has come into our territory. This, you know, yet this you did not do."

Jack looked up quickly. Damn it, she was mad and when Veronique was mad, there was usually no reasoning with her. He'd learned that as a child growing up with her and her younger brothers. He tried to placate her. "Ah, Veronique, you must forgive me, no? This Brickman, this *bête*," he said, calling Brickman an animal with a curl of his lip, "is responsible for the death of many and he has terrorized a friend of mine. I wanted to catch him so badly, I could almost feel his neck in my hands. You understand my zeal, no?"

Veronique knew what he was doing, but nonetheless was drawn in. She relented. "This has become personal for you?"

You don't know the half of it, Jack said silently as he thought about Julie. "Yes, in a way it has. My best friend in Chicago, Brian Keenan—you met him when he came to Paris with me two years ago—is getting married to a real beauty. Her name is Caroline Singleton—"

"The artist?" she interrupted. She sat up excitedly when he nodded yes. "But she is quite talented, yes? I have seen her work in the magazines and galleries. They are calling her the brightest star to hit the art world in years." She didn't feel it necessary to mention that she'd salivated over one of Ms. Singleton's sculptures at a local gallery recently. She was saving as much as she could every pay check so she could purchase the piece. "You know Ms. Singleton? What has this Brickman, this *cochon*, done to her?"

Jack could only be grateful that God had blessed the French with a deep appreciation for artists, an appreciation rivaled by no other culture in the world. Veronique looked mad enough to spit nails as she called Brickman a pig. He leaned forward. "Let's just say that unbeknownst to Caroline, she had possession of something that Brickman wanted last year. If she had realized what she had, Brickman would be in custody even as we speak. Unfortunately for Caroline, Brickman was well aware of the danger he was in and he was willing to go to any lengths to prevent being caught.

"As I mentioned, Caroline is a very beautiful woman and Brickman decided that he wanted to add her to his collection of beautiful things. He planned to kidnap her. He would have probably killed her once he was through with her. It all culminated in the death of one man, the unconsciousness of another, Brickman still on the loose and Caroline understandably terrified that he might come back. We brought in one of Brickman's men, but by the time we convinced him to talk, Brickman had skipped town. I've been tracking him ever since."

Veronique sat back in her chair and studied him thoughtfully. "You would like my help, yes? This is what I will do. I will allow you the use of two of my men for forty-eight hours starting tomorrow. They are all I can spare."

Jack nodded his head. "I hope they will be all I'll need. I have to fly back to Chicago at the end of the week. Brian and Caroline are having their engagement party."

"Now, on to more personal things. You have been in Paris for two weeks, yet you contacted no one, not even my brothers, your childhood friends," she said sternly.

He thought about Tracy, a dark room, helpless, feminine cries, and translated Portuguese. *Eu quero faze amor para você:* I want to make love to you. *Repetidas vezes:* Over and over. *Repetidas vezes.* He could hear her dangerously sexy voice echoing in his head and he wanted to see her again. He frowned when he realized that he was picturing her face as she laughed at something he'd said at the cemetery. The frown intensified when an image of her serious face as she studied a painting came to mind. *What was that all about?* He cleared his throat. "I have been chasing Brickman most of my time here."

"*Most* of your time? What about the rest of your time?" Veronique asked slyly.

Jack frowned. He wasn't usually so transparent. He thought about Tracy again and though he didn't realize it, he got an amorous look in his eyes and his face softened.

Veronique threw back her head and laughed. "You are still the same, eh, Jacques? Still charming the ladies out of their clothes."

Jack didn't smile. He couldn't. Even though what Veronique said had always been true in the past, he felt insulted that she would insinuate that it was the same with Tracy. Somehow, it just wasn't. "I will meet with your men tomorrow at eight. Thanks for your help, Veronique."

Alexander Brickman watched Jack leave the GLEA building. He knew who the bastard was now. It had only been a matter of time before he found out who the man tracking him was. He could handle Jack Winthrop; he'd handled plenty of other federal agents before, only Winthrop would be easier. Winthrop had a weakness that even he probably didn't realize. It was his freelance status. If Brickman killed him, he wouldn't be killing an actual agent of the government. He wasn't on the official payroll.

Brickman's glacial blue eyes took in his surroundings. Pale, thin, short and so blond his hair almost blended into his skin, he looked unassuming upon first glance. His personality, however, commanded attention. Lethally charming, he hid well his desire to hurt, his greed for more of everything, his need to thrill himself by harming others and his cold arrogance. He was perniciously opportunistic when it came to achieving his goals. Even as a child, he'd been truly dangerous to know.

Being a member of one of the most prominent and wealthiest families on the East Coast hadn't held much excitement for him, so he'd decided at an early age to make his own excitement. At the tender age of six, he'd committed his first act of "malicious mischief," when he'd slashed the tires on his teacher's car and written the word *BITCH* in permanent marker on the windshield. The blame had been placed on Charles Wainwright III, a child who was already in trouble.

Even though Charles had actually seen him do it, he'd never been able to prove that Alex was the culprit. Not Alex, the teacher's pet, who never gave a moment's trouble. No, it was more likely that Charles, the kid who had gotten in trouble only hours before for showing his friends how to spell the latest curse word his older cousin had taught him, had done it. Brickman had been bored, had seen his opportunity to bring a little excitement to his day and he'd taken it. He'd had nothing against Charles; in fact, he'd been grateful to him for presenting him with the opportunity. Charles had gotten expelled, yes, but he should have been smarter.

In prep school, he'd graduated to larceny—stealing everything from electronic toys to money from his fellow dormitory mates. Selling drugs on his Ivy League college campus seemed the natural next step to his way of thinking. Now here he was, a successful drug and arms dealer, one of the tops in his field, in fact. He loved the thrill of living on the edge. There was nothing he liked better than pitting his intellect against the establishment. He'd already amassed a fortune larger than anything his blue-blooded family could imagine, and he'd done it by working outside the law his father cherished so much. He agreed completely with Caligula who'd said that a man becomes truly free only when he realizes that the rest of the world simply doesn't matter.

He knew he was taking a chance by coming so near the GLEA building, but this was the first time that any law enforcement agent had gotten so close to him. And he hadn't gotten to his position without taking chances; that's where the thrill lay. Nonetheless, this Winthrop character was starting to worry him. He reminded him of that ex-cop back in Chicago who was marrying that beautiful bitch who had been the cause of him having to flee the city. Winthrop and that cop looked as if they could be brothers. Though Winthrop was much more handsome, they had the same coloring, same build and the same take-no-crap aura about them. Hell, they'd even started out as cops together. He'd always hated guys who looked like them. Their looks made them arrogant.

Brickman watched Winthrop cross the parking lot and slide into a silver Maserati. He signaled for his driver to follow him. Brickman knew that Winthrop was driving the car he always drove when he was in Paris, just as he knew that he stayed in the huge, elegant apartment in of one of the buildings he owned in Paris. He also knew that Jack had a personal fortune that was nothing to sneeze at. For the life of him, he couldn't figure out why the man would turn to law enforcement when he had so much family money at his disposal. Brickman supposed he himself presented the same puzzle to some, except his profession was the opposite. Why turn to crime when he had so much family money at his disposal?

He watched Jack's car as it sped up and disappeared from view after a quick left turn. "Catch up to him," he said to his driver. They followed him as Jack made another turn down one of Paris' beautiful side streets. "Keep up with him!" Brickman yelled over the front seat as they once again lost sight of him as Jack swerved around a huge delivery truck.

"I'm trying, Mr. Brickman, but I'm not going to be able to make it around that truck in time. The space is too small." When the truck finally lurched past, Brickman thought he saw the tail of Jack's car as he made another turn. "There he is! Make a right."

They turned and found themselves at a dead end. The Maserati was turned in such a way that it was blocking any forward movement. Jack Winthrop was casually leaning against the driver's side of the car as he spoke on a cell phone.

Brickman watched as Jack casually tossed the cell phone through his open car window. "Get him and bring him to me!" Brickman said urgently to the two men who served as his bodyguards. "Hurry! The bastard's probably called for back-up."

Jack tensed in readiness as he watched the two huge goons get out of Brickman's car. The arrogant asshole had done exactly as he'd thought he would when he caught his tail as he left GLEA. Come on, he said silently as the men came closer. You're mine. He knew they were carrying guns, just as he knew that they wouldn't want to take a chance on using them in such a quiet, residential area. They were counting on brawn to bring him to heel. Well, they were in for a surprise.

A siren sounded in the distance just as the goons came within a foot of his car. They were a little more than six feet from their own car. Jack pulled his gun from his inside pocket and pointed it at them. He couldn't have timed it better. "Uh, uh. Watch your step, boys. Guns on the ground, please." Jack didn't flinch as he heard the wheels on Brickman's car burn rubber as the driver frantically backed up and screeched away from the trap Jack had set.

"Your behavior, Jacques, was completely unacceptable!" Veronique yelled in French. "How dare you lure this Brickman into a car chase on the streets of Paris? Did you not realize the danger you were putting innocent people in? This…this…" she tried mightily to come up with a term, "…this *cowboy* attitude you have is detrimental to everyone!"

"I had it under control, Veronique. The street was deserted. I knew what I was doing," Jack said placatingly.

"That is just it, Jacques! *You* knew what you were doing, but I did not! Why did you not call me sooner? Why did you not call as soon as you spotted Brickman following you?"

Jack tried another tactic, hedging. "What would you say if I said I only spotted him two minutes before I decided to trap him?"

"I would say that you are lying and that you are no better at it now than you were when you were a child," Veronique said in disgust. "I will say this in English now, just to be sure you understand. What you did was dangerous and unfair, Jacques. And I didn't deserve it, especially after I offered you my help this morning. You could have gotten yourself killed."

Jack knew that that was the true problem. She was worried about him. He looked into her brown eyes. She'd always been his and her brothers' protector. Even though they each towered over her medium frame and probably outweighed her by at least fifty pounds, that didn't stop her instincts as a big sister. "I'm sorry, Veronique. I really am. I just want to catch Brickman and put him away. It's been almost all I can think about."

Veronique threw her hands up, as if to say "I give up" and sat in her chair. "Why did you wait so long to call me?" she asked.

"I didn't want your guys to scare him away with sirens and the chase. I wanted to trap him, which is exactly what I did."

"Yes, but you still did not catch him."

"I know. I was hoping he would get out of the car, but I knew he wouldn't. He's too careful for that. He did, however, send his musclemen after me, and you have them in custody right now. This may not break

Brickman, but it will cripple him for a while. I want to leave him without a net. I'm sure when you run their prints, you'll find that those two guys you have in custody are wanted for something, somewhere. And who knows," Jacques said with a shrug, "perhaps we can get information about Brickman out of them. Maybe they'll give him up."

Veronique was skeptical. "Those two? I do not think so. They are more afraid of him than they are of going to prison."

Jack stood. "Wherever Brickman was hiding out, I'm sure he's long gone now. I'll be leaving in two days myself and if nothing breaks by then, I'll be back."

Brickman seethed with anger as he watched his minions pack things away. He had to run again and it infuriated him. He added Winthrop to the list of people in his head that he owed payback. He was just the fifth. At the top were Ida Martinez, the bitch who'd shared his bed the year before, tried to sell him out and was now on the run; Tony Anders, one of his workers who gave up his Chicago hideout to the police; and Caroline Singleton and her fiancé. He'd get them all. It was just a matter of time before he did.

For now, he had to leave Paris. He knew that Facelli and Peterson were terrified of him and would hold out against telling the police anything about him. But the police had probably already run their prints and had seen that they were each wanted for crimes back in the States. Since Facelli was wanted for murder, he'd probably find it hard to resist a deal and might talk. Brickman wasn't worrying about getting away; he could do that easily. What really angered him was that two of his best men, men who had been in his employ for years, were now unavailable to him. He would kill Winthrop for that alone.

"Mr. Brickman, sir."

Brickman turned around. "Crinkle. Do you have the information I need?"

A fussbudget by nature, Crinkle straightened an already impossibly straight bow tie and flicked an invisible piece of lint from his sleeve. "Yes, sir. A Mr. Jack Winthrop has reservations on a flight to Chicago on Friday. He is expected to arrive in the city at 7 p.m. Central Standard Time."

"All well and good, Crinkle," Brickman dismissed him. *So, you're returning to the States, are you Winthrop?* Brickman thought to himself. Ordinarily, he would have had some of his associates meet Jack's plane, get rid of him and be done with it, but not this time. This enemy, he wanted to handle himself. He could still see the arrogant smirk on Winthrop's face as he set him and his men up to be captured by the police. He normally wouldn't have fallen for such an obvious trap, but he'd been royally pissed. The guy had been on his ass for months and he was sick of it.

Brickman consciously unclenched his fists and took a deep breath. "I'll see you in Chicago real soon, Winthrop, and while I'm there, I'll take care of the other three as well." But first he had a Puerto Rican bitch that he needed to track down and bring to heel.

CHAPTER FOUR

"I just can't get over how happy you look, Tracy," Caroline Singleton said to her friend as she looked through her closet for something suitable for her engagement party. "You're positively glowing. What did you get into while you were in Europe?"

If only you knew, Tracy thought. She laughed nervously. "You keep saying that. I feel like you've been saying it almost every day since I got back."

"Well, if this is what a six-week tour of Europe does for a person, then I say sign me up. I mean, here I am planning a wedding to the love of my life and I don't think I come close to having your glow."

Tracy looked at the stunningly beautiful woman who had been her best friend since preschool. Caroline's long, thin frame would have done any model proud and her blemish-free, dark brown skin was the envy of many. The obscenely long lashes, cocoa-brown eyes, high cheekbones and pouty mouth surely played a role in her fiancé falling for her the moment he saw her. Thinking of Caroline's fiancé, Tracy replied to Caroline's statement. "Whatever, Caroline. You've been on permanent fluorescence since the day Brian Keenan walked into your life.

How many times have I had to ask you to turn down the wattage?"

Caroline chuckled, but gave her a stern look. "Don't try to change the subject." She took Tracy's hand and led her over to the bed to sit down. "Don't you *want* to tell me what happened?" she asked seriously.

Tracy tightened her grip on Caroline's hands in excitement. "My God, I've been dying to tell you, but things have been so hectic since I got back and we've been so busy planning the engagement party, I haven't had a chance. Caroline, while I was in Paris, I met the most incredible man!"

"What?"

"I met this guy, he's French and he's gorgeous! His name is Jacques and we spent three wonderful days together." Tracy didn't realize it, but she was bubbling over with enthusiasm as she told Caroline of their first meeting. "He translated French into Italian for me, took me on a tour of the city and he's so smart and funny that when I wasn't trying to figure him out, I was laughing at something he'd said or done."

"Wow. I'm impressed."

"Wait. You haven't heard the best part yet." Tracy took a deep breath and let it out in a whoosh. "You're not going to believe this, I hardly believe it myself," she said under her breath. "But on my third day of knowing him, we went back to his flat and made all-out, mad, passionate love until I thought I would die from debauchery."

Caroline screamed. It was a combination of disbelief and excitement. "You did what? You're not serious!"

Tracy straightened her back and gave Caroline a look of mock severity. "I am. Perfectly."

"Really?"

"Really," Tracy confirmed.

"After only three days?" Caroline clarified, just to be sure. When Tracy nodded her head in assent, Caroline blew out a breath. "Well, then. He must have been extraordinary."

"Boy, I'll say," Tracy said mildly with a sly grin. The grin became a full-blown smile as she covered her face. "Caroline, I have never, *ever* in my life had such a mind-blowing experience as I had that night. If I could bottle Jacques' skills, I'd be the most sought-after human alive!"

Caroline's eyes grew wide, while her mouth grew slack with surprise. She had never heard Tracy use so much hyperbole—the woman was just so difficult to impress. Usually. "It was that good, huh?" Caroline asked around her shock.

"From the moment he introduced himself, I was sunk." Tracy was so caught up in her memories that she didn't take notice of Caroline's surprise. "I'm still amazed that I was able to keep my hands off him those first two days. The attraction was just that potent. He made me want to gobble him whole. I lost almost all of my inhibitions when I was with him." She paused and said in a low voice, "We almost made love in the hallway of his building. Can you can believe that?"

"Unh-uh," Caroline said dazedly and shook her head. "Definitely not."

Tracy was nodding her head. "Believe it, because we almost did. Girl, things were so hot and heavy between us that I had an orgasm right there in his arms in the hallway! Had my legs wrapped around his waist like a real, honest-to-God tramp and it just happened."

"Whoa," was all Caroline could say, followed up by a soft, "Oh my God."

"Please. God had nothing to do with it. I was so shameless, God couldn't have been *anywhere* in the room that night. Jacques just made me lose all kinds of control. I'd like to say I feel ashamed, but I just can't. Because in true slut form, I don't at all."

Caroline punched her in the arm. "Hey, I'll thank you not to call my best friend a slut. Those are fighting words," she said mildly.

"Oh, sorry," Tracy said, grinning. "I believe the correct term is 'hoochie.'"

Caroline nodded her head sagely. "That's better." She watched Tracy snicker. "But seriously, why should you feel ashamed? You're both consenting adults. I could see it if he were married, but I know he's not, because I know you."

"To be honest, I don't know if I would have been able to hold back, even if he were married. And that scares the holy hell out of me."

Always loyal, Caroline snorted. "Of course you would have. I have no doubts on that score, even if you are a trampy slut or a slutty hoochie, whichever you prefer."

Tracy only smiled uncertainly. "I just thank God I didn't have to put myself to that test. He just made me feel so alive, so different from my usual self."

"Oh, I'm so happy for you, Trace! That's just how I felt about Brian when we first met. When will the two of you see each other again?"

"See each other again? Probably never. I told you, he's French and he lives in Paris. In fact, that's what made the whole thing perfect for me. I wasn't looking for a relationship. I didn't even know I was looking for a fling, but I guess I was."

Caroline's disbelief was plain. "Are you saying that any man would have done for your fling, as you call it?"

Tracy heard the quotation marks around the word fling loud and clear. "No, I'm serious, Caro. I don't want a relationship with him."

"But don't you want to see him again?"

Tracy thought about Jacques' smile, the deep timbre of his voice, his skilled hands. She smiled. "I wouldn't say no, but the odds are totally against it and that's just fine with me."

"But if he's the perfect guy for you— "

Tracy came out of the clouds long enough to realize that Caroline actually thought that Jacques and she had a love match. "Wait a minute, Caroline. Hold your horses. Who said anything about the perfect guy? My relationship with Jacques was nothing like what you have with Brian. You guys had love at first sight. This thing with Jacques was as far away from that as you could possibly get. Ours was just instant animal attraction."

"Well, *really*. Brian and I had that too. There's nothing wrong with it. But that's not all we had and the way you were talking about this Jacques guy, I just assumed—"

"Assumed what? That I'm in love with him?" Tracy laughed gently. She didn't stop to ponder why the laughter tried to stick in her throat. "Caroline, I know that because you're ecstatically happy with Brian, you want me to find a man and have what you have, but it doesn't quite work that way."

Caroline made a disbelieving sound in her throat and scowled. "Tracy Adamson, don't you dare patronize me," she said chidingly. "I simply meant that the way you were going on about this guy, it sounds like it's more than sex. In fact, you didn't even call it that—you called it making love. Add to that, sex wasn't even the first thing you talked about. You talked about how smart and funny he is. You didn't even mention sex until the very last."

Tracy found herself getting a little frustrated and didn't know why. "That's because I wanted to build up to it, Ms. Preemptive Strike! You're reading way too much into it."

Caroline's face belied her skepticism, but she held up her hands and said, "Okay, okay. If you're sure. Do you want to hear something ironic, though? Brian wanted to set you up with his best friend, whose name just happens to be Jacques, too."

Tracy laughed, a combination of relief and true humor. "You're kidding."

"No, I'm not. He's called Jack, though. At any rate, I told Brian not to bother, because you don't like being fixed up and because you're not attracted to white men."

"After Parisian Jacques—a white man, by the way—I can't state that last claim with any truth, can I?"

Caroline was deadpan. "Not unless he pulled a Michael Jackson on you."

Tracy laughed in shock. "Caroline! I'm proud of you. That was incredibly catty."

Caroline grimaced. "I know, and mean too. I shouldn't have said it. Sorry, Michael," she said to the absent star. "Anyway, another reason I told Brian not to try to set you two up is because Jack has given no indication that he will ever settle down. He likes the single life too much and you eventually want marriage and kids. You might have heard of him or met him. He's Jack Winthrop. His family is Winthrop Industries—textiles, toothpaste, soap, diapers, cat food. They make just about everything."

"Of course I've heard of Winthrop Industries. Who hasn't? But I don't think I've heard of this Jack Winthrop."

"I thought you might have because he's in our age group and his parents used to make him squire his cousin to all of those silly debutante and society things we used to attend. I remember seeing him and meeting him on more than one occasion when we were teenagers."

"If he's white, I never would have met him. I was never allowed to attend the society parties put on by white groups, remember?"

"Oh yeah, that's right. Your mom was on her trip about you only attending traditional black affairs. She was determined that you make all of the *right* connections."

"Yeah, and look where that got me—thirty-one and alone, but having just had the most incredible sex of my life with a white man. Mother would drop her surgical tools. And Dad…" She stopped and thought before shrugging her shoulders. "I don't know what Dad would do, except agree with Mother that I shouldn't have slept with a white man."

"Wait. Wouldn't they first have to get over their shock that you'd slept with anyone at all?" Caroline joked.

"Right. Those two still expect me to be a virgin. It would kill them to know that I had my first sexual experience years ago in one of their spare bedrooms under the less-than-stellar tutelage of Arthur Proctor-Smith and a soft-porn video."

"That's right, I remember your telling me that. A psychologist would have a field day with you. You gave up your mother's—whoops, I mean *your*—prized virginity," Caroline said, tongue in cheek, "in your mother's precious Sentry Room with her arch enemy's *dark-skinned* son." Caroline said the phrase in rounded, cultured, distasteful tones, the way Mrs. Adamson always did.

Tracy chose to ignore the psychologist crack. "That's Mother, all right. You know her saying: 'Marry someone light or lighter—things will be better all around.'"

Tracy laughed, but Caroline could see her friend's pain shimmering just behind her eyes. She patted her shoulder. "Hey, don't let it get you down—some people are just foolish like that. I mean, no disrespect to your mother, but for an educated woman, an M.D., for God's sake, she's remarkably silly. I'm still mad that she tried to forbid you from playing with me, simply because I'm darker than you are."

Tracy sucked her teeth as she recalled a conversation her mother had had with her when she was seven. As she recalled, she'd just come home after playing with Caroline, who'd lived only two houses away. She frowned in remembrance.

"Tracy? Is that you?" The vaguely interested voice called after Tracy slammed the back door.

Tracy dismissed the idea of begging some peanut butter cookies off Mrs. Davenport, the housekeeper. She hoped that the silly dress that her mother had made her wear (on a Saturday, no less) was still unwrinkled and that the stupid hair ribbon was still straight around her equally stupid long curls. She wished she were back at Caroline's where she had her very own pairs of jeans and T-shirts that Mama Singleton had bought especially for her. "Yes, Mother. It's me."

"Well, don't dawdle. Come into the breakfast nook."

Tracy twisted her lips and rolled her eyes. You mean that little old closet off the dining room? She walked into the room. "Here I am, Mother."

Her mother, always immaculate, looked up from her medical journal. Penelope Johnston-Adamson was a doctor, just as her father was and just as his father had been. She'd married a doctor. She was fair-skinned, just as her parents were and as their parents before them had been. She'd married a fair-skinned man whose family had followed the same code. Her parents and grandparents had invested wisely and lived well. She'd married a man whose family had done the same and she and her husband had created wealth in their own right. She expected her daughter to follow tradition.

She gave her attention to her journal again. "I understand you were over playing with the Singleton child." The statement was not as mild as it sounded.

Tracy raised her chin defiantly. She knew where this would lead. "Yes, I was."

"As I've already told you, Tracy, there are certain things people of our station simply do not do. Why were you playing with the Singleton child again?"

"You never said I couldn't play with her. You only said the same thing you said a second ago. I didn't understand it then and I don't understand it now."

"Very well," Mrs. Adamson said and snapped the journal closed. "Since you insist upon being obtuse, I'll say it outright. You are not to play with Caroline Singleton again. She's not suitable."

"I've been playing with her since we were in preschool. How come she's all of a sudden not suitable?" Tracy did not trip over the word. She was very familiar with it, as she'd heard it almost every day of her short life. "She comes from a good family. They have a nice house. Her parents are educated and I think they have more money than you and Daddy do, 'cause they own Grandmother's Ice Cream. Their house is bigger than ours and they have more servants." Tracy couldn't fathom why all of this should be so important, but she knew it was to her mother.

"That's enough, young lady! You will not discuss those things. It should be enough that I tell you that Caroline Singleton is not suitable for you to play with. It was fine when you were in preschool, but you're getting older now. You must be seen with the right people."

Tracy stubbornly folded her arms across her chest. Caroline was the only good thing she had in her life; they were like blood sisters, and she'd be damned if she were going to give her up. "No. I won't stop playing with Caroline. She's my best friend and you're not being fair! I wish Daddy were here—he'd make you see how crazy you are."

"Tracy Montclair Johnston-Adamson, you are not to speak to me in that tone again. I won't have it! As I said, you are not to play with Caroline Singleton again and I mean it. She is too dark. You need to find children who look like yourself, your father and me. That will make things better all around for everyone."

Tracy's mouth twisted. "That's stupid. At school, Ms. Clinesdale said that black people who say things like you just said are ignorant, because we're all supposed to love each other, no matter how light or dark we are. She said that it's stupid to try to make a difference between light and dark skin because we're all in the same boat and that black people come in many different colors. You're ignorant, Mother. Ms. Clinesdale said so."

By this time, Penelope was out of her chair. Two spots of red flagged her cheeks. "You are not to repeat what some silly teacher has said to you. Of course Ms. Clinesdale is going to say that. She's dark, poor and unlucky. You, your father and I are the lucky ones.

People who look like Caroline Singleton can't help you."

Tracy was confused. "Why can't Caroline help me? She does all the time. You can't make me be friends with girls like Tiffany Roberts. I don't like her! I like Caroline." Tracy started screaming then. She knew her mother hated it and she could usually get her way when she threw a tantrum. This one was one of mythic proportions.

"I hate you! I hate you! I hate you! I'm going to tell Daddy and he'll make you stop being ignorant! You'll see; he'll make you! If you try to make me stop playing with Caroline, I'll tell Grandma Adamson and she'll hate you even more than she does now!" Tracy didn't know why this was true, but she'd always sensed that her grandmother didn't like her mother. Bringing the tantrum on home, she fell to the floor and started kicking her legs, so that the heels of her patent leather Mary Janes made crashing sounds on the hardwood floor. Out of the corner of her eye, she watched her mother massage her temples.

"You get up from that floor right now, Tracy!"

"Noooooooooo! Not until you say I can still play with Caroline!"

"I can't talk to you when you're like this. Go to your room right now!"

Tracy knew victory when it stared her in the face, so she stood up. Her mother probably wouldn't bring the subject up again for at least a couple of months. She ran up to her room, closed the door and dialed

Caroline's number. "Caroline? You won't believe it, but I had to throw another tantrum. I'm getting sooo tired of doing that!"

In the present, Tracy and Caroline laughed as they reminisced over Tracy's telephone call about her victory. "I couldn't believe your mother let you behave that way. My mother wouldn't even let me look like I was going to throw a fit."

Tracy smiled. "I know, me, either I'll never forget the time I tried my antics on your mom. She gave me such a threatening look that I stopped in mid-scream. Not only that, she looked disappointed. 'Why, Tracy,' she said in that classy way of hers, 'I can't believe a girl with as much sense as you have would act this way. Not someone so smart. I am *thoroughly* disconcerted.' I didn't know what the hell she meant, only that it couldn't be good, and that made me cry for real and apologize through the tears."

"I never knew that," Caroline said in surprise.

"I know. I was so embarrassed that your mother told me it would be our little secret. I love your mom for that and for making me feel like your home was my home."

"Mom loves you. She has since the day you punched Brandon Robinson in the nose for putting glue in my hair when we were three. Remember that?"

Tracy snorted. "Of course I do. It was the start of your life with a pageboy haircut. *And*, we went out for celebration ice cream after school. Celebratory because I'd knocked Brandon on his ass when your mom couldn't and not get arrested!"

They laughed again.

"Hey, can I join in the fun?" Tracy looked over to see Brian Keenan, Caroline's fiancé, filling the doorway. With a jolt, she realized that he looked a lot like Jacques. White, he had the same rangy build, almost the same skin tone and the same longish, black hair. He wasn't as beautiful as Jacques, though, and his eyes were a solid gray instead of that rich blue she couldn't forget. Tracy gave herself a mental shake. She just *had* to stop thinking about the man.

"Brian, you're back!" Caroline said in surprise and rose to greet him, almost running in her excitement. "What are you doing back so soon?" she asked as she wrapped her arms around his neck and they kissed as if they were alone.

Tracy lifted her brow in speculation when Brian's large hands made their way to Caroline's jean-clad butt to pat and push. She cleared her throat once, twice, three times. "Uh, hel-loooh? I know I'm small compared to you two, but I'm certainly not invisible. Nor am I blind."

Brian lifted his head from Caroline's mouth to smile wolfishly over at Tracy, while Caroline pressed her face into his chest and chuckled sheepishly. "You'll have to forgive me Tracy, but I haven't seen my future bride for four days and I missed her."

Laughing as she stood, Tracy said, "It's all right. I understand. I'll leave you to your ... catching up."

Caroline turned in Brian's arms. "No, Tracy, don't go yet. Stay for lunch."

"Caroline, my friend, your desire for me to stay is distressingly unconvincing."

Caroline had the good grace to flush. "No, I do want you to stay. Brian and I can do our catching up later. Honest, we both want you to stay." She moved away from Brian to take Tracy's hand. "I want to finish our earlier discussion."

Tracy looked over at Brian who made the sign of the cross, put his hands together in a praying gesture and mouthed the words *I'm begging you, please go*. The man was obviously jonesing for his fiancé. Tracy's lips twitched as she tried not to laugh at him. She decided to honor his request. "I'm sorry, Caroline, I really do have to go. I'm meeting a colleague for lunch."

Caroline was skeptical. "Yeah, right, Trace. Why didn't you say anything before? Don't let Brian's eagerness keep you from staying."

"It's not, though there's so much sexual frustration in this room right now, I'm surprised one of you hasn't exploded," she said and left the room to walk down the stairs of the two-story loft. Caroline and Brian followed her.

At the door, she turned to give Caroline a hug. "Don't wear yourself out too much. I don't want the two of you too exhausted to attend your own engagement party."

"Whatever," Caroline said in embarrassment as she returned the hug. "You *could* stay and have lunch with us, you know—"

She was cut off as Brian pulled her out of Tracy's arms. "Caroline, she already said no." As he hugged Tracy goodbye, he whispered in her ear, "Thanks, pal. I owe you one."

"You certainly do," Tracy whispered back and left.

Caroline leaned on the closed door and folded her arms. "What did you do to make her leave?" she asked Brian suspiciously. "Her haste was embarrassing."

Brian looked at her long, long legs that were exposed by her cutoffs, her slender, brown arms exposed to him by her sleeveless tank and her face sans makeup. She had her heavy hair pulled back in a ponytail and was obviously dressed to stay inside. She was delectable. He held his hands up, palms outward. "It only took a little persuasion. She, *unlike someone else I know,* can take a hint." He pressed his body into hers.

Caroline turned her face away to avoid his mouth. "I'm serious, Brian. I'm worried about her. She met some guy in Paris and all she could talk about was him, but then she says she's not interested in a relationship, only sex. That's just not Tracy. I think she's fooling herself. Stop that," she said when he buried his mouth in her neck after he'd slid the skinny T-shirt strap off her shoulder so he could trail kisses from the ball of her shoulder to her neck. She grabbed his hair and lifted his head so she could look into his eyes. "I mean it. I'm worried."

Brian groaned. "Sweetheart, you're killing me. Can't we talk about Tracy later?" He boosted her up and placed her legs around his waist. "You should be worried about me and my friend here. We missed you something awful." He pushed his rigid partner right where it would do him the most good. He watched Caroline's eyes slowly close in passion as she wrapped her arms tightly around his neck. He absolutely loved it when she did that.

Saying nothing, Caroline tightened her legs around him and lifted her mouth for his kiss. Brian smiled before obliging her and walking into the living area. He fell so that he was on top of her on the sofa. It seemed that they *could* talk about Tracy later.

It would have surprised Tracy to know that Caroline was worried about her. In her mind, it was over with Jacques. Even if she'd wanted to date him—and she didn't, really—she couldn't. She'd made it a practice to date only black men, and even then she was attracted only to the darker-skinned ones. She'd never been attracted to light-skinned black men, and it was because of her mother's warnings. The idea of marrying someone as light in complexion as she for the express purpose of producing babies who would be "light, bright and damned near white" sickened her. She heard her mother's shrill voice in her head telling her about the benefits of finding a man "who look likes you" and she shuddered.

As Tracy turned the key in the ignition, she thought about Jacques again. No, he definitely wasn't her usual type. But that was okay, because now that she was back home in Chicago, things could get back to normal. And nothing was more normal at the moment than trying to scrounge up a date for Caroline and Brian's engagement party. She'd go through her phone book and select a candidate when she got home.

CHAPTER FIVE

"Hello, Ida."

Ida Martinez turned fitfully in her sleep, trying to escape the soft, deadly voice she'd been hearing in her dreams for the past eight months. She still thought she was dreaming. She moaned. "¡Dios! Alexander," she said aloud from the midst of her dream. "Please don't hurt me. I wasn't going to turn you in. I swear."

From across the room, Brickman watched as Ida's lovely, black hair fell around her shoulders when she finally settled down. Clearly, she'd dreamed of him often since her betrayal. He didn't know what he'd expected to find when he finally caught up with her, but he certainly hadn't expected to find her living in little more than a hovel in the slums of Bogotá. She'd definitely shown a predilection for the finer things in life when she'd been with him. Because it had only been money, he'd given her everything she'd asked for. He moved closer to the bed when she started talking in her sleep again.

"Alexander, I only wanted you—I didn't want you to have that skinny, black bitch. I was only going to warn them, not turn you in."

Brickman smiled. Ida had never been able to understand his fascination with the black artist. She'd hated her. He now knew that she'd correctly surmised that once he had the artist in his hands, she, Ida, would no longer be of interest to him. She was definitely a tigress in bed and she was pretty, but she wasn't the artist. He'd wanted the artist. He still did.

Brickman leaned down and put his mouth to Ida's ear. "Wake up, Ida." He straightened when Ida suddenly jerked awake. He smiled down at her. "Hello, Ida. It's been far too long. Wouldn't you agree?"

Ida thought frantically about what to do as she stared into the eyes of the man she'd alternately dreaded and looked forward to seeing over the past eight months. She'd known that there was virtually nowhere she could go that he couldn't find her. It was just that simple. Brickman's reach was extensive and she was actually surprised that she'd gone this long without being caught. More likely, he'd been toying with her, wanting her to feel safe, when he could have plucked her from her hidey-hole at any time.

She hadn't felt safe since she'd met him. But when she'd been with him, she'd thrived on the thrill of the danger. Alone, she was just plain scared. She'd known he'd kill her once he found her and it wouldn't be a quick and easy death he had in store for her. Several times over the long months, she'd thought about killing herself—just to prevent the torture he was sure to inflict. But she couldn't bring herself to do it, because, perversely, she wanted to see him again. Even now, knowing that her death was a certainty, she felt her stomach quiver in response to his presence. She didn't know what to do, so she just lay there and waited for him to make his move. When it came, it was obscene in its brutality.

Brickman saw the calculation, the lust and then the acceptance in Ida's eyes. None of it surprised him. His hand reached out to snatch her chin. Using it as leverage, he lifted her up into a sitting position, with her hurriedly using her hands and feet to gain purchase. His fist whipped out to deliver a devastating blow to her right eye.

As she began to lose consciousness, Ida thought about what her uncle would find when he made his visit to the room he rented her. He came to brag about his "largesse" and to try to cop a feel. The dirty bastard would be scared shitless when he found her.

Jack couldn't believe he was seeing who he was seeing as he walked into the dining room of the parents of Caroline Singleton. His eyes were not deceiving him—it was Tracy. What was she doing here? She looked gorgeous in a pale pink, strapless dress as she stood in the center of two equally striking guests, one man and one woman. The woman he recognized, the man he didn't. He'd worked up a fine head of steam on his plane ride across the Atlantic as he'd thought about her and how he'd probably never see her again. And that even if he wanted to get in touch with her, he couldn't.

It was on the trip home that he'd realized that she'd deliberately left out the important things about herself when they were together, like her full name and where she was from, so he wouldn't be able to find her. And then she had sneaked out of the apartment like a thief in the night. How do you like that? he'd asked himself. He conveniently neglected to remind himself that he hadn't asked her for any of that pertinent information. Jack's eyes narrowed when she looked up at the man and laughed at something he'd said. Just who in the hell was he? Well, he'd soon find out. He'd go find and greet the couple of honor and then he'd take care of Tracy Whatever-the-hell-her-last-name-is.

Tracy smiled at her friend K.K. Patrickson's joke and then felt a sudden shiver travel through her. Where had that come from? The room was not cold and even if it had been, the shawl she wore over her arms ensured that she wouldn't be affected. But the shiver wasn't from cold. In fact, her skin felt prickly and heated.

"Are you all right, Tracy?" K.K. asked in concern.

Tracy looked at the woman who was known as one of America's most talented columnists and tried to corral her thoughts. "I'm fine, K.K. Why do you ask?"

"You just didn't look it, that's all. I thought that maybe you were about to swoon from the relief of Clifford leaving you for a few minutes. I have to say, Trace, the brother is fine. It's just a damn shame that such a beautiful package holds such a boring mind."

Tracy laughed. "Don't be so mean. Clifford is a nice man. He can't help it if he's clueless when it comes to talking about anything besides cars and his family's dealerships. He was kind enough to escort me tonight when I called on such short notice."

K.K. snorted. "Whatever. Brother probably did a happy dance when you called."

Tracy smiled conspiratorially and leaned in. "I'm so bored with him, I'd rather be at home watching a cat clean itself while a scoreless baseball game plays on television."

"Wow. That's bored."

Tracy joined in her laughter and then abruptly stopped. She felt that prickly sensation again and she considered removing her shawl. She just knew someone was staring at her, but she didn't see anyone when she discreetly looked around to figure out who it was. If she didn't know any better, she would swear that Jacques was somewhere near. She was feeling just the way she'd felt when she'd been in Paris with him.

"Now that right there is what I'd call a fine man," K.K. said with a speculative look in her eye. "And I can tell you from experience that he's anything but boring," she added in a sultry voice. "Oooh, and he's coming this way."

"You are so bad. That had better be your date I see coming towards us when I turn around," Tracy said as she started to do just that. The laughter caught in her throat and everything in her seemed to freeze. It couldn't be! What the hell was *he* doing here?

As if from a distance, she heard K.K. speaking. "Please. I don't think of Harrison Powers in that way and you know it. He's like a brother to me. An annoying, older brother at that. But anyway, doesn't Jack Winthrop look good? He always did know how to wear his clothes."

Jack Winthrop? Tracy thought, still trying to get her bearings. But that was her Parisian Jacques who was slowly making his way through the crush towards them. How could he possibly be Jack Winthrop too? It was slow in coming, but Tracy's intellect finally caught up with what she was seeing; and when it did and all of the implications of what she was seeing sank in, she saw red. *Quel orrendo bastardo!* was her first thought, as seeing him automatically made her think in Italian.

Tracy's chin lifted in challenge when Jacques arrived. She folded her arms and listened with half an ear as he and K.K. greeted each other.

"Jack Winthrop. It's been way too long. Where have you been keeping yourself?" K.K. asked as she returned his hug.

Jack felt a wave of insulted female dignity continually slam into him from a foot away as he greeted K.K. Patrickson. He ignored it and gave his attention to K.K., whom he hadn't seen in more than two years. With her unusual light brown, curly hair and light brown eyes vying for attention against her dark skin, she was the same standout she'd been as a teenager, when he'd see her at those tedious affairs he'd been roped into taking his cousin to. He'd always liked her and her dry sense of humor.

"K.K., it's good to see you. As for where I've been, you know I travel between Paris and Chicago frequently and work has been keeping me busy, but you know how that goes."

K.K. smiled and turned to Tracy, thinking she'd introduce them. The blast of frigid air she felt Tracy throwing at Jack made her hastily rethink that. She looked at Jack whose eyes were so hot with anger as they stared at Tracy that they appeared to be giving off blue electricity. K.K. blew out a breath. "Allll righty, then. I see introductions *aren't* in order. When you hear the signal, come out fighting. No hitting below the belt, though. It's against the rules." When this got no response, K.K. looked around for inspiration. She saw Caroline and Brian and signaled for them to come over.

"Hi all," Brian said when they reached the group. "Has everyone met—ow!" He held his side where he'd been elbowed. He looked at Caroline. "What'd you do that—"

Caroline had read the look of angry betrayal on Tracy's face and had assessed the situation almost immediately. She'd *thought* Tracy felt more for him than she'd let on. Not taking her eyes off Jack and Tracy, who hadn't taken their eyes off each other, Caroline leaned in to whisper in Brian's ear. "Don't be a dolt, Brian. Can't you see that there's something already going on between these two? I think your Jack is actually Tracy's *Parisian Jacques* and she's just found out about it. He let her believe he lived in France." She made a disappointed sound. "What a rat he turned out to be."

"Parisian Jacques? What are you talking about?" Brian whispered back.

"I'll explain later. Right now, take your idiot friend out of here before he hurts Tracy even more."

It wasn't necessary. Tracy found her voice. And though she whispered, it was scathing. "You dirty, low-down son of a dog," she began in Italian, again not thinking about it at all. "How dare you lead me to believe you were someone else! You lousy bastard!" She said aloud what she'd only thought earlier.

Jack slipped into Italian just as easily. "I? I did nothing wrong. You were the one so secretive. Why didn't you tell me your last name?"

"You didn't need to know it, you lying pirate! You pretended to be French, when you're an American. I don't even know who you really are. How do I know that everything else you said to me wasn't a lie as well? You let me believe that I wouldn't see you again. If I had known that you were American and lived in Chicago, I'd have never slept with you. I regret ever meeting you!" Intending to stalk away, she turned around abruptly, causing her skirt to fly gloriously around her knees.

The swishing skirt was like a red flag to a bull. Jack grabbed her arm to keep her there. That's when he noticed that they had an audience. Tracy must have noticed too, because she froze in his grip. Caroline, Brian and K.K. were all looking at them in fascinated confusion.

"Soooo," Brian said into the heavy silence. "My Italian's a bit rusty, but I take it you two know each other?"

Jack was surprised. Italian? They both must have just slipped into the language they had gotten used to speaking in each other's presence. He ignored Brian and turned to Caroline, who was giving him a dirty look, letting him know that she had been apprised of the situation. God, did women have to share *everything* with each other? "Is there a place where Tracy and I can speak in private?" he asked her.

"Tracy's familiar with the house. If she wants to be alone with you, she'll take you someplace," she paused, "*ma petite.*"

Jack flinched and shot Tracy an accusatory look. She folded her arms again and turned her head stiffly away. Her neck was flushed with red, though, and the cheek he could see was suffused with it, so he hoped she was embarrassed. "Well?" he asked, waiting for her to lead him to a private spot.

It was clear she wasn't going to answer, so he looked at Brian, not even bothering to seek help from Caroline again.

Brian looked at his fiancé, who'd adopted Tracy's same stiff pose. He bent his head and whispered a question. "Caroline, some of the rooms are off-limits tonight, right? Where can they go?"

"He can go to hell as far as I'm concerned," she whispered back furiously.

"Caroline. Don't be unreasonable. This is their problem and they have to solve it. You shouldn't get involved."

"But he hurt her, Brian," she whispered plaintively. "If you knew what I know, you wouldn't be trying to help him."

"Maybe he can fix whatever went wrong. It's not our business. Will you please tell Jack where they can find privacy?"

"No. If Tracy wants to, she will. She knows this house as well as I do. I won't betray her."

"Didn't you tell me that Tracy was fooling herself about Jacques? Maybe this will be a good thing," Brian whispered.

Jack, tired of being in the dark during their whispered exchange, said rather loudly, "It's okay, Brian. If Tracy doesn't want to be carried out of here, she'll tell me quickly what I want to know."

Tracy turned her head slowly. "You wouldn't dare," she said through clenched teeth.

"How do you know what I would dare? After all, as you so clearly pointed out, you don't even know me," he said coldly and watched her lips clamp tightly shut.

"Hey, guess what, folks," K.K. said. "I was over here all the time as a kid, and I too know my way around. So, before Tracy falls over from holding herself so stiffly and so Caroline won't suffer for her loyalty to a friend and because I know you're going to soon tire of being the *center of attention*," she emphasized, "I will give you directions." She clapped her hands together. "Won't that be fun, boys and girls?" She ignored the hot looks she got from Tracy and Caroline and told Jack how to get to the Singleton library.

Jack didn't waste time and had them standing in front of the library in less than a minute. They were detained just outside the door.

"Hey! What's going on here?" a handsome man balancing two full plates from the buffet asked.

Jack recognized him as the man he'd seen Tracy with earlier. So she liked them tall, dark and handsome, did she? "I'm sorry, did the lady come with you?" he asked the man.

"Clifford," Tracy said at the same time in some surprise. She'd almost forgotten that he was there.

Clifford looked between the two of them for a moment before deciding to respond to Jack, the one he viewed as a threat. "Yes, the lady came with me. And who, may I ask, are you? Don't I know you?"

"Me? Why, I'm the guy the lady's going to leave with. I'm going to give Tracy a ride home. That's who I am. Have you got a problem with that?" Jack asked arrogantly, causing Clifford's mouth to fly open in disbelief.

Tracy said forcefully, "He doesn't have to have a problem with it, because I do!"

Clifford recovered from his shock long enough to sputter, "Well, of course I have a problem with that!" He turned to Tracy. "What's going on here?"

Tracy patted his arm and tried to smile. "Don't worry about it, Clifford. I'll explain later. Jack and I have some unfinished business. Would you mind taking the food into the dining room and waiting for me? I'll be along directly."

"I don't feel comfortable leaving you here with this man," Clifford said, looking doubtfully at Jack, who made a point of doing absolutely nothing to reassure him.

"It's okay, Clifford, I promise. I'll see you in the dining room shortly. You know, K.K. Patrickson said she was starving and she wanted to talk to you about purchasing a new car. Perhaps you could kill two birds with one stone by going in to find her and giving her my food. I wouldn't want it to get cold," Tracy said, finding a small way to pay K.K. back for directing Jack to the library.

A speculative look came into Clifford's eyes. Tracy could practically hear him counting up a sale in his head. "I think that's a good idea. I'll see you in the dining room," he said, no longer feeling uncomfort-able as he suddenly recognized Jack.

"Nicely done," Jack said as he led her into the library.

"Let go of me!" Tracy snatched her arm from his grip and stalked away as soon as he closed the doors behind them.

"There's a perfect explanation for everything, if you'll just listen," Jack began.

"Oh, I'll just bet."

"There is." Jack reached out to take her arm to lead her over to a sofa. One look from her stopped that idea and he simply held his arm out in an "after you" gesture. Tracy plopped down with ill grace.

Knowing she didn't want to be anywhere near him, Jack sat on the sofa across from her. "Look, Tracy. The initial reason I didn't tell you that I was French-American was because I thought as an American in Paris not knowing the language, you might try to latch onto me."

She made a disbelieving sound. "Of all the nerve! Well, I like that."

"I know, I know. I'm the one who foisted myself off on you. That wasn't something I'd intended on doing, but you just had me so fascinated, I couldn't break away."

"How do I know you don't use that routine on hapless, female tourists all the time?"

Jack let out an explosive breath. "It's not a routine. I'm half French and when I was a child, I spent every summer there and most of my winter breaks, too. So the Jacques you saw in Paris is the real me."

"You could have told me. I feel like such a fool and so used."

He could hear the humiliation in her voice. "I've already explained why I originally didn't tell you. The other reason is because we were enjoying each other so much. You clearly didn't want to have anything to do with me after your trip ended, so I thought I'd let you have your wish. I thought telling you that I was American and lived in Chicago would scare you away. And besides that, I didn't think I'd see you again. You didn't tell me you lived in Chicago, so there was no way I could have known. I'm sorry you were hurt. I didn't mean for you to be. One thing you should know is that the time we spent together was wonderful for me. I don't regret one second of it."

Tracy mulled over what he'd said. Quietly, she said, "All right, Jacques. I believe you and I'm sorry for what I said at the party."

Jack smiled and said expansively, "No harm done."

Tracy stood. "I'd better be getting back."

Jack was startled and stood as well. "Hang on a minute. What about you? Don't you think you owe me an explanation as to why you didn't tell me your last name or where you were from?"

"You know why. Let's not play games. I didn't tell you that information because I didn't want to and you didn't want it. You never asked for it. We both studiously avoided talking about it. As you pointed out, neither one of us expected to see each other again."

Jack was nodding his head slowly. "Okay, I'll agree with that. But what about now?"

Tracy looked surprised. "What about now?" she asked against her better judgment.

"What if I told you that I think we should get to know one another stateside? You know, talk and spend some time together."

Tracy was truly alarmed now and was shaking her head no before he finished speaking. There was no way she could get involved with this man who made her do things she normally wouldn't do. She wouldn't be able to handle it. "No. That wouldn't be a good idea."

"Why not?"

"As I recall, with us, talking leads to other things."

Jack smiled. "I know. What's wrong with that?"

"There's nothing wrong with it. It just can't ever happen again."

CHAPTER SIX

"Well, Tracy. Are you ready to stop all this nonsense about finding yourself and get back to your accounting career?" Penelope Adamson asked, sipping from her china cup of tea. "You know as well as I do that that vice presidency is yours for the taking if you'd only take yourself back to work."

"Hello, to you too, Mother." Tracy sat down across from her in her receiving room. "I'm doing well, thank you. And you?"

"There's no need to be sarcastic, Tracy. I asked a simple question." Penelope didn't raise her voice. She never did.

Tracy held back a sigh as she listened to her mother's passionless voice. She couldn't remember a single time in her life that she'd ever heard her mother express emotion towards her, unless it was disappointment or anger. "I disagree, Mother." Tracy gave the maid a smile of thanks after she served her tea. "You call me this morning and demand that I come over here, and then you don't even greet me properly before you practically call me an idiot because I want to take some time and take stock of my life. There is every reason to be sarcastic. It's either that or say something we'll both regret."

Penelope was used to such outbursts from Tracy. For the life of her, she didn't know where she'd gotten her high temper. It didn't matter, however, for it was just one more thing to dislike about her daughter. She gave Tracy's navy suit and white blouse a quick once-over. At least she had a sense of style. She took a sip from her tea before responding. "Well, I don't agree. As I said, I asked you a simple question."

Tracy looked at the woman who could have almost been mistaken for her twin sister. They looked so much alike, but were so completely different that Tracy didn't know how they had survived living together for eighteen years. They were of the exact same height and coloring and her mother's skin was almost wrinkle-free. The only difference between the two was the color of their eyes. Her mother's were a pretty brown, while Tracy had inherited her color from her father. And of course her mother would never wear her chemically relaxed hair in such an "ethnic" style as Tracy did. She studied her mother thoughtfully—the wrinkle-free linen sundress, the perfectly made-up face, the bob haircut, the mani-cured nails—all presented an unshakable picture of elegance. "Have you had plastic surgery done, Mother?"

A widening of her eyes was the first indication that Penelope was disturbed by the comment. She put her teacup down with a snap and said in a mild voice, "I beg your pardon?"

"I asked if you've had any plastic surgery done. After all, that is your area of expertise and you barely look forty, let alone fifty-eight. You've got that whole Dick Clark thing going on. He hasn't aged a day since he turned forty and he's gotta be at least seventy by now, right?" Tracy kept her face and voice impassive, all the while watching her mother for any sign of emotion. She was to be disappointed.

"Tracy, I do not find the turn in the conversation amusing and your grammar is atrocious. As I understand it, 'gotta' is not a word one would find in the English language."

Tracy only smiled. She didn't know why she always set herself up like this. She'd been trying to get a rise out of her mother over something—anything—since childhood. As a child, she'd done it just to assure herself that her mother cared about her and she supposed that was why she still did it as an adult. Tracy chuckled without humor. "Of course it is, Mother. I've just used it, haven't I? In any case, it's not worth arguing over. Enlighten me again, please. Why the command performance on my part?"

"I simply want to know what you're going to do about your position at the accounting firm."

"Bogotá? What the hell is he doing in Bogotá?" Jack asked in confusion from the phone in his bedroom that Monday morning. He'd just thrown on a pair of jeans and a plain white T-shirt when the phone rang.

"He has been there, apparently, for three days," Veronique said.

Jack sighed and pinched the bridge of his nose. "All right. I'll pack my bags and try to get the next flight out." This would be a definite setback in his efforts to woo Tracy into spending time with him.

"I would not advise that, *mon ami*," Veronique said. "Certain things suggest that he is not there for a long stay."

"What certain things?"

"It appears that he only has one man with him. Is it not his usual style to take a whole entourage wherever he goes, like one of your American pop stars?"

"Yes, but you forget he is severely handicapped since your people nabbed his two bodyguards. He may just pick up more men along the way."

"Perhaps, perhaps not," Veronique said. Jack heard the shrug in her voice.

"What are the other certain things?"

"We think he went to Bogotá specifically to meet someone. He went directly to a rather run-down, dangerous part of the city. It was certainly not up to his usual standards. No, he was definitely there to meet someone."

"Is there anything else that leads you to believe that he will not stay in Bogotá long?"

"Yes. We were finally able to get one of his body-guards, this Facelli person, to talk and he said that Brickman's long-range plans include going back to Chicago. He still wants the artist, Jacques." Veronique's voice was grave.

"Are you sure Facelli isn't just giving you the run-around? I mean, I'm sure he's terrified of Brickman and the last thing he would want to do is tell Brickman's plans. That's tantamount to signing his own death warrant. I'm sure Brickman is even now working to find a way into your agency to get those two killed."

"As to that, it has already occurred. One of the men guarding Facelli attempted to inject him with a lethal dose of digitalis last night. It was lucky for Facelli that another guard heard the struggle and came running. This was when Facelli decided it would be in his favor to tell us about Brickman. The murderous guard had been bribed with 50,000 francs."

"Don't you think that this last piece of informa-tion is the most important and should have been the first thing you told me?"

"Yes, but I decided to indulge in what you Americans call payback. Petty of me, I know, but I could not resist. And it is very little compared to what you did here in Paris," Veronique chided.

"All right, Veronique. We're even. Now, answer a question for me. When the hell is GLEA going to staff an office in Colombia? If you had offices there, Brickman would be in custody by now."

Veronique laughed at his frustration. "Careful, Jacques, your impatient American side is showing again. This, we have been trying to do for more than ten years. You cannot expect it to happen over night just because you wish it so. We tried to work with the Bogotá police, but by the time we were able to work through the language barrier, Brickman had gone again. We know he's in Bogotá, but we do not know where."

The conversation went to personal things from there and Jack hung up when the doorbell sounded. He loped down the stairs of his townhouse to let Brian in.

He could have done without Brian's smirking, all-knowing smile, and he let him know it by walking away from him without issuing a greeting.

Brian stepped into the house and shut the door. He followed Jack out of the entryway, through the living room and into Jack's study. "Hey man," he said as he fit his long length onto Jack's leather sofa. "Don't sulk. After all, I don't let every guy I know almost ruin my engagement party while he fights with his girl-friend."

Across from him, Jack studied his friend thought-fully. Brian had been his best friend since they were rookie cops together on the Chicago force. They hadn't been partnered, but there was no one he trusted more to have his back in a crisis situation. Even when he'd left Brian behind to join the FBI, they'd still been able to maintain a certain amount of closeness. That was the reason he found it difficult to tell Brian about Brickman. "I don't want to ruin your mood, but I just got off the phone with my contact at GLEA. They've tracked Brickman down."

Putting all kidding aside now, Brian sat forward, alert and ready. "Where is he? When are they going to bring him in?"

"That's the problem. They've tracked him down, but they didn't bring him in. He was in Bogotá and GLEA has no jurisdiction in Colombia. By the time they were able to make the Bogotá police understand, Brickman was gone. They believe that he's going to stay in Bogotá for a while, but they also know he'll be heading this way eventually. One of his men broke and told GLEA that Brickman is still determined to get Caroline."

Too antsy to sit anymore, Brian stood up to pace around the room. "This makes no damned sense to me! Everyone's been trying for months to get this man and no one can track him down. How is that possible? Tell me, Jack. Damned useless bureaucrats. It makes me want to gear up and go after him myself."

Jack tried to calm him down. "Hey, you're a computer nerd now. What are you going to do— bring him down with a keyboard?" Brian looked over at him and the anger, love and fear Jack saw in his eyes made him wince with regret. "Look, I'm sorry for making a joke. But there's one thing I can tell you so that you won't worry so much. Brickman probably won't try to come here for months. Because we took out a couple of his bodyguards, he has to take the time to surround himself with people he can trust again. And besides that, he failed to keep one of the body-guards quiet. I would say that gives us a couple of months, at least, before he tries to step foot on American soil again."

Brian's tense muscles relaxed a fraction. "It's just that Caroline is terrified of him after what he did last winter. She's just recently stopped having nightmares and she's finally lost that haunted look she had. She's been so happy preparing for the wedding and looking for a new house. How can I tell her this and take that happiness away? This will just bring all the crazy stuff back."

Jack was sympathetic but said, "You just do it, man. The sooner she knows, the better off you'll both be. It would be unfair to leave her walking around blind. And she doesn't strike me as the type of woman who would let you get away with keeping something like this from her."

"No, you're right about that. She'd kill me." Resigned, Brian rubbed his hand across his face. "At least now we know what he's planning and can be better prepared for him. Before, we had no idea what we were up against."

"I know. Don't worry, we'll get the bastard. You can tell Caroline that I'm still on the case. That I have a personal interest in catching Brickman."

The smirk was back on Brian's face. He sat down again. "I don't know if that will make things better or worse. She's still pissed at you about Tracy. What exactly happened between you two? All I could get out of Caroline was Parisian Jacques, liar and fraud. Those are pretty harsh accusations. What the hell did you do?"

Jack sat back and relaxed. This was the true reason he had called Brian and asked him over. He told Brian about meeting Tracy in Paris. Perhaps he wasn't as detailed as Tracy had been with Caroline, but Brian got the drift. "I just really enjoyed spending time with her. Seeing Paris through her eyes made me fall in love with my place of birth all over again. She's a great girl."

"Uh-huh," Brian said and nodded slowly. "So tell me. What exactly does that mean?"

Jack narrowed his eyes. "What do *you* mean?"

"I mean, what are you planning to do about Tracy being a great girl? What do you want to do about it? In short, what are your intentions? Because you're right, Tracy is a great girl. She's not only Caroline's best friend, but I've come to care for her as I would a sister. So, you understand me when I say I don't want to see her get hurt."

It was a clear challenge and Jack didn't like it. Ironically, he understood why Brian was issuing it. No one knew better than Brian that Jack liked women, and that he never stayed in one relationship long. But how did Brian know that Tracy was looking for long-term? Maybe she was just looking for someone whose company she could enjoy until she grew tired of it. He didn't stop to wonder why he felt irritated at the thought of that. Instead, he said, "You're not in a position to know what Tracy wants or if I will hurt her or not. It certainly isn't up to you what goes on or what doesn't go on between the two of us."

"You're right, it isn't. But it is up to me whether or not you get the opportunity to find out what she wants or doesn't want," Brian said with a laugh, breaking the tension. "That is what you called me over here for, isn't it? To learn more about Tracy? To see if I could maybe arrange a meeting between you two?"

"Intuitive bastard. You're half-right. I want you to get me within proximity of her. The rest, like her full name, her phone number and all the other important stuff, she'll have to tell me herself."

"I have one condition. You have to tell me why. Why Tracy? I've never seen you act this way over a woman. They usually flock to you."

"It's not what you're thinking." Jack was almost panicked at the thought of what Brian might be thinking. "I just really enjoyed my time with her. She's intelligent, has a dry wit, she's kind, honest almost to a fault and sexy—all the things a guy wants. Like I said, she's just a great girl." He shrugged. "There's nothing more to it. I like her."

Why, the poor sod's already half in love with her, Brian thought as he looked at the defensive look in Jack's eyes, and he doesn't even realize it. Brian smiled to himself. This ought to be fun. "Okay. What do you want to know?"

Jack was suspicious of the smile and the sudden, easy capitulation. "I warn you, Brian, don't even think about doing anything. Remember that time last fall when we had lunch and you were trying to set me up with some girl? I told you then and I'm telling you now: not everyone's meant to be whipped over a woman like you are."

Brian laughed outright. "Think back real hard to that conversation, Jack. How did I describe the woman that I told you would be a good match for you? If I recall," Brian continued without giving Jack a chance to answer, "I told you she was candid, smart, witty and I think I said loyal. Ring a bell? How did you just describe Tracy? Uh, I believe you said she was intelligent, had a dry wit, and was honest almost to a fault. Damn, I'm good!" Brian crowed when he saw that Jack realized that he had been trying to set him up with Tracy all those months ago.

"I'll be damned," Jack said slowly, almost to himself. "I guess you know me better than I thought you did."

"Maybe." Brian settled back against the sofa. "So, what else is going on with you, man? How are your parents?"

"My parents are fine. Dad is still working and gardening and *Maman* is always on my case about coming out to the house more often."

"Tell her I know that I'm a poor substitute, but I'll come over if she'll make me some of her delicious *coq au vin*."

A smile flashed across Jack's face. "*Maman* loves it when you come over, because you eat so much. She's happy for you and Caroline." He didn't mention that his father had expressed reservations about Brian and Caroline together.

"I know. She sent us a beautiful bouquet after the announcement ran in the paper. Caroline loved it. I'm sorry they couldn't make the engagement party."

Jack's parents had met when Jack's dad was working in Paris for Winthrop Industries. They'd met, courted and married all within six months. They were still together almost forty years later, both claiming that each was the only one for the other. Jack believed them, but they were the exception to the rule. He'd grown up watching his uncles on both sides indulge in what today would be called serial dating. He had one uncle who didn't marry until the age of fifty-five, and even then it was to a woman thirty years younger.

His mother claimed that the men in her family just hadn't always found the right woman to settle down with and they looked until they did. She said that once they found the woman, they almost always instantly knew that she was the one. Some of the men tried to deny it by continuing their old ways, she declared, but something always drew them back to the woman they were meant to be with. Once they stopped fighting the inevitable, their *destineé*, the catting around came to a halt. This, Jack didn't believe. He liked women, period and he'd always figured that once he was ready to have children, then he'd marry one of them. Love, fate, destiny—those things had nothing to do with it.

"Hello in there. Anybody home?"

Jack pulled himself out of his thoughts when he realized that Brian had asked him a question. "I'm sorry, Brian. What did you say?"

"I asked you how things were going at the office."

About a month after leaving the agency, Jack had opened his own security firm. He had a staff of about seventy-five and most of them were ex-cops or had come from a federal agency. Their client list was small, but intense, and was comprised of large corporations and wealthy individuals.

"I haven't been there much lately, but Joe Rickleby has a good hold on things. I get a report every day on the status."

"I'd like to hire your firm to protect Caroline."

Jack wasn't surprised. It's what he would have done. "Are you sure that that's something she'll go for?"

"I know she won't go for it. In fact, she'll hate it, but I'm not leaving her vulnerable. She'll have to get used to it."

"If you're sure, but I think you should talk to her about it first. If she still balks at doing it, call me and I'll come over and give her a presentation."

"Good idea. That's the way we'll get you in the room with Tracy again. I'll ask her to come over to watch the presentation, so we can both convince Caroline of the need for your company's expertise. Of course, I won't tell her it's *your* company."

Jack pictured Tracy's face as it looked Friday night when she'd told him that they couldn't see each other anymore. She'd looked so resolute. And so beautiful. "Set it up."

CHAPTER SEVEN

Tracy thought about Jack as she looked for parking in the neighborhood around Brian's loft. He'd looked frustrated and then determined when she'd told him that she wouldn't see him anymore. She didn't know why the fact that she didn't want to see him should come as such a surprise to him. After all, that was the definition of a fling, wasn't it? Did he expect her to just jump back into bed with him just because he said so? "I don't think so," she said softly.

She pursed her lips as she began to squeeze her Jaguar in between a mini-van and a huge SUV. "I can just make it…Damn!" she swore aloud as the tail of her car swiped the SUV behind her just as she slid into place. Grabbing her purse, she hurriedly got out of the car to check out the damage. Lowering her sunglasses, she saw that there were a couple of scratches and that some of the paint from her car had marred the black finish of the other vehicle.

She blew out a breath. "Well, hell." Since she had no idea to whom the SUV belonged, she took out a pad and pencil from her purse, scribbled an apology and her name and number and slid the paper under the windshield wiper.

"I swear I didn't know anything about this." That was the first thing Caroline said when she opened the door to Tracy.

"I'm confused," Tracy said with a frown. She adjusted her Chicago White Sox cap over her somewhat messy, twisted hair she hadn't had the time or energy to fuss with after she'd taken her satin scarf off that morning. She'd gone very casual in her choice of wardrobe, wearing jeans, sneakers and a white, short-sleeved shirt of cotton. Her face was without makeup and her tired eyes were hidden behind dark glasses.

"If I'd had any idea what Brian was up to, I'd have told you not to come," Caroline said.

"Wait, Caroline, first I need to empty my bladder and I need to take these contacts out. Anything else will have to wait until I come back." Tracy made her way to the powder room hidden behind the stairs. She took care of her most pressing issue first and then took her sunglasses off and studied her eyes in the mirror. They were red-rimmed and watery. She'd been up half the night figuring out what else she needed to do to get her new business off the ground. And she'd spent the other half reliving her one night with Jacques—*Jack*—in Paris. As a result, she was tightly wrung, tired and sexually frustrated. The last thing she wanted to do was sit through a presentation about high-priced musclemen, but she agreed with Brian about the issue of Caroline's safety and she was ready to double-team her with Brian to gain her cooperation.

She took her contacts out, cleaned them and stored them in her purse. Taking her glasses case out, she plucked her wire rims out and put them on. She checked herself in the mirror again. She certainly wouldn't win any beauty contests, but one did the best with what one had available, she thought as she exited the powder room.

"Okay, Caroline," she called as she took the couple of stairs down into the living area. "What were you—Oh for God's sake," she said in disgust, "not again!" Jack stood in the living area with Brian, setting up a laptop. Jack in close-fitting, black jeans and a black T-shirt was not something her senses needed to experience when her body was already hot and bothered. I will not run, she told herself silently. Since he's Brian's best friend, we'll probably see each other all the time, so I may as well get used to it.

So instead of taking an all-out full sprint to the door as she wanted, she turned to Brian. "I'm ready to get started when you guys are." She walked further into the room and sat down in the lone chair, which was so big two more of her could have fit in it.

Jack said nothing as he watched her, willing her to look at him again. When she didn't, he turned to his presentation. He'd never seen her dressed so casually before and he thought she looked just as sexy in jeans as she did in formal wear. The glasses really turned him on. He refused to let her ignore him. He'd seen the quick flair of desire in her eyes when she'd first looked at him. Otherwise, he would have cut his losses after she deliberately ignored him. The last thing he wanted was to pursue someone who didn't want him. But she did and he was reassured as he set up his PowerPoint presentation.

He noticed how she'd purposely chosen the only chair in the room. As someone who'd been in law enforcement most of his adult life, he appreciated her strategy. Her flank was protected. He couldn't sit next to her if he wanted, not if he didn't want to cause a major social *faux pas*. She thought he wouldn't dare, which just proved that she didn't know him that well. Oh, he'd dare. He'd dare just about anything to get what he wanted. He smiled as he commenced with his presentation.

"So, are you saying that I don't necessarily have to have a bodyguard?" Caroline asked. Jack had just finished his presentation and was taking questions.

Jack noticed that Brian moved out of his slouched position and gave him a warning look, to which Jack could only shrug. "For the situation you might find yourself in, a bodyguard would be your best bet. He or she could be there when Brian isn't able to be."

"In your presentation, you said something about a body alarm. Wouldn't that be just as sufficient? I mean, I know self-defense and we have the dog. Add to that a body alarm, and everything should be covered, right?"

"It's true that body alarms have proven to be very effective in terms of letting people know you're in danger, but if Brickman should somehow get hold of you and—"

"But the body alarm comes with a tracking device, so if he does get me, I can be found."

Brian joined in the conversation. "What if he disabled the alarm? Then what would you do?"

Caroline looked at him in frustration. "What if he disabled a bodyguard? What would I do then? No, I think a body alarm and a new alarm for the house should be sufficient. He would be expecting a bodyguard, so he'd make allowances for that."

"Sweetheart, Brickman is not a stupid man. He'll probably make allowances for everything we can think of and then some," Brian said.

"If that's the case, then I don't see what difference it will make if I don't have a bodyguard."

"Caroline, I can see his point," Tracy said. "I mean, a bodyguard is human and not subject to breaking down or fizzing out on you."

Caroline looked at her. "*Et tu*, Tracy?"

Tracy smiled back at her. "Hey, I'm just trying to help. Now I'm going to go help myself to more water. If you'll excuse me?" she said to the room in general, never once looking at Jack.

Jack left Brian and Caroline to their debate and followed Tracy into the kitchen.

When she turned from closing the refrigerator, he was standing right in front of her.

"I should have expected this." She unscrewed the cap on a bottle of water and took a long drink.

"Yes, you should have," Jack agreed. He got right to the point. "Give me one reason why we shouldn't see each other."

Tracy's eyes widened in surprise. "Well, you're blunt, aren't you?" She moved away from him in agitation to toss the cap into the trash.

"And you're avoiding me. Again."

She turned to look at him. "What do you mean, 'again'? I haven't avoided you."

"Of course you have." Jack stepped closer, trapping her against the cabinets. "You sneaked out the next morning after we made love from sundown to almost sunup. You left like you'd stolen something."

"I wasn't avoiding you," Tracy said uncomfortably. "I simply left. It was morning and time to go."

"Without saying goodbye?"

She looked down at the water bottle. Her fingers were tearing the label to shreds. "Uh, I didn't think it was necessary. I certainly didn't think you'd expect me to."

Jack noticed her nervous fingers as well and wanted to smile. He recalled that when they were in

Paris and she got a little rattled, her long fingers couldn't keep still. He found the habit endearing. "By the way," he said in a low voice. "How were you the next morning?"

Distracted by his nearness, it took a moment for Tracy to respond. "What?"

"How were you feeling the next morning?" he reiterated. "We made love so often and so thoroughly—what was it, six orgasms for you? And if I recall, at least twice it was multiple. Anyway, even if you're an acrobat, your muscles and a certain other more *delicate* part of your anatomy had to be tender the next day. I was concerned."

Tracy had to clear her throat and when she finally found her voice, it came out as little more than a squeak at first. "Don't you worry about my...my... muscles!" she cried for lack of anything better to say.

"I really was worried," he said earnestly. "I became particularly concerned when I remembered one move we executed with me lying between your legs and you lifting said legs so that they— "

Tracy covered his mouth with her hand. Her breathing was erratic, her nipples begging for his special kind of attention, and she had to fight the urge to close her eyes as she remembered all too clearly the move he was referring to. "Stop it, Jacques! For God's sake, I was fine," she whispered desperately.

His tongue flicked out to scorch her palm and she snatched it away. "Well, I'm glad you were okay.

It's just too bad you didn't stick around long enough for me to see for myself. I was all prepared to heat a special oil I have and spread it all over those long, limber muscles of yours. I would have left no part untouched. The oil tastes and smells like cherry, my favorite fruit. After I rubbed you down, I would have then licked my way to paradise. Again, I would have left no part of your body untouched. Starting with your exquisite thighs, I would have laved, licked and thoroughly enjoyed myself." Tracy's eyes were closed by then, and unable to hold back any longer, she let her head fall on his chest as she imagined him doing just what he said he would have.

She moaned. "Please, Jacques, you're not playing fair."

"Fair? Who said anything about being fair?" Jack took the bottle from her and put it on the counter. He clasped her waist in his hands and bending his head, finally got what he wanted. Her mouth. She opened for him and he groaned his approval as his tongue made a wide swath through her mouth. "I've missed this," he said heatedly. "Haven't you?"

Tracy made some small sound of agreement as she stood on tiptoe to fit her mouth to his once again. God, it felt so good. *He* felt so good. She looped her arms tightly around his neck. It was when she felt herself being lifted from the floor that she came to her senses. He was trying to lift her onto the counter. She broke away from the kiss. "Jacques, we can't." She pushed away from him.

Jack let her go and took a step back. And then another. The woman could make him lose all sense of reality. His control almost completely gone, he turned away from her and leaned his head on the refrigerator. He began counting under his breath.

Tracy took the opportunity to slip by him and back into the living room. Brian and Caroline looked at her, both of them arrested by the dazed look on her face. Her swollen lips told everything. She paused in embarrassment. "Uh…I gotta go." She hurried to the chair and grabbed her purse. "Caroline, let me know what you decide to do." She was up the stairs. "I think either choice would be a good one." Her hand was on the doorknob. "Loveyoubye," she said the words quickly and as one and was gone.

"Well," Caroline said into the silence.

"I couldn't agree more," Brian said as he watched Jack walk into the living room with the same dazed look on his face that Tracy had had.

Jack looked around for Tracy. "Where is she?" he asked in a raspy voice.

"Gone," Caroline said.

"Damn." And then Jack was gone as well, leaving all of his equipment behind.

Caroline and Brian looked at each other. "Do you think it was something we said?" Brian asked impassively.

Instead of waiting for the elevator, Jack ran down the stairs, knowing that he was probably too late to catch her. He rushed out into the street and when he didn't see her, he ran to either end, hoping to catch a glimpse of her slim back. He heard a car start and he ran in that direction. Too late. "*Merde!*" he swore in French. This was the third time he'd seen her and he still didn't know any more about her than he did in Paris.

Deciding to get his equipment from Brian later, he went to his car. He saw a piece of paper underneath his windshield wiper. Thinking it was some sort of advertisement, he snatched it off with the intention of throwing it out. After getting a good look at it, however, he smiled, folded it neatly and put it in his pocket. He'd told Brian that she'd be the one to give him her name and number.

Tracy raced all the way home, barely keeping to the legal speed limit. "What the hell am I going to do now?" Her voice echoed throughout the empty car. "I'm more attracted to him than I've ever been to anyone, but I can't have a relationship with him."

She pulled into the designated parking spot in front of her greystone in the Kenwood neighborhood on the city's South Side.

She let herself into her home slowly, not even taking notice of things the way she usually did. Whenever she had a tough day at work or with her mother, she'd come home, look around at the peaceful setting and with a little help from a soak in the tub and candles, she usually felt immeasurably better. This time she shut the door behind her, walked on weak legs over to her nineteenth century staircase, sank down onto a stair and let the turmoil she was feeling overtake her. "Dear God, this is bad," she moaned into her hands in which she had buried her face. The ringing of the telephone startled her and she sighed as she rose to answer it. She knew who it was.

"As always, your timing is perfect, Caroline," she said quietly into the phone.

Caroline chuckled. "As is your intuition." Her voice became serious. "Are you okay, sweetie?"

"No, I'm not and it scares me." Tracy slumped down into the Queen Anne chair she kept by the telephone table.

"What can I do to help?"

"I'm afraid that there's nothing anyone can do about my feelings, but thanks for asking."

"What exactly are you afraid of?"

Tracy bent at the waist so that her forearms were resting on her thighs. Staring at the inlaid diamond pattern of her oak floor, she said, "It's hard to explain, but I'll try. Jacques makes me feel things that I've never felt before. Each time I see him, the feelings increase in intensity and I don't know what to do with them."

"When you came out of the kitchen, you looked like you'd found some sort of outlet."

Tracy surprised herself by laughing. "That wasn't nearly enough. I don't think that anything ever will be and that's what scares me."

"Tracy…" Caroline paused. "Is this just about sex?"

Tracy's voice was just as grave. "I don't know, but I don't think so."

"I know you don't like hearing this, but I felt the same way about Brian and that was what really had me running in the other direction. All of the other things were important, but they definitely took a back seat to all of those powerful feelings he invoked in me."

"It's not that I don't like hearing it, Caroline, it's just that I don't think you should compare your relationship with Brian to my non-relationship with Jacques. They're not the same. You fell in love with Brian almost immediately, while I fell in…in lust with Jacques. You wanted to have a relationship with Brian and I don't with Jacques. I *can't* with Jacques."

"Why don't you and why can't you?"

"Caroline, you know I've always dated only dark-skinned black men. It's just always been that way and it *will* always be that way. I can't date a white man. I can't date a man who's even lighter than I am!"

"Of course he's lighter than you. He's white," Caroline said patiently. She felt that after all these years Tracy and she were finally getting somewhere with the issue of color.

"And therein lies the problem. It's always been easier for you because your skin is dark. No one questioned your loyalty to the black race because of your skin color. No one ever accused you of having 'high-falutin' ways' because of your 'high yellow' skin color. No one ever accused you of thinking you were better than other blacks because of your light skin." Years of pain and frustration came through in Tracy's voice.

"I have to agree with you on all of those points, Tracy," Caroline said quietly, feeling her friend's pain. "But I was and have been accused of those same things because my family is wealthy, because of what my face looks like and finally, because I'm with Brian and he's white. These are all things that I'm not willing to change. I had to learn that I can't live my life worrying about what others are going to say to me or think about me, especially when they have no idea what they're talking about."

"I know when we were kids that you got the same kind of treatment that I did, but I received it in double doses. People disliked me because my skin is light *and* because my parents are wealthy. I was always getting accused of not being 'black enough,' whatever that means, and sometimes, I felt like I just couldn't win," Tracy said. "Don't get me wrong. I don't feel sorry for myself, but people can make your life difficult. I don't want my life to be any more difficult than it has to be."

"I think I understand what all of this has to do with you dating Jack," Caroline said slowly, "but I'm not sure. Will you clarify?"

"Having Jacques in my life would just make things more difficult. Just for the sake of this conversation, say I did decide to get involved with Jacques. Then let's say we have a wonderful relationship and decide we can't live without each other. Well, I want children. Any children I have with Jacques, remember this is just for the sake of this conversation," Tracy reminded Caroline, "any children I have with Jacques would most likely be very fair. What kind of life would they have?"

"All I know for sure is that they'd certainly have a better life than you had with your parents, who, incidentally, also play a role in this."

"Yes, of course they do," Tracy said without hesitation. "They, mostly my mother, did the exact opposite of what strangers did. They wanted me to believe that I was better because of my light skin and rich family. They expected me to act like I was better simply because I was out to lunch the day God was giving out second and third helpings of melanin. My light skin was supposed to be a badge of pride. My mother married my father first and foremost because of his fair skin. Her family has been doing it for generations. That's what she expects me to do. So what if I don't love the guy, so what if he's abusive? As long as he has fair skin and wealth, then he's A-okay with Mother. It's really quite sick," Tracy finished.

"You're right, it is, but should that govern your life?"

"I'm not letting it govern my life," Tracy disagreed. "I simply don't want to make my life more complicated."

"Oh, but you are, Trace," Caroline said gently. "You've made yourself believe that you're only attracted to dark-skinned men, not even opening yourself up to the possibilities of other men. There is absolutely nothing wrong with loving dark-skinned men, but you should be true to yourself about why you love them or are attracted to them. Is it just to get back at your mother, because she wants you to be with someone who looks like her family? Or are you truly attracted to them for who they are and not for what they represent—a slap in your family's face?"

Always honest, Tracy said, "I don't know what to say to that. Why haven't you ever said anything like this to me before? You've obviously thought about it."

"Because as close as we are and always have been, I sensed that you weren't ready to talk about it."

"*Merda!*" Tracy swore in Italian. "Maybe I should be seeing a therapist. Jacques would be a fool to get involved with a loon like me who has so many issues."

Caroline laughed. "I don't know about a therapist, but I do know you need to ask yourself some questions. First, if you could, would you change any of those things about yourself that people give you so much grief over? Second, do you want to get involved with Jack, even with all of the flack you'll probably get? Is he worth it? I mean, what if he's the one man you can spend the rest of your life with? In which case, you need to reach out and grab onto him with both hands."

CHAPTER EIGHT

Brickman walked through the rich estate on the outskirts of Bogotá. One of his colleagues in the business had loaned it to him for the duration of his stay. Like any other large city, Bogotá was beautiful in some places and uncompromisingly ugly in others. He, of course, preferred the beautiful. He thought about Ida and the squalor she'd been hiding in for the past seven months. He'd never understand how she'd done it, but then again, when he'd first met her in Chicago, she'd been living in little more than a slum.

People did what they had to in order to survive, he guessed. Ida had been surviving and nothing else since she'd run that fateful day. Now she could run no more. He'd caught her and taken care of unfinished business. One down and four to go. His brow lifted when his most *private* private line rang. Only one person had the number and he knew never to call him unless it was of absolute necessity. He pulled the cell phone from his pocket. "Jonathan," he said into the phone.

His younger brother heard the myriad of unasked questions in that one word and he answered them all with one sentence. "Mother is dead."

"How?"

"A brain aneurysm. She never woke up. You must come home."

"It's impossible." Brickman said.

"Why?" Jonathan's impatience was clear.

"The authorities will be expecting me to and they'll grab me as soon as I attempt to come home."

"You'll just have to be careful."

"Impossible," Brickman said again and his voice indicated that he would no longer discuss it.

Jonathan sighed. "Father will be expecting you."

"Yes, so he can personally turn me over to the authorities. You know the man hates me, just as he hates you. You'll never be more than his whipping boy. He'll never turn over the reins to the Brickman empire to you. I don't know why you stay and put up with him."

"Mother's gone. There's no reason to stay anymore."

Brickman almost smiled. "I'll make all of the arrangements for your arrival at my next stopping point. You just wait to hear from me. Welcome to the fold, little brother." he said and disconnected.

"Crinkle," he called.

"Yes, sir." Crinkle arrived only seconds later.

Brickman gave him the cell phone. "After you dispose of this, phone ahead to the compound in Fiji and have them ready it for my imminent arrival. Additionally, I need you to make arrangements for transport from Boston to Fiji for my brother. Use your usual discretion while doing so."

"Yes sir," Crinkle said. "May I ask when we will be leaving for Fiji, sir?"

"We will be leaving here in three days' time. I want my brother to arrive there two weeks from today. Of course, no one else is to be apprised of this information."

"Yes, sir. I'll take care of everything."

"You do that." Brickman resisted rubbing his hands together in satisfaction. His brother would make a perfect addition to his organization. He could trust Jonathan.

Jack answered his phone before it could ring a second time. "This had better be good. It's three in the damned morning!" he said by way of greeting.

"Get your ass out of bed, Winthrop. You need to pack for a trip to Boston. Your flight leaves in two hours."

"Why am I going to Boston, Constance?" Jack asked his boss at the agency.

"Because Brickman's mother died four days ago."

Jack was still irritated. "I repeat, why am I going to Boston?"

"Wake up, genius, and listen to me. Brickman's mother is dead. We want you in Boston for the funeral for when little Alexander makes an appearance."

Her middle-of-the-night voice was no more appealing than her daytime voice. It was harsh and sounded as if she'd stripped her throat while swallowing broken glass. Jack groaned, thinking that the only female voice he wanted to hear at this time of morning was Tracy's. "Listen, Constance. Brickman is not going to attend his mother's funeral. He's much too smart for that. He knows we'll be looking for him."

"I know that, you know that and the brass upstairs knows that. You're going to Boston for just-in-case reasons."

"Fine." Jack never wasted time arguing when he knew he would lose. "Give me the information for the flight." He hung up with Constance and dialed another number.

She picked up after the third wing. "Hello?" Her voice was sleepy and sexy.

"*Bongiorno, ma petite,*" Jack said tenderly to Tracy.

Her voice was still slow and sleepy, but now she spoke in Italian. "Jacques? Is that you?"

"*Si, bella.*"

"*Querido,* is something wrong?" she asked.

Unless she'd had a change of heart that she hadn't informed him of, Jack knew without a doubt that she was not yet fully awake. He switched to English. "Tracy, wake up, sweetheart. I need to talk to you."

He heard rustling and then alertly, "How did you get my telephone number? I'm not listed. If Brian gave it to you, I'll— "

"So you're still fighting the inevitable, huh, Tracy?" Jack interrupted. "You don't have to do bodily harm to Brian. He didn't give me your number, you did."

"I did no such thing!"

"Sure you did. I'm the black SUV." He didn't know what she said in Portuguese, but it was definitely not an endearment. He laughed. "That's not the reason I'm calling, at any rate. I'm calling to say goodbye. I have to go out of town and I don't know exactly when I'll be back."

There was complete silence on the other end and then, defiantly, "Why would you think I would care about your going out of town?"

"*Merde*," he swore under his breath, before saying louder, "I liked it better when you were still half asleep and calling me darling in Portuguese. I don't have much time, so please don't argue just for the sake of arguing, Tracy. Okay?"

"I never argue just for form's sake and if you knew me better, you'd know that."

"That's what I'm trying to do—get to know you better. But this trip is unexpected and it's messing up my plans. *Bella*, please answer my questions honestly, with yes or no. Are you still attracted to me?"

Again there was silence, and then a soft rush of breath. "I don't think there's any question about that."

"*Belissimo*. Now, I would like to get to know you better. Would you like to get to know me better?"

The silence was much longer this time and it was filled with indecision and nerves. Finally and very softly, "Yes, but there are— "

"No," Jack said gently, but firmly into the phone. "There will be no buts. Now, I'm going to Boston for work and as I said, I don't know when I'll be back. I called you to tell you that I'll be thinking about you and I'll miss you. Will you do the same for me?"

"Jacques…" She drew his name out in protest.

"Sweet *Bella*, I'm thirty-six years old, I know what I want and I like to think that I can sense when a woman wants me in the way that I want her. Honesty is very important to me and I value it in other people. I'm going to be honest and tell you that I've never before connected with anyone the way I've connected with you. I'd like to explore it further. Will you tell me something just as honest?"

Her voice was hesitant. "I…I…" She cleared her throat. "I'll be thinking about you while you're gone."

"Bravo!" Jacques said. "Now tell me in Portuguese that you'll miss me desperately while I'm gone."

That startled full-throated laughter from her and he closed his eyes and imagined her soft, sexy and warm with sleep. "You don't ask for much, do you?" she asked.

"No," he agreed. "I don't."

"I told you, Jacques," she said, "I only know a little bit of Portuguese."

"Just tell me something, anything. Whatever you say, it will sound sexy and beautiful coming from your mouth."

"Are you serious?"

"Think back to Paris and decide if you need to ask me that again."

"All right," she said and was quiet for a moment. "Okay, here it goes. *Tenha uma boa viagem e se cuido.*" She paused and her voice became softer and huskier, just the way he liked it. *"Querido, por favor volte logo. Vou sentir muito sua falta."*

Jack's voice was filled with urgency. "What did you just say?"

"Have a safe journey; keep out of danger," Tracy translated.

"Thank you. And the rest?"

Softly, she said, "Darling, please hurry home to me."

Tracy replaced the telephone receiver and lay back down in bed. She didn't know if she'd be able to get back to sleep. She'd just taken a big step with Jacques and it scared her, but it was a delicious kind of scary. She still had her worries, but he'd sounded so confident, she'd given in to her own desires and had tried to let her fears go. She'd never been brave when it came to sharing her emotions, but she wanted to try to be now.

Caroline had been right: she had to decide if Jacques was worth it, and the moment that he'd said he wanted to get to know her better, she'd decided that she should see if he was. Thinking of how he affected her, Tracy snuggled into her pillow and fell asleep with a frown on her face. She didn't know if she wanted him to be worth it.

Jack watched as mourners for Rose Brickman filed miserably out of a posh Boston funeral home. Because of who his family was in the Boston area, he actually knew some of the people in attendance, not extremely well, but well enough to strike up a conversation. He was subtle as he tried to get some questions answered. All of the answers were as expected. No, they hadn't seen Alexander. Alexander hadn't been back to the family estate in years, as far as anyone knew.

Jack followed the funeral procession to the burial ground, feeling that this was a complete waste of his time. Getting out of his car, he stood well off and in the back of the rest of the group of mourners, so as to be unobtrusive. He looked around and on his first survey, was able to pick out two plainclothesmen. He assumed that they were with the Boston police, because he had already met up with his Boston counterpart whose presence Constance had insisted upon. Catching the other man's eye, he signaled him.

The two men met near the line of limousines. "Notice anything unusual?" Jack asked the other agent.

"Nothing at all," Bradley Johnson said. "It's a bust. A waste of time and the taxpayers' money."

"Maybe," Jack said noncommittally. "I saw that Jonathan Brickman noticed me and he hasn't really taken his eyes off me since this whole thing began. Makes me think that he was told to expect us."

"You think he knew *we* were going to be here?" Bradley was incredulous.

Jack shook his head. "Maybe not us specifically, just law enforcement, period."

Bradley looked over at the large man with blond hair and blue eyes. Jonathan had taken his size and coloring from his father, while Alexander had gotten his father's coloring, but his mother's small size. Jonathan quickly looked away when Bradley caught his eyes. "He's made us, all right. But he's not even in the business. He's a flunky for his rich daddy. How could he even know what to look for to distinguish us from the other mourners? There must be three hundred people here at least."

"It's obvious that he's been in contact with his older brother. He's been told what to look for. What's he up to?" Jack's question was rhetorical and unheard, as he'd said it to himself.

"You think Brickman would trust that milksop? No way. The guy's a loser. He's let his father browbeat him and run his life for years. He still lives at home because his father demanded it and he's never gotten married because his father made him give up the one woman who would have him. Oh no, not him. The guy's too weak for Brickman's needs," Bradley opined.

"I don't know," Jack said, still staring at Jonathan. "Weak people can prove to be very useful. If he's used to taking orders from his dad, then how hard would it be for Brickman to make him take orders from him?"

"For starters, he's about twice Brickman's size. He could smash him at the first sign of disagreement."

"His father didn't keep him in line through physical force," Jack said. "It was a mind thing. People can be browbeaten for so long that they begin to believe that they can't do anything on their own. We know that Alexander Brickman, Sr., bullied all three of his children their entire lives. They all responded in ways unique to their personalities. Alexander went rebellious at a very early age and finally broke away when he didn't need his parents anymore. He's the most like his father.

"Jonathan is weak, so it was just easier for him to tow the line. The sister, Candace, is somewhat in the middle; she's under his thumb, but she doesn't exactly kowtow. She doesn't live at home and she works for the company for a pittance. However, I know that she insisted that her dad pay for everything, including her home and her cars and all of her expenses. So you see, everyone is different," Jack finished.

"Where are you going with this?"

"I'm saying that Brickman has been in touch with his brother for a reason and we need to be aware and wary of it. Personally, I think Brickman is going to scoop him up and use him to replace some of the manpower he lost in Paris. We need to keep an eye on baby brother," Jack said as he started walking towards his car.

"Hey, where are you going?" Bradley asked.

"Back to my hotel. I'm exhausted. You stay here and keep an eye on things. We can be sure that nothing big is going to happen at least until after the reading of the will. That doesn't take place until tomorrow, so there's no need for both of us to be here."

Jonathan Brickman paced his suite of rooms in the family mansion. He was nervous and more than a little scared. He was sure that the man Alex had told him to look out for had been at their mother's funeral yesterday. He and another agent. He looked at the cell phone Alex had sent him years before, willing it to show some sign of life. He'd only had to make a call on it once since he'd gotten it and that was to phone Alex and tell him that their mother was dead.

Mother. He couldn't believe she was gone. He sniffled into the handkerchief he always carried. He'd just come from the reading of their mother's will, where he hadn't been surprised to learn that she hadn't left his siblings and him anything. His father had forced her to make a will leaving him everything years before, including all of her family holdings. Jonathan didn't fret over it; it was just the way things were.

He looked at the phone again. "Damn it, Alex, will you call?" The phone vibrated in his hand, startling him enough to make him drop it. "Alex?" he whispered nervously into the phone after he picked it up.

"Who else would it be, Jonathan? From this moment forward, don't use my name. The phone is untraceable, but you never know who might be listening at the door."

"The man was there. He was at the funeral," Jonathan said.

"Are you sure?" The question was so urgent, it made Jonathan nervous again.

"Y…yes, pretty sure. At least I think it was. He's tall, dark and has unusual eyes. A dark blue."

"That's Winthrop, all right. I knew he would be there."

Jonathan clutched the phone as if it were a lifeline. "What should I do?"

"There's nothing you can do, except be on the lookout for him. Make sure he's not following when you leave. Here's a new number to reach me by." He gave him an international number. "So, brother, how'd you make out in Mother's will?"

"Abysmally, just like you and Candace," Jonathan said.

⟡

Jack approached Jonathan Brickman the next evening as he was walking towards his car from Brickman, Incorporated. "Excuse me, Mr. Brickman," he said. "I'd like to speak to you."

Jonathan looked up with startled eyes. Recognizing Jack, he panicked. He swung out with his heavy briefcase, delivering a glancing blow to Jack's right cheekbone.

The stunning pain staggered Jack and he fell back a few steps. "Goddamn it!" he roared as the pain caused stars to cluster in front of his eyes.

Jonathan didn't look back as he raced the few feet to his car. Disengaging the locks, he climbed in and started the engine. He roared from the parking lot, his thoughts preoccupied with using the new cell phone number his brother had given him.

CHAPTER NINE

Jack parked his SUV with a satisfied grunt. He'd been driving around the neighborhood for twenty minutes looking for a spot. He'd finally found one a block away from Tracy's house. He wasn't quite familiar with the area, except in a general sense. He knew that the whole neighborhood near the historically fashionable Hyde Park neighborhood had undergone major changes during the past decade or so. The distinguished old mansions, greystones and brownstones in the area had fallen into disrepair until perceptive developers and home buyers had started snapping them up for a song.

As Jack started walking towards Tracy's house, he wondered if she'd been smart enough to buy one herself or if she was in a condo or townhome. She'd told him on the phone that she'd bought her place five years before, so she'd have been quite young when she purchased it. Even run-down, most of the homes in the turn-of-the-last-century neighborhood didn't come cheaply. They'd have been a bargain for what they were—big, beautiful and time-honored—but for what people paid for them, they'd be able to have a house built on a huge lot in the suburbs.

Just what kind of accounting did she practice? Jack wondered as he stopped in front of her address. The place was massive and gorgeous. The façade of the building was made up of huge, gray stones that bulged in the middle, instead of remaining dull and flat. The house was three stories, not including the attic. The front door was painted black and held a gold knocker. Gracing each side of the door were narrow panels of stained-glass windows, each depicting what looked to be two different scenes. Jack opened the black, wrought-iron gate and walked up the stairs to get a closer look.

He smiled at the whimsical pictures of children in various forms of activity. One showed a little girl sitting on a large disk of some kind with other children standing around her. The next one showed the little girl standing and striking what could only be described as a sassy pose as the rest of the children stood back in awe. Her hands were on her hips and she had one leg forward, while the back leg took most of her weight. She appeared to be staring the rest of the children down. The last two scenes on the other panel showed the same little girl with her eyes closed and a look of concentration on her face. As in comics, two curved lines on each side of her indicated that she was moving her hips from side to side. Underneath the last scene were the words "Rise, Sally, Rise."

Jack straightened and rang the doorbell. He laughed out loud as a Vincent Price-like voice intoned:

"'*Tis some visitor wanting entrance at my front door—*

Some new visitor wanting entrance at my front door. This is it and nothing more."

He rang the bell again, just to hear the different take on Poe's "Raven" again.

He waited and then looked at his watch. No, he wasn't early. He was right on time. The door finally opened. Tracy looked at his face, particularly his right eye, which was still a bit swollen and black and blue. "My God, Jack. What happened to your eye? Just what exactly did you get into in Boston?"

"Hi," Jack said, bending his head for a kiss. After a slight hesitation, she rose on tiptoe to kiss him quickly. "Is that any way to greet a man after he's been gone for several days?"

Tracy smiled. "It is when we're standing in the doorway for all the neighbors to see." She motioned him inside, closed the door and looked at him. "Now, what happened to your eye?"

"I'll tell you later. How about a tour of this magnificent house?"

Tracy eyed him with a raised brow. "You're not trying to avoid the question, are you?"

"No, I'm not. The explanation is long and drawn out and we need to be sitting down when you hear it. I'd like to see the house first, if you don't mind. I'm really curious."

"Can't we talk about your eye while I'm showing you around?" she asked and led him towards the staircase.

"I don't want to get distracted. Hey, what is that picture on your stained glass?"

"I'm not telling, not until you tell me what happened to your eye." She started walking up the stairs. "This is the original staircase from when the house was first built in 1896. It's made of mahogany and is a bitch to keep dust-free."

Jack looked at the staircase, with stairs wide and long enough to sleep a four-year-old child and chuckled. The banister curved at the end and was decorated in an ornate swirl pattern. He counted twenty-five stairs before they reached the second-floor landing. They stood in front of a table that looked to be made of cherry. She'd placed a huge arrangement of flowers in the center of the table, next to an old-fashioned telephone.

On one side of the table was a shut door, which he assumed to be a bedroom. When he looked further down the hall to the right, he saw two more doors and another, shorter staircase. The other end of the hall held three more rooms.

"How many bedrooms?" he asked.

"In total, there are eight. Three on this floor, three smaller ones off the back staircase on this floor and two more upstairs off the library. There are five bathrooms—three up here, one upstairs and one downstairs. Any other questions?"

"Yeah. Which bedroom do you sleep in?"

"I've slept in almost all of them at one time or another," she said.

"Which one do you lay claim to now?"

"The one at the end of the hall and no, you can't see it."

He laughed. "Why not?"

"You know why not," she said and laughed with him.

"Can I at least have that proper greeting now?"

Tracy laughed again. She really had missed him while he'd been gone, despite the fact that he'd called her at least three times. Telling her that he didn't want to give her a chance to change her mind about them, he'd reminisced about their time in Paris each time they talked. They'd never really talked about ordinary, everyday things like careers and families and such, because they'd decided that they'd do that face-to-face. Now here they were face to face and all she wanted to do was jump him. Taking him by surprise, she grasped his face, pulled it down and ravaged his mouth. Ending the kiss, she traced the rim of his lips with her tongue before whispering a throaty, "Hi, Jack."

She turned and walked to the other staircase, with him following slowly behind her. They'd also decided via telephone to take things at a slower pace, so he knew that there'd be no hanky-panky during his visit. "Hell, that was just plain unfair," he said.

"I know. Deal with it," she said over her shoulder.

Jack stepped up behind her after she stopped and looked over her shoulder. He found himself looking into a huge, open space that held only a large desk, a sofa, a few floor lamps and books. The place was lined with books from floor to ceiling. She even had a ladder for the stacks. "My God," Jack breathed. "Let me guess. You like to read."

Tracy smiled. "Isn't it gorgeous? It's taken me years to fill it."

Jack walked further into the room to get a closer look. She had different sections labeled, just as in a library. She'd been really thorough. One side of the room held nonfiction and the other side held fiction. Within those sections, there was everything from biographies to history to science to classic literature to mysteries to romance. "How many?" Jack asked

"Close to seven hundred."

"I know you haven't read all of these."

Tracy was shaking her head. "With work and everything, I haven't been able to devote as much time to reading as I would have liked. But that should change now. Now that I've left accounting, I'll have more free time on my hands." She walked to the other end of the room towards a set of back stairs.

Jack followed her. "So you hope. Take it from me, starting a new business will take up a lot of your time."

"I expect that, but it won't always be that way."

"No, it won't," Jack agreed as they reached the first floor. "And you'll feel much better at the end of the day, knowing that it all belongs to you."

"I expect that, too," Tracy said. "Okay, this is the kitchen, of course." The kitchen held a long island in the center and hanging from above it were copper pots and pans on a baker's rack. In one corner of the room there was a small table with four chairs. Her appliances were quite modern and state of the art and her cabinetry looked almost brand new. "Did you gut the old kitchen?" Jack asked.

"Yeah," Tracy said with a grimace of distaste. "It was horrible, all cracked linoleum and '50s décor. It screamed 'Do Over!' It was the first room I tackled when I moved in."

"It looks great."

"Thanks." Tracy started walking out of the kitchen. She stopped and turned right, toward what looked like a short, unusually wide hallway. "I assume that this is where servants used to store dirty dishes and other things between meal courses." She pointed to a sideboard and shelves that were built into the wall. "I'm told the family who originally built the house entertained all the time and even when they weren't entertaining, they were quite formal and four- or five-course meals were not uncommon. Those small bedrooms on the second floor off the back stair-case belonged to the servants." She turned right and walked the length of the hallway, and then turned left into another room.

Jack looked around. He guessed with the computer, desk and other office equipment, that this was her office. She walked across the room, grasped the gold handles on two heavy wooden doors and slid the doors open. "This is the dining room," she said and kept walking to another set of doors. "And for the *piece de resistance*," she said as she opened the second set of doors with a flourish and stepped aside for him to enter. "My parlor."

"'Come into my parlor, said the spider to the fly,'" Jack murmured as he took in the huge room. It held very little furniture, but his eyes flashed in interest. A fireplace took up the left corner of the room and she'd placed cream-colored armchairs on either side. Jack didn't pay much attention to that. The wall next to the bay window held a flat-screen television, at least fifty inches across. Facing the television was an eight-foot-long sofa. He was in love. He turned to Tracy. "Will you marry me?" he asked with a dopey grin on his face.

She laughed. "I figured you'd like it. What guy wouldn't? I bought it for myself for Christmas last year. It was in anticipation of Wimbledon and the Williams sisters. Of course, I was in England and was able to see them live this year. And as you can see," she indicated her collection of DVDs and a DVD player encased in a high-tech-looking, silver entertainment system beneath the plasma television, "I love movies. What are you into? Football, baseball, basketball, hockey or soccer?"

"All of the above. In fact, I think the Cubs are on right now." He went over to the sofa, sat down and picked the remote up off the coffee table.

"Oh, no, you don't." Tracy sat next to him and snatched the remote from his hand. "We're supposed to talk, remember? And besides, I never would have pegged you as a guy who backed a perpetually losing cause."

"Let me guess. You're a White Sox fan."

"Born and bred," Tracy said with a competitive smile. "I like winners."

Jack snorted in disbelief. "They're winners all right. Winners who always choke when it counts."

"At least they don't pin all of their hopes on one guy who *sometimes* manages to hit a ball out of the park."

Jack settled back. He was in his element. "You're talking about Sosa, I presume. Honey, the Sox don't have a man on their team, who's good enough to lace up Sammy's cleats."

"Hah!" Tracy said. "Which team wins the cross-town classic every year? Correct me if I'm wrong, but I don't think Slammin' Sammy," she said the name with a derisive curl of her lip, "is on that team."

"The Sox have just been lucky and the referees seem to have a penchant for making bad calls against my beloved Cubbies."

Tracy laughed. "Yeah, right Jack. Don't hate the Sox just because they have the best team in the city."

"Yeah, they're the best if you consider choking a sport. In that category, they're at the top of their game." Jack grabbed his throat and pretended to be choking.

"Whatever," Tracy said in dismissal as she laughed at his exaggerated sounds and bulging eyes. "Idiot."

Jack smiled. "So tell me," he said, changing the subject. "Why do you need such a big house?"

"I don't *need* it. I just saw it and fell in love with it. At the time, its price was such a steal, I decided to snatch it up."

"What kind of security do you have?" He thought about all the ways in which the house was vulnerable to break-ins.

"I have the usual alarm. You saw the keypad near the front door."

"That's not enough," Jack said immediately. "You need it to be wired to the back door, the basement door that leads outside and the stairs. If someone got in here, they could hide for days if they wanted and you'd never even know. This house is too large for you to be living in by yourself, so you need a better alarm system."

"Would you say that about a man living here alone?" Tracy asked. Her doubt was clear.

"Yes, I would. I would say a man living here alone would need a better alarm system than what you have."

"Would you say that the house is too large for a man to live in alone?"

"It's a lot of house for *anyone* to live in by himself or herself. But since you do, we should get you better protected."

"I've always felt perfectly safe with my alarm system."

"It's an illusion, *ma petite*. A big, beautiful house like this is bound to attract crooks. I'm surprised no one broke in when you were away in Europe for six weeks."

"I had a house sitter," Tracy said with a triumphant smile. She was determined that she wouldn't spend any more money, something she didn't like doing. "And besides, the security sign on the lawn serves its purpose."

"To some degree, yes, but you still need more security."

"I just don't know, Jack. I mean, with my trying to start a new business and everything…I don't want to overspend."

"Hey, I thought you were loaded." He laughed when she only gave him a look that said she wasn't going to talk about it. "I see you have several of Caroline's paintings in here," he said, looking at the right side of the room where the entire wall to the right of the entrance into the room held paintings of varying sizes. The wall on the other side of the entrance was much narrower and held only one painting. In front of the wall full of paintings stood a baby grand piano. "Caroline is extremely hot right now in the art world. They're even talking about her in Europe. Her stuff is quite valuable and in demand. Any enterprising criminal looking in from the street can see what a gold mine you have in here."

Tracy smiled. She still got excited about her best friend since training pants suddenly being a famous artist. Caroline had only had her first showing that past January and things had snowballed from there. She'd always known her friend was talented and had early memories of posing for her. In fact, her collection held one of the first paintings Caroline had ever created. It was her attempt at a still life and she'd painted it when they were 13. Tracy had at least one piece from every year since. The house was full of Caroline's paintings and sculptures.

She'd be a fool not to protect them. It was as Jack had said. It wasn't as if she didn't have the money. She had more than enough. She just didn't like to spend so much at once. She was an accountant, after all. Frugality was in her blood. But this was her home and her best friend's work, work she herself treasured. She sighed and looked at Jack. "Okay, I guess you're right. What'd you have in mind?"

CHAPTER TEN

Tracy sat at one end of the sofa in a lotus position, while Jack sat next to her, facing her. Her face was a mask of disbelief. "So you're telling me that you're a freelance agent and you're trying to chase down the monster who terrorized Caroline last year?"

"That's it in a nutshell," Jack confirmed.

"Well?" This was said with impatience when it appeared he wasn't going to elaborate. "What's the status? When do you anticipate catching him?"

Jack shook his head. "If I could answer that, I'd have him in custody by now. All I can tell you is that we hope we're close. The last place we tracked him was Bogotá. But I'm sure he's gone from there by now."

"How'd you get the shiner? Did it have anything to do with him?"

"Indirectly, yes. His brother did it."

She was horrified. "You mean there's another one like him out there? We didn't know about him."

"Until now, we didn't think we had reason to worry about Jonathan Brickman. We just kept him and the rest of the family under light surveillance. But now, Jonathan has disappeared and we have reason to believe that he's been in contact with his brother and has gone to meet him," Jack said.

"You mean you didn't arrest him after he punched you?"

Jack touched his eye gingerly and winced in remembered embarrassment. "Bastard hit me with his briefcase. Caught me flatfooted and when the stun wore off he was gone. No one has seen him since."

"Poor thing," Tracy cooed. "Should I get you some ice? Raw meat?"

Jack knew she was teasing, but he went with it anyway. "No, not necessary." He unfolded her legs and placed her feet on the floor, effectively turning her whole body. He stretched out and laid his head in her lap. "I could use some tender loving care, though." He took her hand and splayed her fingers through his hair. "I always did love scalp massages."

Tracy laughed in disbelief at his gall. She shook her head and continued to smile as she slowly took her hands through his hair. "You don't have dandruff, do you?"

Jack let his eyes close at the touch of her fingers. "A little more to the left please." He winced when she pulled his hair. "Okay, okay," he said and chuckled.

"Did you know you have gray hair?" she asked in some surprise as her fingers sifted through the hair on the crown of his head. There were several strands of gray.

He grunted without opening his eyes.

"How *old* did you say you are?"

Surely she wasn't serious? Jack opened one eye and peeked up at her. He closed it again when he saw her playful grin. "How's the old saying go? There may be snow on the chimney, but there's still fire in the belly of the stove," he said with a wiggle of his brow.

Tracy's chuckle was confused. *"What?"*

"Whatever. You know what I mean."

"Yes," Tracy said cryptically. "I'm afraid I do and stop talking about it. We promised that we'd take this relationship slowly."

"If I recall correctly, you said it and I agreed. Reluctantly."

"Still," Tracy said, "you agreed." She sighed. "Look, Jack, you said you wanted a relationship. I'm hesitant about it, but so do I. We know we're attracted to each other and we know we burn in bed together. But that's almost the extent of what we know. I can't be in a relationship where the only thing of interest between us is sex."

"There's more than sex and I think you know it," Jack said and sat up to face her. "But let's talk about the hesitancy you have. Why are you hesitant? Don't tell me it's the black/white thing."

"No, it's not that, though I never have been able to see myself dating a white man. You caught me by surprise and even then, I told myself it would just be a one-night stand."

"Then it is the black/white thing that makes you hesitate," Jack said.

"No, it isn't. I don't have anything against your being white. The problem lies with me. Since I was a child, a really small child, I've been determined that I'd grow up and date and then marry a dark-skinned black man. Because of who I am, only a dark-skinned man would do."

"Why?"

Tracy looked at her hands to gather her thoughts. "Ever since I can remember, I've been judged based on my skin color. If it wasn't my mother telling me that I was lucky to be so light-skinned, then it was strangers disliking me because of the color of my skin. I would have perfect strangers, even adults sometimes, calling me names simply because I was shades lighter than everyone else. As a child, that was hard to cope with.

"Almost everyone in my immediate family is as light or lighter than I am. It's been a family practice for generations, especially on my mother's side, to marry other people with fair skin. It was like insurance at first, but then it became more of a matter of pride and something to use to lord over other people."

Jack looked thoroughly confused and Tracy endeavored to explain. "It goes back to slavery. Those slaves who were lighter because the master of the house had done some raping or *seducing*," this last word was said with skeptical disdain, "were given more privileges and were many times made to feel that they were better than their darker counterparts. Light skin was currency then. For instance, my great-great-great-great-grandmother, Lydia Atkins-Johnston, was

given an entire college education because of the light-
ness of her skin. She attended Spelman College and
was in one of the first graduating classes.

"She was given that opportunity because of what
she looked like, not because of how intelligent she
was. But she *was* intelligent, so she took the opportunity and ran with it. I'm the first woman in the family
since then who didn't attend Spelman. Going to
Brown University was part of my rebellion. And my
parents had to pay for it, because I threatened not to
go to college at all if they didn't. And we couldn't have
that. A Johnston without a college degree was just
unheard of. The Adamson side of the family is almost
as bad when it comes to that and other status
symbols."

"I had a colleague who graduated from
Morehouse, the all-male college in Atlanta. All he
used to talk about were the beautiful women who
attended the African-American all-female college
nearby. Isn't that the Spelman you're referring to?"
Jack asked.

"Yes. My mother would have liked nothing better
than for me to go there and meet Mr. Right. Of
course, he would have had to be of a light complexion
and from a well-to-do family. My dad is a Morehouse
man, but they'd met long before college. Both of them
come from a long line of doctors and there was really
never any question that the two of them would
marry."

"So your dad is just like your mom?"

"My dad kind of just goes with the flow. He does what's going to give him the least amount of grief and that means agreeing with my mother. He has never once initiated a conversation with me regarding complexion. I really don't think he cares one way or the other, but I don't know for sure."

"I still don't get it. You didn't want to have a relationship with me, a white man, because...." Jack gave her an opening.

"I guess I've kind of gone in circles. My mother always harped on my being with people of my own complexion or lighter and she insisted that I only date fair-skinned boys. In fact, when I was a teenager, she and her friends got together and constantly set their children up with each other. When I was old enough to realize that the whole purpose was to create fair-skinned babies to 'preserve' our kind, as she called it, I refused to date her choices anymore. In fact, I went in the opposite direction and only dated men darker than I am. I'd convinced myself that they were the only men I could be attracted to. And as for dating white men—no way!"

"Because that would mean satisfying your mom's twisted need even more," Jack guessed.

"Actually, no. Mother would have a fit if she knew I was dating you."

"Okay, I'm confused," Jack said.

"Mother doesn't mind white people, but she would never want you guys in the family. It goes back to the slavery scenario. Yes, people who looked like me may have been treated better than darker slaves, but they were still not given the benefit of being fully human. They were still slaves and when they weren't slaves, they still were treated abominably. In the eyes of the people in power, they were only slightly better than darker slaves because they were closer to looking white. Mother may not want any dark skin in the family, but she definitely wants the family to be considered black. Caroline told me that she used to see you at all the society parties when we were teenagers."

Jack frowned at the irrelevance. "My cousin never seemed to have a date and my mother always guilted me into taking her. What does that have to do with anything?"

"Well, I ran in the same social circles as Caroline usually, but my mother never allowed me to go to parties where there would be white people. She didn't want to take the chance that I might mix and mingle with unsuitables, as she called you guys. I only went to the parties put on by black society organizations and to Mother, even that was risky, because by that time, dark-skinned people had long been allowed in."

Jack rubbed his hand over his face. "This is deep."

Tracy laughed with little humor. "You said it. It's enough to give me a headache and I've been living with it my whole life."

"So, what made you decide to date me? It isn't just to piss your mother off, is it?"

"No," Tracy said. "I would never do that to you or anyone else. If you want to know the truth, it was your late-night call that did it. You were just so honest, that I felt that I needed to be just as honest. Few people besides Caroline have accepted me for me the way you have. Besides all that, I like you and I enjoy spending time with you."

"Ditto, *ma petite*," he said as he kissed her hand. "You know, I had no idea that things could be so difficult. I mean, I've heard about self-hatred in reference to African-Americans, but for things to go so deeply and be so complicated is news to me. I don't know why, because it all kind of makes sense in a twisted way. But slavery was twisted, wasn't it? So why shouldn't the repercussions of it be twisted as well?"

"Exactly," Tracy agreed. "Switch places with me." She stood. After he had, she lay down with her head on his thighs. "Now it's your turn to massage my scalp. While you're doing that, you can tell me about your family."

"Oh, no. We're not quite finished with you yet," Jack said as he let his fingers play with the twists of her hair. "Are you not a doctor because your parents wanted you to be one so badly? Did you have any interest in medicine?"

"As much as my parents would have liked that, I knew by the age of fourteen that I wouldn't be able to do it. I tried reading their medical journals and my dad even arranged for me to watch him in surgery once. I was bored to tears reading the journals and watching him operate made me sick. However, I've always loved numbers and I was good at figuring out complicated equations at an early age."

When he was quiet, she asked, "Is there anything else? Let's see. I'm a 31-year-old ex-accountant turned housing developer, I love children and I have a 13-year-old cousin whom I spoil rotten every chance I get. I'm an only child, love yoga, my favorite color is blue, I love old black and white movies and my favorite movie of all time is *To Kill a Mockingbird*. It's one of those rarities—a movie that's as good as the book."

"I've never gotten the chance to see that movie through to the end. I'm guessing you own it, so what if we watch it tonight?"

"That sounds good."

"Your hair is so cool," Jack said. "I noticed a picture of you when you were younger. You wore it long and straight then. How'd you get it from that to this?"

"My hair was one of the first things I changed when I left my parents' house. My mother used to make me put chemicals in it to get all of the kinks out. It's called a relaxer, and it does almost the reverse of what a perm would do for straight hair. Instead of making the hair curly, a relaxer straightens—relaxes—it. It's a process I hated. But from the time I was little, my mother had my hair straightened. When I was about four, she took me to the hair salon to have it pressed. That's where you take a comb, heat it over a fire and then comb it through the hair."

"Sounds scary," Jack said.

"It was to me. I suffered through that every week until I was about sixteen, and then she took me to the same salon and I got my first relaxer. Every ten weeks, religiously, I was in Madame Yvonne's salon chair getting my hair straightened with smelly chemicals. So when I went away to college, I didn't bother with the touch-ups needed to keep it straightened."

"How'd your mother take that?"

"Oh, when I came home for the holiday break with '*braids,* for heaven's sake,' Tracy imitated her mother's voice, "she tried to drag me back to Madame Yvonne. I refused to go and that was one of the infrequent times my father put his foot down against her. Still, I probably would have been bound and gagged and in Ms. Yvonne's chair if Grandmother Adamson hadn't been visiting. Mother was terrified of her and Grandmother Adamson disagreed with Mother just for the hell of it. Anyway, Grandmother Adamson took my side and I've been natural every since."

"I like your hair in either state, but the twists show more of your face, so I like this style better."

"Thanks. African-American hair is so versatile; I could get my hair in that old style without chemicals. I'd have to do some major blow-drying and curling-iron action, but it can be done. I'm thinking of doing a straight look for Caroline's wedding."

"Speaking of which: how's that coming, Ms. Maid of Honor?"

"It's coming along pretty well. Since the wedding is in November, I still have three months to wrap things up, but all of the major stuff is already taken care of."

"That's impressive. I'm Brian's main groomsman, you know. But all I have to plan is a bachelor party, and I'll just make a couple of calls and we're all set."

"I'm sure there's more to it than that." Tracy turned her body so that she was on her side and facing him, with her knees bent toward the back of the sofa. "I mean, what are you planning on doing? Calling a strip bar and ordering a keg of beer?"

"Bite your tongue," Jack said in an affronted tone. "I'm going to order *several* kegs of beer."

"Oh, I stand corrected." She laughed. "You and Brian met as rookies on the police force, right?"

"Right. We were in the same graduating class from the academy. We hit it off right away."

"I know your parents must have objected to your being a cop. Wasn't there pressure to join the family business?"

"Actually, no. I know it surprises people that one of the scions of the Winthrop fortune didn't pressure his only child to join the firm, but my dad was cool about it. He knew that I wasn't interested. Besides that, I have plenty of cousins who were more than willing to join the family business. My mother, being French, has a very European attitude about work. She didn't care what I did, as long as it was legal and made me happy. She comes from a wealthy media family and again, I have plenty of cousins who clamored to jump in with both feet."

"So, what kind of relationship do you have with your parents?" Tracy asked.

"We're pretty close. My mother thinks I'm the best thing since sliced bread and is dying for me to give her grandchildren. My dad and I have butted heads occasionally, but we usually have a good relationship. He's liberal in his politics and is a compassionate businessman, but he said something that surprised me when Brian and Caroline announced their engagement. We haven't really healed the breach caused by the argument that followed."

"Let me guess," Tracy said with a cynical twist to her lips. "He would hate the fact that we're dating, right?"

Thinking to soothe, Jack ran his hand down her side from hip to her knee. "Apparently so, yes. I don't get it, especially given the way he raised me. When I called him on his comment about Caroline and Brian, he didn't make any sense. He told me that he's not racist, but he just doesn't think that black and white people should have children together. He's like your mother in that he says that each race should work to preserve itself. He sounded perilously close to spouting off Aryan philosophy and it blew me away. I mean, this is a man who marched during the civil rights movement."

"Hey," Tracy said as she made herself more comfortable by folding her hands beneath her face. "Maybe you should try talking to him again. You're disillusioned, I can tell. Maybe there's more to the whole situation than what it seems. Surely a man who had enough sense to see that America can be horribly inequitable to some of its citizenry isn't all that bad. When was the last time you talked to him?"

"It's been a couple of months," Jack admitted. "I've been so angry and he seemed genuinely hurt that I would call him a racist, but what else am I supposed to think when he says stuff like that?"

"What does your mother say?"

"She says we're both being stubborn and should knock it off. It bothers her to see us like this, I know, and she wants us to sit down and talk."

"You should listen to your mother."

"She'd love you and your practical mind."

"Maybe," Tracy hedged, not wanting to talk about meeting his parents at such an early time in their relationship. She changed the subject. "So, is there anything else you want to know about me?"

Jack laughed. "That was a smooth segue." He paused. "Not."

Tracy only smiled. "We're taking things slowly, remember? Any more questions?"

"Yeah," Jack said. "How is it that you, an American, are fluent in—what is it? Five languages? That's what immediately impressed me about you in my uncle's restaurant in Paris. You didn't assume, like a lot of Americans do, that everyone speaks English, just because it's your native tongue."

"Thanks, I've always loved languages. Some of them I learned in school and some I learned on my own. The school I went to from kindergarten through twelfth grade, Benjamin Banneker Academy, required that we take Swahili from third through eighth grades. It was really an immersion program. We also took Spanish in elementary school. In ninth through twelfth grades, we had the option of taking one of three languages—Italian, French or Latin. I took Italian, Caroline took French and K.K. took Latin, figuring we could teach each other, which we never did.

"I learned German for business and Portuguese for pleasure. K.K. gave me some Brazilian music for my birthday and I wanted to know what they were singing about. Two CDs in particular I love. One is called *Bossa Nova Brasil* and the other one is called *Red, Hot and Rio*. The music and the language are so beautiful, I can't get enough of them. What about you? How is it that you're so multilingual?"

"Most of it is courtesy of my *maman*. She insisted that I learn Italian, German and Russian. Spanish was Dad's idea. I'm fluent in French. I learned Swahili and Japanese for the job. I wanted to enhance my résumé, so to speak, before I joined the agency. Given the current world situation, I'd be extremely useful if I knew Arabic."

"I'm sure you would. Anyone who could speak Arabic and who could prove his or her loyalty to America is in demand right now. They'd be in danger too, thanks to our fearless leader who acts like a cowboy who thinks we're all in the Wild West and he's the head gunslinger."

Jack laughed. "He is from Texas, after all."

"You're being unfair to the state of Texas," Tracy said as she studied his face, wondering what his reaction really was. To hell with it, she thought. If they were going to date, she needed to know if they were at least somewhere *near* the same wavelength.

Jack chuckled. "Maybe, but don't hold back. Tell me how you really feel."

"Since you mentioned it," Tracy said, sitting up and swinging her legs to the floor, "our foreign policy is irrational, unforgivably ill-informed and simply too slash and burn. It's ridiculous how we treat other people. Too often of late, America is like a big bully who takes his toys and leaves because no one wants to play his way. But for good measure, he smashes everyone else's before he leaves the playground."

"That's an interesting analogy," Jack said. "I like it. However, you can't completely blame the current head bully for the recent dangerous playground situation where everyone, including our allies, is ready to double-team us and take us down. There were other bullies in power before him who bullied by ignoring and withholding."

"No, I can't blame him for everything, but he has certainly exacerbated things. Thanks to him, the world has definitely become less safe and more volatile."

"I can't agree with that. Not wholly, anyway. The danger was there long before he took over. It bubbled just beneath the surface."

"Maybe, but," Tracy said as she held up her finger, "he has definitely made things worse."

"Yeah, maybe."

"Oh no," Tracy said in horror, "don't tell me you voted for him."

"No, I didn't. But in a sense, I do work for him."

"Right," Tracy said skeptically. "Jack?"

"Yeah?" Jack looked over at her.

"Did you know anyone who was killed in the plane attacks?"

"Yeah, I did. I had three friends in Washington and two in New York. What about you? Did you know anyone?"

"Yes. One of my cousins was in tower one. His parents are devastated. There's so much anger and grief and it's scary, because I don't think we've learned our lesson yet. I believe there are going to be more attacks and next time, they'll be even worse."

"What do you mean 'learned our lesson'? We can't give in to terrorists. Otherwise they'll use the same tactics again and again to get what they want."

"They're going to do it again anyway. I'm simply saying that a whole group of people feels disenfranchised from the world and that they aren't being listened to. The president's tactics clearly aren't working, so what now? I'm not saying that we should give in to terrorists, but I am saying that something has to be done. Something other than dropping bombs. Are we going to have future generations of Americans living in fear, simply because we aren't doing all we can now to try to fix the problem?"

On a roll now, Tracy leaned in. "And I'll tell you something else. The events of September 11, twenty01, did not surprise me."

"What?"

"Let me rephrase that. The manner in which things were carried out *did* surprise me, but the fact that something happened did not surprise me."

"How could it not have?"

"Because I remember the failed attempt to blow up the twin towers in 1993. I remember Timothy McVeigh in 1995 and I remember the story about two men trying to cross the border from Canada with the intent of blowing up LAX or the Space Needle, I can't remember which," she said impatiently. "Anyway, did we think that they were just going to go away because things didn't work out the way they planned the first time? Where did we think their anger would go? A large percentage of the world is still angry with the U.S., justified or not. You must know these things— you've been a G-man."

"Yes, I know these things, but your average American citizen doesn't think like that. A lot of people feel that America has done nothing wrong."

"That's because most of us don't pay attention to what's going on in the world. We don't think globally, we think nationally. Shall we talk about the Kyoto Protocol? The twenty01 World Summit on Racism? How about the International Criminal Court?"

Jack held up his hands. "No thanks. My parents and I have discussed those topics ad nauseam. None of us is happy about America's role, or I should say lack thereof, in the proceedings. Besides, how did we get on this topic anyway?"

Tracy's shrug was guilty. "It just came up, that's all. I wanted to see where you stand," she mumbled as she realized that she'd been looking for an excuse not to see him. If they'd been worlds apart on such important issues, then there was no way they could have a good relationship.

"And?"

"And…nothing. I guess you pass the test."

"Good, because if I didn't, I don't know how I would be able to talk you into making out with me during the movie later on," he joked.

"As to that, I can tell you right now. It's not going to happen."

"We'll see," Jack promised.

CHAPTER ELEVEN

"Mmm." The kiss was slow, sensual and tempting. "*Querido*, you have to go," Tracy said as her lips clung to Jack's. It was four a.m. and they stood in her doorway trying to say goodbye, as they had been for the past five minutes. And as they couldn't keep their hands off of each other, saying goodbye was difficult.

"You shouldn't call me that if you're trying to get rid of me," Jack said between little bites to her lips. "You know what your Portuguese does for me."

"Mm-hmm," she said in distraction as his mouth sneaked behind her ear. She let her neck fall to the side and slipped her arms around his neck. "One last kiss, okay?" she asked softly.

"Agreed," Jack said immediately.

They took their time. The kiss was slow, drugging and quite complete. Tracy tasted hints of the red wine they'd had, her brand of mouthwash and Jack. She closed her eyes at the familiar taste of him and enjoyed herself.

Just as caught up, Jack slid his hands underneath her hair to cup her neck. Placing his thumbs on the undersides of her chin, he gently tipped her head back for better access and plunged his tongue inside. The need to breathe soon took precedence and the kiss slowly ended. Tracy leaned into him and Jack's hands gravitated to her bottom, causing her to arch into him like a satisfied cat.

"That's it," Jack said. "No more movies at home, unless we're planning on having another night like the one we had in Paris. It's going to be at least five minutes before I'll be able to walk straight. Thank God it's too early for anyone to be out."

Tracy laughed. "I'm sorry. I knew this would be hard, but not this hard."

"I knew," Jack said in an aggrieved voice. "I can't believe we sat on your sofa making out for hours. I feel like I'm in some freaky remake of my teenage years."

"That's not true," Tracy corrected around more laughter. "It wasn't just making out. There was some heavy petting involved too, things I never let some horny, teenage boy do to me. And I certainly never did for them what I did for you."

Tired of the game, Jack's tightened his hands on her bottom and watched awareness shoot into her eyes. His voice turned quiet, its softness in tone making it all the more intense. "One day soon, you're going to lie down for me again and I'm going to feel you naked, wet and eager around me. No latex, just you and me. Skin on skin. We're going to enjoy each other so thoroughly that I'm going to catch your cries in my mouth, while your knees squeeze imprints in my waist, your nails score grooves into my back and the heels of your feet dig into the backs of my thighs."

Breath caught in her throat, Tracy shivered with need at the bald truth. "Go home, Jack," she whispered achingly, moving out of his arms and shutting the door with a soft click.

Jack smiled grimly and walked to his car. Desire for her rode him hard. Why shouldn't she be as frustrated as he was? He planned to go home and crash for a couple of hours. Tracy and he had gotten some sleep, but not nearly enough. His eyes narrowed as he thought of her waking up on top of him. Her shirt had been missing, his pants had been unzipped, her skirt had been up around her waist and using fingers, lips, teeth and tongue, they'd immediately started up again where they'd left off.

When his hands had wandered down to urgently grasp her silk-clad behind and her legs had automatically opened, he'd known it was time to break it up. He'd known that more heavy petting wouldn't have been enough to satisfy either of them.

"Johnny…baby brother," Alexander Brickman greeted his brother with outstretched arms. He'd never had much use for any of his family, except for his younger brother. His mother had never been able to share herself, because she'd been too busy being terrified of his father and therefore didn't deserve his love or his respect. His father was a tyrant who cared for nothing but money and position. And his sister, well, he'd had no use for her since the day she was born. He'd seen the pink bow in her hair and had known she'd be useless to him, just like his mother. He'd been five at the time.

However, when he was six, they'd brought Jonathan home from the hospital. He'd known a big change was going to take place and he'd been ready for it. He'd taken Jonathan under his wing from the first and his brother was the only person in the world for whom he felt any kind of affection.

Brickman opened his arms and despite their differences in height and body mass, Jonathan somehow managed to take comfort in his brother's arms. "Alex, I'm so glad to be here," Jonathan said with heartfelt feeling. That incident with the blue-eyed federal agent had frightened him terribly. He'd been afraid that he'd get arrested for assault, so he hadn't returned home. Holing up in a ratty motel, he'd waited anxiously for days until it was time for him to leave to come to Alex. He'd been desperate to get to his older brother. Alex would protect him. Jonathan assured himself as his brother released him.

"Pull yourself together. You're here now on beautiful Fiji. Everything is okay."

"But, Alex," Jonathan said with a worried frown, "that agent with the blue eyes is really determined. I don't think he'll ever give up." He sat down on one

of the expansive lawn chairs that his brother indicated.

Brickman laughed and took the chair on the
other side of the table. "Don't worry about Jack
Winthrop, Jonathan. He's just another agent and
agents have been chasing me for more than fifteen
years. They'll be chasing me for fifteen more. The
only difference with Jack Winthrop is that I'll get
him before he decides to stop trying to get me."

"But Alex, now that I'm here, I'm afraid I'll slow
you down. I don't know how to be...I mean, I know
nothing about your...your business," he finished
lamely.

Brickman smiled and Jonathan had to keep
himself from cringing at the evil that was so
apparent. "No worries there, little brother. I'll teach
you everything you need to know. You'll be my
right-hand man. I know I can trust you, just like
when we were kids. We'll be a team. Of sorts." He
raised his glass for a toast and waited while Jonathan
nervously raised his.

"Now," Brickman said after taking a long drink
from the champagne, "I've got a plan that will take
care of Jack Winthrop. This plan is so brilliant, so
resplendent, that it will not only take care of our
handsome Monsieur Winthrop, but it will also get
rid of all those who would stand in my way. At the
same time, the plan, if carried out correctly, will get
me the one thing I've wanted more than anything
else in the past decade."

Jonathan thought about his brother's lifelong peculiar habit of trying to collect the unusually beautiful and exotic. He recalled his parents discussing a particularly brutal incident with a Japanese college girlfriend after she'd tried to break things off. The girl had needed extensive plastic surgery once Alex had gotten through with her. Jonathan suppressed a shudder.

When he spoke, his voice was hesitant. "And…and you want me to help you with this plan?"

"Yes, of course. You, my dear boy, are an integral part. The plan won't work without you."

Ida stared through the window down at the two men. She wondered who the stranger was. She'd never seen him before, she was sure of it. True, she'd been kept a prisoner in the third-floor room since they'd reached the islands and before that in Bogotá, she'd been shut in recuperating from the vicious thrashing Brickman had given her. Maybe she shouldn't be surprised that she didn't recognize the man. But she'd spent a lot of time with Brickman the year before, prior to things going horribly wrong, so she knew that he rarely let in anyone new. Who was that man?

She made her way carefully away from the window and over to the bed. She still wasn't one hundred percent and had to do everything slowly.

After he'd found her in Bogotá, Alex had taken his time beating her. He'd systematically broken her nose, shattered her cheekbone, dislocated her shoulder and cracked all of her ribs. He'd broken six of her fingers, three on each hand, and then he'd taken a stiletto and abused the sensitive bottoms of her feet. Both of them were still wrapped in heavy gauze. It was the only way she could walk with any degree of comfort.

As she'd passed in and out of consciousness, she'd looked into his eyes and had seen the unholy glee that connoted insanity. As she remembered how his thrill level had elevated as he'd caused her more and more pain, Ida was surprised she still lived. But no matter how fervently she'd prayed for death during his torture, he hadn't killed her. Mercilessly, he'd kept her alive, then had taken her to a doctor to be looked at, and a plastic surgeon to have her face fixed. However, he hadn't done either of those things until after he'd personally and joyfully reset her shoulder. She gently rubbed her shoulder as she remembered his maniacal chuckle just before she'd passed out.

They still had sex. He had, in fact, demanded it a week after he'd beaten her. She hadn't been able to participate fully, but he'd walked away satisfied. Ida began to cry silent tears as she realized she loved Brickman enough to let him kill her. Needing him, she constantly feared that he would abandon her and had nightmares in which she found herself back in

Bogotá without him. She didn't know what she could do to make him trust her again. He kept talking about this master plan he had. She wondered what it was. Whatever he was planning, she hoped he'd let her help him. Maybe she could prove her loyalty to him that way and take care of that bitch Caroline at the same time.

Surprised, Tracy opened her front door and looked at Jack. "Hi! What are you doing here? I told you I had appointments today—" she paused in indecision, "didn't I? I mean, we didn't make plans or anything, did we?" she asked and turned to go into the living room. Where was that briefcase? She could have sworn she'd left it down here…she was going to be late for her first appointment if she didn't hurry.

Jack stepped inside and closed the door. He stood on the landing and watched her rush around the living room in a distracted flurry. She was dressed quite professionally in something he'd never seen before, a black mini-skirted suit with some sort of frilly blouse underneath. He liked it. A lot. After she took a final pass around the room, she rushed up the stairs to where he was standing, heading for the main staircase. Jack snagged her wrist, causing her forward momentum to suddenly stop. She slammed into him.

Jack held her arms and smiled down into her frustrated eyes. "This is a different look."

Tracy smiled. "You like?"

"Of course." Jack took her hand and spun her around in a small circle, so he could take a closer look. The skirt showed just enough skin to have him lifting his brow. The heels gave her about three extra inches and he marveled once again at all the leg she had. She wasn't even that tall. He wasn't complaining, though.

Tracy sighed and blew out a breath, at the same time smothering a chuckle at the licentious way he was looking at her. "Stop it, Jack. I have to leave here in the next fifteen minutes and I can't find my brief-case." She pushed out of his arms and turned to rush up the stairs. "I can feel your eyes traveling," she warned over her shoulder. "Stop ogling me and tell me what you're doing here."

Jack took his eyes off her behind long enough to notice her briefcase near the telephone table. He reached over and picked it up. "*Bella*," he called, "here's your briefcase."

Tracy rushed back down the stairs. Taking her briefcase, she asked, "Where was it? I could have sworn I'd left it…oh, never mind. I'd better get going." She turned to grab her purse and car keys off the telephone table. She paused and turned back around. "Jack?"

"Yeah?"

"What are you doing here? And why are you dressed like that?" He was wearing a navy suit. He hated suits. She felt suspicion sneaking into her mind. She *had* told him about her appointments. She'd told him on the phone three nights before and she remembered now that he'd expressed concern about her going to her first appointment alone because of its location. He'd better not be trying to go... Tracy didn't finish her thought, because Jack confirmed she was right when he spoke.

"I thought I'd go with you to your appointment today," he said with studied nonchalance. "I'd like to see you in action and we could spend some time together. This will just be another step in our getting to know one another better."

"Uh huh," Tracy said, not fooled for a moment. They walked through the door. "And this has nothing to do with the fact that I'm looking at a property in a neighborhood that's fallen on hard times?"

Jack took her keys. "The way you say it makes it sound like this is recent news." He turned to lock her door. "That neighborhood's lived on hard times for the better part of twenty-five years. I don't like the idea of you going there by yourself."

Tracy sighed as he returned her keys. They'd had a similar conversation on the phone. "I'll be perfectly fine. A representative from the city will be there to show me around the property, so I won't be alone. And after that, I'm meeting K.K. Patrickson with one of the girls she mentors and the girl's mother to show them a property I own. And besides," she said impatiently when he didn't say anything, "the neighborhood you're concerned about has been up and coming for years."

Jack made a disgusted sound. "Up and coming," he muttered. "Up and coming, my ass. Just when does the damned thing plan to arrive, is what I'd like to know."

Tracy tried unsuccessfully to stifle her chuckles. She put her briefcase down. "Jack." She put her hand on his cheek and looked into his eyes. "Baby, I appreciate your concern, given your penchant for law enforcement and all, but it isn't necessary. No one's cared for me in this way before, and I kind of like feeling cherished, which is why I haven't called you high-handed and just walked to my car and driven off. However, if you're going to want to come with me every time I go out on an appointment, when will you work? Shouldn't you be out chasing the bad guys?"

Jack looked down into her serious eyes. How to explain to her that he was concerned for her safety because of Brickman? He had no concrete proof that Brickman would come after her, but he knew the jackass would come after him because of what he'd done to him in Paris. He welcomed it, but he didn't want Tracy involved and he knew Brickman wasn't averse to using whatever means necessary to get what he wanted.

She'd come to mean so much to him in the few, short weeks he'd known her that he didn't even want to think about anything happening to her.

He knew Brickman was planning something big, but he could do nothing about it until he knew where he was. And right now, Brickman was completely off the radar. It was as if he'd disappeared. He answered Tracy, "I've got time. The only bad guy I want hasn't resurfaced yet."

"Jack," Tracy said and smoothed the frown from his forehead, "I'll be fine. Anyway, what were you planning to do? Stand around looking like an enforcer from La Cosa Nostra?" She touched a gentle finger to his fading black eye. "That's sweet, but it's not needed." She wrapped her arms around his waist. "You'd scare the little city employee to death. He wouldn't know what to do and he'd be so jealous of this gorgeous face of yours, he might try to jack up the price to make up for his feelings of inadequacy around you."

Jack scowled. "Don't pander, Tracy."

"Me? Pander?" she said, tongue in cheek and trying not to laugh. "Never! You know you're gorgeous and I know you're gorgeous, so let's not pretend others won't." He hated his looks being talked about, so as a consequence, she loved to tease him about them.

"Stop. This has nothing to do with your going to that house alone. Now, are you going to let me come or not?"

"No," Tracy said definitively, and pressed a kiss to the corner of his mouth and lingered there. "Don't worry about me. I'm a very careful person," she said between the kisses she was trailing from one corner of his mouth to the other.

Jack seized her lips with his own, making her go boneless against him when he caressed the roof of her mouth with his tongue. He loved it when he could cause that. He felt her arms tighten around him and he caressed it again.

God, she loved his kisses! Like a hedonist, Tracy fell into the pleasure of it, completely taking what she was offered. His hands slipped under her jacket and pressed into her back, pulling her closer. Tracy obligingly moved in, nestling her heightened nipples into his chest.

"Okay, okay," Jack whispered as he broke the kiss and pressed brief ones to her mouth. "I won't go with you. All you had to do was say no. You didn't have to bribe me." He kissed the top of her head.

"Well, cold, hard logic wasn't working, so I thought I'd try something else. Did it work?" Tracy asked impishly. She removed one arm from around his waist and trailed her hand down the front of his slacks. "Yes, I can see it did."

"Okay, you win. I can't play this game, at least not when there's no apparent relief in sight." He finished with hope as he looked at her.

"Oh, no. Don't look at me like that." Tracy moved out of his arms and picked up her briefcase. "I have to leave for my appointment right now, or else I'll be unforgivably late."

Jack followed her to her car and shut her door after she was inside. He leaned into the open window for another kiss. "Just be careful," he said against her lips. "Be aware of everything around you."

"Will do," Tracy said, just before driving off.

Jack watched with a frown on his face until her car disappeared. She was really getting to him. He woke up with her on his mind and usually fell asleep in the same state. And just witness his behavior today. He'd rushed over to her place like a lovesick fool. He didn't know if he liked the sensation or not.

CHAPTER TWELVE

"Do you think they really liked the property?" Tracy asked her friend K.K. after they'd seen Kenya and her mother off in their mini-van. Tracy turned to look back at the ranch house. It held three bedrooms, two baths and a full basement. The repairs it needed were minimal and would take a little less than a month to complete.

"Are you kidding?" K.K. lowered her sunglasses a bit to look at Tracy. "Mrs. Tinker loved it, and did you see the look on Kenya's face? That's the most animated I've ever seen her and I've been mentoring her for five months. Are you sure you want to rent it to them? At the price you're asking, I mean? You could get a lot more than $700 for a house this size in a middle-class neighborhood like this. Three times as much, maybe."

"I know," Tracy said. "But remember, Mrs. Tinker will be responsible for all of the utilities, including the water bill. I just hope she can handle it. She's a widow raising three children and she has a car note, insurance and other necessities. It could be a stretch for her and she did say she'd like to rent-to-own, so that would take the rent up to $850."

"Oh, Mrs. Tinker can handle it. She told me she's due for a raise at work and she expects that to be at least $2,000. I don't know how much she makes as an administrative assistant, but $2,000 is $2,000."

"She meets my minimum requirement for salary," Tracy said. "In fact, she's over it and that raise will put her just under my maximum."

"I didn't know you had a maximum."

"Oh, yes. I had to. I want to help those who truly need it, not those who can more than afford what I'm asking for, but are just looking for a good deal."

"Mrs. Tinker and her girls definitely qualify for needing help," K.K. said. "She's been struggling since her husband died five years ago in a car crash. This will help her immensely. Kenya told me that before her father died, her parents had been looking at homes. Unfortunately there was no insurance, so Mrs. Tinker has gone through all of their savings. And no bank would talk to her about purchasing a house once there was only one income."

"I know, K.K. You told me all of this last week, remember? How old did you say the girls are?"

"Kenya is fifteen, and there's an eleven-year-old and an eight-year-old. I've met the other two girls only briefly, but they're both smart, like Kenya."

"I could see the intelligence in Kenya's big, brown eyes, but she never spoke around me, so I couldn't really gauge her. She seemed so serious."

"She is. Since her father died, she's had to help her mother out in a lot of ways. She baby-sits, cooks, cleans and helps with homework. In addition to all of that, she gets top marks at school. She has plans for college. Speaking of education, when will the repairs be done so they can move in? It would be perfect if they could move in before the new school year starts."

Tracy bit her lip. "I see. I don't know if that can be done, though. The guy I hired to rehab the place says it would take a little less than a month. That could mean anywhere from a day less to a week less. Doesn't school start pretty soon?"

"Yeah, the public schools start in about two and a half weeks." K.K. was quiet for a moment and then said, "Hey, if I chip in with, say a $3,500 bonus at the end, do you think the guy would guarantee a two-week turnaround?"

"I could ask him," Tracy said. She looked at the woman she'd called friend since the seventh grade. Ever since Caroline and she had befriended K.K. on her first day on the grounds of Banneker Academy, K.K. had had a tough shell. Few people knew the kind, generous person beneath, because K.K. was too defensive to let them. Given K.K.'s family background and the tragedy in it, Tracy was not surprised. "That's really generous of you, K.K. I'm sure I can work something out with the contractor."

K.K. turned her head away from the look Tracy was giving her. It made her uncomfortable. "Hey, it's only money. Don't get sappy on me, now. Save that for when you tell me about your relationship with Jack the hottie."

Tracy studied K.K. The contrast of her light hair and eyes and dark skin made her beautiful in a different sort of way. That wildly curling mane of hair and tall, statuesque figure of hers turned the heads of both men and women. The fact that she dressed like the diva that she was kept eyes on her as well. "Did you and Jack ever have a relationship?"

K.K.'s mouth twisted in disappointment. "Girl, I wish. It never happened, though. Every time we'd see each other at one of those boring society parties, we'd commiserate with one another about how much it sucked that we had to be there and before I knew it, we were friends. Years ago, whenever I was in Europe for a modeling gig, which wasn't all that often, we'd try to hook up with each other, depending on what city I was in and if he was in gay Paree visiting the family. Before Caroline's party, I hadn't seen him in two years or more."

Despite the fact that she came from an extremely wealthy family, K.K. had financed her college education by modeling. But she'd never intended modeling to be her career. Since Tracy had known her, K.K. had been drawing caricatures and writing pithy comments beneath them. Now she was one of the most popular political columnists and cartoonists in the country and she still refused to touch her family's money. She also refused to come into the family business. Given the fact that the family business was Roberts Publishing, the largest and oldest black-owned newspaper and magazine publishing company in the country, Tracy was sure that the fights were more than a little volatile whenever K.K. deigned to see her family.

"What? What are you thinking?" K.K. asked.

"Nothing," Tracy answered. "Just off in a daze, I guess. Want to grab something to eat with me?"

K.K. looked at her watch. "Sure. I have another hour or so before I need to hunker my behind down somewhere and get to work on my next column. Where do you want to go?"

"How about Army and Lou's? It's just a few minutes away from here." When Tracy mentioned the famous soul food restaurant that enjoyed everyone from politicians to celebrities as guests, a huge, greedy smile spread across her friend's face. "I take it that's a yes?"

"That's more than a yes—that's a lead-me-to-that-wonderful-turkey-and-dressing! My thighs and butt too, since they'll get the end result of it."

Tracy laughed. "Okay. Since you're blocking me in, I'll follow you to the restaurant."

K.K. watched Tracy tuck into her catfish and waited for her to finish swallowing before starting her inquisition. "So, what's the deal with you and Jack?"

Never one to prevaricate with friends, Tracy said, "We're at the beginning of a courtship in which we're dating and getting to know each other. We're doing things backwards, though, because we had hot, steamy sex all night long within three days of knowing each other," Tracy finished nonchalantly. She watched K.K.'s mouth split wide with a grin.

"Well, well, well. Tracy Montclair Johnston-Adamson, you lucky girl you! I knew that when you got caught by a man, you'd get caught but good. And I know Jack is good in bed. A man that looks that good just has to be great. Phenomenal, in fact."

"You were always pretty intuitive, K.K."

K.K.'s delighted laughter slowed down and then she asked, "But why are you doing it in the reverse? Shouldn't the phenomenal sex be on the current itinerary?"

"If I were normal, then it would be. But since I'm not, it isn't." When K.K. frowned, Tracy said, "Let me explain."

"With pleasure."

"Okay, Jack and I met in Paris and had wonderful sex, but I didn't know he was American. I thought he was French. I left his apartment thinking that it would be the last time I saw him. And that was fine with me, because, well you know what I've always said about the possibility of my dating a white man—it wasn't going to ever happen. I didn't think I could be attracted to white men.

"But anyway, I was happy to count my one night with Jack as a fling. I was, in fact, glad that he lived in Paris and I in Chicago. That way, I would never see him again.

"You know I'm not the type to sleep with a man I've just met, but the attraction was just so damned hot and potent. Since I was in Paris to figure out what I wanted and to live a little, I decided to let my hormones have their way for one night.

"But when Jack showed up at Caroline's and Brian's party and I realized he was the Jack Winthrop of Chicago and not *zhee Jacques de Paree*," Tracy said with a French accent, "I flipped out. I thought he'd deliberately misled and used me. He was angry because I hadn't given him any pertinent information, like my last name, and that's why we fought at the party. But everything is cool now and we're dating."

"Okay, that explains a lot," K.K. said. "But that still doesn't explain why you're not getting to know the man in the good, old-fashioned, biblical sense. What's wrong with you? What's wrong with him? Hell, what's wrong with the *both of you?*"

"There's nothing wrong. It's just that when we slept together, we didn't really know each other. And he's the one who's insisting on a relationship and since he is, we felt it best to put the carnal side on hold and get to know each other out of bed. If a relationship is going to work, that's what we need to do," Tracy finished.

"Wait a minute. You said *he's* insisting on a relationship. You make it sound like you have no choice in the matter," K.K. said disbelievingly.

"No, that's not it at all. What I meant was that in the beginning Jack wanted a relationship and I told him no and that was because I didn't want to make my life more complicated than it has to be." She sighed. "Since Caroline figured it out years ago, my guess is you probably did too. I'd convinced myself that no one would do for me but a dark-skinned man and that's because of my parents. You know how my mother is. If it weren't for the fact that you come from old money, she would have forbade our friendship, the same way she tried to with Caroline."

Well aware of Tracy's mother's ridiculous way of thinking, K.K. only nodded dismissively in agreement.

"So, anyway, I carry a lot of baggage around because of that. But Jack didn't give up and since I wanted to date him just as badly as he did me, I just stopped fighting it."

"Okay. Good," K.K. said as she finished up her turkey. "So, how are things going for you two?"

"So far, so good. He's a great guy and we have fun together, whether we're discussing politics or seeing a movie. I'm having a great time."

"You sound like you're thinking long-term. Are you?"

"What makes you say that?" Tracy was surprised. "We're definitely taking things slow. However, I told him about my parents and he still wants to meet them."

"Brave man, our Jack," K.K. said. "Are you going to let him meet them? When will you meet his parents?"

"I don't know if I'm ready for either of those things to happen yet, K.K. That would bring in too much reality. Right now, I just want to enjoy being with him without all the outside racial nonsense that we're bound to get from my mother and his dad. But Jack wants me to go out to his family's house in Highland Park for Labor Day. I told him no, but he won't let up on it. I think I'd rather be by myself this year."

"So you probably won't be joining the Singletons for their annual Labor Day pilgrimage to the wilds of Michigan, huh?"

"No, probably not. How about you?"

"I don't know, maybe. How are the wedding plans for the bridal shower and wedding coming along?"

"Oh, swimmingly. Especially since a certain bridesmaid has made it her mission in life to miss several appointments with the seamstress regarding her dress." Tracy's sarcasm couldn't be missed as she shot K.K. a stern look.

"All right, all right, I'll go next week. Happy, now?"

"Ecstatically so," Tracy trilled. "Did you get my invitation? Will you be able to attend Nessie's birthday party?" she asked, referring to her young cousin.

"Of course. How old will she be? Fourteen?"

"Yes, I'm throwing her the party to beat all parties. She begged me to let her have it at my place, since her parents are so 'brand new' when it comes to throwing parties and, horror of horrors, suggested that she have a ballerina theme."

"What the hell does that mean?" K.K. asked. "Brand new? Besides it's usual meaning, of course."

"You mean, after hanging out with all those teenage girls you mentor, you don't know?" Tracy teased. "I'm afraid, then, K.K., that you too, are unforgivably 'brand new.'"

"Mm-hmm. You don't know what it means either, do you?" K.K. asked placidly.

Tracy gave up her farce without a qualm. "Girl, no, I don't. I'm guessing it means square, but I didn't want to seem like a loser and come right out and ask her." After they finished laughing together, Tracy said, "Anyway, she said that I, giver of the party and owner of the 'slammin' house' where it's being held, could invite my friends because you guys are and I'm quoting here, 'straight.' I'm guessing that means 'cool' and doesn't refer to your sexual orientation."

K.K. chuckled appreciatively. "Now that one I know. It does mean cool, so we're safe on that one."

Tracy pretended to wipe her brow. "Phew. That's a load off." She went back to her catfish.

"So how many people are coming to this little shindig anyway? And when is it again?"

"She's invited about fifty people and the party is the first Saturday in September."

"Fifty people! You're planning a party for fifty teenagers, helping to plan a wedding and bridal shower, starting up a business *and* starting a new relationship? And let's not forget the annual Black and White Ball for Chicago's Children." K.K. shook her head. "I don't know, Trace. That seems like an awful lot, even for you."

"It's okay. The ball is little more than a week away, the birthday party's two weeks after that, the bridal shower is in October and the wedding isn't until mid-November. I've got plenty of time. As for my new relationship and business, both of those are coming along just fine, thank you very much."

"Just don't wear yourself out Tracy, that's all I'm saying."

"I won't. Now, what's new and exciting in your life? How's the love life? Still seeing that Jamaican coffee baron?"

"No, he's history," K.K. sniffed. "Idiot started making permanency sounds and I had to let him go." K.K. was genuinely insulted. "As if I'd ever get married."

"The nerve of that guy. Imagine him falling in love with a woman and then expecting, *hoping,* that she might feel the same way. I say send him to the guillotine. A man like that deserves no less." Tracy slammed her open palm on the table for emphasis. "Off with his head!"

"Ha ha." K.K. smirked. She was well aware that she had dating… *foibles,* but she was loath to change them. Could she help it if the thought of marriage or long-term commitment turned her stomach? "Anyway," she said to Tracy, "I'm on hiatus. No more dating for a while. The men are going to have to do without K.K. Patrickson's witty presence for the time being. Listen," she whispered and paused. "If you concentrate, you'll hear the unmistakable sound of male weeping."

Tracy laughed, but she wasn't convinced that K.K was on a hiatus. K.K. had been slaying the male of the species since she'd turned sixteen and had been allowed to date. They were simply drawn to her. Not that she actually dated all of them; many of them were just friends who were doomed to hope for more. She gave her friend a doubtful look.

"What? I'm serious."

"Oh, I know you are, but that doesn't mean that the men will leave you alone." Changing the subject, she said, "So tell me, who's the lucky bastard to get slammed in your next column?"

As their table was cleared, K.K. began talking about her idea for her next column.

CHAPTER THIRTEEN

The letter came in a plain, white envelope and immediately made Jack suspicious. Unadorned script spelled out his name and address, and of course there was no return address. The weight was nominal and Jack held it up to the sunlight at his office window. He could see nothing but thin paper inside.

He knew immediately who it was from and sat on his sofa as he opened the envelope. Brickman had finally made his next move. The wide, satisfied grin left Jack's face as he read the letter. He lunged from the sofa, grabbed his jacket and rushed through his office and to the elevators. The son of a bitch had really gone too far this time. He punched numbers on his cell phone as he left the building.

Brian looked up from a report he was reading as the door to his office was unceremoniously shoved open. "Hey Jack, what are you—What's wrong?"

"Have you talked to Caroline today?"

Jack's urgency brought Brian to his feet. "Not since I left home this morning. Why? What's going on?"

"Let's sit," Jack said. "I need to show you something." He walked over to Brian's sofa and waited until Brian was seated before he sat down. He pulled out the letter from Brickman. "This letter came to my office today. It's from Brickman."

Brian snatched it and read it aloud.

Hello Mr. Winthrop:

Miss me? So sorry we couldn't chat more in Paris. But no matter; you had your fun, now it's my turn. How are your parents? By the way, how is the lovely Ms. Singleton? I understand that she would like to get married. I regret that Chicago is so cold in November.

Goodbye. For now.

"That asshole," Brian said angrily. "Not only does he threaten your parents, but he's letting us know that he still wants Caroline." He rushed over to the phone and dialed a number. "Baby," he said with relief, "where are you? On the expressway? Okay. Do me a favor? Go over to your parents or Tracy's. I don't want you at home alone."

Jack watched Brian as he stood there in silence with a frown on his face listening to whatever Caroline was saying. "Yes, it is Brickman. He sent Jack a letter. It came in the mail today. So you'll go to Tracy's, right?" Brian confirmed. "I'll tell you more about the letter when I see you. You're sure Tracy's at home? Good. I don't want you at home alone," he reiterated. "Yes, sweetheart. I'll see you at Tracy's. I'll be there within the hour. Jack and I both will be there. No, wait, hold on," Brian said as Jack made interrupting motions. He looked at Jack expectantly.

"I have to go to the agency. I'll come to Tracy's a little after you."

Brian spoke into the phone again. "Jack will come later." Another pause. "I will be careful. I love you, too. Bye." Brian hung up the phone and looked at Jack. "She's angry, but I could hear the fear and it makes me want to kill Brickman."

"That's good. Anger and fear make a good combination in this situation. The fear, hopefully, will keep her from putting herself in danger and the anger will keep the fear from taking over enough to make her cower. It's a good thing she decided not to go to her parents' home. She'll be safer at Tracy's. Brickman doesn't know about her."

"What makes you so sure about that?" Brian asked.

"Because if he did, he'd have threatened her instead of or along with my parents."

"He may be trying to throw you off," Brian suggested.

"Maybe," Jack conceded, "but I doubt it. Tracy and I haven't been dating long enough for him to know about her. Obviously, he did a check on me. There's no way Tracy would have surfaced. She and I don't really have a history, there's nothing legal or official on paper and we have not been photographed together by the press. We've been out, yes, but to the movies, dinner and a few shows. Nothing big that would interest the few reporters who cover so-called society functions."

"Have you contacted your parents?"

"Yeah. They're not in town. They won't be back until around Labor Day. That reminds me. Why didn't you answer your cell? I tried calling you several times on my way over here."

"The one you have the number for is recharging. I've got another one so Caroline can always reach me. I'll give you that number. What now?" Brian asked.

"Now I head to the agency and you head to Tracy's, and we'll meet there later to discuss the letter more."

Tracy stared at Caroline as she paced back and forth. "Caroline," she said gently and patted a spot on the sofa next to herself. "Come sit down. You're not doing anyone any good working yourself up like this."

Caroline didn't slow down. "I can't. I have too much nervous energy." She walked over to look out the window. "Where is he, Tracy? Where is Brian?"

Tracy walked over to take her by the shoulders and turn her around to face her. "Look, he said he'd be here in an hour. That was only forty-five minutes ago. If he isn't here in twenty-five minutes, we'll call his cell phone. In the meantime, why don't you sit down and enjoy some of this tea I slaved over a hot kettle to make?"

Caroline's mouth quirked half-heartedly. "It smells delicious." She hugged Tracy. "Thanks for always being here when I need you, Trace." She released her and moved over to sit down on the sofa.

"Hey, it's not a problem. You don't have to thank me." Tracy looked out into the street, wondering herself what the hell was taking Brian so long. She was just as anxious as Caroline for him to get there. When Jack had phoned her earlier to let her know what was going on, she'd been shocked into silence. As she listened to him, she'd realized how much he'd come to mean to her. The thought of him being threatened by or even coming in contact with a cold, ruthless man like Brickman scared her.

The fact that Brickman had contacted Jack had brought the realization home to her. She was just as worried for him now as she was for Caroline, if not more. What did that mean? She was afraid of the possible answer.

She turned from the window at Caroline's call. The look on her face told Tracy that she had said her name more than once. "I'm sorry," Tracy said with a small smile. "I'm a bit out of it. What were you saying?"

"I was saying," Caroline began as Tracy came over to sit next to her, "that I'm sorry for monopolizing the conversation. You must be worried too. For Jack, I mean."

Tracy sighed. "Yes, I am. I'm as worried for him as I am for you. That confuses me because you're the closest thing I have to family. You're my sister in every way but the biological one. So why should I be as scared for him, someone I've known for such a short time, as I am for you? It makes no sense."

"Of course it makes sense, Tracy, if you're honest with yourself." When Tracy continued to look at her with bafflement, Caroline rapped her lightly on the forehead with her knuckles a couple of times. "Hello …is there anything in there besides denial and fear? Is there enough room for reality?" She sighed and became serious. "Tracy, are you in love with Jack?"

Tracy was stunned. "What? Of course not! I mean, I've only known him for a short time. How could I possibly be in love with him…" Her voice faded into nothing as her stomach dropped when certainty hit. She turned frightened eyes to Caroline. "Oh no, Caroline. I can't be. I'm not ready."

For the first time since she'd gotten the call from Brian, Caroline felt a genuine smile cross her face. "Oh sweetie, falling in love is not something you can always get ready for. You just have to be open to it, in both mind and heart. That's all. It's nothing to be frightened of. Just let go and feel."

"You don't understand," Tracy said, a panicky feeling mushrooming through her entire body. She jumped up from the sofa and turned away. "I can't just let go. I'm afraid to," she finished in a small voice.

"But why?" Caroline asked.

Tracy turned back to her. "I'm afraid if I let go, I'll lose everything."

"I should have known that this would be an issue of control," Caroline said in a gentle voice to take the bite out of her words. "You never have liked losing it, even when we were kids. Even those temper tantrums you used to throw were a form of control."

"As they usually are with every child," Tracy interrupted defensively. "Besides, it's not just an issue of control. I'm afraid to love him, to let him in, because I don't want to get hurt again."

"Again? When were you hurt before?" Caroline asked in surprise.

"You're thinking romantically, but that's not what I'm talking about. I'm talking about my parents, Caroline. I tried so hard when I was growing up to get them to love me and it never worked. Every overture was met with resistance or worse, cold silence. Eventually I realized that my parents just didn't want my love and they definitely didn't love me, so I just gave up. Gave up trying to please them, gave up trying to be the perfect daughter and gave up on love."

"I didn't know your dad was like that," Caroline said hesitantly.

Tracy tried to give a negligent shrug, but it came off as shaky. "It doesn't matter because he gave into her. He was disinterested and that was just as bad as dislike. You have no idea what it's like to know that your parents don't…" she stopped and cleared her throat, appalled at the quaver in her voice, "…love you. And worse yet, you have no idea why they don't. They just don't. My whole adolescence I felt as if I was just a fluke of nature, a person who didn't deserve love."

"Oh, sweetie." Caroline rose from the sofa to take her in her arms. "Obviously you were wrong. My parents and I adored you. We still do."

"Oh, I told myself that you were just being nice because you felt sorry for me. And if that weren't the case, then you didn't see the real unlovable me and when you did, you all would realize the mistake you'd made and turn me away. Stupid, right?" Tracy's weak attempt at laughter turned into full-fledged sobbing.

Caroline's arms tightened. "I could kick your parents' asses for this," she said angrily.

A shaky laugh emerged from the sobbing. "Now I know you love me. You never swear, unless you're really angry."

"Son of a bitch, shit, asshole, damn," Caroline litanized readily. "Does that help?" she asked Tracy as she looked down at her.

Tracy laughed harder. "Aw, Caroline. You like me. You really like me," she said dramatically.

Caroline laughed with her as they sat back down. "Now back to Jack. Are you going to tell him?"

"No." The answer was said without panic or urgency. It was just definitive.

"Okay." Caroline nodded. "I guess I understand why not."

"Yeah. I want to be sure of him and his feelings. I know if he ever says those three words, he'll mean them. I'm just not ready to open myself up to possible heartache unless he's willing to do the same."

"So, if he tells you he loves you, you'll tell him you'll love him?" Caroline asked.

Tracy's nod was unsure. "Yes."

"What if he doesn't say it? Maybe he's not the kind of guy to express himself in that way. Or maybe he'll expect you to just know, like it's a given. A lot of people are like that. Or what if he's embarrassed to say the words? Or what if he too, God forbid, is afraid to give up control? What then?"

Tracy laughed at Caroline's frustration. "You're just assuming he loves me."

"No, I'm not," Caroline said, "I know he does. I've seen the way he looks at you even if you haven't. The man loves you and it's apparent to everyone."

"Apparently not," Tracy said with a rueful twist to her mouth.

"Even Brian has remarked upon it. But anyway, back to my original question. Answer it."

Tracy was lost in thought. Could Brian and Caroline be right? Did Jack love her? She realized that Caroline was still talking. "I'm sorry. What?"

"I want to know what you will do if Jack, for whatever reason, doesn't tell you that he loves you."

"I don't know," Tracy said with candor. "It's not something I can plan for. The only thing I know is that I need to hear the words from him before I say anything. I have no experience with matters of the heart and I don't feel secure. So, I'm going to do what people do when they don't have sure footing: I'm going to wait for my, for lack of a better word, my challenger to make the next move."

"Challenger! Tracy— " Caroline was interrupted by the sound of the bell.

Tracy rose to answer the door and then thought better of it. "Do you want to get it? You know it's Brian. The alarm is activated, but you know the new code," she said to Caroline's departing back.

Deciding to give them privacy, Tracy headed for the kitchen to brew a pot of coffee. She knew Brian preferred it to tea. After getting the coffee started, she fixed up a fresh tray. She remembered the tea tray she'd left and retraced her steps to the living room to retrieve it.

Caroline and Brian were standing on the landing holding each other, their grips equally tight. Caroline nestled closer and Brian kissed the top of her head.

Not wanting to interrupt, Tracy left the tray and backed out of the room. Could she have that kind of love with Jack? Did she *want* that kind of love with Jack? Or for that matter, with anyone at all? Could she risk it? She didn't know. She did know, however, that she missed Jack and that she wished he would hurry and arrive.

"So what now, Brian?" Tracy asked. Tracy had taken one of the armchairs from in front of the fireplace and placed it so that she could face Caroline and Brian as they sat on the sofa. He'd just finished telling them what had been in the letter.

"There's really not a whole lot to do, besides what we've already done in terms of security. We just have to wait until Brickman makes his next move."

"So what? We're just supposed to sit around and do nothing? Like sitting ducks? That doesn't make sense!" Tracy was incensed.

From her position of nearly being on Brian's lap, Caroline snorted and threw Tracy a look. "Yes, I can see where that could almost be considered ill-advised in certain situations. Why, it could almost be considered…hmmm…what's the word I'm looking for? Cowardly. That's it, it could almost be considered cowardly."

Tracy gave her a warning look, but felt herself flushing as she realized Caroline was referring to their earlier conversation regarding Jack. Wrinkling her nose in annoyance and saying nothing, she took a sip of her tea.

"Sweetheart," Brian said, turning to look at Caroline, "I think cowardly is a bit strong, don't you? I know you're angry and hate feeling helpless, but come on. Prudent is a better word."

Caroline patted his knee in amends. "Yes, you're right, darling, and I'm sorry. In this instance, prudent is a better word." Muffling a chuckle, she rolled her eyes at Tracy.

"*Mind your own business* is also a good term when it comes to some situations," Tracy said with a side look at Caroline, to which Caroline threw up her hands in acquiescence.

Finally sensing the undercurrents, Brian looked from one woman to the other. "Okay, obviously I came in on something that you don't want to share and that I don't think I want to know about. If you'll excuse me, I'm going to the bathroom before Jack gets here."

"You know where it is, help yourself," Tracy said. Once he left the room, she looked at Caroline.

"Hey, I'm finished talking about it."

"Good," Tracy said. She rose to answer the door when the bell sounded.

"Far be it for me to call you a cowardly chicken shi— "

"Caroline," Tracy said in warning over her shoulder.

"Cursing just shows you how much I love you. Remember?" was the sweet reply.

Tracy smiled and shook her head. She looked through the windowpane of the door. Seeing Jack, her fingers trembled in excited relief as she rushed to unlock the door. The fear she'd been feeling for him overwhelmed her and she hurled herself at him, wrapping her arms around his waist. "I'm so glad you're here," she mumbled.

Jack returned her hug. "I'm glad to be here. Especially with this kind of welcome." He held her away from him, so he could see her face. "What's going on?"

"What's going on?" Tracy repeated on a strangled scream. "What's going on is that a madman has threatened you and my best friend! That's what's going on!"

"Oh, that," Jack said.

"How can you be so calm about this? I mean, I'm no big-time secret agent, but even I know that that note means he's planning something. He wants to kill you, Jack."

"Hey, hey, calm down." Jack took her in his arms again. "It's going to be okay." The unshed tears in her eyes surprised him. Up until this point in their relationship, she'd always kept a careful hold on her emotions. He didn't like that she was scared, but he'd take the proof that she cared any day. "Let's go inside so we can all talk about the letter."

CHAPTER FOURTEEN

"All right, let's get started." This was Jack's greeting to Caroline and Brian as he came in. He sat down in the armchair and leaned forward.

"Wait, I'll get another chair," Tracy said.

Jack snagged her wrist and pulled her down into the chair with him. "No need, there's plenty of room for both of us here," he said it as a joke and was surprised when she didn't object, but settled in and made herself comfortable.

"So, what do you think Brickman is up to, Jack? What will his next move be?" The question came from Caroline.

"I can't tell you what his next move will be. At this point I would only be guessing. I can tell you that by sending the letter to my office, he's letting me know that he's had me checked out and that he knows all about me. Or so he thinks, anyway. The part about my parents is definitely a threat, though."

"Have you contacted your parents?" Tracy asked.

"No worries there, because they're out of the country. Years ago, my parents bought a small place in the Belgium countryside. They use it when they don't want to be contacted at all, not by work and not by family. Very few people know about it. Brickman won't find them because they flew into Paris, stayed a few days and then drove to their place in Belgium, using one of the cars they keep in Paris. That's the way they always do it. So, he may be able to trace them to Paris, but that's as far as he'll get."

"Property records?" Brian said quietly.

"The house is in my maternal great-grandmother's maiden name. My parents gifted it to her about five years ago right before she died, so she could spend her remaining days in peace. Brickman won't find them, trust me."

"That's good," Caroline said. "What else does the letter mean? Dare I hope he means it's too cold here and he won't show up at my wedding?"

"He won't be coming here for our wedding," Brian said. "That would be stupid of him. He knows we'll be expecting that he might and security will be tight. No, he'll try to surprise us, somehow."

"What about our honeymoon? He'll probably try something then, won't he?" Caroline said.

"Yes, maybe," Brian answered. "That's why Jack and I have come up with a plan. We'll keep the tickets and reservations that we already have for the honeymoon, but then we'll go somewhere else. Instead of flying out the day after the wedding, we'll leave three days later and we'll fly in one of the company planes of Jack's family."

"So, no two weeks in Japan?" Caroline asked with a resigned pout.

"No, sweetheart, I'm afraid not," Brian said with regret. "I want us to be able to enjoy our honeymoon, not worry and wonder about when Brickman is going to appear. How does Hawaii sound? Or how about the California wine country? Arizona?"

"Does it have to be in America?" Caroline asked.

"It should be, yes. Knowing that he's done a check on you, we're sure Brickman knows you like to do a lot of international traveling and he would expect us to travel out of the country for our honeymoon. When he realizes we didn't actually go to Japan, we're hoping he won't think to look stateside."

"Let me think about it. I can't decide right now." Caroline frowned. "He probably knows I live with you now. Are we safe there? What about my art studio?"

"We think he's planning something around your wedding and honeymoon, but to be on the safe side, Brian and I think you should have a bodyguard, just for the times when Brian isn't with you." Jack finished hurriedly when he saw that Caroline was going to object.

"That's most of the time," Caroline said. "He has to work. I have to work. We're not together much at all during the day. I don't want a bodyguard. I *won't have* a bodyguard. What if we both just worked at home as much as we can? I won't go to my studio and you won't go into the office."

"It sounds like a good compromise to me," Tracy said into the silence that fell as they all contemplated

Caroline's offer. She stiffened when Brian threw her a looked that fairly screamed betrayal. "What? I can't blame her for not wanting to be followed wherever she goes. A bodyguard would be an invasion of privacy and it would make me feel like I couldn't protect myself, as if I was helpless or something. Besides, why did she take all of those self-defense lessons if she's not going to use them? She's got the body alarm."

"That's right," Caroline said. "Brian, let's just think about it and talk about it some more later, all right?"

"Fine. Back to Brickman then. I stopped by the loft on the way over here and we didn't get a letter from him. But who knows? Maybe one will come tomorrow."

"Or maybe he sent it to Caroline's old place? How would he know she's moved out?" Tracy suggested. "I know it's for sale, but that doesn't mean she can't still be living there."

"Of course she wouldn't live there," Brian said. "Someone was killed there."

"You're thinking as the man who loves her, Brian," Tracy said. "You wouldn't want her there, of course. But how do we know Brickman is thinking like that? Maybe he doesn't know."

"Well, if he did send it there, it will just be forwarded to Brian's place," Caroline said. "So I guess we'll know in a few days."

"You may be right. But the bastard probably knows that you live with me. Hell, he probably even knows that we're looking for a bigger place."

"We can't do anything about it right now," Caroline said as she stood. "So, let's just go home."

Tracy snuggled further into Jack's side and sighed when his arm wrapped around her. They'd moved to the sofa once Caroline and Brian were gone. "Jack?"

"Hmm?"

"You didn't mention yourself. Brickman is going to come after you, too, isn't he?" She didn't lift her head from his shoulder.

Jack didn't try to sugarcoat the situation. "Yes, he is. I would imagine he wants me just as much as he wants Caroline, for different reasons, of course. He wants to kill me. This sick desire he has for Caroline…we just won't let him get close enough to her to get his hands on her." When Tracy remained quiet, he misunderstood and said, "You don't have to worry about him coming after you. He doesn't even know about you. If you are worried, though, and don't want to see me— "

Tracy had stiffened when he'd mentioned the possibility of Brickman coming after her. Now she straightened to look at him. "I hadn't even thought of that, him coming after me. But how do you know he doesn't know about me?"

"Because if he knew, I'd know. Just as I knew all along that he was checking up on me. I'm a security expert," he explained when she frowned in confusion. "He tripped up all kinds of red flags when he searched my background by computer. I was notified by my own people and by the agency."

"Impressive," Tracy said after a moment, "but how do you know he doesn't know about me?"

"The only way he could have known is if he'd had me followed, and I would have known that," Jack said, and then told her what he'd told Brian about there not being an official record. "And besides all of that, if he had known about you, he would have mentioned you in the letter."

Satisfied, Tracy settled back in against his shoulder. "So, if I were worried or scared for my own safety, you'd stop seeing me?"

"What gave you that idea?"

"Isn't that what you were going to say a moment ago?"

"No, it isn't." Now Jack straightened so he could look at her. "You didn't let me finish. I was going to say if you're worried and don't want to see me anymore, then we could discuss what we needed to do so you felt safer, but I didn't think I could let you go."

Tracy smiled and pulled his face down for a kiss. "Do you really mean that?" she asked softly against his lips.

"Of course I do." Jack captured her lips for another kiss. The kiss held much more than just desire. She had been in his thoughts all day. He was more concerned for her safety than he wanted anyone to know, though Brian had probably figured it out. It was true that Brickman had no way of knowing anything about Tracy, yes, but that didn't mean that he wouldn't find out about her.

Jack was angry that Brickman had intruded upon any part of his personal life. He didn't want Tracy touched by the man's madness in any way. As it was, just talking about him in front of her made Jack feel guilty. He was bringing evil into her life and he hated it. A part of him thought that he should do the honorable thing and let her go. He also knew, however, that he would do everything in his power to keep her safe.

Julie Emery had been on his mind during the day as well. He hadn't been able to save her from Brickman all those years ago. The situation with Tracy was different, he knew, but he'd never forgive himself if anything ever happened to her. He'd die before he'd let anything happen to her and that disturbed him. Although he didn't want her to know these things, many of Jack's feelings were in his kiss. The kiss held guilt, fierce yearning, confusion and fear.

Tracy felt the difference and instinctively responded, holding his face with both hands and using her thumbs to caress and soothe. She curled into him as she lifted her leg to hook over his thighs. His urgency kindled something deep inside her and she wanted—*needed*—to get closer to him, to somehow be a part of him.

Jack lifted her and placed her astride his lap, all without breaking the kiss. She was wearing one of the many floaty skirts she preferred, and so in effect had very little protection against the feel of him when she settled on his lap. Moaning, she ground her hips down so that she could feel all of him nestling at the juncture of her thighs.

"Jacques," she breathed against his mouth when he lifted his own hips and pushed against her.

Jack was still lucid enough to realize that she'd gone back to calling him by his French name, something she now only did when she was close to being overcome with passion. He liked hearing her say it in that sexy voice of hers. It brought them to a whole new level of intimacy. His name on her lips became an endearment. As he grasped her hips to set a faster pace, Tracy bent to kiss the sensitive spot behind his ear. His long fingers clinched spasmodically. It drove him mad when she did that and she knew it.

Jack groaned. "Tracy. Sweetheart…don't tease. I won't be able to take much more."

Tracy's tongue continued its delicate exploration behind his ear. *"Pelo contrário, meu querido,"* she said in Portuguese. *"Eu sou absolutamente sério. Eu quero faze amor para você. Repetidas vezes."*

"*Bella,*" Jack said slowly, his voice husky with excitement and passion as his hands tightened at her hips. "You're speaking in Portuguese. I don't understand most of what you said, but those last couple of sentences have become a part of the everyday vocabulary of my memory." He shifted her so that she was lying beneath him on the sofa. Leaning over her, he placed one foot on the floor for balance.

Eschewing the need for speaking, Tracy pulled his head down for a smoldering kiss and then unbuckled his belt, pulled his zipper down and eased his pants past his hips.

Jack pushed the skirt of her dress up and slid her underwear down her legs, leaving her to kick it off. "I can't go slow," he said with apology clear in his voice.

"I don't want you to." Tracy embraced his thighs with her legs. Feeling him probing at her entrance, she said, "*Jacques...querido*, hurry, please. I missed you."

Jack entered her in one, quick, smooth motion, causing her to arch her back and scream at the feel of his possession. He covered her mouth, pushing his tongue in and then withdrawing it over and over, a wanton imitation of what his body was doing to hers. Tracy responded hungrily and twisted her tongue around his while she met the force of his hips with her own.

Feeling his orgasm nearing, Jack slowed down a bit and reached down between their bodies to rub and caress her already hardened nub of desire. "Come with me, *bella*. Come with me."

Tracy made a keening sound, stiffened and then held on tightly to Jack as wave after wave of unassailable pleasure clashed through her body, making her buck wildly beneath him. Jack had held back long enough and he let himself go, groaning and spurting his seed copiously into her.

Tracy stirred beneath Jack and took a peek over his shoulder. She muffled a laugh. From her vantage point, she could see that Jack still wore his shoes and pants, the latter of which barely cleared his naked behind. She could feel her skirt underneath her own bare behind. She wriggled her left foot and gently caressed his butt. "Hey you. Nice ass," she commented in a soft voice.

Jack lifted his head and looked awkwardly over his shoulder. "I've always been satisfied with it," he said and turned his attention back to her with a wolfish grin. "I'm especially pleased with it now, in its current position." He moved his hips and then let out a soft whistle when he felt her internal muscles contract around him. "I can't go again yet, but give me a few minutes." He bent his head and pressed a kiss full of apology and gentleness to her lips. "Are you okay?"

Tracy stretched her arms over her head and sent him a smile that was just as wolfish as his had been. "Never felt better."

"I didn't use anything," Jack reminded her. "It's the first time since I became sexually active, but still, I didn't use a condom."

"I know," Tracy said. "It was a first for me, too. I'm safe as far as pregnancy is concerned." They'd discussed this before, even going so far as to exchange health histories and records. Jack had suggested it, after that first night at her house when he'd so boldly told her that he was going to one day have her naked and wet without the cover of latex. She smiled happily. "I like the feel of you. I like it a lot. It's an exhilarating experience," she finished and contracted around him.

"Stop that."

"What?" Tracy tried to look innocent, even as she helplessly started squeezing him again. "I'm...not...doing...anything. Not really," she said, trying hard not to lose herself to the sensations. She gave up and slowly began to rock beneath him.

About to voice a protest, Jack changed his mind when she executed a little wiggle that had her catching her breath. He watched as her eyes slowly shut and her lips parted as she gave herself over to passion. She was beautiful and he felt excitement stir in him as he watched her take her pleasure from his body. Thinking to help her along, he kissed her as he unbuttoned her blouse and slipped his hands inside to stroke and fondle her nipples.

Tracy's need became urgent and her cries grew louder and more frequent as she tightened her legs around his hips and pushed up against him. Her crisis hit and when the release came, it was long and draining. "*Jacques ... querido!*" A little while later, Tracy stretched in satisfied contentment and opened her eyes to find Jack staring down at her. *Oh God, I've done it again,* she thought with chagrin as she averted her eyes. She sneaked a peek at him from beneath her lashes.

That was all Jack needed. "That's the second time in our relationship that you've gone the distance without me," he said, trying to sound stern. "I'm starting to think that you may not want me for my mind."

Tracy still couldn't meet his eyes and unconsciously pressed closer to him in amends. "But I really did miss you, *querido*. A whole lot," she protested in a small voice to his chin. "Honest."

"Me or my body? Or should I say, *his* body?" he asked with a meaningful look down at that part of himself that she had so thoroughly enjoyed moments before.

"I'm sorry," Tracy said sheepishly as she tried not to smile. "It just felt so good to have you naked inside me. All smooth skin covering hard organ. It was so filling and so and so...so..." Her breath caught on a hitch as she felt him growing inside her again. She lost all track of what she was going to say.

"Would madam care for another refill?" Jack asked simply when she looked up at him. He leaned down to plunder her mouth and started moving slowly.

She wrapped her arms around his neck. "Oh, *Jacques*," she said breathlessly with closed eyes to better enjoy the havoc he was creating. "I'll take as many as you can give me."

CHAPTER FIFTEEN

Later, after they had bathed, eaten and were ensconced in bed, Jack came back to their original conversation. "So far tonight, we haven't used any protection. Are you sure about the whole pregnancy thing?"

Tracy fiddled with the hair on his chest. "Do you remember when you ambushed me at Caroline and Brian's? I knew then that it was likely that we'd be together again, so I went and visited my gynecologist for birth control. But I told you all of this when we talked before, remember?"

"Yes, but nothing is foolproof."

"I know, but in addition to the birth control, the timing for pregnancy just isn't right."

"All right," Jack said and closed the subject. "Now, would you care to tell me about your change of heart regarding us and intimacy?"

Tracy kissed his bare shoulder. "I just wanted to and I thought we were ready for the next step. Didn't you?"

"I've thought that from the beginning, as well you know. What else precipitated this sudden change of heart?"

"It wasn't all that sudden," Tracy mumbled defensively. The conversation was making her uncomfortable, but she knew Jack wouldn't leave her alone about it, so she hedged. "The threats from Brickman today made me realize how short life can be and how tenuous happiness can be as well."

"I figured Brickman's letter had something to do with this." Jack sighed before he lifted her and placed her on his chest so he could see her face. "*Bella*, you don't have to worry. Brickman won't get near you."

She couldn't let him feel guilty. "I'm not worried about myself. I already told you that it hadn't even occurred to me that I'd be a target. It's just that—" Unable to look at him, Tracy laid her head down on his chest. "I just…umm…just…"

Jack frowned. This was new and unusual. Tracy tongue-tied? Jack's mind immediately recalled other times that day when she'd done something unusual. He remembered her greeting at the door and how she'd accepted the seat in his lap. What was this all about? Determined to find out, he lifted her chin so that he was looking into her eyes. "You just what, sweetheart? Tell me."

Tracy kept her eyelids down, shielding her thoughts from Jack's too-perceptive gaze. It was so difficult for her to admit to strong emotions. Emotions brought her one step closer to commitment and commitment meant vulnerability. She just wasn't ready.

"Is that your final answer?" Jack asked when her silence lasted a little too long. "Tracy," he said implacably when his sarcasm got no response.

Tracy let out an explosive breath. "I was worried for you, okay? I was as scared for you as I was for Caroline and that scares me. Are you happy now?"

"Why should this be so difficult for you to tell me? Why should it upset you so much? I would be just as worried for you."

Tracy started to move off of his chest, but Jack tightened his arms around her. "Oh, no you don't. We need to hash this out."

"Jack, while this position may be conducive to other activities, I don't find it a comfortable one for talking. I'll talk, but I need to be comfortable."

Still holding her, Jack suddenly moved, throwing the sheet aside and rising to sit on the side of the bed. He settled her in his lap. "There, we're both more comfortable now."

Tracy yelped. "Jack, I'm naked! I don't usually sit around holding conversations in cold air conditioning while I'm nude."

Jack reached behind them, grabbed the top sheet and settled it around her. "Now talk."

Tracy clutched the sheet to her naked breasts and proceeded to do just that. "It's just so hard for me, Jack. I don't trust emotions because they can be used against me."

Jack kissed the top of her head, which she had tucked under his chin. "Does this have to do with your parents?"

She sighed and nodded her head. "It's hard to let go of lessons learned so early and frequently. They're ingrained now."

"If that's the case, how are you so close to Caroline and her family? You talk about Mrs. Singleton as if she were your own mother."

"I met them when I was three. I hadn't learned those lessons yet, though Mrs. Singleton likes to tell stories of how wary I was when she first met me. And you're right, I do think of Mrs. Singleton as a mother figure. I even call her Mama Singleton sometimes. The Singletons were—and are—much more like parents to me than my real parents ever were. I love them, just as I love Caroline.

"When I was six, my mother decided that I needed a nanny. The woman was a sadistic monster. She would pinch me until I bruised or hit me in the back of my head with the flat of her hand whenever she thought I'd misbehaved. After one particularly grueling trip to the grocery store, my entire right arm, from shoulder to wrist was black and blue. I was in so much pain, I couldn't even lift my arm over my head with any degree of comfort—"

"What did your parents do?" Jack's voice was softly menacing as he imagined six-year-old Tracy, small and defenseless and trying to fend off an adult.

"I didn't tell them. The nanny told me that they wouldn't do anything and prior experience with my parents told me that she was right. So, I told Mrs. Singleton. I knew she would believe me, and better still, she would do something about it. Mama Singleton took me home and confronted both my parents and the nanny. She told them that she'd already called the Department of Children and Family Services and she suggested that my mother report the nanny to her agency."

"So what happened next?" Jack asked when she fell silent.

"My parents had little choice but to fire the nanny, since Mama Singleton knew how abusive she was. A maid started taking me back and forth to school again, and for months afterward, a social worker would appear at the house unannounced to check on me. My mother told me firmly that what went on in our household was none of the Singletons' business. And to help me remember not to share family secrets, she grounded me. I wasn't allowed to go to Caroline's house for a month. I was miserable."

"So, basically you were punished twice. Once by the nanny and once by your mother. Did they at least press charges against the nanny?"

"Oh no, that would have meant publicity and we couldn't have that."

"They actually said that to you?" Jack was incredulous.

"Yes," Tracy said simply. "It's not that big of a deal," she hastened to say when she realized that he probably felt sorry for her. "I only told you that story so you'd understand the kind of childhood I had and why it's so hard for me to trust my emotions to anyone." Sleepily, she dropped the sheet, brought her knees up and curled into him, locking her arms around his waist and nuzzling his neck as she made herself comfortable.

Jack adjusted his arms around her so that he could accommodate her in this new position she had chosen. "I understand, *bella*." He smiled and pressed another kiss into her fragrant hair. She didn't realize it, but on some subconscious level, she already trusted him. How else could she have fallen asleep naked and vulnerable in his lap?

Tracy yawned and stretched herself awake. She blinked rapidly several times and then turned her head to find Jack looking at her. "Good morning," she said with a nervous smile as she remembered everything that had happened the night before, everything she'd told him.

"Good morning," Jack said drowsily. "Glad to see you're finally awake." He moved the sheet aside. "And so is he."

Tracy directed her gaze down to where he was looking. Her smile turned wicked and her thighs immediately went slack and opened for him. "I always say," she began as she made her way on top of him, "that nothing says good morning," she sat astride his hips and took hold of him with her hands, "better than a standing salute." She finished breathlessly as she slowly impaled herself upon him.

Jack made a deep sound in the back of his throat and gripped her hips. As always, feeling himself enclosed within her body filled him with an emotion he had never experienced before. She simply shook his world on its axis.

Tracy bent down to kiss Jack's eyelids as she moved slowly upon him. She loved having him inside her body. Apart from the wonderful physical sensations that this gave her, it made her feel so incredibly full and desired. "God, Jacques, don't stop." She placed her hands on either side of his face and pressed her mouth to his.

Jack sucked her tongue into his mouth and swirled his own around it. He fed on her mouth greedily, possessing it as if it were the one thing he was born to do. Their pace remained slow and torturous, despite Tracy's sudden efforts to speed it up. He could feel her frustration, but the slow pace was increasing his pleasure all the more. She straightened and opened her eyes to look down into his, her black pupils contracting and imploring him.

"Jacques, please… *querido*…" Tracy's voice was ragged. The explosive sensations her body craved were so elusive—they were *just* out of reach. Yet she couldn't make Jack go any faster. The hands on her hips kept the pace maddeningly slow. "Oh God, Jacques! Please!" she heard herself scream.

She bent down and placed her hands on either side of his head again, hoping that that would give her the extra leverage she needed. She pushed and her hips bucked, all to no avail. "Jacques!" she begged, partially pushing herself up so that their faces were only inches apart. She saw that his eyes were narrowed and glinting with pleasure and hard-won control.

Tracy's frustration manifested itself into a painful grimace as she bent her head and used her tongue to find that spot behind his ear. She laved it lavishly. In seconds she felt him jerk in reaction and then his hips began quickly pistoning upward. The resultant sensations were too much for Tracy and she collapsed upon his chest, leaving him to do all of the work.

Jack was only too happy to finish them off. He tightened his grip on her hips and reversed their positions, so that she was on her back. He looked down at her face. She seemed to be out of it. Her hands clung weakly to his sides and her eyes were halfway shut. He watched as her tongue flicked out to lick her lips. Taking one of her legs in either hand, Jack lifted them and held them aloft as he slid into her, feeling himself go deeper and deeper.

Tracy suddenly screamed and dug her nails into his sides. Jack barely noticed the little pinpricks of pain as he gave one last push and exploded into her.

He tiredly settled her upon his chest and joined her in sleep.

"That wasn't fair." Tracy unconsciously pouted at Jack from across the table. They were having a late breakfast of cornflakes and juice, both of which she merely picked at.

"Ah, she speaks," Jack grumbled sarcastically, ignoring the caustic look she threw his way. She'd been in a pissy mood since they'd awakened the second time. A mood she'd refused to discuss with him. And since she'd hopped up from the bed, raced into the bathroom, slammed the door behind her and refused to share the shower with him, he'd assumed what he thought all reasonable men would assume: She'd gotten her period. So he'd thought it best not to push it, but she'd been giving him dirty looks since they'd started breakfast and that had been the reason for his sarcasm. Now he asked, "What wasn't fair?"

"You controlling me like that when we were making love," Tracy accused. She'd been so angry and afraid when she'd awakened that she hadn't wanted to say anything to him until she'd gotten her emotions under control. "Just because you're stronger, that doesn't mean you should have used your strength to control me. What was that all about?"

Jack looked stunned. "It wasn't *about* anything, I assure you. I just felt like a slow pace, that's all."

"What about what I wanted?" Tracy said heatedly. "I wanted to go faster. I *needed* to go faster."

"Eventually, so did I. You just needed to sooner than I did, that's all."

To Tracy, his insouciant answer seemed entirely too cavalier. "Aaagh!" she stifled a frustrated scream as she rose with the intent of taking her dishes over to the sink.

Jack put his arm around her waist and pulled her down into his lap. "Are we really going to fight about this?" he asked incredulously. "It was a great experience for both of us. I honestly don't understand what the problem is."

"You were controlling me," Tracy charged, sitting rigidly in his lap. She couldn't relax; she was too wound up. "I didn't like it. I don't want to be controlled."

"That was not my intent. I was just enjoying the slow pace and wanted to prolong it, that's all. There was nothing sinister or underhanded about it." He was completely taken aback by her attitude.

"I'm serious, Jack."

"So am I. You don't see me getting upset because you found that spot behind my ear and used it to get me to do what you wanted."

Tracy folded her arms in rejection of his reasoning. "That was different."

"I don't see how. It's all a part of lovemaking. It's a give and take situation."

Tracy said nothing. She was irritated and scared beyond words and she didn't really know why. She only knew she had to get rid of him.

Jack placed his hand under her chin and forced her head around to face him. "I'm not going to let you do this, Tracy. I'm not going to let you push me away."

"I'm not doing that," she objected as she lowered her lids over guilty eyes.

"Aren't you? Let's look at it from my perspective, shall we? I'm the man who spent all of last night and half of today buried inside your body, while you screamed and begged for more. Yet you won't even look at me right now. You're running scared, Tracy. You're afraid of the things I make you feel and that's only natural, but I'm not going to let you ruin this relationship because you're scared."

Tracy's startled eyes had latched onto his when he'd accused her of being afraid, but now she said nothing. And then, surprising and horrifying herself and him, she burst into tears.

In addition to shock, Jack immediately felt panic. "Oh no, don't do that," he begged as she buried her face in his neck. "I'm sorry. I didn't mean to make you feel bad." He held her closer and rubbed her back. "Please, *bella*," he murmured softly. "I don't like to see you cry. We don't have to talk about it now, if it upsets you this much," he said over her sobs.

"It's not that," Tracy said as she tried to stop the flow. "Oh, Jack, I'm in love with you and I'm scared to death. I don't know what to do!"

Jack's smile could have lit up the room. "Just don't cry, *bella*. If it will make you feel any better, I'm scared too. You terrify me, because you're the only woman I've ever met who could make me fall in love with her. Before you, I was a confirmed ladies' man. But since the day you walked into my life, I haven't been able to look at another woman. *Merde bella*, I haven't even wanted to."

Tracy's head had lifted from its cocoon. "You really mean that?" Her eyes searched his face for any signs of duplicity.

"Yes, I really mean that. It's not easy for me either, Tracy. I've never really believed in true love between a man and a woman. I mean, my parents love each other, but they're practically the only example I have in my life. I grew up in a family full of philandering men, so I've always had issues about true love. The women in my family just seemed to let the men do what they wanted—it was no big deal. To me, my parents were an anomaly.

"I didn't believe in love, but I did believe in necessity. It was a *necessity* for men and women to find pleasure in each other's bodie, and it was a *necessity* for them to get married for the sake of children. I was always cynical about love, even when my mother would tell me that one day I would find the one woman that I would want to spend the rest of my life with. I would scoff and tell her to call it what it was, lust. She would always laugh and tell me when I found *le grande amour*—true love—I wouldn't know what hit me. And she was right, *bella*. In Paris, it was all I could do to catch my breath when I was around you."

Tracy's smile was radiant, if a bit tremulous. "I just realized yesterday that I was in love with you. But I think I've been in love with you since our night together in Paris." She squeezed him and put her head on his shoulder. "But what do we do now?"

"I don't think there is much that we need to 'do,'" Jack said. "We just relax and enjoy it. My mother always told me that love is not something to be analyzed. Love just is. It's not a puzzle to be figured out. It's just something one enjoys."

"But I've never been in love before, and I could probably count on one hand the number of people who have ever really loved me. I don't have much experience with it."

And there was the crux of the problem, Jack thought with anger as he heard the pensive worry in her voice. Her parents certainly had a lot to answer for. They had succeeded in making her believe that she was unlovable. "Sweetheart, you don't have to have experience. We'll muddle through this together."

"I know I sound foolish," Tracy said, also feeling foolish. "It's just all so new to me, that's all."

"It's all right, *bella*." Jack hugged her close. "Since I'm new at this too, we'll be foolish together. Now," he said, trying to inject a little levity into the situation, "I think these revelations call for a celebration." He drew a deep breath. "What say we go out to dinner tonight? But first," he drew a breath and paused with anticipation, "you have to tell me the meaning behind that scene depicted in stained glass on your front door," he said as if it were a weight on his shoulders. He grinned when she started laughing.

"It's a rhyme, one I've known since I was about six years old."

"What's it mean? How does it go?"

Tracy lifted her head. "It's really bugging you, isn't it?"

"Yes," Jack admitted without hesitation. "It has every since that first day and you wouldn't tell me."

"It's not that I wouldn't tell you. It's just that I forgot."

"Well, I didn't. So give."

"It's called 'Little Sally Walker,' and every black girl I grew up with knew that rhyme. I think it's a Chicago thing. The subject of rhymes somehow came up in college once and a girl from Chicago brought that one up. She and I and the other Chicagoan in the room were the only ones familiar with it."

"If it's called 'Little Sally Walker,' why do you have 'Rise, Sally, Rise' etched into your glass?"

"Because I like what that means. I've been meaning to do research behind the rhyme to find out more about it, because I think it was probably written or made up during a time of oppression. You'd have to hear it to get what I'm saying. I'll have to get up," Tracy began as she rose from his lap, "because there are movements that go with the rhyme."

Jack watched as, in a dress that probably cost several hundred dollars, Tracy got down on her haunches and closed her eyes. *"Little Sally Walker, sitting in a saucer,"* she sang softly in a whisper. *"Rise, Sally, rise,"* she said more strongly as she slowly began to stand. *"Wipe your weeping eyes and put your hand on your hips."* Tracy did both, defiantly and boldly. *"It makes your backbone slip."* Her right shoulder came forward as she pushed the left one back and said, *"Oh shake it to the east,"* Jack's eyes narrowed when she tightened her hands on her hips and thrust them provocatively eastward. *"Oh shake it to the west."* Now they moved westward. *"Just shake it to the one,"* she moved closer to him and stood in front of him with her body in profile, *"that you love the best."* And then she thrust her hips toward him.

Jack reached out and grabbed her. "You'd better shake it at me." He tumbled her back into his lap. "That's an interesting rhyme. I wish I'd known you when *I* was a kid," he mumbled with feeling and kissed her laughing mouth.

"It's not supposed to end like that," Tracy said when she came up for air. "I improvised."

"Improvisation, like change, is a good thing," Jack said and took her mouth again.

CHAPTER SIXTEEN

Ida smiled bravely at Brickman and mentally gave herself a pep talk. *Courage, Ida, that's all it takes, just a little bit of courage.* She cleared her throat. "Alex?" Her voice was soft and meek.

Brickman merely lifted his eyes from his paper and briefly looked across the width of the bed at her. Ida took that for a good sign and bravely pushed on. "Are you going to let me help you with your plan?"

"What plan would that be, Ida?" Brickman asked idly as he went back to reading the *Boston Globe*. He had various American newspapers delivered to him at his Fiji compound, including ones from Chicago, Los Angeles, New York and D.C. His business demanded that he keep himself informed, whether he was in the country or not.

Ida fidgeted nervously. He had just spilled his seed inside of her and all over her stomach, yet he couldn't even bother to spare her a glance. A part of Ida, a part reminiscent of the Ida she used to be, objected feebly to his cruelty. But the thought was fleeting and the new Ida, the Ida who had been broken down both mentally and physically, desperately wanted to get back into Brickman's good graces.

This Ida was deathly afraid of him, but was also afraid to try to live without him. She worried her bottom lip with her teeth and reached out to tentatively touch his arm. "You know what plan, Alex—*the* plan. The plan you have to rid yourself of your enemies in Chicago and to get Caroline Singleton." She mumbled the name resentfully in a hate-filled voice.

Brickman laughed at her and tossed his paper aside. He moved across the bed and roughly pulled her legs apart so he could fit himself between them. He looked down at her. "*You* want to help me get my hands on Caroline Singleton? The woman you see as your rival for my affections? Fascinating," he said with a cruel twist to his lips.

Ida briefly pouted and then looked up at him. "If that's what you want, Alex, I know I can't stop you. I would do anything for you. You know that."

"Hmm," Brickman said noncommittally as he took a handful of her thick, jet-black hair and then let the silky strands flow through his fingers. "I seem to recall, Ida," he said slowly as he very carefully picked the strands up again, "that last year you were one of the people who meant to sabotage my plans to get her. In fact, last year at about this time, you were doing everything in your power to keep me away from her."

His voice and his hands might have been gentle, but Ida had learned that that was when she should be most afraid. She froze and even stopped breathing for a few seconds as everything within her went on alert.

In that moment, she could identify with animals of prey. She thought she knew just how they felt just before their predator attacked. Ida looked up at her own predator and tried to regroup. "Yes, but that was before I knew any better. I just wanted you all to myself, but now I know that it isn't what I want that matters. It's what you want. I've learned my lesson," she said with a dry mouth as she thought about the punishments he'd doled out and continued to give her. "You taught me. I just want to help you now."

Brickman only smiled and pushed himself into her body without having prepared her for his entry first. Her fear turned him on and he got even more aroused by her pain as her body reflexively jerked away from him. He'd always liked having Ida in his bed. She might be terrified of him now, in a way that she hadn't been before, but she was still a wildcat in bed. Even now, as he rammed himself inside her, she forgot her pain and fear and began moving beneath him, moaning and digging her nails into his back.

He knew she loved him; she was too afraid not to. Brickman sped up his pace, not caring if she was with him or not. His orgasm was near and he was ruthless in his driving need to achieve it. Spent, he collapsed on her for but a second and then removed himself from between her legs, giving her cheek a hard, careless slap as he did so. "Don't ever touch me again without my permission," he said, referring to her earlier touch on his arm. He went back to his papers. "You disgust me. Go clean yourself."

Angry that he hadn't answered her regarding his plan and suddenly feeling unclean and unworthy, Ida tried not to balk at his orders, and moved to do as he'd said. "Fine, Alex." She removed herself from the bed and stalked into the adjoining bathroom.

Brickman put his paper down as soon as the bathroom door shut. It wouldn't do for Ida to think that she or anything she said or did to him mattered. He had her right where he wanted her and now he was assured that she wouldn't try to betray him again, the way she'd done the year before.

He paid attention to everything she did and said. And from her request this morning, he knew he'd be able to use her. Yes, she'd be a part of his plan to take care of those saboteurs in Chicago—she would be surprised at how large a role she was going to play. The plan was already in motion, with the first phase already being well under way. Jonathan was ready to perform his duties and his own contacts in Chicago were on standby waiting for his directives. When that time came, that bastard Winthrop would never even know what hit him.

Brickman smiled as he went back to reading his paper. If Ida had been privy to that smile, she'd have gone back to feeling like a trapped animal again.

"*Oui, Maman,*" Jack said into the phone to his mother. "I am doing well."

"And you are not working so much? You are going out more and enjoying yourself?" Lisette Winthrop asked her son from thousands of miles away in Belgium.

"*Oui, Maman,*" Jack said again. "I am going out."

Always savvy, Lisette heard what he didn't say. "You are still working too much, are you not? Darling," she said patiently, "you must take the time away from work. That is the one regret I have about your father being American. He gave to you this reprehensible American need to work and work and work. It is incomprehensible. You should have taken more after me in this regard. We French, we know how to enjoy life while we support ourselves. You must go out and meet someone. How else do you expect to give your father and me the grandchildren we so richly deserve, eh? Your work cannot help you accomplish this," she chided.

Jack smothered a chuckle. "You are absolutely right, *Maman,*" he began. "That is why I'm going to hang up the phone now. I'm going to rush out, find myself a willing woman and then I'll impregnate her. You and Dad can welcome your first grandchild into the world in roughly nine months."

Lisette made a sound of disgust and Jack smiled as he pictured her lips compressed and her nose turned up in annoyance. As always, her French accent thickened when she was excited or upset. "Zhis is funny to you? You find it amusing to tease your *maman* and give her zhee heartbreak as well? You naughty child, you. Zhis is not zhee way a good French son should behave! I am *dévasté,* no? I give up all hope for your redemption!" she finished in a long-suffering voice.

Jack laughed outright. "Ah, *Maman,* I miss you!"

Lisette tried unsuccessfully not to smile. "I miss you too, *chéri.* You should have come to *Belgique.* It is beautiful. You have not traveled with your father and me in years. I miss that very much," she said wistfully.

This was not something Jack could laugh about. She was not being overly dramatic. "I miss it too, *Maman.* I wish I'd been able to spare the time these past few years, but work has just been taking up all of my time."

"It is this Brickman, yes?" Lisette said wisely. "He is what is taking all of your time." She finished sadly, knowing that she could not dissuade him from going after the man. Her son had driven himself for years, trying to bring Brickman to justice. She knew it was personal for him and she wished she knew what demons made him go after him so fiercely. But Jacques rarely shared that part of his life with her. She sighed. "Are you any closer to catching him, *mon chér?* Will my poor *bébé* soon have his heart's desire so he can finally rid himself of the demons that chase him?"

Jack sighed too at the sadness he heard in her voice. "*Maman,* please don't worry. Everything will be fine soon, I promise. I really do miss you."

"And what of your father, *chéri?* Do you miss him as well?" His immediate ominous silence almost broke her heart. "Jacques," she began with tears in her voice.

"I'm sorry, *Maman*. Of course I miss him, just as much as I miss you. I just don't understand him anymore."

"You must know how this saddens me. You and your father must come to terms. No disagreement is worth a breach between father and son. You must force yourself to talk to him again. Surely you do not plan to let this go on for the rest of your lives?"

"Of course not, *Maman*. In fact, the issue will have to be resolved soon, because the woman I'm seeing, the woman I mean to marry, is African-American," Jack said and waited.

Lisette's reaction was immediate. "*Ah, c'est merveilleux, Jacques!*" she said excitedly in her native tongue. "*Qui est-elle?*"

Jack was able to laugh again. "Calm yourself, *Maman*. Yes, it is wonderful—she's wonderful. And to answer your question, she is Tracy Adamson."

"But when did zhis 'appahn? Where did you meet 'er? Jacques Winthrop, 'ow dare you keep 'er from me?"

"It wasn't deliberate, *Maman*," Jack assured her. "It happened in Paris when I was there this summer. She was on vacation and she came into *Oncle Pierre's* restaurant when I was there having lunch. I was drawn to her almost immediately. Lucky for me, she was as drawn to me, and she let me share three days of her vacation with her. I can also count myself lucky that she lives in Chicago. I started courting her when I returned stateside."

None of this seemed out of the ordinary to Lisette. She was French and she knew love could happen very quickly, just as it could happen slowly. "So, when is the wedding?"

"I haven't asked her yet." Jack winced at the sound of disbelief that resonated through the phone lines. "She only just told me she loves me," he said in his own defense. "She didn't have a great childhood, *Maman,* and she's afraid to be in love."

"Afraid to love?" The concept was completely foreign to Lisette. "What is zhis? Zhis, I do not understand."

"It's a long story and we don't have time for it now."

"You will tell it to me soon," Lisette warned. "As you know, your father and I will be back in Chicago next Tuesday to prepare for the Labor Day holiday. When will we meet her?"

"I'm trying to get her to come out to the house for Labor Day, but so far she hasn't budged in her decision not to. She knows about the argument I had with Dad and she's in no great hurry to meet him."

"This is understandable. Your father is not a bad man, Jacques, and I pray that you do not let this one stupid thing that he said make you forget what is wonderful about him."

"I haven't, *Maman.* I'm just glad that you don't feel the same way about interracial marriage that Dad does."

"Bah! Your father has nothing against interracial marriage, *chér*. You have misunderstood him. He feels as I do. What do I care what color skin your Tracy has? Love is love and when one finds it, one should keep it and enjoy it."

"Agreed, *Maman*. Is Dad around? I need to speak to him."

Lisette paused. "You wish to tell him of your Tracy?" she asked curiously.

"No, I'll leave the telling of it to you. It concerns something else."

"Very well, then," Lisette said, disappointed. "I will fetch him from the garden."

"*Merci, Maman. Je t'aime. Au revoir,*" Jack thanked his mother and told her he loved her before saying goodbye.

"*Je t'aime, chéri. Au revoir,*" Lisette said warmly.

Jack's conversation with his father was vastly different. "Hello, Dad," he said reprovingly in response to his father's careful, surprised greeting.

"Son, we need to talk about what happened," Carlton Winthrop said.

"I don't have time for it now," Jack said impatiently.

"That's just too damned bad, because now is when I want to talk about it." Carlton said heatedly. He took a deep breath to calm himself down. "Now, the last time we saw each other, we both said some things we didn't mean."

"Oh really," Jack said sarcastically. "And what was that?"

"You called me a racist, but I'm not and you know that I'm not. I believe people should be able to be with whomever they choose to be with—"

"Is that why you were so disgusted at the thought of Caroline and Brian having children together, Dad?"

"I wasn't disgusted, Jack. You misunderstood. I did and still do think that it could be a mistake to bring a mixed-race child into the world. There's nothing wrong with wanting to preserve your culture, especially if you take pride in it."

"Is that why you married *Maman*? So you could preserve your WASP culture? How could you have done that with her, Dad? She's French and Catholic."

"Your mother has her culture and I have mine. The two combined gave us you. I don't think that we did too badly," Carlton said quietly.

"So, how is that any different than Caroline and Brian combining their two cultures? They're both wonderful and they each have something to offer. A child born of their union would have two cultures to be proud of and to learn from."

"It's different because a biracial child will eventually have to choose what he wants to be. There's usually no in-between. Society makes them choose, especially children of one black parent and one white one. You know that as well as I do. And when that child makes a choice, one culture will lose out."

Jack sighed. "But it doesn't have to be that way, Dad. Not if the parents raise the child to be proud of what he is and not ashamed. All it takes is knowledge, Dad. That's what you and *Maman* gave me. Why are you so against others having the opportunity to do the same? Are you even talking about culture or is that just a polite way of saying color of skin?"

"I resent that, because that's not what I'm saying at all. However, I'm trying to see your point and this is something I have to think about."

"Fine," Jack said. "At any rate, I didn't call to talk to you about this. I called to discuss a case I'm working on."

"Is it still Brickman?"

"Yes. I'm getting under his skin. He sent me a letter, but he was threatening you and *Maman*— "

"I'll kill the bastard myself if he comes anywhere near your mother." There was no mistaking the threat in Carlton's aristocratic voice. "How dare he!"

"Oh, he dares all right," Jack said. "Listen, there's no way he could know where the two of you are, but be on the lookout for strangers. I've posted guards at the house and one will meet you at the airport. I'll send photos by courier, so you'll recognize them when you arrive in the states."

Carlton wanted to object, but didn't. His wife's safety was of paramount importance. "Have you told your mother any of this?"

"No, I thought it would be best if you told her, since you're there and all," Jack said with studied nonchalance. "She may need comforting and I figured there was no need for me to upset her when I can't be there to reassure her."

"Bullshit," Carlton said succinctly. "In other words, you didn't want to hear the fallout when she learns that her baby is closer to danger than he's ever been. As far as she knows, that is. No one could ever accuse you of being slow on the uptake, son," he finished in a wry voice.

CHAPTER SEVENTEEN

"Why don't you just stay home and relax today? You've been running yourself ragged trying to get ready for that ball." It was early Friday morning and Jack was trying to convince Tracy to slow down and take a day for herself.

"I can't," Tracy said as she put her jeans from the day before back on. She grimaced in distaste. She hated wearing dirty clothes, but she had nothing at Jack's to change into.

Jack saw the grimace and the reluctant way she put the jeans on and because he knew how fastidious she normally was, he didn't have to wonder what the grimace was about. He nodded in satisfaction. She was resistant to moving in together or even to leaving a few things at his house. Fortunately for him, they'd ended up at his house last night after spending the evening with Caroline and Brian. It had been too late and she'd been too tired to drive all the way back to the South Side, so she'd spent the night with him.

She'd been pulling back in little ways since she'd told him a couple of days before that she was in love with him. And she hadn't said the words again. Jack admitted to himself that he'd love to hear her say them again, but he couldn't rush her as he himself had turned chicken and hadn't said them again, either. He did, however, admit to her that he wanted to move in together, or at least leave some things at her house, while she did the same at his. She'd been adamantly opposed to the first option, but had said she needed to think about the second one.

Jack watched her actually shudder as she put her blouse on and smiled again. *She'd cave eventually,* he thought, *just from sheer distaste.* "What's the matter?" he asked innocently as he came up behind her and put his hands on her shoulders.

"What? Oh, it's nothing." Tracy was distracted. "It's just that I don't like wearing the same clothes two days in a row. Especially when I've just showered. When I think about all the things I did in this blouse yesterday…well, all I can say is yuck. Plus, thanks to those people at the restaurant last night, I smell like smoke."

"Why don't you wear one of my shirts? I'm positive I don't have any pants that would fit you, but you could borrow some of my boxers. That way you don't have to wear wet underwear." She'd insisted on washing them in the shower that morning.

"Jack! Your boxers?" Tracy turned around to look at him. She was appalled.

"What?" he asked and watched her wrinkle her nose. "I promise I'll give you a clean pair. You wouldn't even have to wear them that long—just until you get home and change. Besides, think of how sexy you would be in my boxers. I know I would be turned on."

"I don't know, Jack—" Tracy cut herself off as a speculative look came into her eyes. "Really? My wearing your boxers would turn you on?" Her thoughts turned inward and it was almost if she were speaking to herself when she said, "It would be sexy, wouldn't it? And almost unbearably intimate. Just think, every time I moved, I could remember that the same part of you that usually resides in the shorts has also been inside me. It would definitely— "

She abruptly stopped speaking as Jack covered her mouth with his own. He undid her jeans and slowly backed her up until she felt the dresser at her back. It was waist high and after he shoved her jeans and panties down her legs, he lifted her onto the dresser. "Kick them off," he commanded. She did as she unbuckled his belt and pulled his zipper down, taking him in her hand to free him from his boxers. She squeezed delicately.

Bracing her feet against the dresser, Tracy opened her legs wide and guided him inside her. Jack's first shot was true and he stopped all motion, closed his eyes and just savored.

Tracy was having none of it and she bit his bottom lip and sucked it into her mouth as she clasped his hips with her bent knees and started pushing, forcing him to move. Climax came for both of them in one explosive punch.

"Did you get the license plate number of that truck that just went through here?" Tracy slurred from the vicinity of Jack's chest minutes later.

Jack's chuckle was definitely on the weak side. "I think we need to shower again," he said as he withdrew and stepped back. "What color boxers would you prefer?" He plucked her from the dresser and strolled through the connecting door.

"You need to take the day off," Jack repeated himself as they walked through his front door. "With starting your own business, planning for Caroline's bridal shower and wedding, your little cousin's birthday party and this Black and White Ball tomorrow, you've been pushing yourself to the limit. You need to sit down before you fall down."

Tracy's answer was the same as it had been earlier that morning. "I can't, Jack. The ball is the biggest fundraising event of the year for Chicago's Children First. I'm on the board and I want to make sure everything is all set to go. We've hired a special events firm and I'm going by their office today for a meeting."

"All right, but what about after that? You're not going to devote all of your time today to CCF are you?"

Chicago Children's First, or CCF, was a service organization that Tracy had been a part of for more than half her life. The organization worked to improve the quality of life for children, whether that be with emergency shelter, tutoring programs, job training for parents or playground equipment. The agency did its best to fulfill its clients' needs and that was why Tracy, Caroline and K.K. had been willing to volunteer in any way they could. Another reason was that Caroline's parents and aunt and uncle had funded the organization's start twenty-eight years before. They'd plunked down $350,000, hired qualified staff and started the ball rolling.

Tracy, Caroline and K.K. had started out volunteering as mentors and tutors when they were teenagers and their responsibilities had grown from there. Tracy and Caroline served on the board of directors, but K.K. had abstained, saying that she didn't have time to deal with adults and their petty squabbles. She preferred to work directly with the children and continued to mentor and tutor.

Tracy smiled. "Jack, I'm having a meeting with the people who organized everything, that's all."

"You just seem so tired. I'm concerned." Jack was silent as he thought for a moment. "Look, why not pamper yourself after the meeting?" he suggested as they began walking down the stairs. "Why not do your yoga thing? You're always saying how it refreshes you." He opened the passenger door of his car for her and saw a thoughtful frown appear on her face. "So, it's settled, then?" he asked as he buckled himself in. "After your meeting, you'll do your yoga thing and relax?"

"Yes, I promise I'll do my 'yoga thing.' But I can't tell you how long feeling refreshed will last. Things will be much better after the ball. Speaking of which, you're sure you don't mind going?"

"No, not at all. After all the work you've put into it, I can't wait to see how everything turns out." Jack started the drive to Brian's to pick up Tracy's car.

"The place looks great, Tracy," K.K. said the next night at the ball. "CCF has outdone itself again." They were standing on the sidelines of the dance floor.

"Yes, they have. The special events firm really knew what they were doing when they suggested a jazz/19twentys theme. I think this year's event will bring in much more than last year's event. I don't have the final tally, but Caroline says it looks good."

"Where is she, by the way?" K.K. asked. "I've been here for more than an hour and I've barely said hello." She straightened a fold in her floor length, white, form-fitting gown.

"She and Brian are off mingling and accepting felicitations. It's funny, but the same people who couldn't wait to talk about them at the ball last year are the ones who are this year giving the heartiest well wishes," Tracy said sarcastically. She took a sip of champagne and studied K.K. "Did I mention how fabulous you look in that gown?"

"Thanks, you look good, too. With your light skin and dark hair and eyes, you always did look good in black, almost spookily so." K.K. stepped back to take in Tracy's flapper-style dress.

"I think thanks are in order, but I never can tell with you." Tracy laughed. "Have you spoken to Kenya lately? Did she tell you they'll be moving in next week?"

"Yes, I talk to the child almost daily. She's so excited, Tracy. She and her mom are so grateful to me for telling you about them and vice versa. It really makes me uncomfortable. I only wanted to help. That reminds me, please don't ever tell them about the bonus I offered the contractor. I'd never hear the end of it."

"Don't you think I know you well enough by now to know that you would be uncomfortable if they knew? I would never tell. Besides, the opportunity to discuss that sort of thing would never even arise."

"True," K.K. confirmed and moved on. "So how's the housing development business going for you, Lady Entrepreneur?"

"So far, so good. I found another property that I might purchase and I have a family interested in that West Side property I was telling you about. They're a young couple with a set of year-old twins. Both parents are just out of graduate school and in social work, so you know their income isn't spectacular. The house is a three-bedroom with a full basement and will be perfect for them, I think. They answered an ad

I ran in the *Daily Nubian News*." Tracy named the paper that was the jewel of the Roberts publishing empire. "I saw Tiffany at Roberts Hall when I went to place the ad."

K.K. didn't bother to hide her distaste. "Did my dear old cousin bare her fangs for you or did she do you a favor and merely ignore you?"

"Neither," Tracy said with a grin. "I saw her, but she didn't see me. I scurried into the elevator before she had a chance. I didn't feel like the drama."

"I hear you." It was no secret that K.K. and her cousin despised each other.

Tracy decided to change the subject. "Have you seen Jack lately? I'm exhausted and I think I'd like to leave soon. At least within the next hour or so."

"No, I haven't seen him. By the way, how's that whole dating thing going for you two?"

"I'm scared," Tracy said baldly. "I'm in love with him and I'm terrified."

K.K. lifted a brow. "You're handling it well. Other than some dark smudges under the eyes, one would never be able to tell that there was anything wrong."

Tracy's laugh was more of a snort. "Am I? Every day since the day I realized I was in love with him, my first urge in the morning is to run—as fast and as far away as I possibly can."

"Interesting." K.K. gave a low whistle at the panic she saw in Tracy's eyes. "Go easy, now. I'm sure he won't bite. Or is that the real problem?" She leaned down and comically checked to make sure there was no one else around before whispering conspiratorially, "Giiiirlll, is he kinky?"

Tracy burst out laughing and couldn't stop for several minutes. And unnoticed by her, her husky laughter caused several male heads to turn and look at her with interest. "You're incorrigible!" she said finally as she wiped tears of mirth from her eyes.

K.K. only smiled and took a sip from her champagne. "So what do you do to control the urge to run?"

"Well, it's only been a few days since I told him, but after I take a few deep breaths and remember that I have responsibilities I can't run away from, I usually calm down. Besides, he's usually in bed with me." Tracy gave a nod toward Jack as she spotted him on the floor with Mrs. Carpenter, a donor who had been giving to the organization since its inception. She waved as he blew her a kiss. "And he does things to … occupy my mind. He has a wonderful ability to turn it on to other pursuits."

"Say no more," K.K. said as she held up a hand. "I get your drift. What I don't get is why you're so afraid."

"It's a long story," Tracy said, "but let's just say I don't like the feeling of vulnerability that being in love with him gives me. It's like I have no choice in the matter."

"I'm no expert, but my sense is that you don't have a choice when it comes to that sort of thing. Ask anyone who's ever been in love, I'm sure they'd tell you that. Hell, don't ask anyone, just look at people in abusive relationships or people who love people who are bad for them. To a one, they'll all say they couldn't help it. However, I do know that you do have a choice in what you do about it." Her voice soft with emphasis, K.K. said, "You can either act like a lily-livered chicken shit and chuck it all away, or you can hold onto it and never let it go."

"Look who's talking. You're a man-slayer. They all fall in love with you and you hightail it out of Dodge, taking their hearts with you."

"Yes, but there's a key difference here. *They* fall in love with me—I don't fall in love with them. And besides, stop exaggerating. I'm not a man-slayer!" She looked as if she could actually be one as she pouted and traced the rim of her mouth with a blood-red fingernail. "Maybe just a man…*wounder*," she said after some consideration.

Tracy laughed with abandon. "Yeah, okay. I'll just call you "Siren" or "Circe," from now on, we'll pretend that it's just an affectionate thing." The two had taken Greek mythology together, so Tracy knew that K.K. caught the joke. "I'm going to the ladies' room. When Jack gets off the dance floor, will you tell him I'm looking for him?"

"Will do," K.K. said. "And I'll even refrain from singing when I'm around him."

As she adjusted her clothes in preparation to leave the bathroom stall, Tracy heard the outer door open. "Can you believe that Tracy Adamson?" The woman spoke in a tone that indicated that *she* clearly could not. The voice was snippy, cultured and instantly recognizable to Tracy. It was Elizabeth Cogsworth, a thrice-divorced, socially connected 38-year-old harridan who had a need for men like most people did for shoes. She was not happy unless she was with one and was notoriously jealous of women who did have them when she was without. She and Tracy had never gotten along. Tracy paused with her hand on the door. This ought to be interesting, she thought.

"What do you mean?" Tracy heard the other woman ask.

"Didn't you see who she was with?" There was a pregnant pause and then, "My dear, she was with Jacques Winthrop. He's sexy, gorgeous, disgustingly wealthy and with all those qualities, what else could he be but white? Of all the nerve! As if someone like her could ever expect to hold on to someone of Jack's caliber. Silly, black bitch." Elizabeth was also a closet racist who didn't really know how to keep it in the closet.

Tracy had heard enough and apparently Elizabeth needed a break to refresh because it sounded as if a lipstick were being opened. Tracy began to open her stall.

"That Singleton girl may have gotten her hooks into one of our boys, but I hope that Tracy doesn't think that Jack's going to marry her— " Elizabeth cut herself off as the mirror image showed Tracy coming out of the stall behind her.

"Ladies," Tracy said, enjoying the looks of stunned surprise on their faces as she washed her hands. She took a hand towel from the attendant. Tipping the attendant and smiling her thanks for the lotion, she said musingly, as if to herself, but just loud enough to be heard, "Hmm, jealous, racist *and* vicious, such a winning combination. It's no wonder she's had so many husbands."

She turned to look at Elizabeth's angry face. "Don't worry, dear. You *are* wealthy, after all," Tracy said in a sugary voice. Then with lips pursed in thought and her head cocked to the side, she pretended to study her. "Men must just wait in line to snap you up." She smiled as she walked toward the door. "You ladies be sure to have a nice night. Ta." She waved her fingers and swung through the door.

As catty exits went, that one was flawless. But Tracy was not as calm as she appeared. "Hateful witch," she mumbled under her breath as she made her way around the periphery of the dance floor on her way to the coat check just outside the ballroom. She was so angry. How dare Elizabeth! She had no right, the worn-out queen of plastic surgery. Tracy's mother's partner had operated on her three times already, so Tracy was in a position to know. "Oomph," she said as she bumped into some immovable object.

She looked up at Jack. "Where have you been?" she asked accusingly.

"What's wrong?" Jack asked instantly. He could tell from her high color, compressed lips and snapping eyes that something had happened to upset her.

"Nothing. Are you ready to leave yet?"

"Come on, Tracy. Don't do that. Just tell me."

Tracy gave in and told him. She'd barely finished telling him what she'd overheard before he got angry. She sighed. "See, *I knew it*. That's why I didn't want to tell you. I *knew* you'd get angry."

"Who was it?" Jack asked.

"It was Elizabeth Cogsworth, but it doesn't matter. I handled it. If you'll let me finish, I'll tell you how." She did and smiled when he laughed. She laughed with him.

"Hey, that was incredibly on the money, as well as catty—the only thing that Elizabeth and those of her ilk understand. You've done well. I salute you."

"Well, I do what I can." Tracy jokingly performed a little curtsy. "So, are you ready to leave yet?"

"Me? Ready to leave? You bet, but there's just something I need to take care of first."

Tracy tried not to look too disappointed. "Do you think it will take long?"

"That depends on you." Jack palmed her shoulders and caressed her bare skin with his thumbs. He slid his hands down her arms, massaging them as he went. Reaching her hands, he used them to lift her arms and place them around his neck.

Starting to feel relaxed, Tracy allowed her body to lean into his. "Depends on me how?" she asked with a lazy smile.

Jack bent and placed a kiss on her nose. "It depends on how long you want to brave the crowd on the dance floor and dance with me some more. I've barely danced with you at all tonight."

"As long as you hold me like this, I think I could brave it for as long as you want me to." Tracy closed her eyes and snuggled into him.

Jack heard the fatigue and wanted to pick her up and carry her away. "Poor baby, you're exhausted. We don't have to. I'll take you home."

Tracy straightened. "No, I want to. We'll just dance a couple of songs and then we'll go. I like it when we dance together."

"All right. Just a couple."

CHAPTER EIGHTEEN

Tracy murmured sleepily as Jack kissed her lips in goodbye. She put her arms around his neck. "Do you have to go now?" she asked without opening her eyes.

"Yes, I do," Jack said and giving in to her tugging, he kneeled beside the bed. "You need rest—you're worn out. And if I stay, rest is the last thing you'll get. After last night and the last few weeks, you probably need to take the whole day to laze in bed." He gently traced the dark circles under her eyes. He was sure that she hadn't had more than twenty hours of sleep over the past five or six days. She was practically running on empty. He meant to see that she recharged her batteries.

Tracy released him and rolled over so that she was on her stomach. She placed a bent arm under her head and used her free hand to cover a yawn. "Last night was a wonderful success, wasn't it?"

Jack climbed into bed and laid his head next to hers, so that they were facing each other. He placed his arm around her and kneaded the smooth skin on her back. "I'd say it was, yes. And I'd say we had even greater success once we arrived home. You were very naughty," he teased. He stopped his massage and slid his fingers into her hand, which was slack near her head. "Which is another reason why you need the rest."

With eyes still closed, Tracy smiled wickedly. "Stay with me."

Jack laughed. "I swear, *bella*, you are insatiable!"

"Only where you're concerned, *querido*," she purred. Her already sexy voice dropped a notch in huskiness. "Only where you're concerned."

"Whoa-ho!" Jack said. "Even half asleep, you're dangerous. I've got to go, my little sex goddess," he said with clear reluctance.

"Kiss, g'bye?" she murmured the question and pursed her lips invitingly.

Jack moved his head until he was close enough to press his lips to hers. Still holding her free hand, he gently and slowly sucked her tongue into his mouth. Tracy indolently participated. After the slow kiss, he rose from the bed. "I'd stay here and work, but everything I need is at home. I'll be back later with dinner. How does Thai food from Star of Siam sound?"

"Yummy," Tracy said and the sleep was so heavy in her voice, the word was slurred. "Crab Rangoon?"

"Sure, I'll get Crab Rangoon."

"Pad See Eiw, too?"

Jack chuckled. "Okay, little glutton. Pad See Eiw, too. Listen, baby, I'll be at home working all day if you need me. I'll be back around six, but I've set your alarm for two, because I know you'll be pissed if you miss a whole day. I've also turned the ringers off on all of your phones."

"'Kay. Thanks." Tracy was slipping fast. She sat up and let the covers fall to her waist and held out her arms. "Hug."

Jack grinned. "Oh, you wonderfully wicked woman." He leaned down into her arms. The feel of her naked breasts, even with his shirt on, almost made him change his mind and climb back into bed with her.

Tracy dropped back onto the pillows. "Just wanted to give you something to think about." Her words were almost unintelligible.

"You certainly did that." Jack bent to fix the covers over her. As she snuggled back into her pillows and fell into a deep sleep, he kissed her again and then shook his head in amazement. She'd carried on that entire conversation and had never once opened her eyes.

The phone rang a scant hour later. The sound jerked Tracy out of her sleep and she looked around in confusion. "Jack...ringer...off," she mumbled unintelligibly. She looked at the phone on her bedside table and realized that it wasn't making any noise. She noticed that the ring was odd, muffled, but shrill. Cell phone.

She stumbled out of bed and towards the window seat, which was where she'd thrown her purse and everything in it the night before. She yanked the phone from her purse. "Yes?" The word was ungracious, angry, impatient and full of exhaustion.

"Good morning, Tracy," her mother said. "I'm amazed to find you still sleeping at this late hour."

"Late hour?" Tracy's eyes found the clock on the wall. "Mother, it's a little after nine on a weekend morning."

"Nonetheless, I expected you to be up by now."

"Well, I wasn't. As you well know, the Black and White Ball was last night. I didn't get to bed until after two."

"Yes," Penelope said noncommittally. "I heard you were there."

"Look, Mother, I know you've never liked the Singletons, so it goes without saying that you wouldn't want to have any part of their organization. But did you really call me to talk about it?"

"Of course not, Tracy. Don't be ridiculous." Penelope sounded bored, but she was really quite angry. Those upstart Singletons had turned that silly ball into one of the biggest events of the social season and she, a Johnston and an Adamson, wasn't a part of it. She thought about it every year and every year, it made less sense to her.

"Then what did you call for?" Tracy asked, still impatient.

"I want you to come to the house. We need to talk."

"Isn't that what we're doing? What's this all about?"

"Don't be impertinent, Tracy. This is not something that should be discussed over the telephone. I'd rather be looking at your face when we speak." When she didn't receive a response, Penelope said, "Come, Tracy, this is not difficult. You come over, we talk and then you leave." Still no response. "Tracy! Tracy!" She spoke loudly into the receiver.

Tracy jerked awake again at the sound of her mother's shrill voice. She'd slumped down into the window seat and had fallen asleep again. She sighed. "Fine, Mother, I'll come over." If she didn't agree, she'd never get back to bed. "When do you want me there?"

"Arrive within the hour, please."

"Sorry, Mother. I'm too tired. What if I come at about three?"

"That won't do, Tracy. This is rather urgent and it must be discussed sooner rather than later. It concerns your cousin, Vanessa Helen. Her parents are here and have entrusted me—"

"Nessi? What about her?" Tracy was alert now. Her cousin's precious 14-year-old face flashed in her mind and she panicked. "Is she all right?"

"Yes, she's fine," Penelope said with little patience. "For now."

"What is that supposed to mean? Mother, will you please stop speaking in riddles!"

"Don't use that tone with me, young lady. We'll expect you by ten-thirty." Penelope hung up.

Tracy gathered clean underwear and clothing and raced to the shower. She had to clear the cobwebs so that she could drive. To help the effort along, she decided to stop and get some coffee. Thirty minutes later she was using her key to let herself into the home she'd grown up in. She had a key because she checked on things when her parents were away on vacation. She never used it otherwise. To her, it would have been like intruding. But this time, she was too impatient to ring the bell and wait for the maid to answer, so she just let herself in.

The maid, who had been dusting her mother's many antiques, looked up in surprise, but recovered quickly. "Ms. Adamson," she said by way of greeting. "They're all in your mother's parlor."

"Thank you, Casey." Tracy hurried toward the room, but stopped long enough to inquire, "How's your son?"

"Oh, Bobby's well, miss." A smile lit up Casey's face. "My husband and I want to thank you again for getting us into one of the CCF child centers. Being with other children has been good for him and now we don't have to worry if he's in good hands while we're working."

"It wasn't a problem, Casey. Didn't I tell you that Roberta Gilchrest is a wonderful teacher and nurturer?" Tracy said, referring to the center's lead teacher.

"Yes, she is. Bobby just loves her. Thanks again."

"Bye, Casey."

"Goodbye, miss." Casey watched her go and shook her head. Such a nice woman. It was too bad she had such a harpy for a mother. Casey had heard Penelope speaking on the phone to her brother early that morning regarding Tracy and before then, Casey had never known a mother who could be so heartless towards her own child.

Tracy pushed the parlor doors open.

"Aunt Tracy!" her cousin Nessi put her teacup down with a rattle, jumped up from the sofa and rushed over to greet her. The girl threw herself into Tracy's arms and Tracy hugged her close and hard. "Oh, I've missed you, sweetie," Tracy whispered feelingly. Though the two were separated in age by seventeen years, they'd always shared an unusually close bond and Nessi had always called Tracy aunt. Tracy just adored the bright-eyed, highly intelligent, serious child. If it weren't for Nessi, Tracy sometimes thought that she'd just cut herself off from the family entirely.

She hadn't seen Nessi much that summer because first, she herself had been in Europe and then Nessi had been away at camp. Nessi pulled back in Tracy's arms to look at her. "I've missed you, too. If I had known you were going to be here, I wouldn't have thrown such a hissy fit when Mom told me we were coming over. I acted like an infant." She smiled mischievously. "You should have seen it."

Tracy laughed and looked at her. But for the hair, mouth and eye color, Tracy could have been looking at herself at fourteen. Nessi was small for her age, but had long legs that promised to be knockouts one day. Her complexion was the same color as Tracy's, as was the shape of her eyes and nose. She had her mother's kewpie doll-like mouth and her father's brown eyes. As for the hair, when she'd been fourteen, Tracy had still been forced to get her hair straightened, whereas Nessi's mother had always allowed her to wear her hair in its natural state. Its current style was in micro braids—those extra-skinny braids that made it difficult to tell where one braid began and the other ended.

"Love the hair, darling," Tracy said dramatically. "And this outfit—it's simply to die for."

"Why, thank you. Mom chose both of them." She went on in a monotone, "Hair braided in complicated style: $450; powder-blue track suit with the ever popular hoodie: an unknown, but surely obscenely high, price; affected look of boredom on teenager's face: priceless!" Nessi finished in a wry tone.

Tracy burst out laughing. Nessi had always been witty. "I don't care who chose the outfit, you look gorgeous! So," Tracy lowered her voice, "tell me what this meeting is about."

"I wish I could, but the three stiffs over there," Nessi indicated her parents and Penelope with a flick of her hand over her shoulder, "are being annoyingly closemouthed about the whole thing. I swear, it's enough to make a girl gnash her teeth. Of course," she paused thoughtfully, "that would be exceedingly difficult with these braces…"

Tracy laughed again. "Never mind, let's just get this little powwow over with."

"'Once more unto the breach, dear friends…'" Nessi direly quoted from "King Henry V" as they approached their family. When Tracy chuckled, Nessi grinned, pleased with herself for remembering the quote from her Shakespearean literature class.

"Uncle Ronald," Tracy greeted her uncle with a kiss on his cheek when he stood to give her a hug. "You're looking good," she said and she meant it. Her uncle was tall with dark, wavy hair, brown eyes that fairly crackled with intelligence and light brown skin. But Tracy wasn't referring to any of those things. She was complimenting him on his physical condition. At sixty years old, he was lean and trim. His stomach was flat and his arms and legs were well-shaped.

"Thank you," Ronald Johnston said.

"So, how are things at your practice?" Her uncle was a pediatrician.

"Oh, I can't complain," he said heartily.

"Regina, how are you?" Tracy said to his wife. Regina was tall and thin, forty-two years old and Ronald's second wife. She had the requisite light skin and good breeding, and they had been married for sixteen years. Nessi was the only child for both of them.

"Hello, Tracy. I'm well, thank you," Regina stated in a soft, cultured voice. "You look well."

"Thank you." She turned. "Mother." Tracy's only greeting to her mother was a nod in her direction before she sat down in an armchair across from everyone else. They all shared a Duncan Phyfe sofa. After raiding the sideboard for another muffin, Nessi wriggled in between her parents, causing them to shift about to make room for her.

Tracy caught the mischievous glint in her eye and grinned. Sassy imp.

"Tracy, as I told you on the telephone, this little impromptu gathering concerns Vanessa Helen. Specifically, your influence over her."

Tracy looked at Nessi and saw that she looked as confused as she felt. "Pardon?"

"Abigail Lynch was at that ball you attended last night," Penelope said.

"Yes, she was. I saw Dr. and Mrs. Lynch and I spoke to them during the early part of the evening," Tracy said when it appeared that her mother wanted her to say something.

"Naturally Abigail was concerned by your behavior and she felt it prudent to call me. As your behavior could have an adverse affect on Vanessa Helen, I felt it best to call Ronald and Regina."

Tracy was still confused, frustratingly so. "Would someone please tell me what this is—" she stopped herself as it dawned on her where the conversation was leading. Or to whom. *Jack*. Angry now, Tracy glared at her mother. "Yes. Go on."

"I think you know." Penelope placed her teacup in its matching saucer.

"I may and I may not," Tracy said. She'd be damned if she'd be the one to introduce his name into this poisonous, sick situation. "Why don't you enlighten me?"

"Very well, if you insist. Abigail reports that you were seen dancing and generally spending most of your time with Jack Winthrop, heir to the Winthrop fortune and a white man. Is this true?"

Tracy tried mightily to control her temper. It almost worked. "So what if it is? I don't believe this!"

Penelope remained calm as she finished her tea. "If it is," she stated with emphasis, "then we have a problem. This family cannot be humiliated by your cavorting with a white man. I will not allow it," she said forcefully, her emotions finally getting the better of her.

Tracy lurched forward in her chair. "Oh, this is rich! You won't allow it! *You* won't allow it? What do you think this is? The 1800s?" Tracy folded her arms and let out a mirthless laugh. "How do you possibly think you can stop me from seeing Jack? I'm not a child anymore."

"As to that, we have an ultimatum for you. You're going to have to make a choice. Stop seeing this Jack Winthrop or Ronald and Regina won't allow you to spend time with Vanessa any longer." Penelope ignored Nessi's outraged, pain-filled gasp. "We cannot allow you to have such a negative influence on her."

"We?" Tracy asked, stunned. She looked at her uncle and his wife. "You two agreed to this? I see," she said through the feeling of betrayal clogging her throat when they remained silent and averted their eyes.

Tracy looked back at her mother and the malice she saw in her eyes hurt and stunned her so much, that she unconsciously wrapped her arms around herself in protection against the agony she felt. "Do you hate me that much?" she asked in a pain-ravaged voice that was little more than a whisper.

"Oh, don't be so dramatic," Penelope said and the cold triumph was so evident in her voice that even Ronald winced away from it. "You've had your way for far too long. First you took up with that Singleton girl, even though I expressly forbade it. In fact, it is my belief that you deliberately cultivated that relationship just to spite me."

Tracy cringed, each one of her mother's words striking her like an invisible knife. "I was three years old…" Her anguished confusion was apparent, even to the cynical eye.

Penelope, however, continued to speak as if Tracy hadn't said a word. "Then you refused to follow family tradition and attended a college other than Spelman. And now this: taking up with a white man!" She spat the words out as if the words themselves carried a distasteful flavor. "Well, no more. You will no longer be allowed to disgrace this family."

Tracy lifted her eyes to look at her family. She vaguely took notice of Nessi struggling to get loose from her father's hold on her arm and of Ronald and Regina's continued avoidance of her eyes. She couldn't look away from her mother, who met her gaze unflinchingly, her eyes daring her to stand after the devastating blow she'd just dealt her. Tracy understood the message her mother was conveying loud and clear: *I've won! This is my family and you either fall in line or get out of it!* For all intents and purposes, Tracy realized, she had no family. For the first time in her life, she felt utterly alone and abandoned.

Nessi watched in torment as her favorite person in the whole world seemed to shrink and crumple right before her eyes. Aunt Tracy, she whispered achingly in her head. Don't believe them. "Don't do this to her," Nessi tried to yell at her parents, but her own pain was so great, the sound barely escaped her lips.

"Hush," Ronald tightened his grip on her arm. "It's for her own good." He didn't sound too sure about that.

This isn't happening, Tracy told herself. It can't be. My mother doesn't hate me. She *can't* hate me—she's my mother. Mothers don't hate their children. They may resent them or even dislike them sometimes, but they never hate them. Tracy tried desperately to console herself, but another look at her mother took away the dubious comfort of denial. Her mother actually despised her. Oh God, she wanted the pain to go away.

Tracy tried to rise from the chair. She had to get away. She had to find a safe place for herself. But her legs wouldn't hold her and she fell shakily back into the chair. Oh God, the pain was a vicious thing. Please God, help me! she pleaded silently. *Please!* God was listening, because on her next attempt, Tracy was able to rise. She looked down at the woman she felt she could no longer consider her mother. "All my life I knew you didn't love me. I didn't know why, but I knew and I learned to live without your love. But until today, I didn't know that you hated me. I'm sorry to have ever bothered you." She looked at the rest of her family. "Ronald, I never knew I was such a problem for you. I apologize."

On shaky legs, Tracy turned to go, never noticing the hand her uncle held out to her.

"Aunt Tracy, wait!" Nessi had finally found her voice and she broke away from her father's loosened grip to catch Tracy at the door. She grabbed her around the waist. "I understand that you need to go away now for your own sake," she said, wise beyond her years. "But please don't think that I knew about this and agreed, because I didn't. I swear I didn't." She buried her face in her chest when she felt Tracy's arms weakly come around her.

"I know, sweetheart. Don't worry. I know." Tracy kissed the top of Nessi's head. "Just remember, I love

you. I always have and I always will." She released her
to open the door.

"I see you've made your choice, Tracy." Penelope's
unemotional voice stopped her in her tracks, but
Tracy didn't turn around. "You know, of course, that
this means you won't be hosting Vanessa's party."

Tracy stiffened, but gave no other indication that
she'd heard her. She opened the door and left.

Nessi took several deep breaths, but she couldn't
stop the sobs from coming. Her entire body shook
with them. "How could you do that to her?" she said
softly as she rushed back into the center of the room
and didn't stop until she was standing directly in front
of Penelope. "What kind of person are you? You
awful, awful woman!"

"How dare you!" Penelope began.

But Nessi ignored her, just as she ignored her
parents' remonstrations. "No, how dare you? You
must be the devil's own servant." She ignored
Penelope's look of outrage and dashing angry tears
from her face, she turned to her parents who had been
behind her, trying to force her to sit down. "And the
two of you are worse than she is. She's going to pay for
what happened here today. You're all going to pay for
it." She tried to jerk away from her father. "No, let me
go! I hate you. I hate all of you." Nessi's words were all
the more powerful for their softness.

"Calm down, sweetheart," Ronald said. "It was for
her own good. Tracy will come around, you'll see."

"For her own good?" Nessi repeated in amazement. "How can you say that after everything that just happened? She's completely shattered. She'll never 'come around,' as you put it. Do any of you even care about what you've done to her? Did any of you geniuses notice that after that vicious, evil witch over there delivered her ultimatum, Tracy never called her 'Mother' again and she never referred to you as uncle," she said to her father.

Penelope gasped. "I will not be spoken about in such terms in my own home!"

Nessi barely spared her a glance. "Oh shut up, you hateful bitch. It's less than you deserve."

"Watch your language, young lady!" Her mother finally got a word in.

"My language? Is that all you're concerned about?" Nessi asked. "I'd be worried about other things if I were you. You used me to try to get to Tracy and you're worried about my choice of language! That's priceless, Mother," she said raggedly. "All of you can go to hell!" She said in a broken voice and then ran from the room. "And you can take your precious tradition with you!"

"Vanessa Helen Johnston! You get back here!" Regina yelled to Nessi's departing back.

"Leave her alone, Reggie," Ronald said. "She's entitled. She's right. We behaved abominably towards Tracy." He sighed and sat down heavily. He suddenly felt every one of his sixty years settle on his shoulders.

"Tracy will be fine," Penelope said dismissively. "And she'll do what's expected of her as a Johnston and an Adamson."

Ronald looked at his sister as if seeing her for the first time. "No, she won't, Pen," he said with absolute certainty.

"She'll do it if she wants to remain a part of this family."

"That's the problem. I'm not so sure she wants to." He'd seen her eyes as she'd left and he shuddered as he remembered them. They'd looked utterly devastated.

CHAPTER NINETEEN

Dazedly, Tracy stood on Jack's front porch, not remembering having made the conscious decision to go there or how she'd even gotten there. A frown marring her brow, she turned to search the street for her car. She didn't see it, but couldn't drum up enough interest to care if she ever found it.

She turned back to face the door again, frowning anew at its familiar presence. *How did I get here?* The thought was fleeting. *A key. She needed a key. Shouldn't she have a key?* She patted down the pockets of her chinos without success. Her loose-fitting shirt was the same: it yielded no results. *Something was wrong, but what? Something bad had happened. What was it?*

It started to rain. Tracy lifted her gaze to a leaden sky she hadn't noticed before. It was raining. *Did she have an umbrella?* No, of course not. She had nothing but the clothes she was wearing. She had no bag, no purse. *Why, she didn't even have keys. Where were her keys?* Not knowing what else to do, Tracy leaned against the porch railing to ponder the question.

Jack saved another report to diskette and closed out of the document. Just as he stood to stretch his muscles, the phone rang. He checked the Caller ID. Charles Singleton. He frowned. Why would Caroline's dad be calling him? "Hello."

"Jack, it's Caroline. Is Tracy there with you?"

"No, she's at home. I turned her ringers off— "

"Her cell phone, too? Because I tried her cell and there's no answer."

"No, I forgot about the cell. What's this about Caroline?" he could hear the agitation clear in her voice.

"It's her mother, Jack. She— " Caroline cut herself off and Jack heard a young, anguished voice say, "Please, Aunt Caroline, you didn't see her face. Let me tell him."

"Hello," Jack said impatiently.

"Mr. Winthrop, my name is Nessi. I'm Tracy's cousin. We were at her parents' house today and oh, Mr. Winthrop, her mother was just an awful witch to her. She basically told her that if she didn't stop seeing you that she would no longer be a part of the family. If you could have seen Aunt Tracy's face—she looked so hurt and so confused. And then Aunt Tracy said to Aunt Penelope that she had always known that she didn't love her, but she'd had no idea that she hated her.

"The light just went out of Aunt Tracy. She looked like her entire world had just fallen apart all around her. Aunt Penelope destroyed her and anyone could tell that she enjoyed doing it. You have to help us find Aunt Tracy, Mr. Winthrop. You just have to!" The child became completely incoherent after that, her sobs apparent through the phone.

Find her? "Caroline! Caroline!" Jack yelled into the phone, scared and worried for Tracy now.

"I'm here, Jack."

"Where is Tracy?"

"That's the thing. We don't know. Her parents live two houses down from mine. After Tracy left them, Nessi came here looking for me, because she knows that Brian and I are usually here for Sunday brunch. Brian's already been to Tracy's and he just called from his cell phone to say that her car isn't in its spot and that the house looks empty. He rang the bell, but there was no answer. He's on his way to our place, but I doubt she's there. I think she's headed your way."

"How long has it been since anyone has seen her?"

"Nessi's been here for at least thirty minutes and she says she left out right after Tracy did."

"If Tracy's been gone that long and she was headed this way, she should be here by now." Jack hoped that she would come to him, but was doubtful that she would because of her fear of her feelings for him.

"Give her time. By Nessi's account, she was pretty devastated. Also, it's summer and people are headed downtown, so traffic is probably a mess."

"What do you think, Caroline? Do you think her mother could really be that heartless?"

"Oh, Jack. The bitch is without heart as far as I'm concerned. She ambushed Tracy. She not only came up with the plan, but she also had her brother, his wife and Nessi in the room when she enacted it. Don't you see, Jack? Except for Tracy's dad, her whole family was in that room today, and all but one turned on her. I'm sure she feels completely abandoned."

"What exactly happened? Tracy's little cousin was so upset, I'm sure she left out some details."

When Caroline told him the whole story, Jack cringed in pain for Tracy. Oh, his poor little *bella*. "Caroline, is there any place Tracy usually goes when she needs to be alone or when she just wants to think?"

"She used to like to go to Promontory Point when we were teenagers. As we got older, she discovered the lagoons in the Auburn-Gresham neighborhood. I remember her saying that they were a beautiful piece of serenity located right in the city. But I really don't think she's at either of those places, Jack. She's coming to you."

"I'll give her another fifteen minutes to get here and then I'm going to look for her." He heard the unmistakable sound of rain and turned to look out of his window. "Oh great. It's starting to rain."

Jack didn't wait fifteen minutes. He barely waited ten before he threw on a light jacket, grabbed his keys and pulled open his front door. He stopped short at the sight of the small form huddled unprotected on his banister. "Tracy?" He watched her head jerk up at the sound of his voice. At first she merely looked at him vacantly. Almost immediately, the blankness cleared and was replaced by unspeakable, heartbreaking knowledge. "They don't want me, Jack," she said in a small, pitiful voice.

"Oh, baby," Jack walked over to her. "I'm so sorry."

Seeing Jack had brought everything back for Tracy. He had been her last thought as she'd left her parents' home. She remembered thinking that she had to get to him and that was the last thing she remembered before she had somehow gotten to his porch. Now the dam broke as memories cascaded over her. She took hold of his jacket front and looked up at him with eyes drenched in misery. "What's wrong with me, Jack? Why don't they want me? Why do they hate me?"

"Oh, baby." He was at a loss for words in the face of her suffering. His own throat clogged with pain. "It will be all right. You and I together will do our best to make it all right. Come inside now." He bent to place an arm behind her knees to pick her up. "Come inside now. We'll make it all right." The words became a litany that he whispered into her hair over and over again.

She curled into him and wept as a child would, unashamedly.

Jack hurried inside and walked to the downstairs bathroom. In the bathroom, he stripped them both, turned on the shower and stepped in with her in his arms. His body blocking hers from most of the impact of the spray, he placed her on her feet and turned her around to face him. "Listen to me, *bella*," he said and gently lifted her face. "People who do such a thing that was done to you don't deserve a wonderful person like you. You are a beautiful person and there is nothing wrong with you. Absolutely nothing."

Tracy stood there mutely, looking at him, but otherwise giving no indication that she believed or even heard him. Finally she spoke. "But they were all there, Jack. All of my family. They can't all be wrong."

"They can be and they are all wrong. And besides, not all of your family was in on your mother's cruel scheme. Your father wasn't there. And I understand that Nessi opposed them."

"How do you know, Jack?" The question was so disinterested, it was almost rhetorical as Tracy stood there docilely while he soaped and cleaned her body.

"Caroline called after Nessi tracked her down at her parents' house."

"Oh."

Jack rinsed her and turned off the shower. He watched her carefully as he dried her off and wrapped her in the robe he kept behind the door. Jack dried himself off and wrapped a towel around his waist. Picking her up again, he carried her up the stairs to his bedroom where he removed the robe and pulled one of his roomy T-shirts over her head.

"Jack?" Her voice was so soft he could barely hear her.

"Yes, *bella*?" He looked up from putting her arm through the sleeve.

"I'm so tired."

"I know, *bella*, and that's why you're going to bed to sleep as long as your body needs you to." He picked her up and carried her over to the bed.

"My head hurts," she said when he laid her down.

"Would you like something for it?"

"Yes, please," she murmured drowsily.

Jack raided his medicine cabinet for pain pills. He took two of them and a glass of water back into the bedroom.

"Thank you, Jack," Tracy said after taking the pills. Her eyes drooped.

"You're welcome, *bella*." Jack caressed her cheek.

She covered his hand with hers. "I love you, Jack," she said just before she drifted off.

Jack sat on the bed and watched her sleep. He was astounded by the change in her. She was so far from the smiling, teasing person she'd been that morning that if Mrs. Adamson had been there in front of him, he would have been hard pressed not to strangle her. The child had been right; it was like a light had been turned off. And what the hell kind of person could do that to her own child? Jack didn't know, but it was time he found out. He strode angrily to the telephone in the guest bedroom.

"Caroline? You had your engagement party at your parents' house, right?"

"Right."

"Tracy's parents live two houses down from your parents, right?"

"Yes, but..."

"Which direction?"

Percival Adamson sat back in his leather easy chair in his den and just enjoyed the knowledge that he would have the house to himself for a while. His wife had her parlor and he had his den. He didn't visit her in her space and she didn't step foot in his sanctuary. He'd gotten home from a grueling morning at the hospital to find his wife had gone out to lunch with friends and the staff had either gone home for the day, or in the case of Mrs. Davenport, gone for her day off. It was at moments like this one that Percy felt comfortable in employing that overused phrase: life is good.

He took a sip of twelve-year-old Scotch and smiled happily to himself. He didn't know how much longer Penelope would be gone, but he knew how to make the most of his time. Picking up a puzzle piece, he fitted it in its correct place. Penelope had never understood his fascination with puzzles. She didn't understand how puzzles relaxed him and helped him to unwind. They didn't ask for much—they just mocked you, daring you to figure them out. He was a simple man who didn't ask for much; just peace to do what he wanted.

He loved the challenge of puzzles and other than golf, they were all the excitement he needed in his life.

This particular one was a part of the Natural Disasters series. It was twelve hundred pieces and would yield a picture of a hurricane when he was finished.

As Percy grinned in contentment, the doorbell sounded.

"Blast it all to hell and back," he mumbled as he rose from his chair. He was a man of average height who kept his figure lean through diet and moderate exercise. He walked quickly to the door with the intent of rushing off whoever it was. "Yes?" he said impatiently as he pulled the door open.

Jack looked at the man who had Tracy's beautiful and unusual eyes in his face. The man looked completely unassuming and harmless. Jack refused to fall for it. "Dr. Adamson? My name is Jack Winthrop."

Percy's brows lifted in surprise. "Carl Winthrop's boy?" And not wanting to be rude to the son of someone he genuinely liked, he offered Jack his hospitality. "Come in, come in," he said as he stepped back and made room for Jack to enter. "I play golf with Carl occasionally," he said as he led Jack into his den. "Great golfer, your dad." He walked over to the Scotch. "Would you like a drink?" He held up the decanter.

Jack shook his head impatiently. "No, thank you. Mr. Adamson, I'm not here to talk about my father—" Jack stopped talking to study the wary look that came into Percy's eyes. "But you know that already, don't you?" he said slowly.

"Jack—may I call you, Jack?" Percy asked.

Jack's nod was curt.

"I heard my wife complaining this morning, something about my daughter being seen with you at the ball last night. Is that what you're here about?"

"In a way, yes. What else did your wife say?"

"Sit down, please," Percy said, indicating another chair in the room as he sat in his own. "I don't know what else she said. I was on my way to the hospital and so was in a rush and she's not home, so I can't ask her. I only know that she was upset about the whole thing." He looked directly at Jack. "I assume you know why."

"Yes. She doesn't like the fact that I'm white and that Tracy and I are seeing each other. But since you don't know what your wife did to express her displeasure, I'll tell you." Jack told him and watched as Percy closed his eyes in realization of what his wife had done.

"Oh, my poor baby girl," he whispered painfully.

Jack scoffed at him. "Forgive me, Dr. Adamson, but it's my understanding, because it's Tracy's understanding, that you don't care one way or the other about her or her happiness. You never have."

Percy opened his eyes and Jack's own eyes narrowed at the pain he saw reflected there. They were reminiscent of what Tracy's had looked like earlier. Percy began talking and Jack leaned forward to listen.

"Jack, I've been married to Penelope for thirty-five years and in all of that time, there were two times when I threatened to leave her. The first time was when Tracy was born, and Penelope wanted to sign her up for adoption, and the second time was when Tracy wanted to go to Brown University and Penelope said she'd go to Spelman College or nowhere."

Jack was plainly shocked. "Excuse me, she wanted to give her up for adoption?"

"I love my wife, Jack, but she is probably the most irrational person I have ever known. When Tracy was born, there were complications and my wife had to have a hysterectomy almost immediately following the birth. She blamed Tracy for the hysterectomy and for being a girl. Penelope has delusions of grandeur and she desperately wanted a boy to carry on the Johnston-Adamson name. Of course, Tracy can still do that, but it's not the traditional way of doing things, is it? Penelope didn't really care that she couldn't have any more children, but she did care that Tracy wasn't a boy.

"She had a plan that involved giving Tracy up for adoption, telling everyone else that Tracy had been stillborn and then a couple of years later adopting a baby boy."

"My God," Jack said. "Has your wife ever gotten any help for her problems?"

Percy smiled sadly. "Of course not."

"That still doesn't explain why you were never there for Tracy as a child or even as an adult."

"I told you that I threatened to leave Penelope when she told me that she wanted to give Tracy up for adoption. She gave up the idea, but after we brought Tracy home from the hospital, I started to notice that if I paid too much attention to Tracy, really, any atten-

tion at all, Penelope would treat her all the more
coldly. As she got older, the situation became worse. So
I backed off. Saying it aloud now, it sounds horrible
and cowardly I know, but I really thought I would be
helping Tracy if I didn't let her or her mother see how
much I cared for her. You see, her mother's hours as a
cosmetic surgeon are much more flexible than mine
and she had the day-to-day care of Tracy."

"How could you have possibly helped her by
letting her think you didn't care for her?" Jack was
outraged and he hurt so much for Tracy. "She grew up
believing that she wasn't lovable, that there was something wrong with her that wouldn't allow people to
love her. Even now, she backs away from love."

"I didn't realize...," Percy began and then grew
quiet. "You see, Tracy doesn't tell me anything. It's
difficult for me, but we have a very distant relationship. She seems to prefer it that way. When she was a
very small child, she'd come to tell me everything. But
that all changed when she was about six. As she grew
older, I was just too afraid to bridge the gap, but I miss
my daughter, Jack, and I regret every day the way I
went about things. If I could take it all back, I would."

Jack sighed, angry because he believed the man.
He'd come there ready to avenge Tracy and he wasn't
going to be allowed that opportunity. He looked
around absently and then looked again more closely.
Every available surface in the room held a picture of
Tracy. Jack stood to take a look around. There was
Tracy as a gap-toothed infant, Tracy as a mischievous

toddler, Tracy in pigtails, Tracy with ringlets, Tracy as an embarrassed teenager as she posed in what must have been her prom dress with a boy who sported a shy smile.

Jack took particular notice of that picture. She looked gorgeous. He had never seen her with her hair long and straight and she was just at that stage that drove so many teenage boys crazy—the stage where the girl is on the cusp of womanhood and looks so innocently beautiful, but so uncompromisingly confident and intimidating. There she was in cap and gown. There was even an oil painting of her at about twelve. Unsmiling, she stared right out of the picture as if she were daring the viewer to say anything.

Jack next noticed pictures of her as an adult. There was one he recognized and he picked it up and looked questioningly over at Percy. "How?"

Percy walked over and looked at the picture. "Yes," he said with a proud smile as he looked down at the picture. "That's at the Singleton girl's engagement party. She looks so beautiful there," he said wistfully as he stared at the picture. He looked back up at Jack. "Charles Singleton gave it to me. He's given me lots of pictures over the years. In fact, most of the ones you see of Tracy as an adult and all of the ones of her and Caroline, I got from Charles."

Jack stared at him for a moment. "Why haven't you told Tracy how you feel and asked her forgiveness?"

"Because, Jack," Percy said, looking down at the picture again, "after what I put her through, I don't deserve her."

"Why don't you let her be the judge of that?" Jack asked. "Or are you still too selfish to see to her needs?"

Percy looked at him. "Very clever, Jack," he said thoughtfully. He cleared his throat and said timidly, "Do you really think I have a chance?"

"You'll never know until you try. She's resting at my house now." He ignored Percy's quick look of disapproval. "Come for dinner. Say six o'clock?"

"I don't know."

The look of fear on Percy's face reminded Jack so much of Tracy and how she looked when discussing their relationship, that Jack could only shake his head. He took a pen from the desk and wrote his address down on a slip of paper. "This is the address. I hope to see you at six, Dr. Adamson."

"What am I supposed to say to her about the way I treated her during her childhood? I can't tell her that her mother wanted to give her up for adoption and that she blamed her for her hysterectomy. That would just hurt her more."

"I can't tell you what to say about that whole situation," Jack said. "I can tell you that you need to tell her how much you love her. That's the only thing I'm positive about right now. I'll let myself out." Jack left Percy standing by his desk looking down at his pictures of Tracy.

Jack opened the front door to find himself confronted by a wall of packages. He saw arms, legs, hands, a fringe of hair, but no face. "Oh, Percy, darling," he heard an older, more aristocratic version of Tracy's voice say. "It's good you're home. You can help me with these packages."

Saying nothing, Jack removed the uppermost ones and sat them down. When he straightened, he found himself staring at Tracy's mother. As she looked a lot like Tracy, he had to grudgingly admit that she was beautiful. But she had none of Tracy's kindness or soft- ness. "Dr. Penelope Adamson, I presume," he said softly.

Her eyes narrowed suspiciously. "I know who you are. What are you doing in my home? Did Tracy send you? I should have known she'd do something like this…," she began furiously.

"Tracy didn't send me. I came on my own after I left her huddled in bed where she'd fallen asleep, exhausted from tears and heartache." He watched something flicker in her eyes. "Are you proud of the work you did today, Dr. Adamson? What a fine, upstanding woman you are," he said with loathing dripping off each word. "Why, society is lucky to have a woman like you."

"This is none of your affair. Please leave," Penelope said through clenched teeth.

"I wonder what the Benningtons would say about the little travesty you orchestrated today," he said, naming one of the wealthiest and most powerful

African-American families in the area. He watched in satisfaction as she hid the quick panic in her eyes. A person couldn't step a foot in so-called high society, black or white, without running into the Benningtons. They had a hand in almost everything. "They're close friends of my family, you know." Then sick of the whole scenario, Jack made a sound of disgust.

Penelope continued looking at him, warily now.

"Dr. Adamson, you have a lovely daughter and I thank God that you and your viperous style of child-rearing didn't have a chance to ruin her before I met her. She is everything you're not and it's a credit to her enduring character and warm heart that she didn't grow up to be the kind of monster you are. Good day," he let his eyes travel insolently over her face as he paused to let her know he couldn't think of an appropriate word for what she was, "…lady." His nasty, insulting tone let her know that that was the one thing he didn't consider her to be. He walked to his car and smiled grimly as he heard the door slam in an angry fit of temper.

CHAPTER TWENTY

Brickman hung up the phone, ending the conversation with his contact in Chicago. He smiled at Jonathan. "We're all set, kid brother. In two hours, Jack Winthrop will get a horrible surprise. What a thrill."

As usual, Jonathan looked nervous. "You're taking a big risk, Alex. I mean, sending someone right up to ring his doorbell? Come on, that's too bold, even for you."

Brickman laughed. "You're new at this, but you'll learn yet, Johnny. Nothing, absolutely nothing, is too bold for me! Just knowing that Winthrop is going to feel tortured is enough to keep me going for days. Now, are you ready for your part of the plan?"

Jonathan ran a shaky hand through his hair. "It won't happen for a while yet, but I'm as ready as I'll ever be, I guess."

"No, don't guess, Johnny boy, be certain," Alex said with hard, glinting eyes.

Jonathan still looked nervous, but shrugged and said, "Okay. *I'm certain* I'm as ready as I'll ever be."

Brickman sighed impatiently. "That's not what I meant. You can't just *say* you're certain. You have to…" He looked at Jonathan, who despite being with him for all of this time, was still frighteningly innocent. "Oh, never mind. You'll learn soon enough."

"If you say so, Alex."

Brickman sighed again. "Find a maid and have Ida brought down. It's time she was apprised of her role in the plan."

"Whatever you say, Alex." Jonathan lumbered off to find a maid.

❧

"Are you sure you're okay? I can stay home today if you want," Jack said to Tracy. They were still in bed and had in fact awakened only moments before. He held her in his arms.

"Jack," Tracy said warningly, "I'm fine. Thanks to you and your taking care of me these past three days, I feel refreshed and better than I have in weeks." He'd been with her since she'd shown up on his doorstep Sunday. He'd gone to her house, packed some of her things and brought them back. He'd worked from home, fed her and tried to keep her from wallowing in sadness. He'd invited Caroline, Brian and K.K. over for the day on Monday and they'd had a movie marathon and ordered in Chinese and pizza. Jack himself had kept her mind occupied with movies, games, music or anything she was in the mood for. Well…almost anything. He hadn't touched her with desire in days.

"Jack?"

"Yes?"

"Do you still want me?"

Jack was surprised. The hand that had been playing with her hair, slowly letting each twist fall through his fingers, stilled. He sat up, forcing her to move as well, as she was lying on his chest. "What?" he asked forcefully, his eyes searching her face for some sort of explanation. "Explain yourself."

Uncomfortable with his piercing gaze, Tracy held the sheet to her naked breasts. "I asked if you still want me."

"What kind of question is that?"

"A legitimate one, I think," Tracy said softly, but firmly. "You haven't touched me, except platonically, in days. And anytime I try to initiate sex, you brush me off with the offer of tea or extra blankets or some other such nonsense. Let me tell you something, Jack Winthrop," Tracy said with flashing eyes as she gathered steam. The more she thought about it, the angrier she got. "There's only so much being plied with warm milk a woman can take, you know!"

Jack stifled a chuckle. She'd kill him if he laughed, but she somehow managed to look adorable and sexy as she sat there demanding sex with nothing but a sheet for covering. "Oh, there is, is there?" he asked.

She frowned impatiently. "Of course, there is! If you don't want me anymore, just say so. But don't pawn me off with offers of tea and sympathy."

Jack saw that she was truly upset. "How can you possibly think I don't want you when I haven't been able to keep my hands off of you practically since the day I met you?" he asked her gently. When she lifted her eyes, he had his answer. Penelope Adamson had done her job well. Tracy's self-esteem still suffered from the woman's cruelty.

"Then why…" She swallowed and started over. "Then why haven't you wanted to touch me?"

"Oh, baby, I have. More than you'll ever know. I guess I was trying to be chivalrous. You know? I didn't want to be pawing you when you were going through such a hard time. I wanted to show you that it was more than sex for me."

"But I've never needed you more," Tracy protested and endeavored to explain. "It's as if I was in shock and I needed to feel alive again and feel that I was wanted. And besides, I already know that it's not just the sex for you. It's not that I need sex to know that you love me, but after what happened, I needed," she shrugged, "I guess I just needed to feel desired as well as loved. Does that make any sense?"

"Yes, it does. It makes perfect sense. And to show you just how much I've wanted you these past three days, I've got a little something for you. Lie back down and make yourself comfortable," he said, rising naked from the bed. "I'll be right back."

Tracy lay back against the pillows and wondered what he was up to. She watched him come back into the room, carrying a compact disc. She frowned as he walked over to his stereo system. What was going on? "Jack?"

"Just relax," he said over his shoulder as he left the room again. "I'll be right back." The next time he came back, he was carrying an armload of candles. She watched with a smile as he placed them around the room, lighting them as he went. He next drew the curtains and the blinds, adding to the intimacy of the room.

"Oh, Jack," she said mistily and reached for him as he joined her on the bed.

"Unh uh." Jack took her arms by the wrists and pulled them over her head where he held them securely in one hand. "Just relax. This is all for you. You don't have to do a thing." He pressed the power button on the remote he was carrying and then tossed the remote gently on the floor and pulled the sheet away from her body. He leaned over her and took a nipple in his mouth just as Cassandra Wilson started singing "You Move Me" in that eerily deep voice of hers.

He suckled there for what seemed like hours, driving Tracy crazy. As the music continued, bluesy and slow, with the singer singing about someone knowing her secrets and being possessed after just one touch, Jack transferred his attention to her other nipple.

"Oh God, Jacques," Tracy said as he swirled her nipple inside his mouth, played with it with his tongue and finally sucked it until it was hard and pouty again.

The singer sang about not being able to breathe for the trembling in her thighs just as he let his mouth trail from her nipples to her quivering belly. Tracy closed her eyes on a long moan as he made love to her navel with his tongue, sliding it in and out, in and out and then stopping suddenly, making her hold her breath in anticipation before he plunged it back in for more.

After Cassandra Wilson's voice of pure sex faded out, Diana Krall's smoky, sexy one slowly filled the room as she sang her version of "Gentle Rain." She sang about lovers being alone in the world in the rain, and Jack pressed his mouth to her stomach in parting before taking his attention down further.

The sound of the piano rose and fell and fingers plucked the bass expertly as Jack parted her thighs and slid his hand inside. Tracy sucked in a breath when he first slipped one finger, then two inside her. She bit her bottom lip and rode his fingers as he pulled in and out while his thumb caressed the hard little nub at the apex. His name became a chant on her tongue, flowing with the rhythm of his hand.

When Peter Gabriel started singing "In Your Eyes" and the wonderful things he found there, Tracy figured that Jack must have been going on pure instinct on that one, because the last place he was looking at that moment was in her eyes. *Thank God!* she thought when his mouth replaced his hand, his head completely filling up the space between her thighs. He'd released her wrists long before and now she took her hands and pressed them to his head as his tongue flicked out repeatedly and teased the spot where all of her pleasure was currently centered. Tracy's eyes rolled to the back of her head.

By the time perennial favorite Barry White moaned into the room with "Never, Never Gonna Give You Up," Tracy had already screamed her release two times. Now Barry White, whose voice she found to be just gifted beyond all reasonable belief, was singing and moaning about keeping his woman pleased in every way he could and giving her as much of him as she could possibly stand. Tracy eagerly wrapped her legs around Jack's hips as he buried himself within her. Slow turned frenzied and hot turned scorching as they kissed ravenously, using lips, teeth and tongue.

Jack looked down at her as he continued to move within her. "I will always want you, want this. Being with you, inside you, is as important to me as breathing. Nothing or no one is more important. Do you understand, *bella*?"

Wordlessly, Tracy nodded and her eyes filled with tears as she realized the full impact of what he was saying. She pulled his face down and looked into his eyes, so he would know the full impact of what she was saying. "I love you, Jacques. I've never loved anyone more," she said in a hushed voice.

The frenzied pace slowed again as the tender moment affected them both and they lovingly kissed. Soon the need to go faster was on them and they picked up their pace, giving in to the need and erupting in unison.

"When did you make the CD?" Tracy asked Jack later as they sat at the table eating waffles and bacon. Jack had decided to take the day off after all. After they were finished with breakfast, they were going to act like tourists and take a trip to the top of the Sears Tower, a favorite spot in the city for both of them.

Jack smiled across the table at her as he felt her bare foot rubbing along his leg, which was bared by walking shorts. "Stop that," he admonished and laughed when she widened her eyes and tried to look innocent. She grinned cheekily, but obeyed and removed her foot. "To answer your question, I made the CD while you were sleeping on Sunday. I wanted to do something special for you."

"Well, it made me feel special and I loved it, thank you. I'll never listen to any of those songs in the same way again. Every time I hear Peter Gabriel sing about finding the answer to all of his endless searches, I'll think about that skilled mouth of yours and all of the wonderfully naughty things it can do to a girl's… composure," she finished wickedly.

"Cut it out, Tracy. Unless you want to find yourself pinned beneath me in bed again."

"Oh, promises, promises," she said breezily and ate the last wedge of her waffle.

Jack grinned, so glad to have her and her wicked sense of humor back that he could have cheered. He chuckled instead.

Pleased with him and with life in general, she reached across the table and fed him her last little bite of bacon. She traced his full lips with her index finger and smiled when he sucked it inside. "As I said, promises, promises," she teased huskily.

"Enough of that, now. Are you ready to talk about your dad?" He'd kept quiet about it, because she hadn't once brought him up since Tracy and her dad had talked three days before. The three of them hadn't had dinner together, because Dr. Adamson had been too anxious to wait and had shown up at four, just as Tracy had been waking up.

And after leaving and finding her car—with the keys and her purse still in it, thank God—Jack had returned to work in his home office, leaving them alone.

Now as a shadow crossed her face and she bowed her head, he was sorry he'd brought it up, but figured she needed to get it out. He watched her fingers fiddle with her silverware. "*Bella*, won't you tell me what happened?"

She looked up at him and her eyes were filled with confusion and longing. "He says he loves me and I want to believe him, but if it's true, why did he wait so long to tell me?"

"Maybe a better question is, why would he tell you at all if he really doesn't love you?"

296 LISA G. RILEY

"It could be because you went over there and scared him."

"No, I didn't. I just gave him a reality check and he realized you needed him."

"But I've needed him my entire life, Jack, and he's never been there. Why now? He gave me a story about not wanting to let *that woman*," she said the words scathingly, the only way she referred to her mother now, "know how much he loves me, because he didn't want her to treat me worse than she already was. He also told me that she'd had complications during my birth and blamed me for the hysterectomy she'd had to have and for the fact that she'd never have the boy child that she'd always wanted."

"How do you feel about that?" Jack asked when it was apparent she wasn't going to say anything else.

Tracy shrugged. "I'm angry, but at least I know now why she never in my life loved me. Knowing the reason doesn't change the situation, but at least I know that there's not something intrinsically wrong with me. It's irrational that she'd hate me for something I had no control over, but that's her problem, not mine."

"That's a good way to look at it."

"I have no choice but to look at it that way, unless I want to feel sorry for myself. What's the point in that? But putting all of that aside, knowing that my father loved me or even that he cared would have made living with that woman much more tenable.

And maybe I wouldn't have grown up all screwed up over the issue of love."

Hating her pain, Jack covered her hand with his. "Tracy, I told you about all of the pictures he has of you in his den. The place is like a shrine to you. He even has pictures that he begged off someone else. I'm surprised you've never seen them."

She shook her head quickly. "No, the only time I go over is when I've been summoned by that woman or when I check on things when they're on vacation. I've never had occasion to go in his den."

"You ought to see it. Maybe then you'll believe he loves you."

"I just don't know, Jack. I used to think that if he ever showed me or told me that he loved me, I'd jump in his arms for joy and everything would be all right with my world. But that's not how it's turning out. I'm really just angry and confused and I need time. That's what I told him and that's what I'm telling you."

"I think you should do what you feel is best for you."

"The good thing is," Tracy said as she rose to clear the table, "that he told me he let that woman have it over what she'd done to me. He also said that he'd talked to her brother and had convinced him to let me continue my relationship with Nessi."

"That is good news. Does this mean you'll still be throwing her fourteenth birthday celebration for her?"

"That wasn't mentioned. But I think even if her parents allowed it, I wouldn't do it. I'm too tired and besides, the whole thing is tainted for me now."

Jack gave a silent cheer over the fact that she realized that throwing the party would be too much for her right now, but only said, "You'll get no argument from me. As I said, whatever you feel is best."

"That's how you really feel, huh?" Tracy asked as she plopped herself down in his lap. "What if I said that I feel it's best that we go back upstairs and make more … music?"

"I think that could be arranged." Jack held her loosely. "Perhaps after our little field trip to the Sears Tower. We both could use some air."

Tracy pouted. "Air-Schmair. Who needs it?"

"You do." Jack chuckled. "You haven't been out in it in three days, almost four."

"Air is highly overrated," she insisted with a sniff as she stood.

"Come on, let's go." Jack stood as well, grabbed her hand and dragged her towards the door.

Just as they reached it, the doorbell rang. Jack opened the door to find a messenger standing on his porch. "Package for Mr. Winthrop."

Jack signed on the line the man indicated and took the package. "Hey," he called after he saw that there was no return address on the package. "Where did you pick this up from?"

"I didn't, sir. The package was brought to the service where I work and I was told to deliver it."

"Can you describe the person who dropped it off?"

"Nope. Didn't see him. I just pick up and deliver. The only question I ask is, 'Where to?'"

Jack dismissed him with a nod and turned to go back inside.

"Jack. What is it?" Tracy asked.

"Feels and looks like photos." He studied the lightweight, white, eight by ten envelope. "They're probably from Brickman."

"Should you be opening it?" Tracy asked worriedly. "Shouldn't you call the bomb squad or some sniffing dogs or whatever?"

Jack smiled at her. "Don't worry, sweetheart." He walked back to his office with Tracy close on his heels. He turned on the light on his desk and held the envelope underneath it. "Just as I thought, photos," he mumbled. He studied it more carefully as he turned it over and over. "There's no powdery substance in there, so I guess I can open it."

"What is that, some special light that lets you see through envelopes?" Tracy asked sarcastically.

"Exactly." Jack sat behind his desk. He looked up at Tracy who was studying the envelope. "Sweetheart, could you go get me something to drink? Maybe a pop with some ice? It's really hot in here and I'm feeling kind of parched. I'd owe you big time if you did," he said winningly, trying to get her out of the room.

Tracy wasn't buying it, and snorted loudly. "No, I won't, Jack Winthrop. If you're so thirsty, get your drink yourself. I'm not budging from this spot until my curiosity has been satisfied, so you might as well open it."

"These pictures could be of anything, *bella*. I'm a professional. I've seen just about every horror you can imagine and there are still some things that give me nightmares. I don't want that for you. Now, will you please move away from the desk?"

Tracy didn't want that for herself either and she slowly walked away from him. But she didn't leave him completely; she went and sat on the sofa on the other side of the room and waited in worry for him.

Jack slashed open the envelope and let the pictures spill out on his desk. He sucked in a shocked breath when he saw who it was. Flicking through them hurriedly, he felt his anger rising with each new one he looked at. He picked up the envelope and looked for a note. He knew Brickman had sent one; he'd never be able to resist taunting him. He found it.

Winthrop:
I understand we knew someone in common.
She was lovely, wasn't she? Unfortunately for her,
you couldn't save her. But if it comforts you,
I should tell you that she enjoyed her last
few days on earth immensely. I should know:
I supplied her with her happiness. Just thought
I'd share.
Goodbye. For now.

Angrily, Jack swiped his arm across the desk and knocked the pictures and everything else in his path to the floor.

Tracy jumped up and hurried across the room. "What is it Jack? What's wrong?" When she received no answer from him, she bent to retrieve the photos that he'd knocked to the floor. There were five in all. The first one she picked up showed a young blonde, green-eyed girl smiling into the camera. "She's beautiful," Tracy said. "Who is she?" She continued to pick up the pictures.

Each picture showed the girl looking progressively thinner and obviously sliding into poor health. In one, her eyes were completely unfocused as if she had no idea what was going on around her and her nose was bleeding, but she had a smile on her face. Tracy looked closer and noticed a line of white powder on the table in front of her. "Is that cocaine?" she asked and looked at Jack.

Jack took his hands from his face and took the photos from Tracy. "Unfortunately, yes." His voice sounded defeated. "Her name is—was—Julie Emery and she was a junkie I met when I was a rookie cop."

"Oh God, Jack. Is she dead?"

"Yes. When I first busted Julie, she was selling her body for drugs and she begged me to help her get clean. I could see that she really wanted to, so I helped her. She was here for college, but was from a wealthy Boston family and said that they wouldn't help her if they knew she was on drugs. She insisted that she had to do rehab here in Chicago. It took two years and a lot of stops and starts, but she did it. And one day when she'd been clean for five months, she told me she was ready to go home.

"I helped her pack. Six months later, I went out to visit her and found her using again. Her high society fiancé had gotten her hooked again. He was her supplier, but he wasn't the main source," Jack finished grimly.

"It was Brickman," Tracy said without a doubt.

"Right the first time," Jack said tiredly. "Four months later, I found out she was dead. I've been chasing Brickman ever since. Now he's somehow found out about my connection to Julie and is using it to taunt me."

"*Querido*," Tracy said and turned his swivel chair around so she could hug him close. "I'm so sorry."

"So am I." Jack took the comfort she offered, his arms tightening around her as she slid into his lap. "So am I."

"So, she's the reason why you're so determined to get Brickman?"

"She's part of it yes, but not all of it. The man is just pure evil, Tracy. He needs to be taken out of commission. Julie was not the only victim of his greed. Over the years, I've come across dozens of them. Sometimes, the victims had no idea who had done the stuff to them, but that didn't make it any less horrible. And just look at how he's terrified Caroline. If he ever gets his hands on her, even if she gets away from him, she'll never be the same. And I'll tell you this much. If he ever does get his hands on her, we'll have a hell of a time getting her back."

Tracy felt a shiver thrill down her back, but said in a calm voice, "But he's never going to get his hands on her. I know it, because I know that you and Brian are doing all you can to protect her and besides that, you're going to catch him."

Jack sighed. "I'm doing my best."

"Come on," she said after a while. "Now it's my turn to take care of you, like you took care of me. How does a massage sound?"

"Wonderful. But I can't," he said with regret. "I have to take these pictures down to the agency to see what they can find out about them."

Tracy was nodding before he finished. "Of course you do, but we have a date for a massage when you get back."

CHAPTER TWENTY-ONE

Officer Tim Dyserly watched intently as the small plane landed on a private airstrip outside of Gary, Indiana. He walked over to meet the passengers as they slowly disembarked from the plane. At first he didn't recognize the man who had hired him, but he soon realized that he had to be the shortest one who had the air of a leader surrounding him. "Mr. Brickman," Dyserly said with a deferential nod. "Welcome back, sir."

Brickman smiled and the mustache he had grown and dyed brown moved in sync with his mouth. "I assure you, Officer Dyserly, it's good to be back." He wore brown contacts, carried ten extra pounds and his dyed hair was longer and reached past the nape of his neck. His new passport named him as Henry Dixon. He motioned behind him and Ida and Jonathan stepped forward. "You may not recognize him, but this is my brother Johnnie. And this is the lovely Ida Martinez."

Jonathan had changed his appearance much in the same way Brickman had and had lost several pounds. Ida wore no disguise. She was not wanted for a crime, only for more questioning regarding Brickman's whereabouts. To avoid any hassle from the police, the plan was to have her just walk into a police station, tell them who she was, that she'd been in hiding from Brickman and that she would try to answer any questions they might have about him. She would do that right about the same time Winthrop was being taken care of.

"Sir. Ma'am." The officer's eyes lingered a moment on Ida before flicking away.

"Tell me, Officer Dyserly. Is everything in order?" Brickman asked.

Dyserly, one of Chicago's finest, nodded in assurance.

Tracy sniffled loudly and sank deeper into her sofa. She felt and looked miserable. She hadn't seen or heard from Jack in more than three days. They'd had an argument and if she weren't mistaken, he had dumped her. What she'd thought was a perfectly logical way to feel had caused a fight and had precipitated her currently being alone and miserable.

She pulled her blanket closer around herself and picked up the remote to turn on the television to break the heavy silence. Needing as much noise as possible, she chose a music video channel to watch. She groaned when "Hopeless," a video with singer Dionne Farris came on. Normally a huge fan of the woman's talent—she could go from sounding haunting to quite earthy, all without missing a beat—

Tracy now closed her eyes in pain. The words of the song reminded her too much of herself and her current predicament. *Love Jones*, the movie in which the song was featured, was a movie Jack and she had recently watched together.

Tracy forced herself to watch the video and grimaced painfully when the singer warbled about being as hopeless as a penny with a hole in it. The song was all about the sometimes-torturous state of being in love, just as the movie had been. As she watched vignettes from the actual movie flash on the screen, Tracy remembered how she had teased Jack about the handsome face of one of the supporting actors. She'd called him one of the "finest men alive."

Jack had only grinned, saying thoughtfully that while he couldn't exactly see the appeal of Isaiah Washington, he could, however, see why so many men found the lead actress, Nia Long, attractive. Hoisted by her own petard, Tracy had laughed and punched him playfully in the arm. He'd countered with a pin to the sofa and the evening had ended on a different note as they'd tacitly agreed to finish watching the movie later.

As the video finished playing, Tracy found herself crying. She felt vastly ridiculous, but couldn't stop herself. She angrily flicked the television off, buried her face in her bent knees and cried until there were no more tears. This had been her pattern since the day Jack had brought her and her things home. She hadn't known that she could miss anyone as much as she missed him. Her body craved his touch, while her heart wanted his gentleness. She replayed their argument over in her mind. They'd been sitting on the couch at his place discussing another house she'd scouted out.

⚜

"Look at that exterior, Jack. Isn't it gorgeous?" Tracy showed him the Polaroid she'd taken earlier that day. "It's terrible that it's fallen into such disrepair."

"It is nice." Jack studied the picture carefully. "Where's it located?" he asked absently.

"I don't think you'd know the area," she said as she avoided his eyes. "It's really far out," she said in protest when he looked at her accusingly.

"I was a cop, Tracy. I know this city almost like the back of my hand. Where is the house located?" he asked again, paying close attention this time.

"It's on Milwaukee Avenue," she said slowly, still hedging. She didn't want an argument.

"Milwaukee and what?"

"It's on Milwaukee near North Avenue," she said reluctantly, not knowing she was pouting. Her voice was soft, forcing him to bend his head to hear her.

He heard nonetheless. "Wicker Park? This house is in Wicker Park? You take too many chances, Tracy."

"There's nothing wrong with Wicker Park, Jack. They've been developing over there for years. It's turning into a really nice area."

"It's still not safe. I don't like the idea of you being over there alone at night, which is when you usually go to look at these places."

"No, I don't," Tracy objected. "I've only done that a couple of times. And besides, I'll be safe. I have my body alarm and I took self-defense classes, too."

"I don't like it, Tracy. You leave these places late at night and then you go home alone late at night."

"Lots of people do that, Jack, and murder and mayhem don't always ensue. I'm not the only one who leaves work late."

"No, but you're in a relationship with me and I'm in a dangerous situation right now. Despite not having heard from Brickman lately we still have to be careful. I want you to move in with me."

Tracy stiffened. "I can't, Jack. I'm not ready for that yet."

"Then, I'll move in with you," he said stubbornly.

"I'm not ready for that either."

Jack bulldozed over that, barely letting her finish her sentence. They'd had this conversation before. "Then give me your keys so I can be at your house when you get home on those nights that you do work late. I'll give you my keys as well."

Tracy stood to pace away from him. "It's too soon for me, Jack. I like having my own space. You know I don't like to share—"

"That's bull, Tracy, and you know it. Tell me something. If you aren't ready to make a commitment to me, why have we had unprotected sex so often? Are you trying to give yourself an *excuse* to commit to me? If you get pregnant, then you can tell yourself that you have no choice but to make a more permanent commitment to me. You wouldn't have to let go of all of the feelings of mistrust that you have because they're a comfort to you. You could tell yourself that the commitment was because you needed to be responsible for the baby and not because you love and trust me. Pregnancy would take the decision out of your hands and make it easy for you to do what you already want to do, but are too scared to admit."

Tracy looked at him in disbelief. He'd obviously been thinking about this. "That's not true, Jack, and you know it." She walked back over to him. "I do love you," she said as she sat next to him and reached out to touch his face. "I'm just not—"

"I know, I've heard it before. You're just not ready," Jack said mockingly as he jerked away from her touch and stood. "I'm tired of it, Tracy. You don't trust me, you don't trust your emotions and I don't know what else I can do to get you to trust them or me enough to let go of your fears. Pack your stuff," he said, turning to walk away from her, "I'll take you home."

Tracy felt tears fill her eyes. "Jack?" she called, but he didn't respond. He drove her home, checked inside the house and left. He didn't even kiss her goodbye.

Tracy sighed and rose from the sofa. She walked to the back of the house to the kitchen to splash cold water on her face and to make herself some tea. Having decided to stop wallowing in self-pity, Tracy was back in the living room and folding the blanket when the doorbell poem recitation signaled that she had a visitor. Hoping it was Jack, she tried not to rush to the door, but made it there in record time. Immense gratitude filled her when she looked out the window. She rushed to disengage the alarm and unlock the door.

She opened the door and walked into the arms that she knew would always be held open in welcome and comfort. "I don't know what made you come, Mama Singleton, but I'm so glad you did." Tracy's voice quavered and her relief was evident as she snuggled in.

"Oh, baby," Patricia Singleton said as she held her close. "How could I not? One of my girls needs me."

Tracy felt the tears coming again, and this time she didn't even think twice about letting them fall. "It just hurts so much," she said.

"I know, sweetheart, but it's going to be okay." Patricia gently hustled her into the house and shut the door behind them. She said nothing else, but just tightened her arms and held on.

Tracy didn't know how long they stood there, but she felt tremendously better by the time she pulled back to look into Patricia's face. "Thank you," she said simply and quietly. She watched as a smile bloomed over the beautiful face that was an exact match to Caroline's. "You've cut your hair," Tracy said in some surprise, studying the thick hair that was settled in a chic bob. "You must have taken off two inches at least."

A graceful dark brown hand reached up to fluff said hair. "More like three, but that's not why I'm here. I'm here for you." Patricia pushed a twisted lock behind Tracy's ear. "What can I do, darling?"

Tracy sighed, moved out of Patricia's arms and walked into the living room. She sat on the sofa and waited for Patricia to follow. She watched as the former model turned corporate bigwig walked gracefully into the room. Patricia wore a gray, slim skirt (she still had fabulous legs) and a turtleneck sweater of the same color, but with cream-colored stripes. The soft, leather, knee-high boots matched perfectly as did the expensive leather purse she carried. The classic ensemble was perfect for the mild October weather.

The cavalry's here, Tracy thought, and her heart filled with such pure love and gratitude at the thought of how Patricia had always ridden to her rescue, that tears filled her eyes at the intensity of the feelings. "Thank you," she whispered again when Patricia sat down next to her.

Patricia took her hand. "No thanks are necessary. I would have come sooner, but I was out of town when that debacle with your mother took place. When I arrived back in town, I had to get ready for Labor Day at the cottage. And then work got in the way. I know we've talked on the phone, but I had to see you. I'm so sorry about your mother."

Tracy frowned. She hadn't thought about the incident with her mother at all lately. First Jack had succeeded in keeping her mind on other things and then she'd been too concerned about the current situation with Jack to think about anything else. "You know, it's weird, but I haven't really thought about *that woman* and what she did. I've had other things to think about."

Patricia smiled. "Maybe that's just a sign of your learning to accept what you can't change. I know it's a difficult thing to do, particularly in a situation like this, but it will make things easier."

"I think that that's the same conclusion I came to sometime along the way. I mean, it's hard knowing that she never loved me, not even before I was born. But I realize that that says something about her, not me. I'm thinking about therapy, but for now I do know that there's nothing wrong with me and that I am worth loving. I'm also trying to learn to trust people with my emotions."

Patricia smiled. "That's impressive and I'm happy for you. But darling, if you've settled things in your mind about your mother, then why do you look like you've been crying as if your heart were breaking? Ohhh," The truth dawned on her. "Is it Jacques Winthrop?" She watched as Tracy first looked surprised and then averted her eyes in embarrassment. "He came to the engagement party, remember?" Patricia reminded Tracy. "Even from across the room I could tell that the man is used to getting what he wants and he wanted you. Desperately. And you, dear heart, wanted him right back."

Despite the embarrassed heat suffusing her neck and face, Tracy looked at Patricia again. "You could tell all of that from where you were?"

Patricia smiled gently. "Darling, you're like a daughter to me. I'm in tune with your emotions. As for what Mr. Winthrop was thinking, well, I *am* a woman and I felt the heat he felt for you from several feet away." She laughed lightly at Tracy's wide-eyed stare and patted her arm. "Now, tell me what that awful man did to upset my baby girl."

Tracy chuckled. "Mama Singleton, I'm surprised at you. Does Papa Singleton know about this ability you have to intercept 'heat' from across a crowded room?"

Patricia laughed too. "As I said, I'm a woman full-grown. After that, the rest is easy."

Tracy found that extremely funny and started laughing uncontrollably. Just as quickly as it had started, the laughter was over and deep, wrenching sobs began to shake her body. "Oh, Mama Singleton, I think he's broken up with me and I think it's all my fault."

"Slow down, sweetheart." Patricia patted her back. "It will be okay, I promise you." She reached for her purse.

Tracy took the proffered handkerchief and cleaned her face. "I'm sorry," she said as she peeked up at Patricia. "I honestly thought I was finished crying over him. The heartless beast," she tacked on in a resentful mutter.

"No need to apologize. Just tell me what happened. Start from the beginning."

Tracy balled the handkerchief and stood. She needed to move and started pacing back and forth. "It happened a few days ago. Jack was already mad at me because I hadn't gone out with him to his parents for Labor Day. He really wanted me to meet them, but I just didn't feel up to it. He and his dad had a problem that they needed to work out and it had only been a few days since *that woman* did what she did, so I was feeling emotionally drained. Jack said he understood, but it was kind of a sore point between us. I think he felt that my not going was just one more way, in a history of ways, the way he saw it, for me to not commit to the relationship.

"Anyway, a couple of weeks after his parents' Labor Day bash, Jack and I were talking about my business. He doesn't like that I work late sometimes and come home alone late. He thinks it's unsafe. He said we should move in together. He'd asked me to right before the ball and I resisted because I wasn't ready. When I told him that I *still* wasn't ready to move in together, he asked me to let him have a key to my house and he'd give me one to his.

"Again, I had to say no. I told him I liked having my own space too much to have to share it with anyone. He accused me of not trusting him and my emotions enough to commit to him." She was too embarrassed to tell Patricia about his pregnancy theory. "I tried to explain further, but he walked away and told me to pack my stuff and he'd take me home." Tracy's eyes filled again as she remembered how painful that last part had been for her. "*He kicked me out!*" she said in a bewildered voice and Patricia could tell she still couldn't believe that he'd done that.

Patricia looked at her and could only shake her head in amazement. This child of her heart had always needed extra assurance of love and had always been slow to give it back. It was no wonder with the parents she had, but Patricia figured it was time to break that crutch. "Tracy, darling, you foolish, foolish girl." Patricia refused to be moved when Tracy raised wounded eyes to hers. She gave her head a negative shake to prove it and to give credence to her next words. "Oh, no. There's no sense in your looking at me like that. I think you're in love with this man and from what you've said, I'm sure he's in love with you.

"You've hurt him and yourself because you're afraid. Think about it, darling," she finally softened. "The woman he wants to protect and love and to whom he's made love—Can I assume you've been intimate?" she asked and bit back a smile when Tracy averted her eyes in embarrassment again. That was answer enough for Patricia. "The woman to whom he so badly wants to commit that he's invited her to move in with him, this woman who ran to him when she felt she had nowhere else to go, the very same woman to whom he's given his heart—she turned him down. And not for practical reasons, either, but because she's afraid of the unknown.

"He knows she loves him, because I know her and she's too honest not to have told him. Yet she won't even meet his parents. She won't accept a key to his home because she then would have to give him a key to hers and that would mean too much access to her, both literally and figuratively. Not only that, she tells him she doesn't want to share her space with anyone. But he's not just *anyone*, is he? He's the man who's been there for her, who's made love to her and he's the man who's *in* love with her.

"What is he supposed to think about all of this? Does this mean he loves her more than she loves him? Was he wrong about her? Does their love mean more to him? Is holding onto past hurts more important to her than their love? Is he wasting his time?"

Patricia stood and walked over to stand in front of Tracy. And by the time she finished speaking, Tracy's tears were flowing again, freely and silently. "Sweetheart, what did you expect him to do when you pushed him as far as he was willing to be pushed?" Patricia asked her softly.

Tracy spoke, "I…I…don't know. That's not what I meant to do. I didn't mean for him to feel that way…the way you said he does. I do love him, but I was just trying to protect myself."

"I think it's about time you did your damnedest to stop being so afraid. Ask yourself what exactly you're protecting yourself from. His love? True happiness with him? What is it?" Patricia demanded.

"How do you know he won't hurt me? I don't know that he won't."

"I don't know for sure that he won't. But I think a better question might be, will he hurt you if he can help it? And isn't unfettered love worth the risk?"

Tracy was quiet as she thought about it. She didn't have to think very long because she knew the answers. She knew that Jack would never, *ever* deliberately hurt her and of course their love was worth the risk. "Oh, Mama Singleton, I've screwed up big time," she moaned.

Patricia smiled. "Yes, you have, but I'm sure you can fix it."

The doorbell sounded again and Tracy went to answer it. She recognized the person standing on her porch instantly. Even if she hadn't seen her picture before, the eyes completely gave her away. "Hello, Mrs. Winthrop," she said when she opened the door. "Would you like to come in?"

Lisette hid her surprise behind a wide smile. "*Bonjour,* you are Tracy Adamson, yes?" she asked. "*Bon,*" she said when Tracy nodded. "*Oui,* I would like to come in." She stepped inside. "I do not mean to be rude by dropping in like this, but I simply had to speak to you. You understand, no?"

"I'm afraid I don't," Tracy said nervously as she studied the woman whose face held Jack's gorgeous eyes, from the deep blue color to the double lashes.

She was of average height, slim and had hair almost as black as Jack's. Dressed impeccably in a black pantsuit and light blue blouse, she studied Tracy as thoroughly as Tracy studied her. Tracy continued, "But I'm willing to listen." She tried to smile and thought, good Lord, what is she doing here?

Lisette studied the girl before her. She was quite striking and her voice…She knew her son and was sure that the girl's bedroom voice was responsible for grabbing his attention in the first place. As for what kept it, it was not difficult to figure that out when one looked in the child's eyes. Black and intelligent, they were hard to look away from. Right now, those gorgeous eyes were questioning and a bit nervous.

"Lisette Winthrop? What on earth are you doing here?" Patricia asked as Lisette entered the room. She stood and walked over to greet her.

Tracy watched as the two women greeted each other like old friends. In fact, they did know each other. They'd seen each other on the social circuit for years. Both women genuinely liked each other, but hadn't socialized much beyond luncheons and parties. They hugged with true affection.

"Patricia," Lisette said as they broke apart. "What a delightful surprise."

"Yes, same here," Patricia said carefully as she considered the look in the other woman's eyes. "Tracy's like a daughter to me. I'm here to make sure she's all right."

"Ah. Then you will understand my reasons for being here. May I sit?" she asked and turned slightly to include Tracy in the query.

"Yes, of course," Tracy said and hurriedly led her to the sofa. "Would you like something to drink?"

"Tea would be lovely, thank you," Lisette said, seeing an opportunity and seizing it immediately. She gave Patricia a look filled with meaning.

"I have iced tea made. Will that do?"

"Yes, please. Thank you."

Tracy turned to Patricia apologetically. "I'm sorry, Mama Singleton. With everything that was going on, I forgot to ask you if you wanted refreshments."

"Iced tea will be fine, dear. While you're at it, why don't you just make up a tray with light snacks? Cheese and crackers would do perfectly. What do you think, Lisette?" She was no slouch and had caught onto Lisette's hint immediately.

Lisette smiled approvingly. "Actually, I know it's very bad of me to come here in this state, but I am a bit hungry. Cheese and crackers sound quite appetizing to me right now. And perhaps you have some fruit?"

Tracy hadn't missed the shared look between the two, but was too distracted to really think about it. She went to do what had been not so subtly suggested. "Yes, I do have fruit. I'll be back as soon as I can," she mumbled.

Patricia came to the point as soon as Tracy was safely out of hearing. "All right, Lisette Winthrop, what are you up to? Why get rid of Tracy for so long?"

"Your Tracy's eyes are red from heartbreak, are they not?" Lisette asked.

"Yes," Patricia didn't equivocate as she went with instinct and trusted Lisette.

"It is the same with my Jacques. He is heartbroken and angry. He told me that his love is too afraid to love him and he knows not what to do. So I decided to help. I called her papa for her address. Jacques told me what happened between her and her parents. No, it is not like that," she hastened to explain when Patricia narrowed her eyes in distrust. "He only told me so that I would understand why your Tracy finds it so difficult to trust others with her emotions."

"That's fine, then."

Lisette smiled in understanding. "So, I called Monsieur Adamson, explained the situation and procured her address. I have not planned what I am going to say, but I felt I had to see if I could help in some way. I cannot stand to see my Jacques, my *bébé*, so unhappy. You understand, no?"

"Yes, of course I do. I assume we are of the same accord when I say we must get those two back together?"

"*Oui,*" Lisette said with feeling and a nod of her head.

"Tracy has already decided that she's made a mistake and that she wants to be with him. As I see it, the only thing we have to overcome now is her pride. And maybe his too?" Patricia asked with a lifted brow.

"Yes, my Jacques has much pride, but he is also in love."

"That helps the situation," Patricia said dryly. "What would these children do without us?"

"I do not know," Lisette said earnestly. "If left to them alone, the world's population would dwindle down to nothing and we would never get grandchildren."

Both women laughed and Tracy entered the room with the uncomfortable feeling that she was about to be handled by a couple of seasoned pros.

CHAPTER TWENTY-TWO

Jack shut the door to his office, locked it and walked through the rest of his firm's office space. He ignored the surprised looks he received for leaving so early. The security guard in the lobby looked up as Jack walked past his desk. "Don't forget to swipe your card, Mr. Winthrop."

Jack turned and retraced his steps back to the desk. "Sorry, Vance."

"No problem, Mr. Winthrop." The security guard went back to his magazine.

Jack left the building and tried to remember exactly where he'd parked his car. Unfortunately, his building didn't come with a garage and he usually parked in one of the nearby secure lots. Thanks to Tracy, he couldn't remember if he'd parked in the one across the street or the one a block and a half down. She was driving him crazy, he thought as he decided to take a chance and assume that he'd parked in the one closest to his building. Pulling out his stub, he saw that he was correct and started walking towards the structure. Thank God, this one only had three levels, but he was sure now that he'd parked on the second one.

Jack frowned again as he thought about Tracy and her constant need to pull away from their relationship and commitment. He knew she would never cheat on him, but how in the hell was he ever supposed to get her to move to the next stage if he couldn't even get her into the second one? He'd thought that he could ease her into the idea of marriage, but at the moment she wasn't even open to the idea of exchanging house keys.

He considered his options as he nodded a greeting to the parking attendant and held up his stub. He could either stick to his stance of all or nothing right now, or he could give in to this desperate need he had to see her again and tell her that he'd take her any way he could get her. Jack knew he was an impatient man, but the second option just didn't sit well with him. What scared him, though, was the possibility that she would never trust him and what they had, enough to truly commit.

On the other hand, Tracy had good reason for her inability to trust and they'd only known each other for a few months. Maybe he was moving too fast and expecting too much. Having no experience with being in love before now, he had no idea how these things worked, but instinct told him that he should push her for everything right now. He remembered how devastated she'd looked when he'd told her to pack her things and he winced. He hadn't wanted to hurt her, but he himself had been hurting. It pained him to know that the woman he loved and who loved him back didn't—or wouldn't—trust him.

He honestly didn't know what else he could do to help Tracy. He knew she was considering therapy and thought that was a good idea. He sometimes wished he could just erase her past with her family. Things would be much easier if he could. But then he would realize that she wouldn't be the woman he loved if not for her past. It had definitely shaped her. All her insecurities notwithstanding, her past hurts were also responsible for her generous spirit and kindness. Logically, he knew all of this, but damned her mother for the royal, unfeeling bitch that she was, anyway.

He missed Tracy. He couldn't escape that fact. Missed her laughter, the sound of her voice in the morning, her quirky sense of humor and the feel of her pressed against him. He missed everything about the woman and was quietly driving himself insane thinking about her every day, every hour, every minute. Jack noticed his car and disengaged the alarm from the pad on his key chain.

Still thinking of Tracy, her laughter as she teased him, he slid his key into the lock. There was a sudden, loud noise, Jack saw sparks and flames and then he saw nothing at all as everything went black.

Brickman's smile was obscenely satisfied as he spoke to Officer Dyserly over the telephone. "You say Winthrop didn't even put up a struggle? He was unconscious? Oh, that's marvelous. And you had no problem getting him away undetected? Lovely. I will see you shortly at the assigned rendezvous point, Officer Dyserly. Goodbye." Brickman hung up and turned to Jonathan.

"Get ready, brother dear. You're up next."

Jonathan drew a steadying breath. "I'm ready, Alex. I have the car and a badge and the woman's address. I hope this works."

"It will. I told you before that this plan is foolproof. Every eventuality has been considered and taken care of. When Officer Dyserly told me that it looked like our two lovebirds had broken up, I knew that it was the perfect time to put our plan in motion. Winthrop underestimated me. He thought that I didn't know about Tracy Adamson. He was wrong and now I'll have two for the price of one.

"Now, Ida has been at the police station for a while now, so she should be leaving within the next twenty to thirty minutes. Soon after her visit with the police, she'll deliver her package. In the meantime, I expect you to pick up your *package* and come to the rendezvous point within the next forty-five minutes. You've driven both routes twice already, so you shouldn't get lost."

"Getting lost is the least of my worries, Alex, but I'm ready."

"Good. I couldn't bring the usual number of men because that would have brought too much notice, so I'm counting on you."

"I know, Alex."

"Then let's get going."

Ida stared malevolently across the wide table at the police detective. He'd been questioning her for more than thirty minutes. This didn't appear to be going the way Alex had planned it. "Look, you know as well as I do that I don't have to be here. I came in because I heard you still had some questions for me."

"And where exactly did you hear that, Ms. Martinez?" the detective asked.

"Like I told you, my sister and my parents said you guys had been to their homes several times looking for me. So when I came back to town, I looked you up." Ida hadn't spoken to any of them since she'd run all of those months ago, but she was sure that the police had visited her family.

"Now, you said you've been in Bogotá all of this time."

"No, I said that I was in Bogotá with my uncle up until a couple of months ago when Brickman tracked me there. Thankfully I saw him before he saw me and I got out just in time." Brickman had decided that she'd stick as close to the truth as possible.

"And where have you been since then?"

Ida sighed impatiently. "Are you listening to me or am I just sitting here wasting my breath? I've already told you this. I went to Puerto Rico to hide out with my cousin. His name is Pedro Lopez." When they checked this, they would find it to be true because Alex had already paid someone off to say that it was.

"And you haven't seen Alexander Brickman since Bogotá when you 'got out just in time?'" That he didn't believe her was obvious.

"That's right," Ida said with a curl of her lip.

"And what made you decide to come back to Chicago now? Aren't you still afraid of Mr. Brickman?"

"Of course I'm still afraid of him." Ida didn't have to fake the fright that came into her eyes, but she did make her lips tremble. "But this is my hometown and I was tired of being away from what I know. And like I told you, I don't think he'll think to look for me here. Besides, he can't come back here because you guys are looking for him. So Chicago is probably the safest place for me."

"And you aren't familiar with Mr. Brickman's business interests?"

Ida really had to lie convincingly now, because she herself had even worked for Alex at one point. "No, I'm not. All I did was sleep with the man for a few months last year. All he wanted from me was sex and all I wanted from him was sex, money and in general, a better life for myself," she said boldly.

"And Mr. Brickman had no problem with this?"

"Well, I told him I loved him and that was that. I don't know if he believed me, but the sex was always fantastic, so if he didn't, he never said anything."

"Umm-hmm." The detective looked down at his paperwork. "And you had nothing to do with the kidnapping attempt of Caroline Singleton?"

Ida's lips compressed at the mention of the name. "No. I don't like the bitch, but I didn't want him to have her. If he had gotten his hands on her, then that would have been the end of the easy life for me. That's why I went to warn her and Brian that day. I thought I could beat Alex's men over there."

The detective stood and Ida had to stifle a sigh of relief. "Okay, Ms. Martinez, that will be all for now. We have your address in case we need to get in touch."

"Fine." She stood. Alex had been right when he figured that they'd pick up on the phony flight plan he'd planted for her. He'd figured that instead of detaining her—or the Ida look alike at the airport— that the police would follow her and try to see if she'd lead them to him. The first part of the plan had gone off seamlessly. The fake Ida had entered a woman's bathroom at a fast-food restaurant after having lunch. Ida herself had been waiting and they'd switched clothing. She, the real Ida, had left the restaurant and had come right to the police station, surprising her police tail tremendously, she was sure. She only hoped that she and her look-alike could pull the same thing off again.

Ida left the police station with the absolute certainty that she was going to be followed.

Jack awoke suddenly and was instantly alert. The pounding in his head almost made him want to shut his eyes again. He was in a large, filthy, barren room. He guessed that he was in a warehouse of some sort. He was lying on the floor with his hands handcuffed and his feet in chains. The length of the chain reached behind him to where it was bolted to the wall. He saw a similar chain nearby. He looked around for a weapon of any kind that might help him. He knew it would do him no good to yell for help. Brickman had made sure that help wouldn't be near, he was sure of that.

"Ah, Mr. Winthrop," a soft, deadly voice said.

Jack whipped his head towards the sound. "Brickman," he said without surprise, recognizing the man instantly, despite his new look.

"I've been waiting months to do this." Brickman walked quickly over to Jack and delivered a malicious punch to his jaw.

Jack sneered around the pain. "It doesn't surprise me that you fight dirty, Brickman. It is, after all, the cowardly thing to do."

Brickman snarled and before Jack knew it, he had kicked him in the ribs.

Through gritted teeth, Jack wheezed, "What else have you got?" He tried not to let his suspicions or interest show when Brickman suddenly smiled.

"Oh, you'll see what else I've got, Winthrop. And I promise you, you won't be smiling when I show it to you."

"I know you're dying to tell me how you did it, so go ahead and gloat."

"If you insist. That bomb in your car? It wasn't meant to kill you, just to stun you long enough to get you here. Why, you hardly show any effects from it at all. I mean, the nasty, little bruise on your head is barely noticeable. Anyway, sneaking back into the country is relatively easy when you're as brilliant as I am. A new look, a new passport, private planes all the way and *voilá*, I'm back."

"Yes, in all your dubious glory," Jack said sarcastically. "Ask yourself this, Brickman. How long do you think you can get away with this?"

"For as long as I need to. Let's face it, you and your coworkers have never been able to keep up with me. Look at your record when it comes to me. It's not a very good one, is it?" He laughed as he walked away to exit the room. "I'll be back with my surprise soon, Winthrop."

Jack frowned. He really was in a tight fix and at the moment, he had no idea how he was going to get out of it, though that wasn't his primary concern. He had a feeling he knew what Brickman's surprise would be. He either had Tracy already or was planning to take her. Either way, Jack knew that she was in trouble. Why else would Brickman look so gleeful? Instinct told Jack that Brickman didn't have his parents and he knew now that Brickman's mentioning them in the letter he'd sent him had only been a ruse.

Yes, he would be devastated if anything happened to his parents. But a man like Brickman would know that he would be equally devastated if something happened to Tracy. Add to that the fact that it would be easier to take one person by surprise than it would two, and Jack had his answer. He didn't know how Brickman knew about Tracy, but he did know. He'd been an arrogant fool to think otherwise.

Jack sighed. He knew Tracy would soon be a captive also and had no idea what he could do to rescue her. Brickman had taken all of his belongings. The only thing he had left were the clothes on his back. No cell phone, no keys, no briefcase...there was nothing. Yeah, he was in a tight fix all right. If he was right in thinking that Brickman's main reason for coming to Chicago was to kidnap Caroline, then there was a chance that Brian would figure out a solution to this mess, if he didn't get caught himself.

CHAPTER TWENTY-THREE

Tracy settled more comfortably in the salon chair and enjoyed feeling relaxed. She'd already had a massage and was getting her hair, hands and feet done. As she sat under the hairdryer sipping wine and flipping through a magazine, she thought more about the impromptu visits she'd received from the two grand dames a couple of hours earlier. It had almost been as if they'd planned to meet at her house.

In the past, Patricia Singleton and Lisette Winthrop had both proven to be ruthlessly single-minded when it came to getting what they wanted. In this case, their shared desire had been blindingly clear: they wanted Jack and her together again. Period. Tracy shook her head as she flipped another page in her magazine. Just how she'd ended up currently sitting in Simone's chair still had her head in a whirl.

"Ah, Tracy darling, it looks delicious," Patricia said as Tracy walked back into the living room with a fully loaded tea tray. "Here, let me help you with that." Patricia rose from the sofa, but Tracy forestalled her.

"That's okay. I've got it." Tracy sat the tray down with a slight clatter. She straightened and looked in surprise at one of her armchairs. It had been moved from its usual spot by the fireplace and was now sitting on the other side of the table, directly across from the sofa.

"I moved it, Tracy," Patricia said as she selected a cracker from the tray. "I just thought we should all be comfortable while we talked."

Since the two of them were sharing the sofa, Tracy assumed that she was meant to sit in the lone chair. Nothing like feeling you're facing a tribunal to make you feel comfortable, she thought wryly and lowered herself into the chair. She looked over at the two women expectantly.

Lisette spoke first. "Tracy," she began. "Oh, I'm sorry. May I call you Tracy?"

"Please do."

"*Bon*," Lisette said with a pleased smile. "Then you may call me Lisette. Tracy," she said as she looked at the tray and selected a small tea cookie, "I came here today because my son is not happy."

Tracy squirmed in her chair when Lisette lifted her eyes and settled them on her. "Yes, well…" Tracy cleared her throat, wondered what she was supposed to say and said exactly what she was thinking. "I'm at a loss. I don't know what you want me to say." She spread her hands helplessly.

Patricia said, "It's just that Lisette is worried about him, just as I am about you. You understand that, right?"

Tracy only nodded.

"My dear, I have never seen my Jacques so miserable as he is now. He came for a visit the other day and he looked horrible. He does not eat, he does not sleep and he does not concentrate well on his work. It seems to me that the only thing he is able to do competently is think of you."

Patricia seemed to be choking in her glass. Tracy took her worried eyes away from Lisette's earnest face for a moment. "Are you all right, Mama Singleton?"

"I'm fine," Patricia said with a weak wave of her hand and ignored the warning, narrowed-eyed look Lisette gave her. "Don't mind me."

Tracy looked back to Lisette and missed Patricia rolling her eyes at Lisette. "Surely, it's not as bad as all that," Tracy said.

"Yes, it is. His father and I are terribly worried about him. We're afraid he may do something desperate."

Tracy straightened in her chair, the worry she was already feeling tripping into outright alarm. "Something desperate? What do you mean?"

"He mentioned something about not being fit for the kind of work he does and I'm worried that he may give up his job, something he's always loved." While Jack had said that he wasn't quite up to doing his work and that he might take a break for a while, he had not mentioned anything about quitting. Lisette chose not to quibble over details, however.

"Give up his job?" Tracy was incredulous. "Jack would never do anything like that. And besides, he's determined to find Brickman and put him away. He's been working on the case for years."

"Exactly," Lisette said, completely reversing her stance without a single qualm. "Imagine how much more danger he will put himself in by going after that monster when his mind is not fully focused on his job."

"Yes, Tracy," Patricia put in, "Jack needs you now more than ever. I understand that they feel closer than ever to catching the bastard." She finished with feeling, hating the man who'd made it his mission to terrify her daughter.

"They are?" Tracy asked. "But no one told me."

"Think about it," Lisette said with an embarrassed wince. "Why would Jacques tell you when you two have fought so bitterly?"

"Yes, dear," Patricia agreed. "How could he even approach you, with the way the two of you left things? He is human, after all, and he does have his pride. Just like you have yours."

Tracy looked down for a moment, trying to think. She bit her lip. "But what should I do?" She lifted questioning, worried eyes to the two women. "I don't want him to get hurt."

"You should go to him," Lisette said instantly. "Immediately."

"No, not immediately," Patricia said. "She should go to the salon first. That way, she can pamper herself and be better prepared to seduce him."

"Mama Singleton," Tracy said in a voice begging her to behave. She was mortified. Yes, she was intimate

with Jack, but she didn't want to talk about it with his
mother in the room. She was barely comfortable
talking about it with the woman she considered to be
her emotional, if not biological, mother.

"No, I am afraid she is right," Lisette said. "I know
my son and he will make it difficult for you to apologize. You have no other choice. You must seduce him."
She said it as if she were directing troops into battle.

Tracy stared at the two of them, the truth finally
dawning on her. "I know what the two of you have
been doing. Oh, please," she said disbelievingly as they
both tried to look confused and innocent of any crime.
"You're just lucky that I want to be with Jack as much,
probably more, than the two of you want us to be
together. So I'll ignore this little double-team and let
you have your victory."

Patricia didn't bat an eye. "I don't know what you
mean, dear. But why don't we go pick something out
for you to wear?"

"Yes, you two do that and I'll call and make Tracy
an appointment at Pleasures for You," Lisette said,
never doubting that the most exclusive full-service
salon in town was the one Patricia had been referring to
when she'd suggested Tracy go.

"Thanks. Please see if Simone is available. She
usually does my hair," she said over her shoulder to
Lisette as Patricia rushed her up the stairs. "I need to
call Caroline, too."

"Tracy!"

Tracy looked up to see Simone standing in front or her with an impatient look on her face. "I'm sorry, Simone. What's up?"

"What's up is that you're done conditioning. You need to move over to the sink so I can rinse it out."

"Oh, okay." Tracy deposited her empty glass on the table beside her and stood. "I want to thank you again, Simone, for squeezing me in on such short notice."

"It was no problem. Pleasures always has time for a few special clients. When Lisette Winthrop said the appointment was for you, my partner and I were still pleased. Lisette is on her list of special clients just as you're on mine."

"Well, thanks, Simone, I didn't know."

"You, K.K. and Caroline have been with me from the beginning. Of course you're on my list of special clients. Now," she said as Tracy settled in the chair in front of the sink, "are you sure you want me to straighten your hair? It's not too late for me to put it back in twists."

"Yes, I'm sure."

"What brought this on?" Simone asked.

Tracy suddenly felt shy. "I'm seeing someone and he's never seen me with straight hair. I want to surprise him, that's all."

"What, he doesn't like your hair in its natural state?" Simone asked defensively.

"He likes it fine. In fact, he loves it. I just want to do something different. So don't read anything into it."

"Okay, I'll do it the way you want, but don't forget to come back for your twists next week. With all the heat from the dryers and curlers, I'll need to apply today, I'm going to have to give you another deep conditioner next week. I hope this guy is worth all the trouble, girl."

"Oh, he most definitely is." Tracy's smile held all kinds of secrets.

Tracy hurried through her door, locking it behind her. Jack was in for the surprise of his life, she thought as she pulled her black shawl closer around herself. She was wearing the exact dress and shoes she'd been wearing the night they'd made love in Paris. She even carried the same purse. Her new hairstyle swung against and brushed the tops of her shoulders and Cathy at Pleasures had done an amazing job on her eyes, making them look smoky and more mysterious. Her fingers and toes sported coral polish and her lips matched them perfectly. In short, she looked amazing. Jack wouldn't know what hit him.

Tracy skipped lightly down the stairs with a shiver of anticipation. She was reaching for the latch on her gate when she noticed a large man walking toward her.

Jonathan tried to look official and not nervous as he approached the gate. Was the woman standing on the other side of the gate Tracy Adamson? She didn't look like the picture he'd seen and she didn't fit Alexander's description of her at all. Alex had described her as merely pretty, but this woman was a knockout, Jonathan thought to himself as he came abreast of her. Alex had also said that she wore her hair in one of those funny, twisty hairstyles that black women seemed to like so much nowadays. The picture had also shown her with her hair like that.

Jonathan raised his eyes to meet hers. They were black as night and quite startling in such a light face. Yes, she was the one he was looking for. He cleared his throat and watched as she took a couple of steps back, looking at him warily. "Excuse me, ma'am. Are you Tracy Adamson?" He tried to make his voice as non-threatening as possible.

"Why?"

Jonathan was taken aback by the question for a moment and then he remembered. He lifted his hand and flipped open his wallet to show his badge and waited with bated breath while she decided whether or not to step closer for a look at the badge. He did his best not to let his relief show when it appeared she'd made up her mind to come closer. He didn't know what he'd do if she decided not to come with him. They hadn't planned for that possibility. While the street was a quiet one, he still couldn't take a chance and snatch her. "I'm Detective Miglionne, Ms. Adamson. I need to speak with you," he said carefully.

He watched as she came closer and waited while she carefully studied the badge and his picture. "*Are you* Tracy Adamson?"

She said nothing for what seemed like hours and then finally, "Yes, I am." She took a deep breath as if preparing herself. "What can I do for you, detective?" she asked, but her eyes told him that she thought she already knew. "It's Jack, isn't it? Where is he? Is he okay?" The questions came bullet-like, not leaving room for breath.

Jonathan opened the gate and took her elbow in his large hand. "I hate to tell you this, ma'am, but Jack was involved in an accident. He's hurt pretty badly, but the doctors are saying he'll make a full recovery. I used to work with Jack at the same precinct and the captain thought it best that you see a friendly face when you were told about the accident. Come with me and I'll take you to the hospital." He drew her out of the gate. Almost there, he thought to himself.

But Tracy halted and grabbed his arm tightly. "What happened? It's that monster, Alexander Brickman, isn't it? He did something to Jack. Please, you have to tell me." She was almost hysterical.

Jonathan was jolted at the sound of his brother's name being said in such a hate-filled voice. It reminded him of how his father sounded whenever he'd mentioned Alexander over the past few years. "Please calm down, Ms. Adamson. We don't know that the accident was the fault of Mr. Brickman, but it is something we're looking into. Jack will be okay, I promise you. Please just come with me. My car is parked right at the corner."

He looked at her from the corner of his eye as they began walking. She looked a bit dazed. "You know, Ms. Adamson, I've known Jack for several years. We all miss him down at the job. But on his last visit, he was bursting with happiness. He told us all about you and how lucky he felt that he had met you. And Jack's such a great guy that we were all thrilled for him."

Tracy let herself be led to the detective's car. Tears rolled down her face. Jack was hurt. Her Jack was in the hospital. What had the detective said? She tried to remember as he opened the passenger door, helped her into the car and belted her in as one would a small child.

It came to her as he started the car. The detective had said that Jack had been in an accident and that they were looking into the possibility that Brickman was responsible for it. Oh God, her mind screamed. Don't panic, Tracy, she told herself silently. The detective had also said that the doctors thought Jack would be okay.

She thought about how thoughtful it was of Jack's old captain to send someone to take her to the hospital. And Detective Miglionne was nice to take on the task of coming to get her. She'd have to tell Jack how nice he was. What else had Detective Miglionne said? Tracy frowned and tried to remember. She was so upset that she had a hard time remembering her own name.

Ah, she had it. Detective Miglionne had said that he'd been thrilled for Jack when he'd told everyone at the precinct about her—Tracy's thoughts came to a screeching halt as she realized that the man was lying to her. Jack hadn't told anyone about her because he'd wanted to protect her. The only people he'd told about their relationship were his family and Brian. She turned to look at the man—she was sure he wasn't a real cop—just as the car stopped for a red light.

She quietly unsnapped her seat belt. "You're a liar!" She screamed and fingers curled like talons, she dove for his face.

Nessi rode her bike industriously and tried to control her breathing. "Only a few more feet to go," she whispered softly as she saw the sign indicating Tracy's block a few feet away. She'd been visiting one of her school friends in the city and had come up with the brilliant idea to ride to her Aunt Tracy's house. She'd only spoken to her a few times since the incident with her mother and she really missed her. She didn't worry about not being welcomed because, as Tracy had told her more than once, there would always be room in her home for her favorite cousin, who, incidentally, just also happened to be one of her favorite people.

Nessi turned onto Tracy's street and pedaled a few feet before she noticed that Tracy was outside. She started to wave and call out, but didn't. She slowed and then stopped altogether. She wondered who the strange man was. Tracy looked upset. Something wasn't right, she could tell. But instinct told her not to call notice to herself. She slowly followed as the two walked to an unfamiliar car and continued to follow a couple of paces behind as the man pulled away from the curb.

She wished she could see inside the car, but didn't want to chance getting close enough to be able to. Nessi stopped at a red light, relieved that she'd get to catch her breath for a few seconds. She was not much of an athlete and told herself that she'd sign up for track and tennis at school as her mom had practically begged her to do. Maybe then she'd develop some endurance. She frowned when the car Tracy was in didn't move when the light turned green. The drivers of the cars behind them started honking their horns.

When the light switched to red again without Tracy's car moving, Nessi bit her lip, debating whether or not to approach the car. She told herself that if they didn't move when it turned green again, then she'd catch up and see what was wrong.

A relieved breath escaped her lips when the car moved as the light changed to green. Nessi started pedaling again. She hoped they wouldn't go onto any really busy streets. She wasn't all that experienced with riding her bike in the street and she stayed close to the curb. Watching the back of the car Tracy was in, she saw the right turn signal blink on. Criminy, where the heck were they going? She huffed to keep up.

Traffic thinned a little while later, but not so much that Nessi worried that she'd be that noticed. She just hoped that the man wasn't looking at his rearview mirror often enough to notice her. As the structures on the streets changed from homes to old warehouses, Nessi began to worry. The neighborhood didn't look too safe and it was going to get dark very soon. She stopped as the car turned down a side street. It was way too risky to follow; he'd definitely notice her. She'd have to put some distance between them.

Nessi counted to sixty before turning onto the side street. She was too anxious to count any further. She wanted to cry when she didn't immediately see the car. While she frantically tried to figure out what to do, she stopped her bike beside what looked to be a storage facility and swore in frustration. "Damn. What am I going to do now?" Tears filled her eyes. When she heard a car door slam, she looked up, startled. Her eyes tracked the noise across the street and she saw the car parked in an alley at the side of the building. "That's why I didn't see you," she murmured softly. "You parked in the alley."

A gasp flew from her mouth as she watched the large man go to the passenger side, open the door, bend in and then straighten with a limp Tracy in his arms. Nessi squeezed herself against the side of the building when the man took a nervous look around. She prayed he didn't notice her bike pressed against it.

Her first instinct was to rush him and rescue her cousin. She was on the verge of doing just that when the door to the building opened and another man appeared. "Shit, I can't take two of them," she whispered, her language deteriorating as her fear and nervousness mounted.

"What took you so long, Jonathan?" she heard the new man ask impatiently.

"As you can see," the man called Jonathan said sarcastically, "I had to use the injection to subdue her. Look what she did to my face, Alex. She's got nails like a she-cat."

Nessi couldn't see the damage to his face, but knowing her cousin, it had to be extensive. "Good for you, Aunt Tracy," she whispered fiercely.

When the door closed behind the two men, she hit her head lightly with her fist. "Think, Nessi, think," she told herself. "They must have covered something like this in one of those safety lectures at school. Let's see…drugs are bad…stop, drop and roll…don't talk to strangers…police officers are your friends—" That's it! I need the police!" She looked around for a telephone. "Nessi, you dope!" She reached into her pocket and triumphantly pulled out the cell phone she'd just gotten for her birthday.

CHAPTER TWENTY-FOUR

"Now tell me exactly what happened," Brickman told Jonathan as they walked into the building.

Jonathan placed Tracy on a nearby table. "She was wary of me from the first." He told him what had happened in front of Tracy's house. "And then she attacked me in the car." He touched both sides of his face gingerly. Tracy had left four deep grooves on each side. "I had to smack her to stun her a bit and that's when I put the needle in her arm. She went out like a light soon after that."

"Good, very good." Brickman said as he studied Tracy. "She's going to have a nasty bruise," he said softly, already seeing it form on her right cheek. "She looks different. Are you sure this is Tracy Adamson?"

"Yes, I am. I asked her twice."

Still, Brickman lifted an eyelid. Though the pupil was unseeing and blank, it *was* black, and satisfied, he gently released the lid. "The plan is coming along beautifully. Ida has returned and she says her plan went off almost without a hitch. She's not happy about how long the police detained her, but that's over and done with now. The police are following her look-alike back to that flophouse on Belmont and they'll probably sit there for hours.

"Now, pick Ms. Adamson up and follow me. It's time we started the second phase of our plan."

Jonathan picked Tracy up and followed Brickman down a squalid hall to a locked door. He waited patiently while Brickman selected a key and fit it in the lock, then stepped forward into the room when Brickman stepped back and held the door open.

Jack looked up alertly when he heard the key in the lock. He'd been waiting for Brickman to come back. Maybe if he could get him talking again, he could find out just how extensive this operation was. He swore when he saw Tracy.

Brickman smiled in delight. "You remember my brother Jonathan, don't you, Winthrop? I understand he gifted you with a black eye a couple of months ago. And of course you know the lovely Ms. Adamson." He indicated with a wave of his arm that Jonathan should put her down.

Seeing that he intended to put her on the floor, Jack moved so that her upper body and head were cushioned on his chest. He watched as Jonathan chained her feet.

"Look at that. He wants to protect her from the rough floor. Isn't that lovely?" Brickman said with a smarmy smile.

"What did you give her, Brickman?"

Brickman chuckled. "Oh, it was just a little something to calm her down. As you can see, she gave my brother a rough time." He indicated Jonathan's face.

Jack felt a surge of pride at Tracy's handiwork and he smirked. "Your 250-pound brother couldn't handle a 110-pound woman. That's interesting, to say the least." Ridiculing him did nothing but give Jack a short spurt of satisfaction.

"Don't laugh, Winthrop. The little lady will pay for those scratches, just as surely as you will pay for what you did in Paris."

"Why is she here? You have nothing to gain by bringing her here."

"Oh, on the contrary. I can watch you suffer as I take her away from you. That's what I have to gain." Brickman turned to leave.

"What do you want?"

Jack's question made Brickman pause but he didn't to turn around. "There is nothing you can give me, Winthrop. So don't waste your breath and my time asking." He and Jonathan left, slamming the door behind them.

"Stay and guard the door. I don't trust Winthrop, even if he is restrained. And don't be afraid to use that gun I gave you."

"Whatever you say, Alex."

"Ida will be leaving soon and then things will really be underway."

Jack bent his head down. He could reach just far enough to place a kiss on top of Tracy's head. They'd handcuffed her slim wrists and chained her ankles, just as they'd done his. His only consolation was that Brickman hadn't handcuffed their hands behind their backs. Gently jostling Tracy, he lifted his arms and placed them around her. She let out a breath and snuggled in as her subconscious recognized him even in drug-induced sleep.

He studied her, for the first time taking note of her changed hair and the clothing she wore. She looked as if she'd been on a mission. He was sure that mission had been him. It better have been. That was the dress she'd worn in Paris the night they'd made love. He didn't know if she'd seduced him or if he'd seduced her. He preferred to think that it went both ways.

Tracy shifted, making her usual disgruntled, waking-up noises. She pushed her face into his chest, trying futilely to stay asleep. It was the same thing she always did when they were in bed together. He usually kissed her out of it. He couldn't do that this time, so he settled for speaking. "Tracy. Wake up, baby. There's no use fighting it. Come on, sweetheart. Wake up and let me see those beautiful, obsidian eyes of yours. I've missed them terribly."

Tracy struggled awake to the sound of Jack's voice and to the feel of various aches and pains. Her lashes fluttered a few times to clear her vision. She saw a filthy door just about the time she realized that she was handcuffed and that her feet were chained. She also realized that Jack was holding her rather oddly. "Jack?" Full of panic, fear and confusion, her voice wavered as she called his name.

"I'm here, baby," she heard him say, and stretched her neck backward to look at him.

Jack couldn't help himself; he bent his head and covered her mouth with his own. The need to touch her was stronger than his common sense and heedless of where they were, Jack kissed her carnally, in the same slow, thorough way he did before he made love to her.

Sensing his need and having the same need herself, Tracy pushed herself upward, opened her mouth and let him take what he wanted—what he needed. The kiss was a reaffirming of the connection they had to one another. It brought assurance to both of them. Their lips slowly broke apart and Tracy brushed her cheek against his lovingly and nuzzled his chin with the top of her head before she settled her head in the notch between his neck and shoulder.

"It's Brickman, isn't it, Jack?" she said softly.

"Yes, *bella*, I'm afraid it is. I'm so sorry for getting you into this."

"It's not your fault, *querido*. We just have to figure out a way to get out of here."

From a room down the hall, Brickman watched the scene play out on closed-circuit television and crowed his delight. "That's perfect," he said to Ida. "I think we've got enough." He reached down to remove a tape from a VCR. He'd placed a camera on the wall directly across from where Jack and Tracy lay and arranged for it to start recording as soon as Tracy was brought into the room.

After rewinding the tape, he placed it in its sleeve, which had a note taped to it, and gave it to Ida. "You know what to do."

Ida took the tape and left. "It's about damned time," she mumbled as she walked to the car. She wanted this over and done with. She felt anxious. She just knew something was going to happen.

From across the street, Nessi watched the woman get into the car and drive away. She recognized her. She was the same one who'd terrorized her Aunt Caroline the year before. So, if she was there, then that must mean that that Brickman guy was involved. "Oh my God, oh my God," Nessi whispered. She decided to try her cell phone again. She'd been unable to get a signal before and had been dithering about for the past five minutes. Once she'd realized that her major hope for saving Tracy wasn't going to work, she'd experienced a tremendous letdown and had been paralyzed with inaction. She couldn't decide what to do. Ida's sudden appearance made her decision for her. She hopped on her bike, making sure to take note of the address of the building as she rode off in search of a signal.

Tracy pushed in closer to Jack and tried not to scream from the unadulterated fear blocking her throat. They were bound and in Brickman's clutches. As far as she was concerned, life couldn't get much worse. Jack had been honest with her and had said that he was basically incapacitated, saying wryly that he wished he'd paid closer attention to *MacGyver*. It was an old television show in which each week the hero found ingenious ways to get himself out of perilous situations, using just what was available to him at the time.

Jack could feel Tracy's fear and he agonized over it. Absently, he sniffed her hair and realized how he could distract her. "What did you do to your hair? It's different. And isn't this the dress you wore that night in Paris? Why are you dressed so sexily?" he asked craftily, which was a clear indication to Tracy that he already knew why and was gloating.

She decided not to give him the satisfaction. She turned so that she was on her back and shrugged her shoulders. "I just felt like dressing up, that's all."

"Oh, really?" Jack said, playing the game, anything to take her mind off their current situation, even if only momentarily. "Were you going to go anywhere? I mean, anywhere so that a certain someone could see you in this sexy, little number?"

"Maybe." Tracy shrugged again.

"Maaaaybe that certain someone was me, hmm? And you do understand, don't you, that I'll have to tickle you until you scream for mercy if you give me any other answer?" Jack had his hands cupped over her stomach and poised to commence with their torture. She absolutely hated being tickled. His tickling had actually made her cry once.

Tracy grinned and caught his hands in a tight grip. "And what if I choose to give you no answer at all?"

"Then I'm afraid I'd have to do the dirty deed anyway. A non-answer is the same as the wrong answer."

"In that case," Tracy said with her tongue caught between her teeth as she turned her head to look at him, "my answer is…" She whispered it so softly that he had to lean in and bend his head to hear it. It was a long, seductive answer, but it was the one he wanted.

He cleared his throat. "You got that answer in right under the wire and saved yourself from a hell of a tickle bout," Jack said in a husky voice.

Tracy smiled because she knew what he was doing, but the smile crumpled around the edges and she started crying. "I'm sorry, Jack. I don't mean to cry, because I know it doesn't make it any easier, but I really need to. Just give me a few minutes, okay?" She awkwardly shifted again, curled into his body, turned her face into his chest and let her tears soak his shirt.

"It's all right, *bella*," Jack said painfully. "You cry as long as you need to." Jack stared at her handcuffs as she brought her hands up to cover her face.

Ida stepped off the elevators and into Inclusion Integrated Marketing, her old office where the beginning of the end for her had started last year when that bitch had come in for an interview. She saw that they had a new receptionist and walked over, pleased that the woman wouldn't know her. "Hello. Is Brian Keenan in?"

"No, I'm afraid not, ma'am. He's gone for the day. He usually leaves early on Thursdays and Fridays," she said with a smile, volunteering entirely too much information.

But Ida had counted on Brian sticking to old habits. She smiled. "Oh, okay. Is Justin Hartley in?"

"Yes, he is." The receptionist reached for the telephone. "May I tell him who's asking?"

"No, that's okay," Ida said with a smile, deciding just at that moment to deviate a bit from Brickman's plan. She'd thought she'd be able to follow it, but she just couldn't face Justin, her old boss who also happened to be a decent man. She laid the package on the desk. "Could you make sure he gets this right away. Tell him it's from his old friend Ida and that he should see that Brian gets it immediately." She turned and left.

CHAPTER TWENTY-FIVE

"Hello?" Caroline said into her home phone's receiver.

"Aunt Caroline, thank God you're home. I've been trying for forever to find a signal so I could call you," Nessi said.

Caroline straightened at the worry and fear she could hear in Nessi's voice. "What is it, Nessi? Is it Tracy? Did your Aunt Penelope do something else?"

"Yes, I mean no, I mean yes." Nessi stopped talking altogether and counted to fifteen before talking again. When she did, she was almost a completely different person. "Okay, Aunt Caroline, here's what's going on. It is Aunt Tracy and she is in trouble, but it's nothing to do with Aunt Penelope. Aunt Tracy's been kidnapped. I followed the car, so I know where she is, but I can't go in alone. There are too many of them. I've seen three so far, but there could be more."

"Wait, slow down." Caroline stood up now and started pacing. There was no doubt in her mind that Nessi was telling the truth and that she wasn't seeing things.

Alert to Caroline's every mood, Brian looked over at her from across the room. His eyes narrowed when she said, "What? Tracy's been kidnapped? And you saw it happen? Nessi, are you sure?" Caroline closed her eyes on a shaky sigh.

Nessi relayed how she'd come to be in the right place at the right time, covering everything up to her current phone call. She wound down with, "I think it was that Brickman guy because I saw that Ida lady who caused you so much trouble last year."

Caroline sank back down in her chair as her knees gave out. "Brickman has Tracy?" she said in a small voice as she realized that they should have thought of this possibility. "Where are you, baby?"

"I'm in an area that has a lot of warehouses and storage facilities. I'm not familiar with it, but it isn't too far from Aunt Tracy's. I rode my bike here from there. The address is…"

Caroline grabbed a pen and her sketchpad and scribbled down the address. She looked up at Brian, who had come to stand near her. She leaned her head into his leg for support and cuddled in when his hand came up to tangle in her hair. "Nessi, just tell me that you're okay."

"Oh, I'm fine, Aunt Caroline. Those idiots never even saw me."

"Okay, listen, baby. Are you in hiding? I mean, can they just walk out their door and see you?"

"Actually no, they can't. I had to ride a couple of blocks away before I could get a signal. I'm in front of a McDonalds."

"All right, you stay there. Go inside the restaurant. Don't go back to the warehouse. Did you call the police?"

"No, I started to, but then I thought about you and Uncle Brian and that it might be better to call you guys. I didn't think they'd believe me."

"That's good, baby. You did the right thing," Caroline said, wanting to alleviate some of the worry in the girl's voice. "Brian and I will take care of calling the police. Now remember what I said. Stay right where you are. We're coming to get you. What's the address of the McDonald's?" She took the address down. "Okay, now go inside right now. We'll be right there. I love you." Caroline clicked off.

She rose and turned to Brian. "Brickman has Tracy. Nessi saw everything. We have to do something, Brian. I told Nessi that we'd call the police, but I don't want them to come in with sirens blaring and possibly get Tracy hurt if Brickman panics. Come on, Brian, we have to go."

"Calm down. *We* don't have to go anywhere. I'll go." He laid his hand on her flat stomach when he saw that she would object. "Remember the possibility. I don't want you or her or maybe him hurt," he said and pulled her close. "I'll call the police, too. Don't worry, I know whom to call. They'll do me this favor and kill the bells and whistles."

"What if I go, but only to the McDonald's to pick up Nessi? I'm sure she's terrified."

Brian started shaking his head no even before she finished speaking. "I don't want you anywhere near the place. Please. I don't want you to get stressed for any reason. I'll have one of my friends pick Nessi up." He released her and went to the highest shelf in his closet. He pulled down the gun he'd gotten from a cop friend just about a year ago. After he left the force, he didn't think he'd ever need a gun again in his life. He'd been wrong.

Caroline didn't try to fight him. "What about Jack? Shouldn't we call him?"

"That's what I'm doing now," Brian said, sitting on the bed as he dialed the phone. "His assistant says he's left for the day," he said, just before he disconnected and tried Jack's cell phone. "His cell phone is out of range. I don't think he's home, but I'll try there. *Hi Jack, it's Brian. I need you to call me on my cell or Caroline at home as soon as you get this message. Call me immediately,*" he stressed and hung up.

"I'm scared, Brian," Caroline said quietly. She walked over to him, sat on his lap and held him tightly around the waist. "Please be careful."

Brian slid his hand through the hair at the back of her head to palm and massage her scalp. He could feel her soft breath on his neck. "I will. Don't worry. I'll be back before you know it." He put his arms around her.

Caroline gave him one last squeeze and stood so he could stand. She didn't beg him to stay home, though that was exactly what she wanted to do. "I love you, Brian." She leaned up to kiss him.

Brian allowed himself one last taste of her before leaving. "I love you," he said against her lips. He turned to go. "Keep calling Jack and tell him where I'm going. I'll keep trying to call him on his cell."

A short time later, Justin Hartley greeted Caroline uncomfortably and hurriedly when she answered the door. "Hi Caroline. Is Brian in?"

"No, I'm afraid not." Caroline wondered what Justin wanted. She wanted him to leave. Now was not the time for visitors.

Justin grimaced. "I hate doing this, but Ida stopped by the office today and left this. It's addressed to you, but she said to give it to Brian." He handed over the package.

Caroline pulled out the videotape and the note. She read it aloud. "'Ms. Singleton, watch the tape, get in your car, drive to the entrance of Eggers Woods at 112th and Ewing and wait in your car. Be there at seven tonight and I might let your little girlfriend live. Do not bring Mr. Keenan and don't call the police.'"

Caroline was oddly calm. She walked over to the entertainment center and slid the tape in the VCR. "Justin, would you hand me the telephone?" she asked as images of Tracy and Jack flickered on the screen.

She watched as Jack tenderly held Tracy in his arms, despite his handcuffs. Watched as Tracy slowly awoke and finally, watched as the two kissed. She dialed Brian's cell. "Brian? Brickman has both of them. He has Tracy and Jack."

"How do you know that?" Brian demanded.

"Ida delivered a tape to Justin at the office today and he brought it here. The tape shows Jack and Tracy handcuffed. The tape came with a note and it says that I should drive to Eggers Woods. I guess he wants to trade Tracy for me because the note said if I'm there by seven tonight, he might let Tracy live. I'm not to bring you."

"Caroline, don't you dare leave the house!" The panic was clear in Brian's voice.

"I won't, darling. I promise. I just wanted you to know that Brickman has Jack as well as Tracy."

"He's in for a surprise. By seven, he'll be in handcuffs. The police are meeting me there and I should arrive at his little hidey-hole in less than five minutes."

"Is someone going to pick up Nessi?"

"Yes, I took care of that, too. Call her and tell her to expect Detective Sheila Bracken."

Officer Dyserly watched the entrance to Brian and Caroline's building from across the street. He'd followed Hartley from his office and watched him go in, but so far no one had come out. It had been at least twenty minutes. He pulled out his cell phone and called Brickman.

"Mr. Brickman, I'm sorry to report that Ms. Singleton has not come out of the building yet. It's been twenty minutes since Hartley entered."

"Not so strange, Officer Dyserly. I'm sure they're inside floundering and trying to decide what to do. They're probably even trying to figure out how they're going to outsmart me. Let's give them a few more minutes. Call me back in, shall we say...five?"

"Yes sir," Dyserly said.

"Tracy," Jack whispered urgently as her crying wound down.

"Yes?" Tracy lowered her hands from her face to look at him.

"Do your handcuffs feel loose? Do you think you could slip one of your hands through?" Jack was still whispering. He didn't intend to count on Brian and Caroline somehow rescuing them. If Tracy could get her hands free, perhaps they could take an unsuspecting Brickman by surprise with a blow to the head. Jack only hoped the arrogant son of a bitch was carrying the keys to his handcuffs on him.

Tracy followed his lead and whispered as well. "I can try."

"Okay, very slowly, I want you to turn until you're completely facing me. I just noticed that there's a camera on the wall across the room. It's well hidden, so I didn't see it at first, but I noticed the red light flash a moment ago."

Tracy did as he bade and slowly tried to slide her right hand through its cuff.

"Everything went according to plan?" Brickman asked Ida after hanging up with Dyserly.

"Yes. As I told you, Brian usually leaves early on Thursdays and Fridays. He did just that today. I asked for him first when I talked to the receptionist. When she said he wasn't in, I asked for Justin. Justin has the tape and I watched him leave the building in a hurry about two minutes after I left."

"And what was his reaction to seeing you?"

Ida didn't hesitate. She lied. "Just as we expected, he was shocked. Too shocked to do much of anything but take the package from me. I'm sure I was long gone by the time he came to his senses."

"Yes, I imagine to him it was like seeing a ghost. I would have loved to have seen that."

Ida smiled. "You were so right not to have me take it straight to Brian and Caroline. I'm sure they have some kind of security at their house. I'm probably on a list of people to look out for."

"I'm always right."

Tracy tried not to moan as the handcuff painfully bit into her hand when she tried to squeeze it out. It had been easy to move the cuff at first. The difficulty came when she had to slide it over the knuckle in her thumb. Now she was trying to move it over her other knuckles. "I've almost got it." She'd been working at it for at least twenty minutes.

Jack forced himself to keep his eyes on her face and to talk about other things.

He was sure Brickman was still watching. "When I get you home…," Jack said in a normal voice when he noticed from the corner of his eye that her hand was free. He lowered his head to whisper, "You're wonderful. I'm so proud of you."

"Please. It was easy," Tracy said so dryly that it was obviously a lie. "Now what?"

"Sir, they haven't come out yet," Dyserly said to Brickman from his cell.

"Are you sure? Perhaps they went out the back way."

"I don't think so, sir. The cars they normally park on the street are still here. Their other ones are in the garage, but I haven't heard any others start up."

"Stay on your post, Dyserly, and wait to hear from me." Brickman, all his patience gone, hung up.

"She still hasn't left?" Ida asked him.

"No, according to Dyserly, she hasn't."

Ida tried to hide a smirk. She was sure Brian had realized that Brickman wanted Caroline alone so he could snatch her. How could he not have? There was no way that Brian would let Caroline leave to go anywhere that would put her in danger. Ida had tried to tell Alexander that, but he'd insisted that Caroline would do it to save her friend.

He'd failed to understand that there was a world of difference between a man keeping his woman safe and a woman keeping a *friend* safe. A man like Brian would be fierce when it came to protecting the woman he loved.

Brickman frowned. He'd counted on Keenan coming with Caroline, despite his instructions to the contrary. He'd figured that Keenan would come specifically because he'd told Caroline not to bring him. He'd wanted to goad him into coming and had looked forward to his arrival. He hadn't counted on them not doing anything at all.

The plan was to kill Keenan, along with Winthrop and his lady friend. But it seemed as if the plan weren't going to come to fruition.

"Perhaps it's time I give Ms. Singleton a call," Brickman said.

※

As Brickman was talking to Dyserly, Brian was crouching low against the building, feeling as if he were back on the job. Getting into position and palming his gun had been as natural to him as getting dressed had been that morning. He wouldn't go back to police work for anything in the world, though. The rush of adrenaline was a powerful thing, but coming down from that high had always been difficult for him.

"You ready?" He looked quickly over his shoulder at one of his old partners.

"As ever." Kirt Pendergrast smiled his usual cocky smile. "I still think I should take the lead. You're a civilian now."

"I know it goes against the grain, but those are my best friends in there. I promised my Caroline that I'd do everything I could to bring them out safely. So I take the lead."

"I just hope that cushy desk job of yours hasn't made you go soft," Kirt joked. He'd often joked when they'd been in tense situations together in the past. "You didn't turn all girlie and forget how to use that gun I gave you, did you?"

"Oh, honey, you wish," Brian played along. "Just stand back and let a real man show a little girl like yourself how the job is done."

"Will you two knock it off and let's just do this!" Jeff Connelly said from the other side of the door, directly across from Brian.

"Yeah, losers," his partner for the day said. "Stop wasting time and get this thing started."

Brian reached out and tried the door. Of course it was locked, but it had been worth a shot. Most crooks really were stupid and he'd been in busts before where they'd actually left their doors unlocked. "Okay, guys," he said as he took his tools out of his pocket, "there's only one way out of this place and we're looking at it. So, maybe we'll be lucky enough to snag the bastard this time. You guys will get a collar for the

Chicago police, beating out those lousy feds, and I'll have the satisfaction of knowing that my future wife will be able to sleep peacefully," he finished just as the lock turned for him.

"Okay, we go in quiet. On my count." He held up his fingers one at a time and after he put the third one up, they went in. Brian and Jeff went in low, while the other two came in high.

There was no one in the front area at all. Brian noticed several doors at the end of a hallway. He started towards them and that was when he noticed the large man with brown hair. He stood there in front of a door with his back to them. Obviously he was guarding it. Brian got the others' attention and pointed. Using his hand, he silently directed the others to go to different parts of the building. He stealthily crept toward the guard.

When Brian was within a foot of him, the man suddenly turned around. The man looked surprised and afraid, but he raised his gun anyway. Brian was quicker. "Alex, it's Keenan," the man yelled just before he went down.

The police officers came running towards the shots. "Check the other rooms." Brian started to bend down to get the other man's gun. But Kirt stopped him just in time.

"Uh, let me do that." He kneeled down, retrieved the gun, and checked the man's pulse. "He's still alive. You still got it, Keenan," he said, noticing that the bullet had gone in right above the man's heart. "I think he may make it."

Brickman froze with his hand on the dial pad when he heard his brother yell. "Get to the tunnel," he whispered fiercely to Ida.

Ida ran to the other side of the room, shoved a rug back, opened a hatch and started the climb down. "What about your brother?" she whispered from the top step.

Brickman's hesitation was brief. "There's nothing I can do for him now. It's too risky to go back for him, even if he's still alive." He followed Ida down, and turned and closed the latch. He padlocked it behind him. "That will barely give us enough time to get away to Gary, but it will have to do."

As he and Ida ran forward, Brickman thought about his baby brother and hatred for Brian Keenan filled him. He'd take care of him at another time. He'd take care of all of them. The tunnel was crudely made and was about a half a mile in length. The other side held another empty warehouse. He'd left a car parked there, but when he'd done it, he'd envisioned a different escape scenario. In that one, Caroline was with him.

Inside the room, Tracy and Jack looked at each other in stunned joy when they heard Brian's name being yelled. When they heard the shots next, however, neither one of them could smile.

"It's going to be okay, *bella*," Jack whispered to Tracy when she flinched and pushed in closer to him, burying her face in his chest. "Brian is okay." He tried to convince himself of that as they waited in agony for what was going to happen next.

"I just wish they'd come in, so we can get this over with," Tracy said into his chest. Her voice was heavy with unshed tears. She was so frightened. She prayed that Brian was okay. She wrapped her arms around Jack's neck, past caring about Brickman noticing her freed wrists. Not knowing if it had been Brian or the bad guy who had gotten shot was terrifying. "I love you, Jack."

"I love you, too, sweetheart." He said and awkwardly stood, bringing Tracy with him. He was determined that if he were going down, he'd go down fighting.

They heard the key turn in the lock and Jack bent his head to kiss Tracy's forehead as her arms tightened around his neck.

Tracy lifted her head. "Brian?" She called in excitement. "I'm so glad you're okay!" She wrapped her arms around his neck and kissed him full on the mouth.

"I'm glad to see you too, sweetie. " He lifted her and buried his face in her hair in relief. "A certain friend of yours is waiting by the phone for your call."

"It's about time you got here," Jack said with a huge grin.

Brian looked up. "Yeah, well, you know," he said with an 'aw, shucks' grin, "had to form my posse and all." He released Tracy and she went to Jack's side to hug him around the waist.

Jack lifted his arms. "I'd hug you, but I'm a bit restricted right now."

Brian grinned as he let his eyes sweep over Jack from head to foot. "Guess we'll have to fix that."

"Brickman?"

Brian shook his head at the unasked question. "No, we don't have him. We're checking the building, but I think he's on the move again."

"Damn it. That's what I thought." Jack was furious. Once again, Brickman had slipped through his fingers.

"Let's get out of here," Brian said.

"Yes, let's." Tracy agreed. "Hey, Brian? How did you know we were in trouble?"

"You probably know this already, but that Nessi of yours is one courageous, little girl…"

EPILOGUE

"Jack," Tracy said. They'd both gone to the hospital to be checked out and had been home for less than an hour. Tracy's right hand was badly bruised. Her cheek carried a bruise from Jonathan and her wrists were sore. Jack sported a black eye and sore ribs. They lay across his bed, so tired that they hadn't even undressed yet. "What will you do about Brickman now? I mean, are you still going to try to catch him?"

Brickman had gotten away and they hadn't been able to trace him. "Yes, but it will be like starting all over. I'm sure he'll assume his brother is alive and telling us where they've been hiding all of these months." The bullet had gone straight through Jonathan Brickman and he'd lived. He was currently in the hospital. The police and federal agents were only waiting for him to wake up. "Plus, he has a contact on the police force, I'm sure of it. I think that's how he found out about you."

"It's wild how far Jonathan was willing to go for his brother, isn't it?" Tracy said. "I mean, up until recently, he was a mild-mannered guy who never got into trouble."

"Yes, but he was also insecure and needed someone to tell him what to do. Once his mother died, he willingly followed Brickman and did whatever he wanted him to do."

"Will Brian be in much trouble for shooting him?"

"No, I don't think so. After all, he did call the police when he realized he was in trouble. He was just defending himself. That's the story he'll give and that's the story his friends will back up."

"Good," Tracy said in relief. "Can you believe what Nessi did? I mean, her following me on her bike is what saved us," Tracy said, still in awe.

"Yes, I can believe it. She admires you, she loves you and she needs you in her life. Your family is so crazy, she'd be lost without you."

"Ha-ha," Tracy said around a yawn. "When will you look at the tape that Brickman sent Caroline? I know you're dying to and to read the note." Caroline had come to the hospital, bringing Nessi, who had been delivered by the police to Caroline. They'd called Nessi's parents who'd given her permission to spend the night with Tracy. Because Nessi had called them from her cell phone earlier and had made up a story about being with Tracy, her parents didn't know the true story and hadn't been worried. Nessi was currently sleeping in one of Jack's extra bedrooms down the hall.

"I'm going to Brian's tomorrow to view it before they hand everything over to the authorities."

"Hmm-hmm," Tracy said in a slurred voice and settled comfortably against him, ready to sleep.

Jack knew the signs and shook her shoulder gently. "Oh, no you don't. We still have other things to discuss."

"What?" Tracy whined and moaned when he pulled her into a sitting position and folded her legs in front of her. "Jaaaack. I'm tired."

"I know, so am I. But I'm not willing to let this particular subject go for another night. We've waited too long already."

Tracy heard the determination and slight anger in his voice and knew exactly what he wanted to talk about. She looked at him. "I love you, Jack."

"That's already been established," Jack said, determined not to be easy with her.

He was fighting for their future together and he knew if she didn't open up now and just release everything, he might not ever get her to do it. It was essential that she do it if they were going to be together.

"I was wrong for what I said when you asked me to move in with you. It was cowardly and I'm sorry."

"It sounds good so far. Go on, I'm still listening."

Tracy looked at him. "I didn't mean what I said. I was just scared and trying to protect myself. But I know now that I don't have to be."

"Why not?" Jack asked.

"Because you love me and you would never intentionally hurt me. But knowing that you could because I love you so much is a chance I'm willing to take because I do love you—" Tracy's words were forced down her throat as Jack pressed his mouth to hers. She held on tightly and took what he offered.

Jack made love to Tracy's mouth tenderly, so happy that she'd finally realized the truth that he wanted to cry. He'd almost lost her twice in the past few days. The first time had been when he'd taken a calculated risk and left her and the second time had been when Brickman had had them. His heart had lodged in his throat when Jonathan Brickman had carried her limp body into the room. It had been no different for him when he'd left her in her foyer with her things and a devastated look on her face.

Cupping her face and holding it still, he sipped tenderly from her mouth, taking in her essence. "I love you, *bella*," he murmured into her mouth.

"*Je t'aime, Jacques. Ne me quitte pas,*" Tracy lovingly spoke the French Caroline had taught her earlier.

Hearing her speak in his native tongue flamed Jack's blood and made him narrow his eyes at the heat. "Again," he demanded right before he greedily took her mouth.

"*Je t'aime, Jacques. Ne me quitte pas,*" Tracy told him when she was able to talk… to breathe. She let her head fall back as his lips scorched her neck and shoulder, pushing the skinny strap of her dress aside as they traveled. "J-Jack," she tried to say as he took her collarbone between his teeth, "Nessi…"

"Soundproofing," Jack growled as his hands pushed her dress above her waist and his mouth found her nipples through her dress. He sucked hungrily. His fingers found their way between her thighs and under the elastic of her panties. They found her wet and ready. He squeezed two of them inside and watched Tracy arch her back. "Again," he repeated, taking her high ruthlessly and quickly.

"*Je t'aime, Jacques,*" Tracy obliged him breathlessly, knowing what he wanted. "*Ne me quitte pas.*" She finished as she felt herself explode around his fingers.

Jack pulled his pants down, pushed her panties to the side and filled her completely on the first try. "Again. In English," he said as he moved inside her.

"*I love you, Jacques. Don't leave me,*" Tracy said breathlessly and held him as he took his release.

"This is a killer dress," Jack said later. "That's twice it's made me lose all sense of reason."

Tracy chuckled. "It's not just the dress, is it?"

"No, but let's say it helped matters along. So tell me, what were you planning to do before you were so rudely interrupted? Were you going to seduce me, Ms. Adamson?"

"Yes, that was the plan," Tracy said. "Besides the dress, I have a nice little bag of tricks I was going to pull out. You wouldn't have stood a chance."

Jack picked up strands of her hair and let them slide through his fingers. "A bag, huh? As in an *actual* bag with *actual...*" he cleared his throat "... tricks in it?"

Tracy laughed at the lusty interest in his eyes. "I'm sure it's not what you're thinking, but yes it is an *actual* bag. It's my purse, you horny dog."

"What exactly is in this bag?"

"I'm glad you asked," Tracy said as she slipped from bed and went to get her purse. "Just give me a few minutes." She reached inside her purse and then walked over to the CD player and inserted a disk. She tossed him the remote. "Don't press play until I tell you to." She backed into the connecting bathroom, with her hands behind her back, holding something out of his view.

"Now," Tracy called through the door, just before she opened it.

Jack pressed the button and Anita Baker's "Caught Up in the Rapture" slinked through the speakers, slyly, sexily and slowly. The remote slipped through numb fingers as Jack's eyes fell on Tracy. He gulped. She wore nothing but a black, sleeveless, silky-looking, one-piece…*fantasy.* That was the only word his frozen brain could come up with. She had on matching sheer, thigh-high stockings and he watched, agog, as she bent to slip her feet into the shoes she'd kicked off earlier.

Tracy smiled at Jack's look and walked slowly over to the foot of the bed. She tossed something on his chest. Her smile grew wider when she saw that he realized what it was and chuckled in appreciation. "I like cherries, too, Jack." She said huskily as she swayed gently to Anita Baker's crooning about being caught up in the rapture of love.

She placed one leg on the bed and began to roll one stocking down her thigh. Macy Gray's raspy voice, on the wave of a strong, almost lazy beat, entered the room singing about her love for her lover being as broad as the universe, as deep as the earth and the only thing able to move her.

Jack watched with narrowed eyes and bated breath as Tracy, completely in tune with the music, took her time with the stocking. By the time Macy Gray started singing about her lover's love being as encompassing as the wind and how she'll forever have enough love for her lover, the stocking was only at mid-thigh. Jack broke out in a cold sweat when Tracy finally kicked the shoe off, which also landed gently on his chest. Just as the singer finished the song off with a passionate tribute to having enough love to last forever, despite the complications of being *in* love, Tracy pushed the stocking off.

Slow, mournful and sweet, another Macy Gray song eased its way into the room. While she whispered and crooned that though life was crazy, she was absolutely sure about being her lover's lady and loving him forever—the other stocking started to come off. Tracy made short work of it and was finished with it long before the next song started. It was in Portuguese and Jack almost whimpered in pain as Tracy let her hands trail up her thighs to finger the silk and slowly raise it. Jack saw the brief, black panties beneath and closed his eyes in entreaty or appreciation or both. He really didn't know which.

The beautiful wail of a single guitar filled the room, followed by a pure, feminine voice singing simply and beautifully. A male voice came next and it was just as powerful for all of its scratchy simplicity. The song was slow and sensual, so Tracy moved slowly and sensually. She turned so that her back was to him and continued to raise the silk, criss-crossing her arms and wrapping them around her torso so that Jack saw her hands as they slowly revealed her skin to him. She swayed with the music, making all the saliva in Jack's mouth dry up. Finally, she took the garment off, whipping it over her shoulder.

It landed on his head, sliding down to completely cover his face. He felt the bed dip, felt skin on skin and by the time he uncovered his eyes, she was there, leaning over him. "Now. Want to use that cherry-flavored, cherry-scented oil first, Jack, or shall I?" She asked with a feline smile.

A long time later, Jack asked, "What was that last song?"

"It's called "Preciso Dizer Que Te Amo." In English, it's "I Must Say that I Love You." What did you think of it?"

"Even though I didn't understand a word of it, I think it's a beautiful song. As for the rest of your bag of tricks, all I can say is thank you." He knew that she'd chosen each song carefully. Each one affirmed her love for him and let him know she was willing to trust him and what they had together.

"Anytime, *querido*," Tracy said softly.

Jack took his fingers through her hair. "I like the hair. I didn't know it would be this long."

"Well, take a good look now, because it won't be this way for long. I go back to the hairdresser next week for my twists."

"What did you have done to your eyes? Before you started crying, they looked even more mysterious and darker than usual. I felt like I could drown in them."

"It's just a bit of makeup," Tracy said.

"You put together a beautiful package for my planned seduction, Ms. Adamson. But you should know it would have been just as easy to accomplish if you'd come over in a ratty T-shirt and faded jeans."

"I know that," Tracy said, "but I wanted it to be special."

"It always is," Jack said.

Tracy was quiet for a moment and then lifted her head. "You are going to marry me, aren't you, Jack?"

Jack's hand stilled in her hair. "That's supposed to be my line."

"I love you and I want to spend the rest of my life with you."

"I want that as well," Jack said and frowning playfully, released a sham, long-suffering sigh.

"Jack!" Tracy said laughingly as she pinched him.

"All right, all right. I'll marry you on one, no, make that two conditions."

"What are they?" Tracy said suspiciously, but couldn't quite hide the joy she was feeling.

"First, you have to let me propose on bended knee, with a ring and romance—the whole bit." He looked seriously into her eyes.

"All right, that's doable. What's the other one?" She climbed on top of him, folded her arms on his chest and rested her chin on them.

Jack brought his hands down to rest on her butt. "Now listen carefully, because the entire deal hinges on this one thing." He became quiet, as if he were thinking. "Are you listening?" he finally asked after a long pause.

"Yes!"

"I want you to promise me that you'll recite my new favorite rhyme, "Rise, Sally, Rise" whenever I request it. Only, I want to hear it in Portuguese." He grinned when she collapsed upon his chest with laughter.

Tracy raised her head. "*Algum tempo, querido,*" she said softly and pecked him on the lips. "Anytime."

2009 Reprint Mass Market Titles

January

I'm Gonna Make You Love Me
Gwyneth Bolton
ISBN-13: 978-1-58571-291-5
ISBN-10: 1-58571-291-4
$6.99

Shades of Desire
Monica White
ISBN-13: 978-1-58571-292-2
ISBN-10: 1-58571-292-2
$6.99

February

A Love of Her Own
Cheris Hodges
ISBN-13: 978-1-58571-293-9
ISBN-10: 1-58571-293-0
$6.99

Color of Trouble
Dyanne Davis
ISBN-13: 978-1-58571-294-6
ISBN-10: 1-58571-9
$6.99

March

Twist of Fate
Beverly Clark
ISBN-13: 978-1-58571-295-3
ISBN-10: 1-58571-295-7
$6.99

Chances
Pamela Leigh Starr
ISBN-13: 978-1-58571-296-0
ISBN-10: 1-58571-296-5
$6.99

April

Sinful Intentions
Crystal Rhodes
ISBN-13: 978-1-585712-297-7
ISBN-10: 1-58571-297-3
$6.99

Rock Star
Roslyn Hardy Holcomb
ISBN-13: 978-1-58571-298-4
$6.99

May

Paths of Fire
T.T. Henderson
ISBN-13: 978-1-58571-343-1
ISBN-10: 1-58571-343-0
$6.99

Caught Up in the Rapture
Lisa Riley
ISBN-13: 978-1-58571-344-8
ISBN-10: 1-58571-344-9
$6.99

June

Reckless Surrender
Rochelle Alers
ISBN-13: 978-1-58571-345-5
ISBN-10: 1-58571-345-7
$6.99

No Ordinary Love
Angela Weaver
ISBN-13: 978-1-58571-346-2
ISBN-10: 1-58571-346-5
$6.99

2009 Reprint Mass Market Titles (continued)

July

Intentional Mistakes
Michele Sudler
ISBN-13: 978-1-58571-347-9
ISBN-10: 1-58571-347-3
$6.99

It's In His Kiss
Reon Carter
ISBN-13: 978-1-58571-348-6
ISBN-10: 1-58571-348-1
$6.99

August

Unfinished Love Affair
Barbara Keaton
ISBN-13: 978-1-58571-349-3
ISBN-10: 1-58571-349-X
$6.99

A Perfect Place to Pray
I.L Goodwin
ISBN-13: 978-1-58571-299-1
ISBN-10: 1-58571-299-X
$6.99

September

Love in High Gear
Charlotte Roy
ISBN-13: 978-1-58571-355-4
ISBN-10: 1-58571-355-4
$6.99

Ebony Eyes
Kei Swanson
ISBN-13: 978-1-58571-356-1
ISBN-10: 1-58571-356-2
$6.99

October

Midnight Clear, Part I
Leslie Esdale/Carmen Green
ISBN-13: 978-1-58571-357-8
ISBN-10: 1-58571-357-0
$6.99

Midnight Clear, Part II
Gwynne Forster/Monica
   Jackson
ISBN-13: 978-1-58571-358-5
ISBN-10: 1-58571-358-9
$6.99

November

Midnight Peril
Vicki Andrews
ISBN-13: 978-1-58571-359-2
ISBN-10: 1-58571-359-7
$6.99

One Day At A Time
Bella McFarland
ISBN-13: 978-1-58571-360-8
ISBN-10: 1-58571-360-0
$6.99

December

Just An Affair
Eugenia O'Neal
ISBN-13: 978-1-58571-361-5
ISBN-10: 1-58571-361-9
$6.99

Shades of Brown
Denise Becker
ISBN-13: 978-1-58571-362-2
ISBN-10: 1-58571-362-7
$6.99

2009 New Mass Market Titles

January

Singing A Song…
Crystal Rhodes
ISBN-13: 978-1-58571-283-0
$6.99

Look Both Ways
Joan Early
ISBN-13: 978-1-58571-284-7
$6.99

February

Six O'Clock
Katrina Spencer
ISBN-13: 978-1-58571-285-4
$6.99

Red Sky
Renee Alexis
ISBN-13: 978-1-58571-286-1
$6.99

March

Anything But Love
Celya Bowers
ISBN-13: 978-1-58571-287-8
$6.99

Tempting Faith
Crystal Hubbard
ISBN-13: 978-1-58571-288-5
$6.99

April

If I Were Your Woman
La Connie Taylor-Jones
ISBN-13: 978-1-58571-289-2
$6.99

Best Of Luck Elsewhere
Trisha Haddad
ISBN-13: 978-1-58571-290-8
$6.99

May

All I'll Ever Need
Mildred Riley
ISBN-13: 978-1-58571-335-6
$6.99

A Place Like Home
Alicia Wiggins
ISBN-13: 978-1-58571-336-3
$6.99

June

Best Foot Forward
Michele Sudler
ISBN-13: 978-1-58571-337-0
$6.99

It's In the Rhythm
Sammie Ward
ISBN-13: 978-1-58571-338-7
$6.99

2009 New Mass Market Titles (continued)

<u>July</u>

Checks and Balances
Elaine Sims
ISBN-13: 978-1-58571-339-4
$6.99

Save Me
Africa Fine
ISBN-13: 978-1-58571-340-0
$6.99

<u>August</u>

When Lightening Strikes
Michele Cameron
ISBN-13: 978-1-58571-369-1
$6.99

Blindsided
Tammy Williams
ISBN-13: 978-1-58571-342-4
$6.99

<u>September</u>

2 Good
Celya Bowers
ISBN-13: 978-1-58571-350-9
$6.99

Waiting for Mr. Darcy
Chamein Canton
ISBN-13: 978-1-58571-351-6
$6.99

<u>October</u>

Fireflies
Joan Early
ISBN-13: 978-1-58571-352-3
$6.99

Frost On My Window
Angela Weaver
ISBN-13: 978-1-58571-353-0
$6.99

<u>November</u>

Waiting in the Shadows
Michele Sudler
ISBN-13: 978-1-58571-364-6
$6.99

Fixin' Tyrone
Keith Walker
ISBN-13: 978-1-58571-365-3
$6.99

<u>December</u>

Dream Keeper
Gail McFarland
ISBN-13: 978-1-58571-366-0
$6.99

Another Memory
Pamela Ridley
ISBN-13: 978-1-58571-367-7
$6.99

Other Genesis Press, Inc. Titles

A Dangerous Deception	J.M. Jeffries	$8.95
A Dangerous Love	J.M. Jeffries	$8.95
A Dangerous Obsession	J.M. Jeffries	$8.95
A Drummer's Beat to Mend	Kei Swanson	$9.95
A Happy Life	Charlotte Harris	$9.95
A Heart's Awakening	Veronica Parker	$9.95
A Lark on the Wing	Phyliss Hamilton	$9.95
A Love of Her Own	Cheris F. Hodges	$9.95
A Love to Cherish	Beverly Clark	$8.95
A Risk of Rain	Dar Tomlinson	$8.95
A Taste of Temptation	Reneé Alexis	$9.95
A Twist of Fate	Beverly Clark	$8.95
A Voice Behind Thunder	Carrie Elizabeth Greene	$6.99
A Will to Love	Angie Daniels	$9.95
Acquisitions	Kimberley White	$8.95
Across	Carol Payne	$12.95
After the Vows	Leslie Esdaile	$10.95
(Summer Anthology)	T.T. Henderson	
	Jacqueline Thomas	
Again, My Love	Kayla Perrin	$10.95
Against the Wind	Gwynne Forster	$8.95
All I Ask	Barbara Keaton	$8.95
Always You	Crystal Hubbard	$6.99
Ambrosia	T.T. Henderson	$8.95
An Unfinished Love Affair	Barbara Keaton	$8.95
And Then Came You	Dorothy Elizabeth Love	$8.95
Angel's Paradise	Janice Angelique	$9.95
At Last	Lisa G. Riley	$8.95
Best of Friends	Natalie Dunbar	$8.95
Beyond the Rapture	Beverly Clark	$9.95
Blame It on Paradise	Crystal Hubbard	$6.99
Blaze	Barbara Keaton	$9.95
Bliss, Inc.	Chamein Canton	$6.99
Blood Lust	J.M.Jeffries	$9.95
Blood Seduction	J.M. Jeffries	$9.95
Bodyguard	Andrea Jackson	$9.95
Boss of Me	Diana Nyad	$8.95
Bound by Love	Beverly Clark	$8.95
Breeze	Robin Hampton Allen	$10.95

Other Genesis Press, Inc. Titles (continued)

Other Genesis Press, Inc. Titles (continued)

Other Genesis Press, Inc. Titles (continued)

Intimate Intentions	Angie Daniels	$8.95
It's Not Over Yet	J.J. Michael	$9.95
Jolie's Surrender	Edwina Martin-Arnold	$8.95
Kiss or Keep	Debra Phillips	$8.95
Lace	Giselle Carmichael	$9.95
Lady Preacher	K.T. Richey	$6.99
Last Train to Memphis	Elsa Cook	$12.95
Lasting Valor	Ken Olsen	$24.95
Let Us Prey	Hunter Lundy	$25.95
Lies Too Long	Pamela Ridley	$13.95
Life Is Never As It Seems	J.J. Michael	$12.95
Lighter Shade of Brown	Vicki Andrews	$8.95
Looking for Lily	Africa Fine	$6.99
Love Always	Mildred E. Riley	$10.95
Love Doesn't Come Easy	Charlyne Dickerson	$8.95
Love Unveiled	Gloria Greene	$10.95
Love's Deception	Charlene Berry	$10.95
Love's Destiny	M. Loui Quezada	$8.95
Love's Secrets	Yolanda McVey	$6.99
Mae's Promise	Melody Walcott	$8.95
Magnolia Sunset	Giselle Carmichael	$8.95
Many Shades of Gray	Dyanne Davis	$6.99
Matters of Life and Death	Lesego Malepe, Ph.D.	$15.95
Meant to Be	Jeanne Sumerix	$8.95
Midnight Clear (Anthology)	Leslie Esdaile	$10.95
	Gwynne Forster	
	Carmen Green	
	Monica Jackson	
Midnight Magic	Gwynne Forster	$8.95
Midnight Peril	Vicki Andrews	$10.95
Misconceptions	Pamela Leigh Starr	$9.95
Moments of Clarity	Michele Cameron	$6.99
Montgomery's Children	Richard Perry	$14.95
Mr. Fix-It	Crystal Hubbard	$6.99
My Buffalo Soldier	Barbara B.K. Reeves	$8.95
Naked Soul	Gwynne Forster	$8.95
Never Say Never	Michele Cameron	$6.99
Next to Last Chance	Louisa Dixon	$24.95
No Apologies	Seressia Glass	$8.95

Other Genesis Press, Inc. Titles (continued)

No Commitment Required	Seressia Glass	$8.95
No Regrets	Mildred E. Riley	$8.95
Not His Type	Chamein Canton	$6.99
Nowhere to Run	Gay G. Gunn	$10.95
O Bed! O Breakfast!	Rob Kuehnle	$14.95
Object of His Desire	A.C. Arthur	$8.95
Office Policy	A.C. Arthur	$9.95
Once in a Blue Moon	Dorianne Cole	$9.95
One Day at a Time	Bella McFarland	$8.95
One of These Days	Michele Sudler	$9.95
Outside Chance	Louisa Dixon	$24.95
Passion	T.T. Henderson	$10.95
Passion's Blood	Cherif Fortin	$22.95
Passion's Furies	AlTonya Washington	$6.99
Passion's Journey	Wanda Y. Thomas	$8.95
Past Promises	Jahmel West	$8.95
Path of Fire	T.T. Henderson	$8.95
Path of Thorns	Annetta P. Lee	$9.95
Peace Be Still	Colette Haywood	$12.95
Picture Perfect	Reon Carter	$8.95
Playing for Keeps	Stephanie Salinas	$8.95
Pride & Joi	Gay G. Gunn	$8.95
Promises Made	Bernice Layton	$6.99
Promises to Keep	Alicia Wiggins	$8.95
Quiet Storm	Donna Hill	$10.95
Reckless Surrender	Rochelle Alers	$6.95
Red Polka Dot in a World Full of Plaid	Varian Johnson	$12.95
Reluctant Captive	Joyce Jackson	$8.95
Rendezvous With Fate	Jeanne Sumerix	$8.95
Revelations	Cheris F. Hodges	$8.95
Rivers of the Soul	Leslie Esdaile	$8.95
Rocky Mountain Romance	Kathleen Suzanne	$8.95
Rooms of the Heart	Donna Hill	$8.95
Rough on Rats and Tough on Cats	Chris Parker	$12.95
Secret Library Vol. 1	Nina Sheridan	$18.95
Secret Library Vol. 2	Cassandra Colt	$8.95
Secret Thunder	Annetta P. Lee	$9.95

Other Genesis Press, Inc. Titles (continued)

Shades of Brown	Denise Becker	$8.95
Shades of Desire	Monica White	$8.95
Shadows in the Moonlight	Jeanne Sumerix	$8.95
Sin	Crystal Rhodes	$8.95
Small Whispers	Annetta P. Lee	$6.99
So Amazing	Sinclair LeBeau	$8.95
Somebody's Someone	Sinclair LeBeau	$8.95
Someone to Love	Alicia Wiggins	$8.95
Song in the Park	Martin Brant	$15.95
Soul Eyes	Wayne L. Wilson	$12.95
Soul to Soul	Donna Hill	$8.95
Southern Comfort	J.M. Jeffries	$8.95
Southern Fried Standards	S.R. Maddox	$6.99
Still the Storm	Sharon Robinson	$8.95
Still Waters Run Deep	Leslie Esdaile	$8.95
Stolen Memories	Michele Sudler	$6.99
Stories to Excite You	Anna Forrest/Divine	$14.95
Storm	Pamela Leigh Starr	$6.99
Subtle Secrets	Wanda Y. Thomas	$8.95
Suddenly You	Crystal Hubbard	$9.95
Sweet Repercussions	Kimberley White	$9.95
Sweet Sensations	Gwyneth Bolton	$9.95
Sweet Tomorrows	Kimberly White	$8.95
Taken by You	Dorothy Elizabeth Love	$9.95
Tattooed Tears	T. T. Henderson	$8.95
The Color Line	Lizzette Grayson Carter	$9.95
The Color of Trouble	Dyanne Davis	$8.95
The Disappearance of Allison Jones	Kayla Perrin	$5.95
The Fires Within	Beverly Clark	$9.95
The Foursome	Celya Bowers	$6.99
The Honey Dipper's Legacy	Myra Pannell-Allen	$14.95
The Joker's Love Tune	Sidney Rickman	$15.95
The Little Pretender	Barbara Cartland	$10.95
The Love We Had	Natalie Dunbar	$8.95
The Man Who Could Fly	Bob & Milana Beamon	$18.95
The Missing Link	Charlyne Dickerson	$8.95
The Mission	Pamela Leigh Starr	$6.99
The More Things Change	Chamein Canton	$6.99

Other Genesis Press, Inc. Titles (continued)

Dull, Drab, Love Life?

Passion Going Nowhere?

Tired Of Being Alone?

Does Every Direction You Look For Love

Lead You Astray?

Genesis Press presents
The launching of our new website!

RecaptureTheRomance.Com

Ignite
The Flame!

Order Form

Mail to: Genesis Press, Inc.
P.O. Box 101—
Columbus, MS 39703

Name _____
Address _____
City/State _____ Zip _____
Telephone _____

Ship to (if different from above)
Name _____
Address _____
City/State _____ Zip _____
Telephone _____

Credit Card Information
Credit Card # _____ ☐ Visa ☐ Mastercard
Expiration Date (mm/yy) _____ ☐ AmEx ☐ Discover

Qty.	Author	Title	Price	Total

Use this order form, or call 1-888-INDIGO-1	
Total for books	_____
Shipping and handling: $5 first two books, $1 each additional book	_____
Total S & H	_____
Total amount enclosed	_____

Mississippi residents add 7% sales tax